continued ...

D1007016

Heir of the Dog

A DOG WALKER MYSTERY

JUDI McCOY

AN OBSIDIAN MYSTERY

OBSIDIAN
Published by New American Library, a division of
Penguin Group (USA) Inc., 375 Hudson Street,
New York, New York 10014, USA
Penguin Group (Canada), 90 Eglinton Avenue East, Suite 700, Toronto,
Ontario M4P 2Y3, Canada (a division of Pearson Penguin Canada Inc.)
Penguin Books Ltd., 80 Strand, London WC2R 0RL, England
Penguin Ireland, 25 St. Stephen's Green, Dublin 2,
Ireland (a division of Penguin Books Ltd.)
Penguin Group (Australia), 250 Camberwell Road, Camberwell, Victoria 3124,
Australia (a division of Pearson Australia Group Pty. Ltd.)
Penguin Books India Pvt. Ltd., 11 Community Centre, Panchsheel Park,
New Delhi - 110 017, India
Penguin Group (NZ), 67 Apollo Drive, Rosedale, North Shore 0632,
New Zealand (a division of Pearson New Zealand Ltd.)
Penguin Books (South Africa) (Pty.) Ltd., 24 Sturdee Avenue,
Rosebank, Johannesburg 2196, South Africa

Penguin Books Ltd., Registered Offices:
80 Strand, London WC2R 0RL, England

First published by Obsidian, an imprint of New American Library,
a division of Penguin Group (USA) Inc.

First Printing, October 2009
10   9   8   7   6   5   4   3   2   1

PUBLISHER'S NOTE
This is a work of fiction. Names, characters, places, and incidents either are the
product of the author's imagination or are used fictitiously, and any resemblance
to actual persons, living or dead, business establishments, events, or locales is
entirely coincidental.
   The publisher does not have any control over and does not assume any responsibility for author or third-party Web sites or their content.

This book is dedicated to the angels of the animal rescue world, the amazing team of veterinarians, aides, trainers, and volunteers at Best Friends in Kanab, Utah.

And to the members of Chesapeake Romance Writers in Chesapeake, Virginia. Your support has carried me through many difficult times and writing disasters. Thank you all for being kind, giving, and understanding.

Acknowledgments

A huge thank-you to attorney Lewis H. Fishlin, who phoned me from his home on a snowy day in New York City and answered all my questions on wills, estates, and inheritance law.

Without his kind assistance, Rudy wouldn't have been able to inherit a fortune, and I wouldn't have had a story to tell.

Chapter 1

Ellie and her dog Rudy stood next to a uniformed officer, staring in mute horror at the red sneakers pointing skyward from a pile of leaves scattered on the forest floor. Though she didn't want to believe it, she'd know those toes ... er ... feet ... er ... shoes, anywhere.

She glanced around the clearing, noting it crawled with patrolmen, suited detectives, crime scene investigators, people carting video cams, news vans, and reporters, along with the usual flotilla of gawkers who sensed something newsworthy was going down in Central Park.

Apparently, the Big Apple was so proud of the way it had cleaned up one of the most isolated areas of the city, the fact that a lone homeless person had died in the Ramble under suspicious circumstances was cause for a media circus.

When a suited official caught her eye through the gloom, she cringed inside. The detective, part of the mob circling the cardboard box that made up Gary's home, appeared to be in charge, which she hoped would be a blessing in disguise. There was a better chance she could maintain her dignity and self-control with this officer than she would if on the hot seat with her single-fling lover, the dastardly Detective Sam Ryder.

"Miss Engleman?" The short, stocky man stood in front of her and flashed his badge. "Detective Art Gruning. I understand you found the body and called it in."

Ellie knew better than to offer her hand in greeting. "Actually, my dog did."

Gruning raised a brow.

"I don't mean 'called it in.' I called it in, but Rudy is the one who found Gary's body." Great. She sounded like an idiot. "What I'm trying to say is my dog and I were taking a stroll, and he sort of dragged me in here. Since we'd visited Gary before, I figured Rudy wanted to stop and say hello. When I saw feet sticking out from the leaves in front of his shelter, I knew right away who it was."

"You recognized the guy by his feet?"

She peered over his shoulder and got a view of Gary's red, size sixteen or better high-top Nikes. "Well, sure. How could anyone miss those shoes? They're huge."

"You saw a pair of oversized athletic shoes and figured out who was lying there, just like that?" Gruning retorted, his voice nasal, flat, and pure New York.

"Gary's not a big man, so his shoe size always amazed me. I suspected it was him, but I stooped down and brushed the leaves off to be sure. When I saw he was dead—"

"How did you know he was dead?"

Was that a trick question? She opened and closed her mouth before stuttering, "Uh ... by the bullet hole in his chest?"

"So you disturbed the scene?"

"I checked to see if there was anything I could do to help, as I assume any normal human being would. When I realized there wasn't, I sort of lost it—"

"That would be your vomit next to the shelter, then?"

Sniffing back a tear, she wiped her nose with the used tissue. "Afraid so. Then I called 911."

Gruning scribbled in his notebook. "You say you've been here before." He gazed at a rocky hillside against which Gary had established his cardboard home. "This is a fairly isolated area for someone to visit on a regular basis."

"We didn't stop often. Just when Gary invited us."

His eyes narrowed at the word "invited." "How well did you know the victim?"

Striving for composure, she took a deep breath. "Not very. But Gary is . . . was a really nice guy. Harmless. He wouldn't hurt a fly. I can't imagine anyone wanting to kill him."

Gruning's expression held a nasty edge, as if he didn't believe a word she said. "So you were more than acquaintances?"

"Not really. He was just someone I talked to once in a while when I walked my dogs."

"That dog?" he asked, pointing to Rudy, her gray-and-white Yorkiepoo.

"This one and others. I'm a professional dog walker."

He consulted his palm-sized spiral pad, a must-have, it seemed, for all detectives in the city, and again raised a brow. "Hold on a second. Engleman . . . Engleman . . . Are you the woman who was involved in that dognapping homicide a couple of months back? The one Sam Ryder worked on?"

"That would be me." She blew her nose, then dabbed the crumbling tissues over her damp forehead. Though it was cooler here in the shade of the park, mid-July in Manhattan was brutal, especially since temperatures had hovered in the midnineties for the past week. "I discovered the professor's body."

"Appears as if discovering dead bodies is becoming a habit of yours. Why do you think that is?"

It was obvious from his memory of Buddy's disappearance that she would never live down her involvement with Sam. Now, here she was again, innocently finding a body, and this guy was rubbing it in. "I have no idea, but Detective Ryder took me off his list of suspects after his first round of questioning."

"But you knew who did it?"

"I *figured out* who did it. I didn't actually know the man."

"The way I heard it, you did," he insisted, loosening his garishly patterned tie. Rivulets of sweat trickled down his ruddy cheeks and disappeared under the collar of his shirt.

"I only knew him to see him," she went on. "What does this have to do with Gary?"

Detective Gruning proceeded to take her elbow and lead her farther from the scene. Situating her in front of a stand of trees, he folded his arms and glared. "You look nervous, Ms. Engleman. Any particular reason why?"

"I'm not nervous, just upset. It happens when you lose a friend."

"You just said the victim was an acquaintance. Someone you barely knew."

"I still considered Gary a friend. We spoke several times a week when I walked my dogs."

"How often did you come here, to his hole?"

"Not often."

The detective ran a hand over his face, then wiped the sweaty palm on his suit coat. "Let me put it this way—when was the last time you were here?"

"Before Rudy and I got here tonight?"

"Yes."

"About two weeks ago."

"And why was that?"

"Gary wanted to show me something he'd found . . . a treasure, he called it."

"And what exactly was this treasure?"

"A dog dish. He was proud of the fact that it only had a single chip along the edge. He found it in an alley where he did a lot of Dumpster shopping and brought it to his shelter so Rudy could have a drink of water when we stopped to see him."

"Rudy, as in your dog?"

"Yes."

"So Gary liked your dog?"

Ellie remembered how the homeless man and Rudy had bonded on their second or third meeting. For some unexplainable reason, Gary had picked up on their unique manner of communication and was able to speak with Rudy exactly as she did. "He told me he'd always wanted a dog, but his mother wouldn't allow it."

An officer walked over and handed Ellie her tote bag. "It's clean, sir."

"Hey, Gruning, I think you should see this," a man's voice called from the scene.

The detective nodded at the purse-toting patrolman, who moved to Ellie's side. She waited until Gruning plodded to the cardboard shelter, then accepted her bag and asked her guard, "What's happening?"

"Don't know, and I couldn't tell you if I did."

"I don't like the look of that detective, Triple E." Sounding unsure and a bit frightened, Rudy's voice invaded her mind. Karma had brought her and the spirit of her first dog together at the ASPCA shelter, where she'd gone to celebrate her divorce. Still, hearing his thoughts continued to surprise her when she was stressed—like now. *"I get the feeling he's gonna make trouble for us."*

"He's just doing his duty. Gary is dead, remember."

The officer sneered. "Funny you should notice."

Ellie squatted on the pretext of brushing off her buddy's fur. She didn't mind being thought of as eccentric, but being labeled "crazy" by the cops was something else. "How about you take a walk over there, scope out the site, and report back?" she whispered. "Just don't let anyone see you."

"Like I would."

The terrier mix took off at a trot, his leash trailing in the underbrush. The interior of the park was dank, alive with the scent of decaying leaves, vegetable matter, and putrefying flesh. How long had Gary lain there, bleeding and alone? Standing, she turned her back on the officer and moved to block her dog's disappearance.

"Hey, Ellie?"

"This is a crime scene," the officer said at the same time.

She shifted her stance and spotted her favorite hot dog vendor standing a few feet away. "He's a friend," she said to the patrolman.

"Hurry up," he responded. "This isn't a tea party."

Pops edged closer, his nut-brown face set in a frown. "Heard it was Gary, so I came running. Had to leave the cart chained to a lamppost or I'd'a been here sooner."

She gave him a watery smile. "He was shot. Can you believe it? Why would anyone shoot a nice guy like Gary?"

"Beats me, but um . . ." He glanced over his shoulder, then reached in his pocket and passed her a grimy envelope. "This is for you. Gary told me to give it to you if anything ever happened to him."

She stared at the gift. "To me? What's in it?"

"Beats me, but there's weight to it. Feels like it might be a key of some kind," said the vendor, taking a step in retreat. "Just said he wanted you to have it. I gotta be going. I'll talk to you tomorrow." He ambled off with a wave of his hand.

Trying for casual, she stuffed the envelope in her tote bag. She'd take a peek as soon as the coast was clear. "So, what happens next?" she asked, turning back to the guard, though she had a good idea. The last time she'd found a body, she was immediately labeled the prime suspect and hauled in for questioning. She'd been finger-printed and had her hair and clothes checked for fibers and whatever else the authorities considered necessary to implicate her in the crime.

"What did that old guy just give you?"

"Something personal. When will I be able to go home?"

"When Gruning gives the okay. Why?"

"Because it's getting late."

At the sound of a commotion, they focused on Gary's home. An officer walked from behind the shelter with what appeared to be an empty plastic soda bottle on the end of a pencil. Gruning scanned the item, then glanced at her while more pictures were taken.

"What's going on?"

"Looks like they found something," said the officer, without volunteering a thought on what it might be.

"They got part of the murder weapon." Rudy's voice came from below.

"What?"

"No idea. Too soon to tell," the officer added, unaware he was participating in a verbal ping-pong match with a canine.

"A plastic bottle. They think it was used as a silencer for the gunshot that killed Gary."

"A soda bottle as a silencer?"

The officer folded his arms across his protruding belly. "If you know what they found, why are you asking me?"

"Ah, I don't know. I'm merely speculating." Accustomed to brushing past the conversations she held with her dog, she said, "I think I saw it once on—on television."

"Really? Mind telling me what show that might have been?"

Great. She never watched cop shows on TV or went to any type of movie with violence or mayhem, so she had no idea where she could have viewed the scenario. "Um . . . an episode of *Law and Order*, maybe. I don't remember."

"*Try* CSI," Rudy encouraged. "*Real cops hate that show.*"

"Like I need to get on anyone's bad side."

"You'll only be on Gruning's bad side if you know something and don't tell him," the officer intoned.

When her overseer came to attention, Ellie assumed Gruning had returned, so she pasted a smile on her lips and faced him. "What was all the commotion about?"

"Police business." He glared at Rudy. "We don't need any mutts mucking up the crime scene, so keep hold of his leash, Ms. Engleman, or I'll be forced to impound him. Got that?"

"My dog is probably cleaner than a lot of the people rifling through here, and this is a park with birds, rabbits, squirrels. I don't see how a little dog hair—"

A technician approached, holding a set of tweezers and a plastic bag. Before she could stop him, the man bent and plucked a clump of Rudy's fur.

"*Yeow!*" Growling, Rudy lunged forward, and both the tech and Gruning jumped back. "*Easy with the police brutality.*"

Ellie knelt and ran a soothing hand along her boy's coat, then threw both men a glare. "I would have done that myself, if you'd asked."

"Just control your animal," Gruning warned. Still eyeing the Yorkiepoo, he said to her guard, "Escort Ms. Engleman home so she can drop off her attack dog, then bring her to the station."

Sam nodded at a group of officers shooting the breeze around the water cooler. Instead of calling hello or shouting a string of joking insults, they merely nodded in return. But when he headed down the hall toward his office, a whisper of comments buzzed behind him.

What the hell was going on? Did he have toilet paper stuck to his shoe? Maybe he'd split the seam in his pants or—

"How many times do I have to say it? Gary was a friend. I didn't meet him until after I started my dog-walking business."

Stopping short, Sam kept his feet glued in place. He'd recognize that female voice anywhere, even in the dark. In fact, it had been the dead of night the last time he'd heard it, and it still made his gut clench with desire.

What the heck was Ellie Engleman doing here?

Swamped with guilt, or maybe regret, he crossed to the other side of the hall, as if passing directly in front of the interrogation room would alert her to his presence. He didn't doubt she'd be unhappy to see him. Technically, she had every right to call him a creep and slap him, or worse, pretend he didn't exist.

The one night they'd spent together flashed in his brain, as it did from time to time when his mind wandered, or on nights when he was alone and feeling sorry for himself. Other than that, he hardly thought about her at all.

Striding to the office he shared with three other detectives, he closed the door, took a seat, and shuffled through a mound of paperwork. Then he swung his desk chair around to his computer and logged on, preparing to finish the six reports he should have filed a week ago. After hitting the command keys, the template showed on the screen and he focused on the pink sheets, but Ellie's perfect features continued to pop into view.

He palmed his face, rubbing his eyes. Damn, when would he be able to put her out of his mind and get back to business?

Minutes passed while he concentrated on the computer screen, but it was no use. The question continued to nag him. Why was Ellie being held in an interrogation room? She'd been his own personal bad penny when she'd stuck her nose in Albright's investigation. Now she was in the precinct again, just a few months later, only this time she wasn't horning in on his case. Still, she had to have done something to get her ass hauled in for questioning.

His partner, Vince Fugazzo, sauntered through the door wearing a neatly pressed shirt and matching tie. One of the benefits of having a wife, Sam supposed.

"Hey, did you hear about the guy they found in the Ramble?"

"What guy?"

"Some homeless dude, Gary somebody-or-other, lived in the bowels of Central Park. Seems he got shot, and your girlfriend found the body."

Girlfriend? "What the hell are you talking about?" Sam asked, though he guessed the answer even before Vince spoke.

"You know, the doll who got in your face about those dognappings. The one who helped you wrap the case." His partner snorted a laugh. "The case a couple of the other guys have hinted she solved for you."

He heaved a silent sigh. There was no need to explain things to his partner. Vince knew he was dedicated, even if Ellie had done a lot of legwork on the Albright murder.

"Those other guys can go to hell," Sam muttered, squinting at the screen. Who the fuck had come up with the idea of a computer anyway? Damned plastic boxes were nothing but a nuisance, with a mind of their own and a dozen ways to screw with a normal man's brain.

"I second the sentiment, buddy. Just the same, you can't stop the talk." He sat at his desk and pulled a stack of pictures from his shirt pocket. "Hey, want to see the latest photos of Angelina? Took 'em myself with that fancy camera Natalie bought me for Father's Day." He tossed the pictures on Sam's desk. "I got one beautiful baby there, pal. Pretty soon, I'll have to beat the boys off with a stick."

Sam flipped through the photos and had to agree.

Angelina was about five months old, with a pixie face, a tuft of dark curly hair, and her mother's striking doe eyes. His sister Susan was having a girl, too. Didn't it figure? Pretty soon women would rule the world.

"You're becoming a regular pro with that Nikon. What are these, pics number one thousand through one thousand fifty?"

"Very funny. Just wait till you have a kid of your own. You'll be singing another tune, I promise you." Vince scooped up the photos and tucked them in his drawer. "So, you want I should take a trip down the hall and get the scoop on that Engleman babe?"

"Makes no never mind to me," Sam said with a shrug. "I have paperwork to do."

"Sure, no problem." Vince's face creased in a smirk. "I'll even get the skinny on how she looks."

She probably looks as terrific as ever, thought Sam, though Ellie would never admit it. She was forever covering her curves, thinking she had to hide them instead of show them off. But she hadn't been able to hide them from him, a fact that either made him smile or frown, depending upon his mood.

He ground his molars. This was not the time to dwell on the past, not now, not ever. He'd already fucked up one woman's life because of this job. There was no need to fuck up a second. Fugazzo was lucky. He and his wife were in love, and Sam would bet his last bullet their marriage would survive the taxing mental and physical tolls this profession took on a person. Vince wasn't like most of the men in their department, screwing around on his wife and bragging about it. But women like Natalie Fugazzo were few and far between.

Ellie already had one "failed" on her scorecard, just like he did. She deserved better than a guy who worked twenty-hour days and put his life on the line while doing so. The job of an NYPD detective had driven plenty of good women to divorce court or caused them to cheat on their husbands. He cared for her too much to see her share the same fate.

Vince swaggered back inside, loosening the knot in his tie as he walked. Sitting at his desk, he whistled as he tapped a couple of keys on the computer, then dug through a pile of folders. When he found the one he wanted, he flipped it open and logged on to the system.

Sam drummed the desk with his fingers.

His partner stared intently at the screen.

Leaning back in his chair, Sam heaved a sigh. "Okay, so how is she?"

"I was on family leave when you had the Albright case, so I never got a good look at her before tonight. How come you didn't tell me she had legs up to her armpits and a rack that would wake a dead man? Nice face, too. Innocent, high-class, yet sexy as hell."

"Did you find out why she's here?" Sam asked, not about to comment on the man's spot-on description.

Vince swiveled his seat around. "Your girl found the vic's body in the park while walking her dog. He was shot at close range, once in the heart with a forty-four. The shooter covered his body with debris. They found the silencer, a one-quart plastic soda bottle, but no weapon."

"So why are they holding her?"

"Officially, it's just routine questioning, but you know Gruning. If there's an easy way out, he'll take it, and right now she's it."

No way in hell would Ellie ever commit murder. The woman was so averse to violence she refused to watch a crime show on television or go to a shoot-'em-up movie. She was such a softy she cried when a dog owner died, and not for the owner. She wailed for the damn mutt.

"Why would he think that?"

"It's Gruning. There doesn't need to be a reason."

"Then it's definitely his and Smith's case?"

"Yep."

The pair might be assholes, but they were damn lucky assholes. The incompetent dicks always seemed to get a case that solved itself. Even more annoying, ever since Sam had tied a murder he was investigating to one that was on Gruning and Smith's list a couple of years back, both men had it in for him. Especially Gruning.

"And they didn't find the murder weapon?" He couldn't imagine Ellie holding a gun, let alone firing it.

"Nope, but they're looking. Seems your girlfriend mentioned that she knew an empty plastic bottle would act as a silencer, and that got Gruning's attention."

"She actually told him she knew how that worked?"

"Not Gruning, but she mentioned it to the cop standing guard, and he relayed it to the lead detective, just like he was supposed to."

Sam hunched over his desk. It didn't make sense. Ellie had probably babbled nonsense, not given her expertise on the creative criminal use of a plastic soda bottle. Hell, she talked to her dog as if the mutt was human, a fact he knew to be true because she'd done it enough times while she was on his tail about Albright's murder. She'd probably thrown out a stupid remark when she saw them dig up the bottle, without realizing anything she said could be used against her.

"There also seems to be another small problem."

Fuck. "And that would be?"

"She's refusing to hand over her tote bag. Says they already took a look and cleared it once, so they now need a warrant for a second inspection. Not a good way for someone who claims they're innocent to handle themselves," Vince added.

Sam pushed away from his desk and headed for the door. What in the hell was wrong with her? Ellie knew better than to act as if she had something to hide. "I'd better see what I can do."

"Don't get involved," his partner warned.

"I have to. She isn't guilty."

"Gruning will have you up on professional charges if you interfere. You know that."

"To hell with that asshole. I'm not going to let him pin a murder on an innocent woman just because he's a lazy SOB. Besides, without a murder weapon or eyewitness, they can't legally keep her here."

He charged into the hall, knocked on the holding room door, and let himself in. Ellie saw him, and her complexion bled white. "What's up, Murphy?" he asked, focusing on the officer on duty.

"Just waiting for Gruning to file the paperwork for a search warrant. The lady isn't cooperating, so it's either that or arrest her."

Sam frowned. "Give us a second, okay?"

"It's your funeral," said Murphy. "I'll be right outside."

The door closed, and Sam inhaled a breath for self-control, then met her glare. "What the hell is wrong with you? Why can't Gruning look through your bag?"

Ellie held her tote close on her lap. "It's a pleasure seeing you again, too, Detective Ryder. Now go away."

"This is serious," he began, but he could tell from the set of her lips she wasn't going to talk unless he made nice. "How have you been?"

"Fine."

"You're pissed because I didn't call—"

"Me? Pissed? Whatever gave you that idea?" She raised her nose in the air. "Just because we slept together doesn't mean you owe me anything."

He gazed at the ceiling. This was not the time or place to discuss the past. "You know things will go easier if you cooperate."

Her shoulders straightened. "I want a lawyer."

"Why? Did you shoot that guy?"

"Of course not."

"Then tell me what's in your purse." He sat across from her at the table. "We'll find out anyway."

"Gruning already had a cop search my bag in the park, and he didn't find anything. If they want a second look, they need a warrant ... Don't they?"

"That's debatable," Sam intoned. Then he got the message. "What are you hiding?"

She huffed a breath, opened the bag, and dug around until she pulled out a grubby business size envelope. "Pops gave this to me tonight, in private I might add." She set it on the table. "It's from Gary."

"Gary?"

"The victim."

"Oh, hell." He ran a hand over his jaw. "What's inside?"

She shrugged. "I haven't had a chance to open it, so why should I give it up? Pops said it was for me."

"If it's from the victim, it could be evidence."

"That patrolman guarding me probably blabbed," she ground out. "What nerve."

"Wait a minute. A cop saw someone hand this to you while you were standing right there, and it was after they'd searched the bag?"

"That's what I'm telling you."

He picked up the envelope and held it to the light. "Looks like there's a key inside."

She leaned forward, as if trying to see through the paper. "I don't have a clue what it is. Honest."

"Well, somebody has to take a look." He slid a finger under the flap and gauged her response. "You mind?"

"No, go ahead," she said, pouting. "I just wanted to see it before Gruning. That's all."

Sam thought about calling Murphy in as a witness, then decided against it. Ellie might hate him, but she'd never leave him hanging out to dry. If she gave her word, she'd keep it. She was too honest to do anything else. "I'm going to inspect it, but I want you to promise that whatever it is, you won't say this was an illegal search, you got that?"

"I got it."

He slit the envelope and pulled out a sheet of paper and a key. After reading the handwritten page, he tucked the envelope and its contents into his pants pocket. Then he scowled at her. "Christ, Ellie. What have you gotten yourself into this time?"

Chapter 2

Sam kept his tone neutral while he spoke to Gruning, in case the idiot decided to be a bigger asshole than usual. "Put her in my custody, and I'll take full responsibility," he said to the detective. "The woman wouldn't slap a mosquito, never mind pop a homeless man."

"If that's true, she has nothing to worry about if we do another search of her bag," Gruning responded in a smarmy tone.

Sam stuffed a hand in his pocket and wrapped his fingers around Ellie's envelope. Rarely did he break the rules, but this was a special case. "It's the principle of the thing. Claims you already took a look in her bag at the crime scene, and you didn't find anything, so you don't get another search without a warrant. It's late, and we're all tired. You can hold the tote and have a look-see in the morning, when she comes back with her lawyer."

Gruning fished a mint from his jacket pocket, stuck it in his mouth, and chewed. "Did I tell you that bum's shelter was a mess? Mattress was shredded, boxes emptied—the killer even tore up the moldy carpet squares padding the floor. There's no doubt he was searching for something, probably drugs. The dead guy wasn't a known dealer, but nothing else makes sense."

He chomped on the mint. "We'll get a better idea after the toxicology screening."

"Do you seriously think Ms. Engleman deals drugs?" Sam did his best not to laugh. From his perspective, he could see that the candy Gruning just ate was covered in lint.

"Little Mary Sunshine could be into anything." Crunch, crunch. "Sometimes the ones that appear the most innocent are the most guilty."

"Take it from me, this lady is lily white," Sam insisted, wondering how a mouthful of fuzz tasted. "I'll have her back here bright and early, okay?"

Gruning pursed his full lips. "Eight a.m. and not a minute later. And I want that bag before she leaves."

Sam walked into the interrogation room and nodded at Ellie's tote. "Here's the deal. Gruning will hold the bag until morning, but he swears he won't look inside until you come back with a lawyer for the unveiling. Remove your keys, wallet, and cell phone, before he changes his mind."

Ellie pulled out what he suggested and passed him the tote, but Sam stopped her before she followed him into Gruning's office. "Seeing you will only irritate him. I'll be out in a second." Striding through the door, he dropped the bag on Gruning's desk. "I let her keep the keys, wallet, and cell phone."

"Just remember, she's your responsibility for the next eight hours. That means you stick to her like dog shit on a shoe, and get her back here on time tomorrow or it's your funeral."

Sam nodded and made it into the hall in time to see Ellie striding away like a power walker at the Olympics. Taking off at a jog, he caught her as she skipped down the precinct steps.

"So, where's your dog?"

"Gruning let me bring him home before a cop drove me here."

Sam had done the same thing the morning he'd met her at Albright's apartment and dragged her in for questioning. Was Gruning getting soft? Couldn't be, he decided. Besides, he had his orders from the hard-boiled investigating officer and he couldn't chance screwing them up.

"I'll take you home."

She kept on walking.

He leaned into her, steering her toward the police lot. "My car is over there."

She crossed the street on the diagonal, and he mumbled a curse. When he reached her side, he clasped her elbow. "Come on, Ellie. I said I'd see you home."

She jerked her arm free and continued plowing down the sidewalk.

Deciding to give it one more try, he double-timed his steps and danced in front of her. She sidled left, then right, and he followed. Finally, she stood still and crossed her arms.

"What do you want?"

"I'm taking you home."

"I'll pass on that. I'm beat and not up to another round of questioning."

"You're missing my point. You were released into my custody." She wasn't going to be any happier when she heard the rest of it, but that could wait until they got to her place. "I'm your official escort."

"What? Why?"

"Because you're a 'person of interest.' Gruning let me vouch for you, so you wouldn't have to spend the night in a cell, and you can be present tomorrow when they search the bag, with or without a lawyer."

She ducked into the doorway of a deli that was closed for the night. "I need time alone. Give me the envelope so I can check what's inside. I promise to report to Gruning in the morning, as requested."

"You're not listening. I have to make sure you go

to your apartment and nowhere else." The words shot from his lips before he knew the reason why. "Now let's move."

He again took her elbow, relieved when she didn't pull away, and steered her to his car. In five minutes, they were driving uptown. "Did this Gary have friends? Other homeless people you met when you were with him?" Sam asked, trying to get a handle on her relationship with the victim.

She shook her head. "I don't usually speak to street people, but Gary was different. He liked Rudy, so he stopped to chat whenever he saw us at the park. It was harmless."

"Had you been to his shelter before tonight?"

"A couple of times," she said with a shrug. "I gave him an umbrella for his birthday a few months back, and he brought me to his place whenever he got something new for his cardboard box. That's all."

"And you didn't worry that he or somebody else might take advantage of you while you were in the bowels of the park?"

"Of course not."

Sam clenched the steering wheel. "Don't you realize what might have happened to you?"

"I know. I could have been robbed—raped—worse, but Rudy was always with me, and Gary is . . . was a gentle soul. He wouldn't have hurt anyone."

Now at their destination, he double-parked the car in front of her building, and she hopped out. He raced behind her, prepared to tell her she was getting an overnight guest, but before he spoke she undid the entryway lock and turned.

"Go home, Sam. I appreciate the help, but I don't need you in my life, and I'm fairly certain I'm not welcome in yours."

Instead of answering, he followed her up the steps and waited until she unlocked her apartment, where she held out her hand and said, "I'll take that envelope now."

Annoyed, he grabbed her wrist, removed the keys, and headed for the street, calling over his shoulder, "You can read it when I come back."

"What's he doing here?" Rudy asked, standing on his hind legs when she opened the door. *"And did they figure out who killed Gary?"*

Ellie heaved a sigh. Why the heck was Sam holding that envelope? What was he trying to pull? Rudy nosed her knee, and she glanced at him. "Hello to you, too. Have you been good?"

"Good as I can be when I'm worried about you. Viv walked me a couple of hours ago, but didn't give me dinner, so I'm starving."

She grinned. "I'll take care of it as soon as I—"

"Just tell me what's going on? Why's the defective dick here? What does he have to do with all this?"

"You don't need to worry about it."

"Then what took you so long?"

"Questioning. The same way I was in Professor Albright's death."

"They think you had something to do with Gary's murder?"

" 'Fraid so. Come on." She grabbed his leash from a hook beside the door. "We'll go downstairs and wait for Sam."

Rudy stiffened his legs, refusing to move. *"Whoa, Nellie. Why do we have to bring that Bozo along?"*

"He drove me home."

"Okay, now you're home. Say adios, arrivederci, aloha, buh-bye, boobie. Slam the door and click the lock behind him."

"It's not that easy," Ellie answered, leading him down the stairs. "The policeman standing guard at the scene told Gruning I received an envelope from Pops, and he demanded to search my bag a second time. I said no, and they hauled me in. Later, in the precinct, Sam took a look at what was inside the envelope, tucked it away, and convinced Gruning to let me come home tonight and go back in the morning for a bag check."

They made it to street level and walked toward the corner. "I don't know where he went just now, but he's coming back."

"Isn't that special?"

"Sam still has the envelope, you dope. We have to let him inside so we can take a look at whatever it is Gary left us before Gruning jumps to conclusions."

"I guess it's better than nothing."

She gazed up the street and spotted the detective heading in their direction. "He's almost here, so be nice." She took note of the gym bag slung over Sam's shoulder when he neared. "What's in there?"

Rudy dragged her across the street, purposely, she thought, to be a pain.

"This?" Sam kept pace beside them. "A change of clothes I keep in the car. Never can tell when I might have to pull an all-nighter."

"Where are you headed after this? A stakeout?"

"You might say that."

They walked to a group of trash cans, which Rudy watered, and returned to the brownstone. "I'll take my keys now, and that envelope," she said, climbing the front stairs. "I promise to be at the station by eight."

He followed her up the steps, unlocked the outer door, and kept on going. Ellie caught him on the second floor landing. "I said I'd take it from here. Hand over my stuff and go home."

On the third floor, he pushed open her apartment door and strode inside before she said another word. Ellie removed Rudy's leash, then raced into the kitchen and found Sam at the sink, drinking a glass of water. "This game's gone on long enough. Give me my keys and the envelope, please."

Swiveling in place, he reached into his pants pocket and pulled out the envelope. "You realize that when I took this, I put my badge on the line?"

"I know, and I'm grateful." She sat at the table unsure of where this would lead. Was there something against the law in that envelope? Something that might send her to jail? "Can I look now?"

He took a seat and passed it over.

She raised the flap and pulled out a sheet of paper and a small silver key. She had to scan the note twice before she understood exactly what she held. "This is a will."

"I know it's a will. Read it again. Carefully."

A minute later, she shook her head. "This can't be real. It says the key belongs to a safety-deposit box at a bank somewhere near Rockefeller Center."

"Looks like, and the will is notarized and signed, so my best guess is it's genuine."

"But it says Gary left everything he had to Rudy, and I'm the executor. That means my dog owns what was in his shelter."

"Say what?" Rudy yipped from beneath the table.

"More importantly, your dog owns whatever is in the box that belongs to that key."

"There's a box? Where?" Rudy stood on his hind legs and scratched at her thigh. *"What else does it say?"*

Placing a hand on his head, she ruffled his ears. "Hang on a second." She focused on Sam, who was grinning. "Rudy's a very sympathetic canine. He's reading my emotions."

"It figures, but concentrate. Did Gary ever mention a will or say anything about a safety-deposit box when you spent time together?"

"Not that I remember."

"Me neither."

"And he never said he'd left you anything?"

"What could he leave me? He lived like a pauper, scavenged for food, clothes—everything."

"Well, apparently he had something he thought valuable enough to protect. And whatever it is, it's in that box."

"This is ridiculous. We don't want his junk."

"Correction—I don't want his junk."

"You're not the least bit curious?" Sam asked, raising a brow. "What if he found something in one of those Dumpsters, something valuable, and hid it for safekeeping?"

"Then I'll give it to charity or—or—"

"Charity? No way. Not until I know what it is."

Ellie frowned at Rudy, remembered Sam was watching, and said, "I can't think about this now. I'm going to bed." She stuffed the will and key back in the envelope and left it on the table. "I'll walk you to the door."

Sam hoisted his duffel, but instead of heading for the front door he ambled down the hall and turned into her guest bedroom. She stormed after him. "What the heck is wrong with you? Stop being a jerk and go home."

"Sorry, no can do." He tossed his bag on the double bed. "Gruning had one more requirement in order to let you leave the precinct. I have to babysit you until morning."

Ellie swallowed a gulp of air. Her stomach heaved and her face heated. She stared at the floor, said a silent "Well, crap," and put her hands on her hips. "If this is your idea of a joke—"

"No joke." He sat on the bed and toed off his shoes. "I'm here for the night."

"What a putz. How about I bite him?"

"I don't have anything to hide. I won't leave town."

"I know that, but Gruning doesn't." He undid his tie and started unbuttoning his shirt. Standing, he pulled it out of his pants and reached for his belt. "I said I'd watch over you, and I mean to keep my word. Besides, I wouldn't put it past him to have a patrolman watch the building, just to make sure I stayed here."

Her insides tightened. Had Sam suggested this to Gruning, just to be irritating? "What are you doing?"

His smile sent a jolt straight to her gut. "Getting ready for bed. Are you planning to stay and tuck me in?"

"That isn't funny." She huffed out a breath. "I'm using the bathroom first, so don't get any ideas."

When he slipped off the shirt, their single night together swept into her brain like an X-rated movie, calling to mind the way she'd skimmed her fingers over his muscled shoulders, across his rock-hard chest, and other . . . important places.

He dropped his shirt on the bed and raked her with a gaze. "If you don't want me to get any ideas, go to your room, because the longer you stand there, the more I remember, and all of it was good."

Like a warning bell, her insides tingled, as if priming for another chance to ride him to climax. She sucked in a breath. "If it was so good, why didn't you—"

"Clam up, Triple E. Clam up now!" Rudy yipped.

"Never mind. I'm outta here." She flounced from the room, muttering while her dog trotted beside her. "Thanks for the sass, big boy. It kept me from making a total fool of myself . . . again."

"That's what I'm here for."

She undressed and slipped on a sleep shirt, then hurried through her nightly ritual in the bathroom. What the heck had happened tonight? It was bad enough she was in her ex-lover's debt for saving her from a night in the slammer. Sam had also put his job on the line by knowingly withholding something the police would probably consider evidence.

Settling under the covers, she continued the single-sided conversation. How was she supposed to fall asleep with Sam in residence just a few feet away? And even if he weren't spending the night, she still had Gary's death and that stupid will to worry about.

"It'll be okay, Ellie," said Rudy, curling on the pillow next to her. *"I'm here. I'll watch over you."*

She rolled to her side and laid her hand on his head. Never in a million years did she think a dog would be her best friend, her confidant, the one thing in her life she could count on. "I know you will."

"We don't need that copper. We don't need anyone."

She closed her eyes and sighed. She loved Rudy more than anything, possibly more than Georgette or Vivian or Stanley. But he couldn't give her children or make her toes tingle and her thighs shudder with longing. So far, Sam was the only person who'd been able to do that.

Which was sad, because Sam didn't want her—not the way she wanted him.

Sam punched his pillow for the tenth or was it the eleventh time? He'd done a lot of dumb things in his life. Getting blind drunk at sixteen and falling asleep behind the bleachers at his high school; wrecking his father's three-month-old car the day he'd turned eighteen; taking up smoking in college . . .

And those weren't the worst of his sins. He'd married Carolanne at twenty-five, even though he had a pretty good idea they weren't right for each other, and ruined both their lives, something his mother and his sisters had predicted well before they'd tied the knot.

But he'd learned from his mistakes. Other than an occasional beer or glass of wine, he rarely drank alcohol. He'd sharpened his driving skills and kept his car running like a marathoner, no matter that the outside needed cosmetic work. And he'd stopped smoking two years ago, difficult but necessary according to the documented health data.

As for Carolanne, the divorce had been good for both of them, even if it had taken him a while to realize the end of their marriage was more because of her cheating than his neglect. Which led to the tricky part.

He truly liked Ellie Engleman, enjoyed her sense of humor, her way of phrasing a question, her habit of calling him on whatever he said or did that didn't meet with her approval. He admired her work ethic, her loyalty, her sense of fair play. And that was just the tip of the iceberg.

Because along with all her stellar qualities, she had a body that absolutely turned him on. They'd fitted together like the proverbial hand and glove, a lock and key, peas in a pod—hell, all the sappy stuff written in poetry books. Plain and simple, that single night with her had been the best sex of his life, before, during, and after marriage. So good, in fact, he couldn't imagine doing the deed with anyone else.

And that really pissed him off.

Thanks to that lone night in Ellie's bed, he'd probably never have sex again. His dick might as well rot and fall off from lack of use. And it probably would, if he didn't erase her from his mind and find someone else to scratch the itch he got whenever he thought about her.

Unfortunately, he'd set himself smack in the middle of her problems, and he couldn't desert her now. He'd already gone to bat for her with Gruning and put his job on the line by withholding what he knew was evidence. But he would swear on his life she was innocent of murdering that homeless man, which meant he had a duty to protect her.

Footsteps sounded in the hall. He smiled at the idea of his fantasy wide awake and annoyed with him, just like he was up and annoyed with her. If he had a brain, he'd pull the pillow over his head, count to a thousand, and stay put.

Too bad his brain had taken a vacation the moment he'd heard she was in trouble.

He swung his legs over the side of the bed and tugged on his jeans. Padding to the door, he stepped into the hall and followed the dim glow coming from the kitchen.

Standing in the doorway, he propped himself against the frame and admired what he could see of her under a knee-length sleep shirt. Her curvy hip hitched to the side, and those damned touchable curls reflected the kitchen light while she put a cup in the microwave.

Darting out of sight, he rested his head against the wall, preparing a speech in case she caught him snooping. After a second, he heard her say, "Shh. Keep quiet or you'll wake the dastardly detective."

He peeked around the corner and spotted the dog staring up at her.

"Stop that. He means well. He can't help it if he's a jerk." She tapped her fingers on the counter. "Most men are."

Rudy put a paw on her calf.

"I know you're not, but you're not human, either. It's different with male dogs . . . sort of."

A couple of seconds passed before the microwave dinged and she removed the mug. "Not with me you don't, but what about Lulu? I bet you'd be in that little Havanese's pants as quick as lightning if you had balls."

Sam about conked his head against the plaster. He knew she had a habit of making comments to her dog, but he'd swear that right now, she was holding a full-blown conversation.

"Don't blame me for your lack of testicles. I wasn't the one who had them removed. And neutering is the right thing to do with strays, male or female. The world doesn't need any more unwanted dogs or cats."

He stifled a laugh. It figured. Even in the dead of night, and with her own dog, she couldn't climb down from her soapbox on the proper way to care for an animal.

A drawer opened and closed, then she said, "I'm fine. Go back to bed if you want."

A moment later, he glanced down and his gaze collided with the gray-and-white hound's. A low rumble sounded from deep in the animal's throat. Sam stiffened and raised a finger to his lips, as if the mutt understood. Damn if the dog didn't grin at him before it growled again in a more threatening tone.

"What's your problem?" Ellie called in an exaggerated whisper.

He debated: stay and get bit or walk away like a coward.

Half a heartbeat passed, then he raised his head and saw Ellie in the doorway, her mouth open as if ready to scream. Fist to her bombshell chest, she heaved a breath, but she looked mad enough to chew nails. "Are you spying on me?"

He lifted both hands in a motion of surrender. "Call off Cujo. I'm just looking for something to help me sleep."

She gave him a "yeah, right" glare, then crossed her arms and poked the dog with her toe. "I thought you were on your way to bed?"

The grumpy mutt stared him up and down, growled one more time, and took off down the hall. Sam didn't breathe again until the dog disappeared through the bedroom door. When he swung his head around, Ellie was gone, so he walked into the kitchen, where he found her having a second go at the microwave.

Sitting at the table, he waited while she made another cup of tea and brought it to him. Then she pulled out a chair and took a seat. "You scared the crap out of me," she chided. "Why didn't you announce yourself?"

"Jeez, you're bossy. I'm here to help, remember." He dunked the teabag a couple of times, then fished it out with a spoon and set it on a napkin. "I apologize if I frightened you."

She fiddled with the envelope, opened it, and removed the sheet of paper. "Are you sure this is the real thing?"

"Looks real to me. Besides, if Gary was as nice as you

say, why would he yank your chain about something so serious?"

"I don't know." She sipped her tea, then took another look at the will. "I still can't believe he had anything worthy of a safety-deposit box, let alone a will. And to leave whatever it is to a dog? I know Leona Helmsley willed a bundle to make sure her pooch was cared for, but this isn't the same. Rudy is mine, and I care for him, so why did he do it? And can a dog really inherit anything?"

"Beats me," said Sam. "In my opinion, you need a lawyer."

She folded the will and returned it to the envelope. "Gary's last name was Veridot. I didn't know that."

"I'm sure Gruning does by now. Tell me again, what did the old guy—the man who gave you the envelope—say?"

"Pops? Just that Gary gave it to him a couple of months ago and asked him to pass it to me if anything happened to him." She leaned back in the chair. "Pops heard the commotion in the Ramble, arrived at the scene, and did what Gary asked."

"It would have been smarter to give it to you privately. That way, Gruning's man wouldn't have seen the transfer."

"I doubt Pops had any idea the police would demand a look." She took another swallow of tea. "Now what?"

"First off, if Gruning comes straight out and asks about the envelope, you have to decide what you're going to tell him."

"You mean I can lie."

"You could say it was nothing and you tossed it. Or you could come right out and show him. There is a bright spot in all this. Because the will is in your possession, the police can't take it from you without a court order, which means you'll have time to get to the bank and check out that safety-deposit box first. I'm pretty sure, if you register the will with the Surrogate's Court, you'll be covered."

"I really do need a lawyer, don't I?"

"It's a good idea."

She stared into her mug. "Any suggestions on the best way to handle Gruning?"

"Act as if you know what you're doing, and don't let on that you're scared shitless." He smiled. "Sorry, that usually works for most people."

"I don't want to get you in trouble, Sam."

He raised his shoulders in a "who cares?" motion. "I've been in hot water before. It's nothing I can't handle."

"Still, I appreciate what you did for me. I know staying here wasn't the way you wanted to spend your evening. You probably had a date ... or something."

He drained his cup and set it on the table. Why the hell not confess? Maybe she'd offer a little personal information of her own in return. "I haven't been with a woman, not even out to dinner or a movie, since we celebrated putting the Albright murder to rest."

"Overworked?"

"Always."

"Sorry to hear it."

"Yeah, I'll just bet you are."

Pursing her lips, she carried both cups to the sink, and he followed, positioning himself directly behind her, so close he could smell the flowery scent of her shampoo.

She turned and almost smacked into him. Hand to her throat, she opened her eyes wide. "It's really late. I have to get to be—sleep."

"Yeah, me, too." He wrapped one of her wayward curls around his finger. "You have terrific hair."

She drew away and the curl unfurled, then sprang back in place. "It's hard to manage, especially in this humidity."

"Looks good to me," he continued, edging closer. "The color is ... interesting." His breath fluttered the tendrils spiraling across her forehead. "Red, gold, brown, all at one time. Is there a name for that color?"

She inched to her right, and he followed. "The kids in school used to call me 'carrot top.' It's calmed down to a dull copper now that I'm an adult."

He raised a brow and lowered his gaze to her lips. "The name doesn't do it justice. I know women who'd kill to have hair that shade."

"I found a gray one the other morning," she said with a pout. "Talk about a downer."

Sam smiled at her honesty. How many women would admit to such a thing? "You don't need to worry." Again, he caught a curl, but this time he used it to tug her near. "It doesn't show, and you'd be attractive even if it did."

Before he could stop himself, his eyelids lowered, and he bent forward, hungry for the taste of her mouth.

Instead of welcoming his kiss, she splayed her fingers against his chest, moved sideways, and stumbled toward the door. "I'm exhausted. I—I'll see you in the morning."

She hurried from the room, and he propped his butt against the counter. Closing his eyes, he muttered a silent curse. So much for his good intentions. And so much for keeping his hands to himself. He was in this too far to step back now, even if he wanted to. Ellie needed him. He'd be a fool to let her down.

Chapter 3

Ellie awoke in a fog, showered, dressed in jeans and a lemon yellow T-shirt, and tiptoed out the door at seven to walk Rudy and Mr. T. Thanks to her upcoming morning with the police, the two dogs were doomed to spend the day inside, because she had no idea when she'd return. Of course, if Gruning arrested her, she'd have a bigger problem. There'd be dozens of dogs going walkless today, which would translate to angry customers and a heck of a lot of cleanup.

She definitely needed an assistant.

Her midnight encounter with Sam had kept her awake for too long. Every time she drifted to sleep, his sexy dimples, cocky smile, and coffee-dark eyes popped into view. Then she'd envision his naked chest and the open snap on the waistband of his snug-fitting jeans, and her heart would trip to jackhammer speed. Unfortunately, no matter how hard she tried to erase the tempting features, they kept returning to haunt her. In fact, if she lingered on any one thing long enough, she'd swear she felt his mouth, firm and demanding, covering her lips, his tongue tasting hers, his hands cupping her—

"This is gonna cost you," Rudy yipped from below, breaking into her daydream.

Talk about dropping to reality like a popped balloon. "What if we take a long walk after dinner tonight? If Viv has a date, we'll even bring Mr. T."

"It better be to the dog park at Carl Schurz, fool," Viv's Jack Russell groused, *"or Mr. T won't be a happy camper."*

Though Carl Schurz Park was a hike from their building, Ellie and her best human friend sometimes walked the dogs there on evenings when Vivian didn't have a prior commitment. Since she hadn't spoken to Viv about this current mess, tonight would probably be a good time to sort through it all.

Minutes later, she opened Viv's apartment door, heard the shower running, and left a note on the kitchen table suggesting the evening walk. It was the best she could do until tonight—if she was still a free woman.

When she returned to her unit, coffee was brewing. In the kitchen, she found her houseguest fresh from a shower and dressed in a clean shirt and chinos, setting out mugs. "Thanks," she told him. Walking to the kibble cupboard, Ellie took down a container and poured Rudy his morning nibble. "Here you go." She set his breakfast on the placemat. Then she gave him fresh water, aware of Sam's eyes on her all the while.

"Did you decide what you're going to say to Gruning?" he asked after she dropped two slices of cinnamon swirl breakfast bread in the toaster.

She poured milk in her mug and added artificial sweetener, anything to avoid meeting his gaze. "I decided to leave the will at home. If he wants to see it, I'll tell him to get a court order. I just have to figure out a time to go to the bank with that key. If they won't let me in the safety-deposit box, I'll call Stanley."

"Stanley?"

"My mother's latest husband. He's a retired judge, so he'll give me good advice." When the toast popped, she walked to the counter, buttered it, and passed him a slice. "Sorry there's no time for a better breakfast."

He finished the toast in three bites. "Not a problem. I don't usually eat in the morning."

Ellie tried to nibble daintily, but she was a breakfast person. Heck, she was a lunch and dinner person, too. After swallowing her coffee, she dabbed her mouth with a paper napkin and brought their empty cups to the sink. Then she tucked the key into her front pocket, just in case she had time to visit First Trust today. "Okay. Guess we're ready to go."

Sam nodded and let her walk ahead of him out the door. When they got to the car, she spotted a sheet of paper tacked to his windshield and burst out laughing. "Still collecting those tickets, I see."

He unlocked her door, then marched around the car and tossed his duffel in the backseat. After snatching the parking violation from the windshield, he slid behind the wheel. "There's too damn many cars in this city. Don't people know about mass transit?" Leaning over, he shoved the paper in the stuffed-to-overflowing glove box, then started the car. "I'll take care of them—one of these days."

"You aren't supposed to park in front of a fire hydrant. As an officer of the law, I assume you know that."

"It was late. I didn't see it." He pulled into traffic and stepped on the gas. "So sue me."

"One of these days, someone is going to check the records. Then you'll be in real trouble."

"You sound like my mother," he griped, his tone that of a five-year-old. "I can handle it."

They shot south while Ellie continued to badger him about his refusal to find legal parking or own up to the fines. After turning into the police lot, he took her elbow and escorted her into the station.

"As soon as we step inside, I've done my duty. I'll hang out in the bull pen in case you need me."

Ellie walked to the reception desk. "Hi. I'm Ellie Engleman. I'm here to see—"

"Detective Gruning. He's waiting for you," said the clerk. "I'll buzz him."

A minute later, a female officer showed her to the interrogation room, a useless effort because Ellie figured she could get there blindfolded by now. If this murder business kept up, she could probably demand a free pass into the bull pen, as Sam called it. The officer nodded to a chair, and she sat at the gray metal table. It matched the depressingly gray tile floor, gray walls, and three gray plastic chairs situated around the perimeter.

The door opened and Gruning walked in with her bag. "Good to see you're on time," he said, slamming down her tote. He popped a mint and chewed.

"There's no need to be surly. I'm here, as promised."

He continued to stare. "I see you decided against bringing an attorney."

"I don't have anything to hide, Detective Gruning."

Before he responded, another officer came in carrying the standard recorder. Gruning turned it on and began his spiel, giving the date, time, and names of those present. Then he reached inside and began taking her bag apart, item by item.

"Brown leather date book—"

"It's espresso—"

"I beg your pardon?"

"The color. It's not brown, but it isn't black either. The tag called it espresso."

He huffed out a breath. "One *espresso* date book containing"—he flipped through the pages—"a calendar, address list, and blank paper." He set the book aside and continued. "One package of tissues, one lipstick labeled"—he squinted at the bottom of the tube—"Apricot Delight. A folding mirror, a bag of dog biscuits, one red dog leash, a plastic folding cup, a container of sandwich bags—"

"For my business," she explained. "You know, pet cleanup."

He crunched the mint, then swallowed. "Three pens, one pencil, one hair brush, one black—"

"Uh, no," she interrupted.

"One *espresso* leather credit card case, one can of Mace." He tossed each item onto a pile. "One copy of *Best Friends* magazine, two bottles of water." He stood the bottles upright next to the growing mound and dug deeper. "One cylindrical container."

Heat rose to Ellie's cheeks.

Gruning snorted. "Containing feminine hygiene products. A tube of lip balm, a box of throat lozenges, one bottle of Advil, a package of sugarless chewing gum, a palm-sized spiral notebook, and ..." Upending the purse, he counted out the change after it clattered to the table. "Sixty-eight cents."

Finished with the inventory, he took a seat across from her, pulled a handkerchief from his pocket, and wiped his sweaty brow. Since the temperature in the station was just a couple of degrees warmer than a meat locker, she guessed it was the absence of the envelope that had him so hot and bothered.

"Leave the recorder running, Murphy," Gruning ordered. "You're excused." The patrolman left, and the detective leaned into the table. "It came to my attention last evening, after we did a preliminary search of your bag, that you were approached while waiting at the crime scene by a hot dog vendor who goes by the name of Pops. Pops handed you an envelope. Is this correct, Ms. Engleman?"

"Do you mind if I collect my things while we talk? I have to get to work."

Gruning nodded.

"Yes, Pops gave me an envelope." She gathered her stuff into the tote, then added her wallet, cell, and keys.

"Mind telling me what was in it?"

"I would have shown it to you last night, if you'd asked." So there, you jerk. "But you didn't."

"I'll only pose the question one more time. What was in the envelope?"

"A . . . piece of paper from the deceased."

"From Gary Veridot?" The detective's eyes bugged. "And you didn't think it was relevant to the murder?"

"Of course it wasn't. It was something personal, left to me by Gary. How did you find out his last name?"

"We ran his prints."

"He had a police record?" No, not Gary.

"They were on file for a reason."

"A reason? What sort of reason?"

"Let's stay on topic, Ms. Engleman. The envelope."

"Oh, well. It's at home."

"You didn't think to bring it?"

"Nuh-uh. Of course, if you'd come right out and said that's what you wanted—"

"Ms. Engleman, I have a right to inspect the contents of that envelope. If you refuse, I'll get the court order you claim I need."

"Sure thing. Just let me know when you have it." She stood and hoisted the bag over her shoulder. "Now, if you aren't going to arrest me, I have dogs to walk."

He popped a second mint.

"Okay, then." She waggled her fingers. "See ya."

Ellie started her round of walks only a few minutes late. Since all of her charges were safely housebroken, she didn't think she'd have a problem. She hit the Beaumont, said hello to Natter, the agreeable doorman, and took care of her charges without incident. When she arrived at the Davenport, Randall greeted her and asked how her life was going. Ellie couldn't resist telling him about Gary's death and Rudy's inheritance, ending with, "Gary was so *not* Leona Helmsley. I can't imagine what he left to my dog."

"Mrs. Helmsley isn't the only wealthy woman who bequeathed money to her dog," confided the dapper doorman. "There was a tenant who lived here a few years ago, a Mrs. Levine. Had family money by the truckload, and she absolutely adored her little white poodle, Coco. She owned homes in England, Florida, Hawaii, and California, but she lived here most of the year. Her country house was in the Hamptons, where she stayed on weekends during the summer."

"Wow. What happened to her?"

"She passed on a few years back, but her housekeeper, Elsie Hogarth, still lives in the building. Elsie was given complete charge of Coco, and both she and the poodle have a very healthy allowance."

"Um . . . how healthy? If you don't mind my asking."

"I heard tell two million for Coco's upkeep, and that money is handled by an attorney, but Elsie gets seven hundred dollars a week and the right to live in the apartment with the poodle. I'll have to introduce you sometime. Who knows, Elsie might decide Coco needs a professional walker."

"Even though Rudy will probably get a couple of dollars and change, I'd like to talk to her sometime. So keep that in mind."

"Will do," said Randall. A tenant walked to the counter and he went back to business while Ellie waved good-bye. After taking care of the pooches in the Davenport, she finished her morning rounds and planned to go to the bank, but every time she thought about it she just couldn't do it.

To Ellie, running to First Trust to see what she and her dog inherited was tantamount to stealing from a man sitting in a wheelchair and selling pencils to passersby. So she decided to take it easy, get her second round of walks done early, and go home to think.

After arriving at her apartment, she took Rudy and Mr. T for a quick out, nuked a Lean Cuisine for dinner, and sat at her computer. The nagging questions wouldn't let go of her brain. Who, she continued to ask herself, was so despicable they'd kill a soft-spoken man like Gary? Had he gotten involved in something illegal and was made to pay the price?

Either way, his death was a dismal reminder of the frailty of life. If he had no relatives, she planned to claim the body and see to it Gary had a proper good-bye. But for now, there was only one thing she could think of to do: tackle his past on the Internet while Rudy slept like a baby on the sofa.

An hour later, her worries paled in comparison to what she'd found out about her deceased friend. She'd read the details of his life in newspaper articles from decades ago, and unearthed a dark but fascinating story so disturbing it was worthy of a television movie on the Lifetime network.

Garick Robert Veridot, son of Robert and Sylvia Veridot, now deceased, was fifteen when his older brother, Thompson, had been sentenced to prison for shooting their parents in a drunken and drug-induced rage.

Gary, the sole witness to the killing, had testified for the prosecution at his brother's trial. The brother was convicted, and Gary was sent to live with a grandmother who died just after his eighteenth birthday. A short while later he disappeared, and even the most diligent thrill seekers and tabloid reporters lost his trail.

She teared up when she read the stories centering on a gentle yet intelligent kid too sensitive to adapt to city life alone. His nasty brother was ten years his senior, and he'd become a drug addict soon after puberty. Their wealthy parents had sent the older boy to treatment centers, as they were called back then, and, in the end, were forced to resort to their version of tough love.

An incensed Thompson had discovered their plan to disinherit him and offered to disappear if they gave him his share of the family fortune. When his parents refused, he'd blown them away with his father's gun while his brother looked on in terror.

According to the last story, Thompson had been given the fairly light sentence of thirty years as a result of diminished capacity. The state hadn't been able to prove premeditation because he hadn't brought a weapon to the scene, and his clever attorney had convinced the jury that Thompson was so hopped up on drugs he wasn't responsible for his actions.

Ellie guessed at the rest of the tale while she drank a cup of brandy-laced decaf. Poor Gary had lost a mother, father, grandmother, and brother in the space of three years. Completely alone in the world, he'd probably suffered a form of post-traumatic stress disorder, though at the time the condition didn't go by that name, and chose to hide from anyone who knew of his tragic past.

She bit her lip every time she thought of the gentle, quiet soul who'd lived a hermit-like existence instead of coping with reality, all because of his brutal older brother. She recalled the day he'd seen a group of young men across the street from hers and Rudy's usual park bench, and taken off as if he'd been running a race. Whenever he spotted someone he thought looked suspicious, he'd felt threatened and acted as if the entire world was after him. It was obvious now that he didn't want to be found, nor did he want to deal with real life when his own had wound up badly.

She was so engrossed in Gary's story, she jumped a foot when she heard the knock. Vivian, she thought, ready for their walk. She went to the door and opened it to her best friend, wearing black spandex biking shorts and a sleeveless, hot pink shirt. Her mile-long legs led to a pair of stylish running shoes.

"Hey, you ready?" Viv asked, perky as ever.

"In a second. Just let me hook up the big guy." Squatting, Ellie frowned at her faded denims and sweat-stained T-shirt, then gave herself a mental pep talk. She walked dogs; these were her work clothes. Viv received all the male attention when they were out anyway, so why should she change?

By the time they arrived on the front porch, Ellie was in the midst of filling Viv in on all that had gone down.

"I told you it wasn't safe to be around that guy." Her friend waited while Mr. T watered the side of a building. "Just think what might have happened if you'd been at his shelter when the killer paid him a visit."

"I still can't believe someone murdered such a nice guy."

"The unbelievable thing is the cops think you might have done it."

"After dealing with Gruning, there isn't a doubt in my mind I'm number one on his suspect list. Remember how suspicious the cops were when the professor died? Well, triple their interest in me for this case."

"Good thing Sam was smart enough to know you were innocent once he started investigating Albright's death for real. And speaking of Sam—"

"Leave him out of this."

"But the dreamy detective spent the night." Viv grinned. "Think of the opportunity you blew by remanding him to the guest bedroom."

"Maybe so, but I had no intention of encouraging hanky-panky." Viv didn't need to hear about hers and Sam's heated exchange in the kitchen. "Not ever again."

"Okay, we'll drop the hottie discussion for now and get back to Gary. The man was a nutcase, a beggar. What reason do the police give for thinking you shot him?"

"I was the one who found the body. Seems that's a red flag to the cops. I think the only reason I haven't been arrested is because they haven't found the murder weapon. Once they do—"

"That still won't be enough to assume you're guilty. Who in their right mind would kill for a bunch of junk from a homeless person's makeshift shelter? If it were mine, I'd take it all to the nearest Dumpster."

"It's not the junk in the shelter that has me worried. When Gruning learns there's a safety-deposit box involved, and it could contain something of value, I'm toast."

"I hate to keep repeating myself, but what makes you think there'll be anything worthwhile in that box? Gary had nothing." They hit Third Avenue and headed east toward York. "And remember, they need a murder weapon."

Ellie frowned. "I read a short article in today's paper, and there was no mention of them finding one. There was also no gunpowder residue on my hands—a point in my favor, I might add."

"Whoa. Now you're creeping me out, talking like one of those television cops. Either you've started watching *CSI* or you've switched from reading romance to true crime."

"Neither, but I have learned to keep my eyes and ears open when I'm in the precinct. If you pay attention, it's easy to figure out what's going on."

"Sounds to me like they're fishing. You know, giving subtle hints and hoping you'll incriminate yourself."

"Gruning can fish all he wants—this pond is empty."

They hit York and turned left to get to Eighty-sixth. On the way, she told Vivian about Gary's past and his incarcerated brother, ending with, "Next time I feel like having my own private pity party, I'll put myself in Gary's shoes."

"I don't think I've ever heard a story that sad," Viv stated. "It *would* make a great 'movie of the week.' "

"Now that he's gone, some greedy journalist at one of those gossip tabloids will probably find a way to exploit him all over again. No wonder he went into hiding."

"Not to belabor the point, but what did Sam have to say about Gary's past?"

"I didn't find any of the info out until tonight, but I'm sure Sam knows by now. The stories I read on the Internet explain what Gruning meant when he said Gary's prints were on file." She stopped to let Rudy nose a trash can. "Don't worry. I'll handle things on my own."

"Hang on a second. This sounds like another Professor Albright situation. Don't tell me you're going to play Nancy Drew again."

"Finding out who killed Gary is an idea."

"Ryder is going to lock you up and throw away the key."

"Sam has no right to an opinion on anything I do. It's not his case, and since he left me hanging a couple of months back, I don't owe him any explanations."

"That might be the way you see it, but I bet he's going to have a different view."

"Well, good for him."

"Hey, don't get angry with me. Just be careful."

"I know how to take care of myself."

"Great. I can see the shingle hanging outside our building now. '*Ellie Engleman, Detective-in-Training.*' "

"I have a right to some answers, especially if the police try to pin Gary's murder on me." She brushed a curl from her forehead. "The man was my friend, and a truly nice guy. I want to find the person who did this as much as the cops."

"I'm sure Groaning—"

"That's Gruning."

"Whatever. I'm sure he'll be happy to hear it."

"Stop being a pain. Besides Gary, I have a lot on my mind. I've got so many new customers, I need an assistant. I'm thinking of running an ad."

"Why don't you ask around first, or hang a flyer on a couple of the university bulletin boards? A college kid would work for less than a professional, and they usually need the money."

"I guess I could do that on Monday. I'll have time between rounds. But I still have to get to that bank."

"I'd go with you, but I have meetings scheduled for the entire day."

"Don't worry. I'll let you know what I find, and what's happening with Gruning. I swear, I've never met anyone more obnoxious. He has a partner named Smith, but I don't know a thing about him."

"First Ryder, then Gruning and Smith," Viv said with a giggle. "Before you know it, you'll be on a *last*-name basis with every detective in Manhattan."

Ellie rolled her eyes. "It's bad enough Georgette's going to have a conniption when she finds out I'm involved in another murder. Between my career as a pooper-scooper and my penchant for finding dead bodies, I'm her cross to bear."

"How are she and the judge doing?"

"Fine. According to Georgette, he makes her blissfully happy, and I know she's the light of his life. It's sweet, really, finding a soul mate at their age."

"I sure hope I don't have to wait that long to find my Mr. Right." Viv raised a brow, her smile little more than a naughty leer. "Do you think they have sex?"

"Ewww." Ellie shuddered and set her sights on the park ahead. "I don't want to think about it."

They entered the gates of Carl Schurz Park and took the dogs off leash, then walked to the iron railing. To the north lay the Triborough Bridge, its majestic expanse bright in the waning evening light. Ellie rested her bottom on the railing and watched Rudy and Mr. T play tag with a couple of other dogs.

"What are you doing tomorrow?" Viv asked.

"I'm picking up my two Chihuahuas and boarding them until the middle of the week. Then I plan to go clothes shopping."

"It's about time," Viv responded, her tone teasing.

"Please pick something that fits, instead of things that hang off you like a shroud."

"My clothes fit the way I want them to fit. It's not like I'm model-sized anymore."

"I bet Detective Dreamy doesn't think so."

Ellie's face warmed at the memory of last night's kitchen encounter. Sam had complimented her hair and said she was attractive. The slug.

"He's just like other males of the species. He'll hump anything that's available." It had taken weeks to convince herself she was over the deceitful detective. He was the one who hadn't called as he'd promised after their single night of sexual exploration. She hadn't dumped him—he had dumped her.

At first, she'd assumed the reason for his disappearing act was her fault. She was too fat, too obnoxious, or too dumb, all failings her dickhead ex had mentioned time and again during their divorce battle. But on really bad days, she told herself it was more basic than that.

She was simply a lousy lay.

It had taken her months of self-exploration, but she now realized she'd been wrong to automatically think Sam had bolted because of her, when he was the one with the problem.

"Wow, you really are on a downer," said Viv, breaking into her musings.

"Sam was just doing something nice yesterday, to make up for his being a jerk in April. The last thing I want is him in my pants again, because all that will get me is another night of slam-bam-thank-you-ma'am. I'm worth more than that."

"You certainly are. And it's about time you noticed." They stood side by side for a few more minutes, lost in their own thoughts, before Viv asked, "Why do you think Gary left whatever's in that box to Rudy and not you?"

"Who knows. Gary always talked about how he'd

wanted a dog but his mother never allowed it. He and Rudy got along fairly well." Now was not the time to tell Vivian of her unique talent of dog telepathy, or the fact that Gary had it, too, at least where Rudy was concerned. "Most of the time, he acted like a big kid. He probably thought it was cute, leaving whatever to a dog. Besides, as the executor, I'm fairly certain I have all the power. I need a lawyer, I guess."

"Someone has to read you rights as an executor."

"I plan to talk to the judge about it, if I can get him to myself."

"In case help from Judge Frye doesn't pan out, remember I have that cute corporate attorney I want you to meet. I'm sure he'd give you free legal advice if you went to dinner with him."

"Thanks, but I'll pass," Ellie said, as she'd done a couple of zillion times before. "I'm just afraid asking Stanley for help will make Mother angry. She'll rag on me about my distasteful profession, which will lead to an argument, which will lead to another version of World War III."

"The ex-terminator rides again." Viv gazed out at the park and nodded. "Looks like the boys made a friend."

An older gentleman dressed in jeans and a plaid, short-sleeved shirt squatted in front of Mr. T and Rudy, talking as if they were old pals.

"It's time to go home. We might as well collect them and say hello," said Ellie.

Ellie and Viv ambled to the trio. The man, who looked to be in his sixties, had thinning brown hair and a potbelly. "Evening, ladies. These dogs belong to you?"

"The Jack Russell is mine, and the yorkie mix belongs to Ellie," said Vivian. She shook the man's hand. "I'm Vivian. Do you have a dog?"

The man grinned. "Name's Benedict, and no, I don't. But I like these little guys. I know about Jack Russells, but what's a yorkie mix?"

"He doesn't need to know, Triple E," said Rudy, standing rigid at her side.

"Rudy's part Yorkshire terrier, part poodle. At least that's what they said when I found him at the shelter."

"He seems smart. Is he a biter?"

Rudy growled low in his throat, complete with bared teeth. *"I am where you're concerned!"*

"Hey, stop that," Ellie ordered. "Sorry, he's just tired. Normally, he's meek as a lamb."

"Good to know." Benedict stuffed his hands in his pockets. "You two come here often?"

"A couple of times a week," said Viv. "It's a long walk, but the dogs like it."

"I imagine so. Well, see ya around." Turning, he headed south toward the Cherokee Apartments.

"Nice guy." Viv clipped the leash onto Mr. T's collar.

Rudy snorted. *"I didn't like him."*

Ellie swallowed her canine pal's comment and hooked him to his lead. These days Rudy seemed suspicious of everyone. But really, growling at a nice old guy in the park who just wanted to say hello? He needed to get a grip.

Chapter 4

"Why do I have to take part in today's so-called mission of mercy?" Rudy asked as they left the apartment the next morning. *"Saturday's our day to sleep in."*

"Because you need fresh air."

"I'd rather be snoozing," he grumped. *"And I'm in mourning for Gary."*

Ellie heaved a sigh. After everything that had happened in the past day and a half, catching a few extra winks had been her first choice, too, but she'd promised the Fallgrave sisters she'd babysit their Chihuahuas while they were out of town.

"I feel the same as you, but I have things to do, and this is our only chance for exercise today."

"So take me for a walk and bring me home. I'm not looking forward to this stop."

"Cheech and Chong will be our houseguests for the next couple of days, which means you are their host and I their host*ess.*" She waited while Rudy raised his leg against a trash can. "And no smart comments allowed. I expect you to be on your best behavior both at their home and ours."

"I keep tellin' you those hairballs are illegals. We'll be lucky if INS doesn't raid us . . . or Homeland Security."

"You're being ridiculous. Janice assured me they purchased the boys through a reputable breeder here in the states."

"Right, sure. Heaven forbid she be truthful and tell you they came from some puppy mill south of the border." He snorted. *"You are such a pushover."*

"Why would she lie? Besides, if by any chance they are here 'illegally,' they probably miss their homeland. So we need to be extra nice to them."

Twenty minutes later, they sauntered through the doors of the Beaumont, an upscale apartment complex that had been the second building she'd acquired on her client list. Nodding to the weekend doorman, she held up her key and entered the elevator. On the top floor, she took note of the ear-shattering music playing inside the suite and rang the bell. When no one answered, she used her key to open the door and peeked inside.

"Hello! Patti! Janice? Anybody home?"

She stepped into the foyer and waited. With the blaring rock instrumental, it was no wonder she couldn't be heard.

Rudy pulled on the lead. *"I say we tiptoe in and surprise 'em. I bet we catch those scrawny bean eaters doin' something against the law."*

"Readjust your attitude, mister," said Ellie, holding him in place. "Or I'll leave you in the hall."

"Jeesh! You take the fun out of everything," he groused. *"Okay, I'll mind my Ps and Qs, but don't make me play hide and seek with 'em or anything else cutesy, and remember, I do not share my sleep space. I draw the line at getting intimate with the hairless wonders."*

Ellie frowned. "I'm sure they'll bring their own entertainment, and you sleep on *my* bed, so you don't have a thing to say about it." Inspecting the foyer, she spotted two dog beds and a tote filled to overflowing with, she imagined, treats, toys, and special food. "Look, they're all ready. They even have their own sleeping bags, just like kids going to a slumber party. We'll bring everything home, and they can settle in while you nap."

She walked into the living room and sat on the forest green leather sofa, sinking into luxury. Supermodels made big bucks, she figured, but she doubted Janice's fledgling singing career could compare. They usually slept late when she gave the boys their first walk, but one of them was up when she arrived for the second outing. Since they were both leaving town, she was certain one of the sisters would make an appearance soon.

"I think this mission of mercy exempts me from going to your mother's tomorrow. You know I hate spending time at the ex-terminator's." He hopped onto the sofa and gave her a pleading look. *"Georgette treats me like a fifth wheel ... or something she had to scrape off the bottom of her shoe."*

She ignored his use of Vivian's pet name for her four-times-divorced parent. "Mother made a special point of inviting you to Sunday brunch, so you're going."

"That alone smells like a rancid liver treat. She'll probably find a way to kick me or give you another lecture on filthy animals and your demeaning job."

"You're wrong. I think she's finally coming to accept the fact that we're a matched pair. I've told her often enough, if you aren't welcome in her home, neither am I." She picked up the latest issue of *Vogue*, which featured Patti on the cover, and thumbed through the magazine. "By the way, I'm still waiting to hear about what really happened between you and Mother the week the D and I were on our honeymoon."

"Why does something that took place ten years ago matter? Karma reunited us, and we'll stay together for a long, long while, right? That's what's important."

"Maybe so, but—"

"Ellie, hi." Patti strutted into the massive room with Cheech in her arms. "Who are you talking to?"

"Me? Oh, ah, no one. Hey, the cover of this magazine is fabulous."

"Hang on a second." She went to a wall of bookcases, fiddled with the sound system, and set the music to a more bearable level. "Sorry, that racket is Jan's thing at the moment, not mine. What did you say?"

"This cover." Ellie held out the *Vogue*. "It's wonderful."

Patti cocked her head as if seeing the publication for the first time. "It turned out all right." The supermodel ran a hand through her fall of chestnut hair. "Though I still can't believe that's me, plain ol' Patricia Fallgrave from Union, New Jersey, featured on the front."

Ellie couldn't imagine anyone thinking Patti plain. At six feet tall, with killer cheekbones, smoky hazel-green eyes, and a smile men swooned over, she was striking, even dressed in her current outfit: tight ratty jeans, a baggy red sweater, and a pair of knee-high leather boots Ellie guessed cost more than her monthly mortgage.

"Mind answering a question for me?"

"For you, my baby's number one caregiver?" Patti nuzzled nose to nose with Cheech. "Anything."

"Do you ever get to keep the clothes you wear in these photographs?"

Patti laughed as she sat on the sofa and gave Rudy's ears a rub. "Once in a while. Why, do you want to borrow something?"

"Me? Borrow something that fits you?" Ellie grinned. "I don't think so."

Janice took that moment to enter, carrying her own Chihuahua. "Hey, Ellie, what's up?"

"Jan, please tell our friend here how great she looks. If I could eat, I'd want a figure just like hers."

"I believe the operative phrase is 'if I could eat,'" Janice, her petite sister, responded. "What did you have so far today? Three cups of black coffee and half a bagel?" She screwed her doll-like face into a pout. "I worry about you. Who's going to take care of you in Madrid?"

"You're going to Madrid?" Ellie had always wanted to see Spain, but aside from their week-long honeymoon in Jamaica the D had never taken her away for more than a long weekend, no matter the time of year. "That's great."

"I think so, too," Patti answered, ignoring her sister's pointed question. "But it's only for three days. I'll be back on Wednesday night, which means you can return the boys after their Thursday morning walk."

"Forgive me for being nosy, Jan, but where will you be while Patti's in Spain?"

"LA," said the singer. "I'm interviewing a couple of songwriters to decide if they've written anything that fits the theme of my first album. Jackson's flying with me, so I won't be alone on the big bad West Coast."

Ellie had met Jackson Hall, Janice's manager, a few times since she'd begun walking Cheech and Chong, and he'd made no secret of the fact that he wasn't a dog lover. Consequently, she and Rudy didn't think much of the man. "Where are you staying?"

"I don't have a clue. Jackson made all the arrangements. He always does. I'm lucky to have him."

"You mean, he's lucky to have you," Patti said, wrinkling her nose. "His other clients can't hold a candle to you in the talent department."

"You're just saying that because you love me. Jackson gave up managing several singers to take full charge of my career."

"So he says," Patti reminded her. "I still think you should run a background check on him, talk to a few of his former clients, too. You don't know what kind of skeletons might be lurking in his closet."

Janice turned to Ellie. "What do you think?"

Ellie gave her a blank look. "I don't have the faintest idea, but your sister makes sense. Maybe you should do some research. Especially since you'll be alone with him for the next week."

"No worry there," Janice answered. "Jackson's gay, so I'll be safe."

"There are more ways to be in danger from a man than sexual," Patti pronounced. "He might steer you to a lousy song writer or convince you to buy a crappy tune from someone who's giving him a kickback. And don't let him bring you to any of those outrageous Hollywood parties. I hear they're a hotbed of drugs and debauchery. Next thing, pictures of you naked will show up on the Internet, and he'll claim it's great publicity."

"You're warning me away from celebrity parties? You, who sometimes attend festivities with Kate Moss?" Janice rolled her eyes. "I may be younger, but I can take care of myself."

"Okay." Patti sighed. "But do me a favor. Let my lawyer study any contract before you sign. Fax it to Jacob, and he'll give you his expert legal opinion."

Janice shrugged. "Anything, if it'll get you off my case."

Patti spoke to Ellie. "I made a dozen calls, got advice from models and their agents, and I read the in-depth report I was sent by an attorney organization before I hired Jacob Brenner. I even had him investigated by a private detective, just to be on the safe side."

"A private detective?" Ellie asked, impressed.

Patti buffed her fingernails on her faded sweater. "You bet. When I found out how much that type of attorney charged, I made sure I was going to get my money's worth. Jackson is taking twenty percent of Jan's paycheck plus royalties in a couple of different capacities. She should be positive he's earning every penny."

"You do make sense." Maybe she could use this Jacob guy to help untangle the mess with Gary's will. It would give her an excuse not to meet with that lawyer Viv kept trying to introduce her to.

"As an attorney for people in the entertainment field, he's the best," the supermodel added.

Oo-kay, scratch Jacob, Ellie decided. She was as far from being in the entertainment field as her ex was from being a faithful husband. "Are the boys ready to go?"

"They're ready," said Jan, hugging Chong to her chest. "I'm going to miss my little man."

"Oh, brother."

Ellie ignored Rudy's whine. "I take it their gear is in the foyer? Shall I call the doorman, or can one of you lend a hand?"

"I'll do it," said Jan. "Patti's still packing."

"A girl needs her supplies." Patti gave Cheech a final kiss, and passed him over to her sister.

Janice snapped a leash on each Chihuahua's rhinestone-studded collar and led them to the door. She then commandeered the tote bag while Ellie grabbed the beds and Rudy's lead, and they rode the elevator to the lobby.

"Have a great time in LA," Ellie told her while the doorman hailed a cab. "I want to hear all the Hollywood gossip when you get back."

"You know, that might be fun. Come over and have dinner. The three boys can have a play date, and maybe you can convince Patti to eat more than a couple of lettuce leaves."

"I don't want no stinkin' play date with them illegals," Rudy gruffed. *"A guy's nothin' without his ethics."*

Ellie stored Cheech and Chong's belongings in the kitchen pantry, put out fresh water, and gave each of the dogs a chew treat. "I'll be back later, and we'll go on a nice long walk," she promised. "Be good, okay?"

The little guys latched onto their treats, climbed into their beds, and curled up obediently. Neither one had said a word to her since she'd started walking them a few months ago, but Ellie assumed they understood her, unless . . .

"Now you're gettin' it," Rudy said, following her to

the door. *"They don't communicate with you because they* no habla *English, just like I said."*

"Puh-leeze. Go take that nap you've been yapping about. We'll talk more when I get back from Bloomingdale's."

"Just make sure to buy something your mother will approve of, because I swear I'm gonna bite her if she makes another nasty comment about your clothes."

Fighting a grin, Ellie narrowed her gaze. "Nip Georgette's ankle and I guarantee it'll be the last visit you make to her penthouse."

"Is that a promise?"

"I don't have to promise. If you bite Mother, she'll never let me forget it. And if that happens, I'll see to it you suffer as much as I do." She opened the door and hoisted her tote bag over her shoulder. "Now go to sleep. And leave those two Chihuahuas alone."

A half hour later, she walked through the pricy department store flipping through racks of expensive and, to her way of thinking, unattractive clothes. Why was everything cut for the size-four figure when the average size of the American woman was a fourteen? And since when had "fashionable" become the code word for uncomfortable?

Rudy had been correct when he'd groused about her mother. Georgette always found fault with her clothing, no matter how perfect Ellie thought her outfit. And though her mother might have approved if she bought designer originals, she would never accept the fact that her daughter wore a double-digit dress size.

Searching through the various departments, she finally found mix and match ready-to-wear made of natural linen fabric in bright colors with a flattering cut. After buying several pieces, she made her way outside, where she caught a cab for home. She'd promised Rudy and the Chihuahuas a long walk, and she couldn't disappoint her pal or her charges.

*   *   *

Ellie spent the night going over the Internet articles she'd found on Gary. Reading the stories depressed her, but she couldn't seem to get the sad tale out of her mind. What kind of son would kill his parents, and do it with his younger brother watching? And how had Gary felt as the key witness in a trial that would put his brother away for thirty years?

She went to bed after walking the dogs, exhausted from worrying and still wondering what Gary might have left them in his will. She couldn't wait for Monday, the day she would stop in the bank and check out that safety-deposit box.

"You thinkin' about my inheritance?" Rudy asked from his place on the pillow next to her.

"You're reading my mind again, or pretending to, and it creeps me out. So stop it."

He yawned, then gave a doggie shrug. *"It's not my fault we have a special bond. Besides, you should be thinking about what Gary left us. It could be something great."*

"Uh-huh. Dream on, big boy. Now, good night. We'll talk more tomorrow."

The next morning, when she said good-bye to the Chihuahuas, they simply stared, giving credence to Rudy's theory.

"See. What'd I tell you? They don't comprende *English."*

"Maybe they're still insecure around us, or they miss Patti and Janice." She gave him a look. "I'd expect you to be off your feed and missing me if I gave you to Viv without any warning."

"Missing you, yes. Off my feed—never."

"That could very well be the reason they're not opening up to us now."

"Doesn't make sense. They don't speak to Bruiser or Lulu or any of the other dogs, either. Can you imagine a male canine who doesn't make small talk with Lulu?"

"That Havanese is nothing but a tease. I'm surprised you're taken in by her feminine wiles."

"She's got a right to be picky. She's a dish. Told me she's earned enough points to compete at some big whoop-de-do dog show this November and she intends to win."

"She thinks she can make it at a national competition?" The forecast sounded exactly like something Lulu would say. "Well, I agree she's a cutie, but her attitude is a little too femme fatale for me. Be careful before you lose your heart. Being in love with someone who doesn't feel the same way about you can be a devastating blow to your ego."

"Then it's a good thing you found out about the dime store detective before things went too far, huh?"

"Exactly," she muttered. "I have so many more important things on my mind right now, I don't have five free minutes to even think about Sam." Which was a partial truth, because she did need Sam if she wanted more official information about Gary. Were there any distant family members who should be made aware of his death, and was it the police's job to notify them or hers? And what about his brother in prison? Would he want to know that Gary had died?

They took Fifth to Seventy-second, turned right, and kept walking to cross Madison and ended up on Park, where they entered Georgette's high-rise. As usual, Orlando was at the door. "Ms. Engleman," he said, tipping his hat as they passed.

Did the man ever sleep? "Orlando, you on duty again?"

"Yes, miss."

"I thought the union saw to it you had regular days off?" She headed for the elevator. "Like normal people."

"I do what I have to, miss."

The doors closed, and they rode to the top floor. Orlando was either the most dedicated doorman in the city or a ghoul. How could anyone be on duty twenty hours a day and still be polite and professional? Her mother thought he was a saint, but Georgette said that about most of the service people with whom she dealt. Then again, they'd have to be on the list for canonization to keep her mother happy, so maybe the man was a Gandhi clone.

She eyed her reflection in the elevator mirror, straightened the collar on her new, gauzy white blouse, tugged at the hem of her bright yellow linen vest, and smoothed the front of her beige linen slacks. The tailored vest hugged her waist, imparting an illusion of slimness. She'd added peach lip gloss to her mouth, a sweep of mascara to her lashes, and a dab of styling gel to her corkscrew curls. Just let her mother find fault with her mode of dress today.

"Corinna," Ellie said, clasping the expert housekeeper's hand when she opened the door. "How are you?"

"If it isn't Ms. Ellie and her faithful companion." Shaking her head, Corinna grinned. "And lookin' good, I might add." The woman stooped and ruffled Rudy's ears. "Come on in. The guests are waiting."

Guests? A knot of concern twisted in Ellie's stomach. Though she'd gotten the impression this would be a private affair, she knew her mother's semimonthly brunches were popular with a group of residents living on the Upper East Side. Yes, Georgette had reminded her daughter to dress appropriately instead of appearing in the clothes Ellie wore for her job, but that was her mother's usual order. It hadn't caused any alarm bells to ring ... until now.

When she heard muffled voices coming from the direction of the living room, she dropped to a squat and held Rudy's muzzle. "I don't like the sound of this, so please be on your best behavior."

"I'll try, but I'm not promising anything."

After smoothing his fur, she stood and headed toward

the clamor. Surrounded by the smell of bacon and a variety of other pleasant aromas, she hoped that Corinna had prepared her phenomenal blueberry French toast or perfect eggs Benedict. She could handle small talk with the upper crust if sampling the housekeeper's delectable culinary offerings was her reward.

"My darling daughter, there you are," said Georgette. Wearing an elegant, pale blue Carolina Herrera morning gown, she glided across the room on her size six Manolos and air-kissed her daughter's cheeks. Then she stepped back and inspected Ellie's outfit with practiced eyes. "We've just been talking about you."

Ellie figured the non-comment about her clothes was a good thing, and looked past her mother's shoulder into a corner of the room. Seated on chairs was an unfamiliar older couple speaking with Georgette's latest husband, Judge Stanley Frye, while beside them stood a tall younger man.

"I wish you'd told me there would be guests."

"I didn't tell you because I was afraid you wouldn't come."

"That's probably true." Ellie jerked her chin. "So, who are they?"

"Maydeen and Alan McGowan. You've met them before."

"Uh . . . no."

"They were at my Easter brunch."

"But I wasn't, remember?" Instead, she'd attended a breakfast thrown by one of Viv's coworkers.

"Oh . . . well . . . my Memorial Day celebration, then?"

"Sorry, didn't make that one, either."

Georgette frowned. "Hmm, now that we're counting, it appears you've missed more of my get-togethers than I thought."

"Don't change the subject, Mother. Who are those people?"

"Alan's a founding partner of a huge law firm here in the city. He and his wife have known Stanley for ages."

"Then they're the judge's friends."

"We were passing acquaintances, but now that I've married Stanley, they're my friends, too," she corrected.

"And the tall guy?"

"Ah, so you noticed." Georgette gave a knowing smile. "Isn't he adorable?"

"Since I only have a side view, I wouldn't know." Though the sight of his molded butt and broad shoulders held promise. "Who is he?"

"Kevin McGowan, their son. He's an attorney, too, by the way, and heir to a fortune. Come along and I'll introduce you."

"Lawyer joke! Lawyer joke!"

Ignoring Rudy's plea, Ellie took her mother's hand. Georgette was in such a hurry, she tripped over Rudy and righted herself with a hmmpf of disapproval. "Oh, you brought your dog."

"See what I mean? She doesn't want me here."

"You did say Rudy was invited. If he's not welcome, I'll be happy to leave."

"No, no." Georgette patted her artfully tousled hair. "But do try to keep him out from underfoot."

"How about if I put him the corner and tell him to stay? I'm sure Corinna has something to keep him occupied."

"She did mention a trip to the pet store this week. There she is." Georgette nodded toward the dining room. "I'll ask her while you settle him somewhere . . . out of the way."

"How about I go play in traffic?" Rudy snarled as Ellie led him to a sunny area of the living room. *"Maybe that would make the old bat happy."*

"If Corinna doesn't have something for you to snack on, I promise we'll leave. If she does, you need to curl up here and be good. Deal?"

"I'll try, but it's gonna be tough. Seein' all these legal types brings to mind about a dozen lawyer jokes."

Ellie played along to keep him quiet. "Okay, I'll listen to one. Shoot."

Rudy gazed at the carpet, as if thinking. *"Okay, here's a good one. Why are animal testing labs starting to use lawyers as subjects?"*

"I haven't the faintest idea."

"Because lawyers will do things even rats won't try."

She stifled a giggle. "That is so bad."

"Yeah, I know." He curled into a comfortable position on the plush white rug. *"If that woman gives me one of them lousy Nylabones, I'm outta here."*

Georgette returned and handed Ellie a white cashmere throw. "He can sit on this, and I'll have Corinna take it to the dry cleaners tomorrow." Then she passed over a cloth napkin. "Corinna said this was his."

Ellie unwrapped the napkin, and Rudy licked his muzzle. *"Yum, yum, yum. A Beefy Bone. I love those things."*

"Good. Then you're all set." After arranging the throw, she set the treat in front of him. Standing, she smiled at her mother. "Remind me to tell Corinna thanks."

"Fine. Now come along."

Georgette again took her hand and practically dragged her across the room, leaving Ellie to wonder what was up.

"Kevin McGowan. Why is that name so familiar?" asked Vivian over a late-night snack of Häagen-Dazs in Ellie's kitchen. "I'm sure I've met him or heard some gossip about him somewhere, but I just can't place the name."

Ellie helped herself to another spoon of Caramel Cone. "Beats me where. Unless you've been arrested and haven't told me about it." Kevin McGowan was her mother's maiden attempt at matchmaking, which had shocked Ellie to her core. Was she really that pathetic or needy a daughter? "I got the idea he specialized in criminal law, but we didn't discuss his cases or anything."

"Describe him again. Maybe it'll jog my memory."

"He's over six feet, with black curly hair and sexy gray eyes." Kevin was also charming and a good listener, and he seemed inordinately enthused when he heard where she walked her dogs. "He wasn't the usual buttoned-up lawyer type. Instead of a suit, he wore white slacks and a dark green open-collared golf shirt—no logo—and a pair of Italian leather slip-ons, but nothing flashy."

Viv scraped the bottom of her carton. "Anything else?"

"He has very white teeth. Looked like veneers, but I'm no expert. No jewelry except a Rolex, and he isn't a smoker, thank God. That would have been the big no-no for me."

"Sounds like you think he has dating potential." Viv grinned. "You're sure he knows you're a dog walker?"

"Positive. Seems he lives near Museum Mile, so he knows the area I walk. He was even interested in Rudy."

"The guy had more raging pheromones than I care to remember," groused the Yorkiepoo from under the table. *"Just like you-know-who."*

"How did Rudy like him?"

"Fine. He even accepted an ear scratch."

"So you got the impression Kevin is an animal lover?"

"I did, though he doesn't own a pet. Said his job makes it too difficult to devote the time needed to care for one. But he asked questions about my charges, as if he really cared."

"Sounds like he's worth a second look." Viv swallowed the last of her ice cream. "Will you say yes if he asks you out?"

"I guess so. I haven't had a free dinner in a while."

"With any luck, it'll develop into more than food. A little bedroom activity might be exactly what you need."

"Just let me get through a dinner first, please. I really don't want to think any further than that."

"And who knows, if this thing with Gary and the will goes sour, you might be needing his services."

"Oh, yeah. That'll be a real conversation starter. 'So, Kevin, I've been arrested for murdering a homeless man in Central Park. The cops think I did it because he left my dog all his worldly possessions.' "

"I take it you're going to the bank tomorrow?"

"That's the plan. But, eventually, I'll have to go back to Gruning and tell him about it. Besides, I have a few questions of my own that need answers. I want to hear if they've gotten any leads or found the murder weapon. That sort of thing."

Vivian stood and set her spoon in the sink. "Remember what I told you about being careful. If Sam finds out you're working the case, he's going to lock you up and throw the key in the East River."

"We've been all over this. Sam has no right to an opinion, and I don't owe him any explanations."

"Hey, don't get angry with me."

Ellie propped an elbow on the table and rested her chin in her palm. "Gary was my friend. I want to find the person who did this as much as the cops. If I had more free time—"

"I thought you were hiring a helper?"

"I'm giving it serious consideration."

"Good. Going to try the colleges, like I suggested?"

"I guess I could. Problem is, what with going to the bank and all, I don't know when I'll manage it."

"It's important, so make the time." Viv headed for the hallway. "You and your charges want to take a final trip around the block with me and Mr. T?"

"Mr. T? So you're finally coming around."

Viv heaved a sigh. "I had to. Whenever I called him Twink, he stared at me as if I were a flea. The little shit."

"He may be a shit, but he's *your* shit," Ellie reminded her. "And you love him."

"Yeah, I do. So, you up for a walk?"

"Just give me a few minutes to slip on my shoes and clip leashes on the herd." She nodded toward Cheech and Chong, sitting upright in their designer doggie beds. "I'll meet you out front."

Chapter 5

PAWS IN MOTION IS LOOKING FOR
a part-time employee for their dog-walking service
Hours flexible, salary negotiable
MUST LOVE DOGS
For details, call the number below

Ellie tacked a flyer on the bulletin board in the Lerner Hall bookstore at Columbia University. Last night, after returning from her walk with Viv, she'd quickly put a job sheet together on her computer, and she left the house extra early this morning to take them to a few of the local colleges. She'd written her name and phone number on a row of fringes at the bottom of the page so interested prospects could tear them off and call her.

Plenty of people registered for summer courses, and students usually needed extra money. If she lined up a couple of responsible young adults as assistants, she wouldn't have to squeeze her personal business between scheduled walks. Her client list had grown over the past few months. When word got out about Bibi, the Goth-girl dog walker, and her involvement with the man who had stolen Buddy, Ellie acquired several of her charges, and most of them expected two walks a day. Coupled with her original daily doubles, her workload was, to put it simply, overworked. With a helper or two, she might even be able to take a sick day or go on vacations without worrying about her customers.

Now finished with the help wanted postings, she was going to catch a cab to a new client's apartment and come to an agreement on her dog's schedule. After that, she would gather the other canines in the Cranston Arms, including an adorable snow-white poodle Hilary Blankenship had just purchased. The woman was going through a difficult divorce, and since Ellie knew exactly where Hilary was coming from, she'd been giving her a hand training the new puppy.

"Miss! Excuse me! Miss!"

Ellie turned to see if she was the "miss" in question.

Huffing and puffing, an older man jogged to catch up. "Is this yours?" he asked, holding a ticket from her sheet.

"Yes. Do you know someone who might want the job?"

"Name's Milton Fenwick. I'm retired, but I like dogs." He squatted and held out his hand to Rudy, who sat like a statue by her side. "I was roaming Columbia thinking I'd take a course or two to keep busy, but dog walking might be more fun."

"It's a great job," she agreed when he stood. "Do you have questions?"

"How about I ask the questions?" Rudy ruffed.

"It says 'hours flexible.' What does that mean?"

Ignoring Rudy's cranky observation, she said, "It means I walk dogs in several building south of here, so we'd have to figure out which would be most convenient for you. If I hire you, we'll go over the schedule, and you can choose the shifts you think would work best."

Milton ran a hand over his full head of gray hair. He didn't appear old enough to be retired, but she knew some people made their money and stopped working, then grew bored and needed something to keep them busy.

"Would I have to do anything else, like take a couple hours of instruction?"

"In a manner of speaking. You need to be insured and bonded, so I'd accompany you on the walks while I waited for the bonding firm to send their approval, and you could learn how I take care of my charges. After that, you'd have your own route."

His florid face grew redder. "Bonded and insured? Why'd I need that?"

"It's required in this city, and the customers feel better knowing you've been checked out. You'll have a key to each apartment, which means you'll be on your honor to respect their personal space and privacy."

He glanced at Rudy. "And are they all small and easy to handle, like this guy, or big and unwieldy? I see some walkers toting those pony-sized pooches, and it looks difficult."

Rudy stood on his hind legs and growled. *"Easy to handle? I'll show you easy to handle!"*

Milton jumped back, and she jerked Rudy's lead. "Enough!" She smiled at the frowning man. "I only walk small dogs, and though none of them are difficult, some can be a handful, as you can see."

The older man pulled his baggy chinos up by their belt. "Uh, okay. I'll call you." He took a few steps backward before turning and, with a wave of his hand, hurrying away.

"I didn't like that guy," Rudy groused as Ellie hailed a taxi.

"Lately, you don't seem to like anyone. What's the problem with this man?"

"He was worried about getting investigated by the bonding company, which says he might have something to hide . . . like a criminal record."

"Getting bonded is very personal." She opened the cab door and let him hop inside ahead of her before giving the driver the address. "Not everyone wants to be checked out by strangers."

"Maybe so, but still . . . It's this business with Gary that gives me the willies. Every stranger I see is a suspect."

"He was simply a nice retired gentleman, nothing more."

"Are you gonna hire him?"

"The ball's in his court. He has my number, and he knows what the job entails, so he has to call me."

Minutes later, they entered the Cranston Arms, stopped to visit her new client, a woman named Mariette Lowenstein and her dog, a hefty pug named Sampson, and told her they'd return after they picked up the other dogs. Then she and Rudy took the elevator to the fourth floor and Hilary's apartment.

"Please be nice to Cuddles," Ellie reminded Rudy. "He'll learn by your example."

"Yeah, sure. I just love havin' my ears bit and my butt sniffed six ways to Sunday. It's a real treat."

"Cuddles is a puppy, full of energy and dying for attention. Surely you remember what it was like to be young?"

"Barely. I had to spend a month in the big house waiting for you, and I didn't have anyone spoiling me while I hung out."

Rudy, she realized, was almost as good at piling on guilt as her mother. "Cuddles is a great companion for Hilary. She's going through a rough spot and needs his support. Ours, too."

The door opened, and she frowned. Hilary's red-rimmed eyes and runny nose were evidence of her unhappiness. "What's wrong?" Ellie asked, leading Rudy into the apartment.

Shaking her head, the tall, slim woman pressed a crumpled tissue to her lips. "I can't—can't talk about it." She sniffed as she waggled a finger, indicating Ellie should follow her.

"Is it Cuddles? He's not sick, is he?"

Hilary dropped onto her barge-sized sofa, and Ellie took one of the matching chairs. The furniture in the apartment was high-end and arranged with a decorator's flair. It was evident the Blankenships had money, and not just because they lived on the Upper East Side.

"Cuddles is asleep in his crate, the little darling. I took him for a walk about two hours ago. I'm glad you're here because he should be waking soon, and I simply cannot appear in public looking like this." She dabbed at her shiny nose. "You'll take him out for me, won't you?"

Ellie checked her watch before answering. "If he's up in the next fifteen minutes, yes, but remember what I told you. Cuddles is your responsibility. I'm just here as an advisor. Puppies need to do their business every hour, two if you're pressed for time. And he should always go out after he's played hard, eaten, or just awakened from a nap. It's the only way to train him properly."

Hilary nodded, then blew her nose. Dressed in a tired-looking fuchsia silk pantsuit and faded Prada pumps, she resembled a wilted rose desperate to retain its petals. With her patrician looks and faintly lined skin, she appeared to be in her midforties. Ellie knew the woman was in the throes of a wicked divorce because Stanley had told her that Mr. Blankenship was a hedge fund manager who had no intention of sharing his fortune with his soon-to-be ex.

"Please forgive me for this overly emotional display," Hilary said with a sob. "Richard's lawyer just informed *my* lawyer that I must produce receipts for everything I buy in order to coordinate the amount Richard will be offering in support."

"And you don't have receipts?"

"I have them, but it's an insult, forcing me to hand them over as if I were out to steal from my husband.

I earned a good part of our money when we were first married, and he certainly knows my expenses."

"You worked during your marriage?"

She straightened on the sofa. "I put Richard through school as a legal secretary until he got his MBA, and I continued the profession after we wed. My salary helped pay the rent and, later, gave us money to invest. I only quit after he was able to get investors involved in his new venture and made his enormous salary. Then, when his father died, we were able to buy this place. I thought we were happy but—but—"

Fresh tears ensued, and Ellie waited while the woman calmed herself. Why did everything always have to boil down to money? Her own divorce would have been much more civil if the D hadn't been so cheap and so unrealistic about their finances. And how come men always screwed the women who'd supported them during the bad times?

"I did whatever he asked, whenever he wanted. Now he's trying to humiliate me," Hilary continued, her voice wavering.

Ellie sighed, admitting the woman's hassle sounded a lot like the one she'd had with the D—except for the "enormous salary" part. "Is there anything I can do to help?"

Hilary bit her lower lip. "If things go the way my husband wants, I'll be lucky if I keep this apartment. I need a job."

"A job? Really?"

"Don't be stupid, Triple E," said Rudy. *"This dame isn't responsible enough to walk her own dog, never mind one of ours."*

"You're being silly," Ellie told him.

"I'm perfectly serious," said Hilary.

"I'm sure you are," Ellie added, giving Rudy a glare.

"You're a working woman. Do you know of someone who might be looking for help?"

"Stanley is the only person I know in the legal profession. Have you asked him about job opportunities?"

"I could never go back to work in a law office. Richard has so many connections in the field, I'd be sure to run into someone who knows him." She crumpled her tissue and plucked another from a box on the coffee table. "I'm willing to do anything, short of selling myself on the street, to accrue a little spending money."

"Well, as a matter of fact—"

"Uh-uh-ah."

"I could use some help in my business."

"Your business?" Hilary wrinkled her nose. "Are you suggesting I walk dogs for a living? And pick up their . . . their leavings?"

"Bad idea, very bad," Rudy muttered.

"The job would only be part-time, but it's off the books, and I'd pick up the charges for getting you bonded and insured. You'd receive a 1099 at the end of the year, and it would be your decision on how to handle the taxes."

"Where exactly would the dogs come from?" She leaned back in her seat. "I wouldn't have to go far, would I?"

"No. In fact, I have several clients in this building, and I contracted a new one this morning." She mentioned Mariette Lowenstein and Sampson.

"I know Mariette. Her dog is rather . . . rowdy."

"Not a good match, Triple E."

"Sampson is a pug. That sort of dog can be rambunctious, but we'll work on teaching him better manners. I'm sure you could walk him and the other two."

"Do you think so?"

"I do not."

"I'll show you how," Ellie offered. "But you have to fill out forms with my bonding and insurance companies. While you're waiting for approval, you can accompany me on their morning walk. They get picked up at ten; we can take them together."

"But you said I could make my own hours."

"In a manner of speaking. Sampson, Millie, and Dilbert are scheduled to go out by nine, and you can bring Cuddles. And since he'll accompany you, you'll save that money, as well. I'm sure you'll be fine on your own when I get the paperwork. There's just one thing."

"Yes?"

"If I have an emergency, you have to promise to cover for me on *all* my rounds."

"All? How many would that be?"

"Four buildings in total, and about twenty-five additional dogs."

Hilary's eyes widened to saucers.

"But I'm a very healthy person. Haven't gotten sick in years," Ellie assured her.

"You mentioned emergencies."

"I might have an appointment run late, but that rarely happens. It's just that sometimes—"

"The cops run you in for murder?" Rudy suggested, sniggering.

"I need to take care of personal business."

Hilary closed her eyes, and Ellie imagined the scenario rolling around in the woman's brain: yapping dogs, entwined leashes, and the number one deterrent—thirty mounds of poop to scoop. When seen in such a glamorous manner, even she would shy away from the job.

She was about to rescind her offer when Hilary smiled. "I'll do it."

"Great. Freakin' great," Rudy yipped.

"That's wonderful," Ellie said. A pathetic-sounding whine echoed from the kitchen, prompting her to add, "Sounds like Cuddles is up and ready to go. Put on your sneakers—"

"Sneakers?"

"Or walking shoes. Whatever you wear to trek the city."

"I haven't *trekked* this city or any other in years."

"Then now is a good time to start. Find your most comfortable flats and slip them on. I'll get Cuddles, pick up the other dogs, and meet you downstairs in fifteen minutes."

Hilary continued to stare as if Ellie had lost her mind.

"Ticktock," groused Rudy.

"Go on, hurry up. If you want the job, think of this as your interview."

Hilary jumped to her feet and skedaddled from the room.

"You're unleashing an idiot on those poor canines. They're gonna hate you for it."

"Give Hilary a chance before you doom her to failure. And think of Cuddles. If her husband has his way, she could be forced to move, which means she might have to put Cuddles in a shelter. You don't want to see them separated, do you?" Ellie walked to the kitchen and grinned at the white, four-pound toy poodle standing on his hind legs inside his crate. "Hey, baby boy. How are you today?"

"Ellie, Ellie, Ellie. I'm holding my wee like you told me, but I gotta go bad."

She took him out of the cage. "I'll carry you, just to keep you honest. We'll be outside in a few minutes."

"Rudy, you gonna let me walk next to you today? Are ya, huh? Are ya?"

"Only if you promise to keep your nose out of my privates."

"Aw, gee. Do I haf'ta?"

Ellie hurried to the elevator, smiling as she listened to the canine squabbling. She had the best job on the planet and wouldn't trade if for all the money in the world. Maybe if the cops knew she planned on giving anything of value she received from Gary to charity, they'd realize she didn't care a fig about amassing wealth. But she never wanted to lose this unique ability she had with her pooch and the others. For whatever reason, the gift was hers to treasure . . . even if it drove her nutty once in a while.

Ellie's phone rang right before she stopped for lunch. She'd been debating—eat a hot dog or make that bank run and check on the contents of Gary's safety-deposit box?—for the past thirty minutes, with the wiener in the lead by a nose. She really didn't want to see a bunch of junk Gary thought was valuable sitting in the bottom of a metal box. The items, whatever they were, would probably be too dirty to sift through, impossible to get rid of, and equally painful to keep.

"Hello."

"Ellie, it's me."

"Sam?"

"You busy?"

"Sort of." She plopped onto a bench. "What do you need?"

"I was wondering, have you gone to the bank yet?"

"I've been thinking about it, but I haven't worked up the courage. Why?"

"Because I'm offering my services as your escort. I'll come along and see what's what. Besides, I found out a few things you need to know."

"What 'few things'?" She hated playing twenty questions, especially with Sam. "Do they have something do with Gary?"

"Yep, but I can't talk about them here."

She realized they had yet to discuss what she'd found on the Internet. Was that what he wanted to tell her? "If it's about Gary's family history, I already know what happened to him as a teenager."

"That's part of it. How did you find out?"

"I have a computer, remember? I just googled his name and the newspaper articles came up. I'm no psychologist, but my guess is he suffered some form of post-traumatic stress disorder after he witnessed his parents' murder."

"It's possible," Sam agreed. "But I can't say any more about it right now."

That meant he was going out on a limb for her again, sharing information she wasn't supposed to know about. "I don't want you to keep doing this."

"Doing what?"

"Putting your job in jeopardy for me. If Gruning wants to call me in and tell me about Gary's past, that's fine. You should stay out of it."

"I'm already in too deep. Besides, I have info you need to know but Gruning probably won't tell you. Ever since you pissed him off the other morning, he's been threatening to get a court order on that envelope."

"Oh, that."

"Yeah, that. You annoyed the hell out of him when you danced out of here without handing it over. Not knowing what's in that envelope is practically giving him an ulcer."

"You sound happy about it."

"Let's just say there's no love lost between me and Gruning. It's about time he snagged a case where he has to dig a little." A moment passed before he added, "So, can I tag along?"

Ellie glanced at Rudy, who was gazing at her with a frown on his doggie lips. "Okay, but I have to take my dog home first. Meet me at the apartment in about twenty minutes."

"You dumping me for that idiot detective?" Rudy asked when she hung up.

"Don't be ridiculous. It's time I went to the bank. Sam just offered to come along for moral support." She led him across Madison and headed toward home. "Besides, they only allow Seeing Eye dogs or service dogs in a bank."

"So tell 'em I'm a service dog. I can do everything they can, and then some."

"I'm sure you can. It's just that no one would believe me if I listed your accomplishments. You know that."

"It's not my fault humans love a stereotype. And they lack imagination. Oh, and let's not forget whimsy— today's humans have absolutely no idea of fun."

"Aren't you being a bit hard on us?" She quick-stepped to Lexington and headed south.

"Gary understood. He was a champ."

"I agree. And don't worry, I'll bring home everything in that box and let you have a look before we dispose of it. He did leave it to you, remember?"

"He did, didn't he?" They jogged up the front steps of their building. *"So hurry up and get back here. I wanna show those Mexican hairballs what I own."*

Sam spotted Ellie sitting on her front stoop from a block away. No doubt about it, the contrary woman had worked her way into his fantasies. He only wished there was an antidote, a cure for his addiction to Ellie Engleman.

She stood when she saw him. "Hey," she said, not smiling.

He took in her curvy figure and tightened in all the right places. Good thing he'd made up his mind he had no business going back to where they'd left off three months ago. "Hey, yourself. You ready?"

She eyed the red canvas duffel bag slung over his shoulder. "Planning another overnight stay?"

"This is for you, not me."

"You're sending me on a vacation?" She raised a brow. "Gee, thanks. It's been a while since I had a couple days off."

He clasped her elbow and steered her down the sidewalk. "This is for whatever we find in that safety-deposit box."

They crossed Lexington and walked south. "I still don't understand why Gary's box is at this bank," she said. "There are a dozen closer to where he lived."

"Maybe First Trust offered a free toaster with every new account."

"Come on, why do you think he used a bank so far from his stomping grounds?"

"It might have been the bank his parents used, so he just left everything the way it was when they died. Could be he didn't want anyone he knew to see him doing business at a financial institution, or he figured it best that whatever he had was far away from where he lived. You said he sometimes acted a little paranoid. Maybe he thought he was being followed."

"He mentioned that exact thing to me a time or two, but when I asked him about it he took off for home. If I'd known he had a reason to be afraid . . ."

Sam blew out a breath. "My guess is he could count."

"Count?"

"The trial took place in 1979. His brother got thirty years." They stopped at a crosswalk. "You do the math."

Ellie sucked in a breath. "His brother is out of jail?"

"According to the records, he was released the beginning of May. I heard Gruning talking about it this morning."

"That means—"

"He could be here in the city, right now. He might have been looking for his brother, hoping Gary would lead him to the family money. Or he could have found Gary and decided to go after him for the hell of it."

"Anyone in their right mind would have seen that Gary didn't have a penny to his name."

"The key phrase is 'in their right mind.' Thompson was in the joint for thirty years, and from the sound of it, he wasn't wrapped too tight when he got there. Thirty years is a hell of a long time to sit and think about a younger brother testifying against you in a trial."

"So it's possible Thompson came to the city to confront Gary and they argued? He wanted the family money, because he thinks he earned it by spending time in prison?"

Earlier, Sam had come to the same conclusion. It figured that Ellie, with her logical mind and penchant for trouble, would arrive there, too. "Stranger things have happened between family members. It's something to think about."

He slowed as they approached a Jamba Juice. "Did you eat?"

"I grabbed a hot dog and ate it on the way home. Why?"

"Because I didn't have time." He dragged her into the shop. "Come on, I'll buy you a smoothie."

Tripping beside him, she tsked. "I have to get back to work in less than"—she glanced at her watch—"two hours."

"It'll only take a minute. We can slurp while we walk." He strode to the counter and ordered a peach-coconut smoothie for her and a strawberry-banana for himself. Ten minutes later, they were back on the sidewalk. He sucked down a swallow and let out a satisfied "ahh." "That hits the spot."

When Ellie wrapped her lips around her straw, he focused forward and asked, "Good?"

"Peach is my favorite. Thanks for remembering."

Unfortunately, he remembered a lot more about her likes and dislikes than her favorite smoothie flavor. "No problem. Only three more blocks," he said, looking at the street sign.

Minutes later, they stopped at a trash can and deposited their empty cups, then turned into the bank. The setup was typical for a staid financial institution: tellers along a far wall, a row of desks occupied by account executives, and a couple of freestanding counters holding pens, deposit and withdrawal slips, and information on the bank's latest promotions and interest rates. Taking a fast glance around, he walked to a woman sitting at a desk marked RECEPTION.

"We're here to open a safety-deposit box," he said. "But first we need to speak to whoever's in charge."

"In charge? You can see any of the customer service reps to open a safety-deposit box."

"I mean someone in charge of the bank. A manager."

"But that's really not—"

Sliding his ID case from his pocket, Sam snapped it open. "It's important."

The woman, a dark-haired fiftyish matron in a drab gray suit, puckered her lips. "I'll see if he's available."

She took off at a gallop, and Ellie cocked a hip. "Do you always have to be so—so pushy, flashing that stupid badge wherever you go?"

"It gets things done," he told her. "I don't have the patience to play games."

"I still say I could have done this myself."

"Maybe so, but my being here should get them to move a little faster."

The receptionist returned with a distinguished-looking man wearing a navy suit. He offered his hand. "I'm George Butterworth. I understand you have some questions regarding a safety-deposit box?"

Ellie shook his hand, then Sam did the same. "Is there somewhere private we can talk?" he asked.

"Ms. Hampton said you were here to open a safety-deposit box. We have account executives who can help you with that."

"Not open, as in start a new account," Sam explained. "We're here to open a box we've never seen."

Mr. Butterworth straightened. "And you're from the police?"

"I am. Ms. Engleman is the box's new owner."

He focused on Ellie. "May I see the paperwork that makes you think you have a right to the contents of this box?"

Ellie pulled out the envelope and handed it to Butterworth. "A friend—a man—was killed. He left this for me."

When Butterworth pulled out the will and took a long look, he smiled. "If you'll come this way."

Sam raised a brow at Ellie as they followed the banker, who led them to an office in a far corner of the lobby. Inside, he nodded toward two chairs opposite the massive desk. "Please, take a seat. I'll be right back."

"So far, so good," she said, watching the door.

Mr. Butterworth returned with a card. After opening the envelope, he spread the will on his blotter, set the card beside it, and steepled his fingers. "Can you show me some identification, Ms. . . . ." He took another look at the info. "Ms. Engleman?"

She pulled out her wallet and removed her driver's license. "I also have a couple of credit cards and a social security card with my name on them."

"This will be fine." Butterworth lined the driver's license up with the signature card and studied it. Raising his gaze, he said, "The signatures match."

"Signatures? My signatures?" She furrowed her brow. "But I never—"

Sam squeezed her fingers and pulled her to her feet. "Great. Lead the way to Ms. Engleman's box."

Butterworth handed Ellie her paperwork. "If I may ask, how well did you know Mr. Veridot?"

"Is it necessary Ms. Engleman answer the question?" Sam interjected. "Or does she need a lawyer?"

"No, no. Her signature and identification are enough. It's just that Mr. Veridot's case is . . . was unusual. I heard about his mur—his passing—and expected someone would be here soon."

"You knew Gary?" said Sam. "When did you last see him?"

"About five months ago, but I've known Mr. Veridot for three decades, possibly more."

"Then he was a regular customer?" asked Sam.

"Not exactly, but he did drop in from time to time. He kept several different accounts open, but on that last visit he closed them all and rented this safety-deposit box. A few weeks later, he showed up with this fully executed signature card. He told me he was leaving everything to a friend he trusted completely. And here you are."

"Then you know about his parents?"

"Tragic, wasn't it? I met Mr. Veridot when his grandmother brought him here and introduced us. I was just a junior account executive back then, so it was quite an honor to assist one of First Trust's biggest depositors. The family's money has been sitting in accounts here, earning interest, for many years. From the day Mrs. Benedict brought Mr. Veridot in, he's been welcome, even with his inappropriate mode of dress and unusual circumstances."

"I haven't seen an attorney—"

"But you probably should. Because of the now-reduced dollar amount involved, there won't be any inheritance taxes to consider, but you should record the will with the Surrogate's Court, if you haven't already done so."

"You said 'now-reduced dollar amount.' Before we go any further, can you tell us what Ms. Engleman now owns?" asked Sam.

"You mean you don't know?"

"I haven't a clue," Ellie said. "I wasn't even aware of the will until after Gary was mur—died. He never told me a thing."

"Ah, well then. Come along. You should take a look at what's in that safety-deposit box."

Chapter 6

Standing in the vault room, Ellie stared at the square metal container. According to Mr. Butterworth, it was one of the largest the bank supplied. "Why didn't you let me tell him I never signed that signature card?" she asked Sam, who seemed to be thinking hard about something.

Frowning, he said, "There's no reason asking for trouble. The only thing places like this care about is following the rules. Your signature matched the signature on the card, the card was on file, therefore you're a legal owner of the box. But there's another problem."

Ellie closed her eyes. "Now what?"

"Because there's money involved, your alibi for not killing Gary just got weaker. Gruning will look at it the same way the bank does. You signed the card, therefore you were aware of the box. He'll assume you knew exactly what it held, and whatever it is will be your motive to commit murder."

"Even if it's a few pennies?" she asked, recalling the "reduced dollar amount" Butterworth had quoted.

"People have been killed over less."

His grim expression did nothing to allay her fears. "But I didn't sign a card. I'd have remembered if I did something like that for Gary."

"Okay, so what did you give him with your signature?"

"Nothing. I—oh—"

"Oh?"

"I gave him a birthday card a couple of months back, and I might have signed it Ellie Engleman. Do you think he—"

"Copied your signature? Possibly. He was off balance enough to do something like that, right?"

"I guess." She let out a breath. After wiping her damp palms on her linen slacks, she said, "Can we stop talking about what's inside and just take a look?"

He crossed his arms and hitched his hip on the table. "That's what we're here for."

She swallowed, and her stomach heaved. "I think I'm going to throw up."

Sam held out his hand. "Give me the key. I'll open it if you can't."

"I'm being a baby, I know, but it's—"

"A big step?"

"Major."

"You'll never know how major until you use that key."

She gazed at him, then slid the key in the lock, turned it, and lifted the lid. It took a few seconds for the contents to register. "Oh, my God."

Sam peeked inside. "That's some 'reduced dollar amount.' "

With a trembling finger, she touched the heart-stopping pile of what appeared to be hundred dollar bills banded into bundles. "How many packets do you think there are?"

"Best guess, more than fifty," he said, giving the mound a quick mental calculation. "I'm not a mathematician, but Butterworth closed out the accounts, so I'm sure he knows how much it was, even if Gary spent some since then."

She hefted a bundle. "Maybe we should ask him?"

"Probably a good idea."

Plopping into a chair, she held her head in her hands. "I'm going to hyperventilate." When Sam placed his palm on her shoulder, she trembled. "I mean it. I can't pull any air into my lungs."

"Easy, soldier. Take a deep breath and let it out real slow. Do it until you stop shaking."

She did as he suggested, then peeked inside again. "What am I supposed to do with all that—that—cash?"

"Hell if I know. Go on vacation, pay off your mortgage, splurge on a shopping spree—whatever people with money do."

"I don't have money. This is Gary's, not mine." She stared at him. "I can't take this."

He grinned. "Sure you can."

"But—"

"Look, Gary wanted you to have it. If you don't keep it for yourself, make a donation to charity in his name."

"I already told Ru—I mean, I thought I might, if I found anything of value. I just never—"

There was a knock on the door. Butterworth poked his head around the corner. "Is everything all right?"

Ellie met his inquisitive gaze. "Um . . . fine. It's just—I had no idea—"

"Did you read the note?"

"There's a note?"

"Mr. Veridot wrote a note and told me to make sure you saw it. It might have shifted to the bottom of the box. I'll give you a few more minutes."

Sam began removing bundles and setting them on the table until he found a folded sheet of paper and passed it to her.

"It's addressed to Ellie and Rudy," she muttered. Gary was probably thrilled to add Rudy's name to the letter, knowing her Yorkiepoo would understand his message.

"Only proves the guy wasn't wrapped too tight." Sam

stood beside her and gazed over her shoulder. "You going to read it, or just stare at it?"

The single sheet of heavy white paper had the bank's logo on top, and below, a neatly handwritten note, dated back in March.

> *Dear Ellie and Rudy,*
> *If you're reading this letter, it means I'm dead. And if I'm dead there's a good chance my brother killed me. I'm counting on you to find him and see to it justice is served once and for all. There's no one I want to have this money more than you and my pal Rudy, but I have a request. See that I'm cremated, then bring my ashes to where I lived and sprinkle them around or maybe keep them in your closet. Just don't let Thompson get them. After that, Rudy, buy yourself a lifetime supply of bones, and Ellie, do whatever you want with the rest. It's no good to me now, and it never has been.*
> *Thanks for being my only friends,*
> *Gary*

Ellie sniffed back tears, handed Sam the note, and fished a tissue from her bag. "Isn't that the saddest thing you've ever read?" she sobbed. "We were his only friends."

Sam took the sheet and read it for himself. "This note will go a long way in proving your case to Gruning. It pretty much points to Thompson as the killer, and he makes it sound as if you didn't know about the bequest." He folded the paper and stuck it in her tote bag. "But I don't like what he's asking you to do."

She blew her nose in the tissue. "What's that supposed to mean?"

"It means I don't want you involved in the investigation. It's not your job to find Gary's brother or whoever killed him, and even if the brother did the deed, the detective work is not up to you." He frowned. "The guy was off his rocker."

"Gary was as sane as you are—"

"No smart-ass comments. You know what I mean."

"He probably wrote and told me to take care of things because of what happened with Professor Albright's murder, that's all. He couldn't really know his brother would kill him, and why would he expect me to find the guy and bring him to justice? It doesn't make sense."

"A lot of things that happen in this world don't make sense. Meanwhile, I'll talk to Gruning, see if they're ready to release the body, and get the status on the toxicology reports. You need to find a lawyer and register the will with the Surrogate's Court as soon as possible, so you can become a person of record for Gary Veridot. That means you're responsible for his debts, his assets, and his body. You willing to do all that?"

She nodded. "Of course I am. He didn't have anyone else."

"Then we're all set. If I were you, I'd go slow with making a decision on how to handle the cash. Creditors might crawl out of the woodwork once they hear Gary's dead. You can use the money to settle up, pay for the cremation, that kind of thing. Wait awhile before you spend any of it on yourself."

She threaded her fingers through her curls. "I'll never be able to spend this much money."

"Okay, invest it, or invite friends to dinner, or do as Veridot suggested and buy your dog a bone."

"Easy for you to say," she replied, crossing her arms. "We—I don't deserve this. How can I take it?"

Sam dropped to his knees and gazed into her eyes. "Except for you, I don't know a single person who wouldn't be jumping for joy if they received this kind of gift. It only proves that, nutty as this Veridot guy was, he knew what he was doing."

She smiled through another round of tears. "I just

don't see how anyone can be happy when they lose a friend. Not that I considered Gary a friend like I do Vivian, but he obviously thought highly of Rudy and me." She blew her nose again. "None of this feels right."

"Look at it this way." Sam tucked a strand of hair behind her ear. "Gary trusted you enough to make certain you got the money. Have him cremated and do whatever feels right with his ashes, like he asked. Then let the cops find his killer while you do whatever makes you happy with the cash."

She heaved a sigh. "You think so?"

"I know so." He stood and began returning bundles to the box. "Maybe you ought to talk to Butterworth about opening an account here. Might as well earn some interest while you decide your next move."

She folded the duffel bag and laid it on top of the money. "I have to think that over. Until I make a decision, can I keep this with the cash, in case I decide to take it out one day?"

"A person could get in trouble, carrying that amount of change without a bodyguard."

"I was only joking. Unless there was some kind of dire emergency, I'd never cart this money home. I just need to think about it for a while."

"You sure?"

"I'm sure. Besides, if I don't get moving I'll be late for my second round of walks." She closed the lid and turned the key. "I guess we need to call Mr. Butterworth."

A knock at the door announced there was no need. Sam let the banker in and told him Ellie had decided to keep things as they were for the moment. Butterworth took the box back to its resting place, then led them into the body of the bank.

"If there's anything else I can do—"

"There is one thing," said Ellie. "We—I didn't count it but I'd like to know. How much money is in there?"

"When Mrs. Benedict died there was over three million dollars in the accounts. Over the years, Mr. Veridot has made many withdrawals and given the money to various charities around the city anonymously. When he cashed out the accounts, there was approximately one million six hundred fifty-seven thousand dollars and eighty-three cents. His final act was to give several hundred thousand to a homeless shelter, and a bit more to a mission that runs a soup kitchen. He also made a generous donation to a local boys' club."

"And you know this because . . . ?" Sam let the question hang.

Butterworth smiled. "Because Mr. Veridot trusted me enough to confide what he was doing. I wrote the cashier's checks for each of his gifts and kept a running tab on the money, in case he forgot, which he did on several occasions."

"So what's in the box now—give or take?"

"At last count there was approximately eight hundred fifty-seven thousand dollars at his disposal."

Ellie grabbed Sam's arm to keep from falling over.

Clutching her elbow, Sam said, "Okay . . . well then . . . Ms. Engleman will let you know if she decides to do anything more with the cash." They walked outside, where he clasped her shoulders and propped her against the building like a rag doll. "You're white as a sheet. Are you sure you're all right?"

Staring at the sidewalk, she took several deep breaths. "Guess I'd better find that attorney everyone keeps telling me I need. I have no idea how to go about registering a will or getting someone cremated."

"Surrogate's Court is the place to take care of the will, and the cremation is a process any funeral home can handle. And Ellie?" He held her clammy hands between his big, warm palms and squeezed. "I'll get back to you if I hear anything more about Thompson Veridot. In the meantime, be careful. If the guy's out there, odds are he's trying to figure out a way to sink his teeth into the family fortune. If you think you're being followed, call me."

Heading home later that afternoon, Ellie raised her gaze skyward. The humid July air had grown heavier and hotter as the day progressed, until the clouds looked ready to pop. Her pink cotton T-shirt stuck to her bra, and she was damp in places she didn't want to think about. Walking might be great exercise for toning legs and building endurance, but it was hell on one's appearance, especially when the surrounding atmosphere was as friendly as the inside of a pot of bubbling spaghetti.

The trip to the bank had worn her out. She needed a jolt of java to perk her up and help her think straight, so she stopped at a Joe to Go and stood in line.

"Hey, Ellie," her pal Joe Cantiglia said when she reached the register. "What brings you here so late in the day? You're usually a morning drinker."

"I need a shot of my regular—including the caffeine," she told Joe. Too bad the two of them were better suited as brother and sister than boyfriend and girlfriend, or she might have been raising a gaggle of dark-haired, black-eyed bambinos instead of walking dogs for a living. "And I'd like two cookies, one chocolate chip and one coconut." Rudy was probably pouting because she'd left him home all afternoon. The coconut cookie would be a treat, even if he had to share it with Cheech and Chong.

"Sure." Joe slid the cookies in a bag and passed them to her. "They're on the house."

"You don't have to do that."

"Accept them as a thank-you. Look what I started." He handed her a business card with the company logo in the center, circled by eleven miniature coffee cups. "It was your idea, and it's a hit."

The card announced a new buying plan. "Purchase eleven coffees or bags of beans at any Joe to Go and get the twelfth one free." She stuck the card, already half-punched, into her bag. "Thanks. I appreciate it."

"No problem. The program only began a couple of days ago, and business is up ten percent."

She moved to the service bar to collect her caramel bliss. "I'm glad I helped someone this week."

Joe nodded to a worker bee, who took his place at the register, and sidled to the far end of the counter. "What's with the long face? Something bothering you?"

"Something," she muttered, walking toward the door. "Can we talk outside?"

He followed her onto the sidewalk and scanned the sky. "Wow, we're gonna get hit with a monster storm."

"I guess," she agreed, smiling hesitantly.

"Hey, you look as miserable as those rain-filled clouds. What's up? Can I help?"

"You can't, but maybe your uncle can."

"I got ten of those. Father's side or my mother's?"

"I'm not sure. Which side has the attorney?"

"Ah, that's Dad's side, and it's his oldest brother, Salvatore." He grinned. "I know, we Italians don't have much imagination when it comes to names."

"Is he accepting new clients?"

"That ambulance chaser? You're kidding, right?"

"I'm serious." She'd almost said "dead" serious, but caught herself. "I need some legal advice."

"Don't you have a judge in the family now?"

"Yes, but he's retired and, at eighty-three, too old to get involved." Never mind the fact that Georgette would disown her if Stanley had another stroke while taking care of her disappointing daughter's problems.

"Uncle Sally's not the sharpest knife in the drawer, if you get my drift. As long as it's simple stuff, he'll do a good job." He wrote his uncle's name and number on the back of a card. "Just don't say I didn't warn you if things go FUBAR with him."

Since it didn't seem like things in her life could get

any more "FUBAR" than they already were, she stuck the card in her tote bag. "I just need someone to answer a couple of questions."

Joe took a seat at an empty table and Ellie joined him. "Care to tell me about what?"

She drank a long swallow of coffee, letting the hot, sweet liquid soothe her jangled nerves. "Did you hear about the man the cops found dead near the Ramble a couple of days ago?"

"That homeless guy? Lived in the bowels of the park?"

"That's the one."

He quirked up a corner of his mouth. "You involved in another crime?"

"Sort of."

"Jeez, Ellie, what the hell's gotten into you, messing in murder again?"

"I'm not 'messing in murder,' but I knew the man." She took another drink and decided there was no way around the next sentence. "Rudy and I found the body."

"You what?"

"Found the body, sort of by accident. We were on a walk, Rudy caught a scent, and when I didn't let him go, he dragged me behind until we found the body."

"You're blaming your dog? You are shameless."

"I'm not blaming—" She gave up making excuses and forged ahead. "Either way, I called 911. The cops arrived, swarmed the place, and brought me in for questioning. Then things got . . . complicated."

"I'm almost afraid to ask."

"The dead man went to the trouble of leaving a will, and he named Rudy as his heir and me as the executor."

"Holy crap. Rudy? What did this homeless man collect—bones?"

"Would you believe a safety-deposit box full of money?"

Joe opened and closed his mouth—no wisecrack this time. "You're kidding."

"I wish I was. And when the police find out Rudy and I are the ones who will benefit from the man's death—"

"Ellie, Rudy's a dog."

She raised her nose in the air. "I know he's a dog."

"People don't leave cash to a dog."

"Normal people don't. Gary is . . . was—different."

"You mean whacko, like a lot of homeless people?"

She swallowed down more coffee. At least Gary wasn't a mean-spirited whacko. "He was lonely, confused, and maybe a little frightened. Rudy and I treated him like a normal person, and he appreciated it."

"Interesting." Joe grinned, his complexion dark against his perfect white teeth. "And that's the reason you need a lawyer."

"I have no idea what my legal duties are with a will. Do I have to pay an inheritance tax? Does Rudy? Does the will need to go through probate? That sort of stuff." She took a final slug of coffee. "I can't afford to do anything that would make the police suspicious, and I certainly don't want to break the law."

"Don't worry. Uncle Sal's a good enough attorney to put your mind at ease." He returned to the entrance of his shop. "Let me know what happens, okay? And tell Uncle Sal I said to treat you right."

Ellie arrived home and headed up the steps just as the sky opened and rain splattered the sidewalk. Certain Rudy would be waiting for her with his knees crossed, as would Cheech and Chong, she got ready to pull her umbrella off the hook next to the door.

"What took you so long? I've been worried sick. If you weren't here in the next ten minutes, I was going to call your cell," Rudy chimed when she tromped into the apartment.

She grinned. "You are such a knucklehead. Since

when did you learn to wrap those doggie paws around a phone?"

"You know what I mean."

"Sorry, it's been an enlightening afternoon. I suppose you and the boys need to go out."

"First off, tell me what Gary left me. Is it big? Does it have a mouth-watering aroma? Is it full of tasty flavor?"

She walked to the kitchen and sat on a chair. "No such luck. The safety-deposit box was full of money. Over eight hundred thousand, according to the banker." She stared into space. "I still can't believe it."

Rudy was silent for a beat; then he rolled on his back, wriggled his legs in the air, and yipped out a raucous laugh. *"Eight hundred thousand smackers,"* he wheezed. *"Hah! That's a good one."*

"According to the will, it's yours now. I'm only the executor. But Sam says it doesn't matter, the cops will still think I did it for the cash."

Rudy snapped to attention in a straight-up sitting position. *"Leaving that much cash to a dog only proves Gary was a nut job."*

"Maybe so, but there was a note." She pulled the folded paper from her bag and read it out loud. "Isn't that the saddest thing you've ever heard? We were his only friends." She sniffed. "The poor guy."

"What makes him think you'd be able to find his brother? You don't even know what the guy looks like."

She shrugged. "Sam says Gary was crazy and I should ignore that part of it."

Rudy put his nose on her knee. *"I hate to admit it, but the dopey detective is right. So why are you cryin'? Because Gary didn't leave the moolah to you?"*

"I simply can't understand why Gary didn't use the money for himself. He shopped in Dumpsters, ate whatever he could scam from restaurants or people. When I think of how he lived, alone in a cardboard box, when he could have had a decent life . . . Maybe I should have taken more of an interest in his past, asked him about his childhood, that kind of thing."

"I remember you invited him here to cool off a couple of weeks ago, when the temperature was close to a hundred, and he turned you down."

"I could have insisted, but I let it slide. If Gary had only asked, I would have told him to leave his money to Best Friends or some other animal rights charity. He just did what he wanted to do, and the police will believe we knew he was leaving us the money and we killed him for it."

"But the money was locked away."

"Maybe so, but we got the key and the will from Pops, and it appears Gary forged my signature on the official depositor's card." She scratched his ears. "Sam is certain I'll be a prime suspect once Gruning finds out."

"But what about Gary saying his brother was probably the killer?"

"Gruning will believe what he wants. He's going to look for an easy out."

"Gary left the fortune to me. Does that mean Gruning will think I was the hit man?"

"No, silly. I'm the trustee. That means I'm the one in control of the cash. I don't know much about estates and the rights of inheritors, but I think as long as I follow the instructions listed, I can pretty much write my own ticket."

"Are you saying you aren't going to give me a cut?"

"Be serious. What would you do with all that money?"

"Plenty. Just think of the treats. Dingo Bones, Greenies, pigs' ears . . . Heck, I could buy a butcher shop and get one of those big ol' marrow bones to chew every day."

"Maybe we should split it between Best Friends and the ASPCA where I found you. They can rescue a lot of helpless puppies and kittens with that amount of cash."

"Say what?"

"You heard me. We don't need it, at least not that badly. Besides, eating too much of the junky stuff is bad for you."

Rudy grumped out a growl. *"How about a party for the gang then, in Gary's memory? I don't think anyone but the dogs we care for are gonna miss him, do you?"*

"That's probably true."

"Good. Now let's take that walk. My back teeth are floatin'."

"Fine. Get the boys, and we'll leave."

"You call 'em. They never listen to me."

"Where are they?"

"Last time I saw them they were in your bedroom, snooping in your closet."

Ellie took off down the hall, fairly certain there wasn't anything toxic in her closet, but she did have some very nice shoes she planned to wear in the fall. "Cheech! Chong! Come!"

Rudy's nails clicked on the hardwood as he followed her. *"They probably did their business in one of your leather purses."*

She swung around the corner of her bedroom, spotted the open closet door, and shot across the room. "Hey, get out of there, both of you!"

A second later she raced back to the kitchen with Cheech in her arms and Rudy and Chong skittering behind.

Chapter 7

"He's not going to die, is he?" Ellie asked Dr. David Crane, veterinarian to many of the pampered pooches and cosseted cats on the Upper East Side.

Dr. Dave rose from in front of the sheepskin-lined doggie bed tucked in a corner of the kitchen. "Not today. But it's a good thing you followed my directions when you pulled that shoelace out of his mouth." He shook his head. "I could tell you horror stories about the things some dogs have ingested. Loose change, screws, antique keys, even razor blades. The items read like a shopping list for a hardware store."

The last hour had passed in a haze of panic. All Ellie remembered was finding Cheech on her closet floor, limp as a boiled noodle, with the tip of a shoelace hanging from his muzzle. She'd called Dr. Dave, and he'd kept her on the line, calmly repeating instructions as he raced to her apartment in the driving rain.

She'd extracted the shoelace slowly, inch by inch, being careful to stop if she felt any resistance. Dr. Dave had charged through the door just as the final bit of string slipped from the Chihuahua's lips.

"I never want to go through anything like that again," she said, heaving a sigh. A round of thunder shook the building. "Now look at the little stinker." She nodded toward a perky Cheech, who'd climbed out of his bed and was lapping water from his designer doggie bowl. "He acts as if nothing happened."

"To him, it didn't." Dr. Dave sat across from her at the table. "Dogs live in the moment. Unless they're constantly abused, they're amazingly optimistic, always wanting to see the bright side."

"I like to think that's true. Then I read frightening articles about pit bulls and other bad-blood breeds getting put down for harming a human. Most of the time, the human was the one who taught the animal to be ferocious. Instead of putting down the dog, I'd lock the trainer in a crate for a couple of months without food or water and see how he likes it."

Dr. Dave smiled. "Canine mouth-to-mouth is sort of disgusting. Can I be a mooch and beg a drink? Cold water will be fine."

"Oh, gosh, I'm sorry." She stood and opened her fridge. "I've got Diet Coke, soda water, wine, a couple of Bud Lights . . ."

"Club soda's fine."

Ellie took down glasses, filled them with ice, poured the seltzer, and brought their drinks to the table. "I should have thought of this myself. I'm not usually such a poor hostess."

The vet swallowed half his drink before saying, "This hits the spot. Saving lives is hard work."

"I want to thank you again. I couldn't have handled it by myself."

He glanced at Rudy, who had hovered under the table during most of the action. "Your guy seems to be doing great since that incident in Queens. I take it he's no longer in pain?"

"It only hurts when my home is under siege by illegal aliens," Rudy grumped.

"He's doing great. He doesn't wince anymore when

I give his sides a rub, so I guess his ribs are healed, and he's back to jumping for joy in front of his kibble cupboard."

"That's what I want to hear. He's a great dog, very loyal to his owner."

Ellie sipped her soda water. Why, oh, why couldn't she find a kind, caring dog lover like David Crane who was also able to make her insides melt and her heart dance to a rumba beat? The vet had warm brown eyes, a pleasant face, and a really nice butt. Though he was sweet and attractive in his own horizontally challenged way, he did absolutely nothing for her seriously parched libido.

"I just wish the judicial system had a way to punish animal abusers the same way they do those who take advantage of people. Maybe if they spent a few days without food and water, or locked in a tiny cage, they'd find out what it's like." A knock at the door kept Ellie from expounding further on her disapproval of people who mistreated animals. "I'll be back in a second."

She opened the door to a smiling Vivian, wearing designer rain gear and holding a leash attached to Mr. T. "I just got home from a dinner meeting." She slipped into the foyer. "Did you find time to go to the bank today and check out that box?"

"I did, and you won't believe what was in it."

"So tell me," Viv ordered, following Ellie to the kitchen.

"In a minute. There was a little mishap, and the doc's still here."

"Doc? You needed a doctor? Who's sick?"

"Not me. It was Cheech." She nodded toward the two Chihuahuas, now curled side by side in a single bed. When Viv didn't respond, Ellie turned to find her best friend and the charming vet eyeing each other with expressions of unabashed interest.

"I don't think you two have met. Dr. David Crane,

this is my best friend Vivian McCready. Viv, this is Dr. Dave."

The vet held out his hand, and Viv gave it a shake. "Ellie's told me so much about you, I feel like we're old friends," she said in a silky tone.

"So you're Mr. T's mom. He's a lucky dog," the vet said.

"Say what, fool?" snapped the Jack Russell.

"Don't look now, but the doctor's makin' a play for yo momma," Rudy informed him. *"Smell the testosterone wafting in the air."*

"I want to thank you for bringing T up to date on all his injections this past spring. Ellie is such a pal for making the appointment."

Dr. Dave squatted and patted Mr. T's head.

"Get your hands off me, fool!" T growled.

Viv yanked on the leash. "Hey, cranky pants. That's not nice."

Standing, the vet said to Ellie, "Guess I'd better be going." He turned to Viv. "If you're taking Mr. T for a walk, I'd be happy to come along." He reached for the umbrella he'd tossed in a corner of the kitchen. "You'll need this. It's lousy out there."

"We don't want to be any trouble," Viv said, batting her lashes. She arched a brow and gave Ellie a look. "Maybe you and the dogs want to join us?"

Ellie knew a false invitation when she heard one. It had been a while since she'd seen Viv so smitten—an old-fashioned word but the only one she could think of to describe her friend's attitude. "Uh, not right now. I still have to make sure Cheech is okay. You two go without me."

It was only after she'd said good-bye to her guests that she realized Dr. Dave hadn't given her a bill.

When Ellie picked up Mr. T the next morning, she heard Viv's shower running but didn't see any sign of

Dr. Dave. Had the four-alarm fire she'd sensed burning between them been a false blaze or a warm-up for things to come?

Either way, she was happy for her best friend and the good doctor. Viv had deep-sixed her last boyfriend a few months ago and, aside from some one-shot dating, hadn't found anyone new. To her knowledge, Dr. Dave wasn't attached, but he was definitely a nice guy. Though Viv was a head taller and seemed more sophisticated, it was possible the two would work well together.

She left a note on Viv's kitchen table asking her for details, dropped the Chihuahuas and T at home, and, after making certain all the closet doors and kitchen cupboards were firmly shut, set out with Rudy. Once outside, she removed her cell and called Joe's uncle, who agreed to meet her that afternoon.

"It's about time you arrived," said Randall when Ellie and her Yorkiepoo strolled into the Davenport. "You have an interview with a prospective client." The doorman's usually stoic face held the shadow of a smile. "They're in 11-D."

"Has Eugene gotten to them yet or am I the first?" asked Ellie, frowning as she spoke the name of her archrival.

"I haven't recommended him, if that's what you're asking, but I'll probably have to if you don't meet this person's needs."

"And they're home now?" she asked, striding toward the elevator.

"The last name is Chesney. And give them a second to answer the door, as they keep very . . . unconventional hours."

She waggled her fingers as the car door closed. Her old friend Randall had been instrumental in growing her business, not to mention offering support when her life slid into chaos faster than a one-man luge. They had yet to discuss the contents of the safety-deposit box, but he was sure to have practical advice when he heard. If this gig panned out, she'd owe him two herbal teas per week instead of one. The dog in 11-D would bring her count to eight in the building; any more customers and she'd have to walk her Davenport charges in two groups.

She hit the button for the eleventh floor, straightened the sleeves on her aquamarine linen shirt, and inspected her face in the back wall mirror. Before she left home, she'd swiped mascara on her lashes, blush on her cheeks, and dressed a step-up from her usual T-shirt and shorts. The fact that the makeup and shirt color brought out the blue in her eyes and the gold in her curls was a bonus. She had to look her best for Joe's uncle Sal at their after-lunch appointment.

"Okay, we're here." She glanced at Rudy when they reached the apartment. "Remember, best behavior," she reminded him, knocking on the door.

"Who is it?" warbled a voice from behind the panel.

"Ellie Engleman. The doorman said you were looking for a dog walker."

A series of dead bolts rattled; then the door swung open. She looked up . . . way up . . . and locked gazes with an attractive woman wearing perfect makeup, a pale pink peignoir, and matching satin mules. The tiny cream-and-black dog in her arms squirmed joyfully at the sight of a new friend.

The woman stepped aside, allowing Ellie to enter. "I'm so glad you're here."

The deep musical voice, almost lyrical in tone, made her think the woman was a singer or maybe an actress. "Thanks for going to Randall for a recommendation. I hope you'll give me a chance to take care of your dog."

"Uh . . . Ellie?" Rudy interrupted. *"There's something you should know."*

"Randall's a sweetie," the woman said, holding out a manicured hand. "I'm Bobbi Chesney. Come into the living room and we'll talk."

A dancer, Ellie decided, following in the blonde's wake. With legs that long, the woman had to be in the entertainment field. Sitting across from Bobbi on a buff-colored leather sofa, she gave the pooch a once-over and decided it was probably a Yorkie-Chihuahua mix. "What's your dog's name?"

Bobbi smiled, showing perfect white teeth, and tossed her head, causing her long blond locks to swing behind her shoulders. "This is Bitsy, the most precious thing in the world to me." She nuzzled the dog's head. "Aren't you, baby doll?"

"Oh, boy," muttered Rudy. *"We have to talk, Triple E."*

Ellie passed the woman a card. "I walk several dogs in the Davenport. Feel free to ask their owners about my quality of service."

"I've already done that," Bobbi said. "Besides Randall, everyone gave you an A plus. They said you're dependable and caring, exactly what I want for Bitsy."

"Then maybe we should discuss my rates?"

"No need, honey. I want the best for my baby, and money is no object. When can you start?"

"That depends. How many walks per day does Bitsy need? I'm here by nine each morning, and I stop again at four to do a second round."

Bobbi leaned back and crossed a shapely leg over her knee, showing off a fresh pedicure and toenails painted the color of a ripe plum. "Two is perfect. Due to my current job, I'm never awake before noon, but I made an exception this morning when Randall told me you'd be by. I'm usually up and about at four, running errands or getting ready for my job, sometimes even making plans for the evening." She gave her head another toss. "A working girl's entitled to some fun, don't you agree?"

"Yeah, sure," Ellie answered, though she wished it were true for *all* working girls, especially because it had been a while since she'd had a night of cutting loose herself. She mentioned her rates, including the discount for two walks per day, and the woman wrote a check for the rest of July and August. "How about if I hold Bitsy while you find her leash? That way, we can get acquainted before we go out."

Standing, Bobbi gently set the dog in Ellie's lap. "I'll be right back."

She gave Bitsy a once-over, noting her nails were painted the same shade of plum as her mistress's. "So, are you ready to meet a few canine friends?"

The diminutive dog gazed at her, its brown eyes wide. *"Wow. How do you do that?"*

Ellie grinned, happy to connect with her new pal. "It's a gift. I'm glad you understand me."

"I understand Bobbi, too, but when I speak I never get this direct an answer. I wish I did."

"You're still a puppy. As you get older, she might get wiser. This is Rudy, by the way." Ellie held Bitsy close for his approval. "Say hello, big man, and be nice."

The two dogs connected with the usual round of sniffs and snorts. *"You must lead one heck of an interesting life,"* Rudy commented.

"You don't know the half of it," the pup said, her voice almost a giggle.

Pleased the dogs were getting along, Ellie stood when Bobbi walked in with a purple leash attached to a rhinestone-studded collar, and said, "We'll be back in about forty-five minutes. That okay with you?"

"Whatever, and here's a key. Randall said it's par for the course, so I already signed the permission slip allowing you full privileges." She raised a pencil-thin eyebrow. "I assume my secrets are safe with you?"

Secrets? "Um, sure. I'm one hundred percent trustworthy. See you later."

She tucked the key in her bag and led the dogs to the elevator, pleased to see Rudy and Bitsy whispering like old friends. After seven more stops, and a lot of canine interaction with the newcomer, she guided her charges to the lobby. Randall was speaking with a deliveryman, so she gave him a wave as they stepped onto Fifth Avenue and crossed to the park.

The herd behaved admirably for its size, no growling, smart-assed comments, or nasty nips. Ellie almost preened at the positive influence she had on the pack. After they took care of business, she returned each dog to its home with a biscuit, and left a daily message, noting that her newest client was nowhere in sight when she let Bitsy into the apartment.

"I see you and the new tenant came to an agreement," said Randall, still with that odd half-smile on his face.

"She's a nice woman. Thanks again for the recommendation."

"No thanks needed, my dear. Just remember this moment later, if things don't go well."

"What's that supposed to mean?"

"Nothing. But you never can tell about people." Randall tipped his hat to a passing resident. "Did I mention that Eugene asked about you earlier?"

"Really? What did the dipstick want?"

"Don't you mean dipshit?" chimed Rudy.

"Nothing in particular. Merely asked if you were still walking dogs, as if there was a reason you wouldn't be."

Ellie gazed at her feet. Had the gay dog walker found out about her involvement with Gary and the fact that she was the executor of his estate? It was time she told Randall the rest of the story. Maybe he'd heard gossip about her, too.

"Is there something you're not telling me?"

"Not exactly. But remember that murdered homeless man Rudy and I found? The one who named us in his will? I went to the bank yesterday and got a look at what he left Rudy . . . and me."

"You mean it was something of value?"

"Over eight hundred thousand dollars of value," she said in a hushed tone.

Randall's mouth flapped like a broken shutter in a hurricane. "My, my. That's quite a bequest."

"I know. He also left me a note with instructions on what I was supposed to do if he turned up dead."

"Now you're worrying me. Explain, please."

She gave a brief sketch of Gary's request, finishing with, "Far as I know, the police don't have another lead. There's a good chance I'll be pinned to the wall once they find out about the money in the bank box, even though Gary says his brother will probably kill him."

"I see your problem with the police, but more inconceivable is the fact that a man of Mr. Veridot's station would not have made use of the money for himself."

"He did give a ton of it away, but not all of it."

"I hope you're going to hire an attorney," the doorman advised. "There are several in the building I can recommend. They'll see to it the police don't harass you."

"I have the name of a good friend's uncle, and we're meeting after lunch, but if things don't go well, I'll take you up on it. Right now, I just want to stay in last place in the 'Who shot Gary?' derby."

"I'll keep my ears open, but you know I don't hear much about what goes on in the outside world. The tenants here seem to take up all my time. Please be careful."

She grinned at Randall's modesty. He usually knew more about what took place on the surrounding streets than the pigeons. "Don't worry about me. I'll be fine."

Ellie stood outside the Jacob Javits Convention Center, waiting for Salvatore Cantiglia. They'd picked an area midway between their businesses as a meeting place because it was a straight shot down the West Side to Chambers Street, headquarters of the Surrogate's

Court, where they would file the will with a probate clerk.

He'd instructed her to bring the document, along with two forms of identification, which they would need to register her claim. According to Uncle Sal, as he wanted to be called, the task would be "a piece a cake." And because she was Joey's good friend, his fee would be nominal.

Unsure of what the "nominal" amount was these days, she stopped at an ATM, withdrew ten twenty-dollar bills, and stuffed them in her wallet. If Sal wanted more, he'd have to accept a check or bill her.

Ten minutes past their appointed rendezvous time, her cell rang, and she figured it was the attorney calling to tell her he'd be late.

"Hello."

"Is this Ellie?"

"Yes. Who's this?"

"Kevin McGowan. We met Sunday, at your mother's brunch. I was the tall guy who wasn't wearing a suit."

"Kevin, hi. I didn't recognize your voice. Sorry."

"That's something I'm hoping to rectify. Are you free for dinner?"

Kevin McGowan was asking her out? On a date? "Tonight?"

"I'm sorry it's short notice, but I had a client cancel and I thought about you. Unfortunately, it'll have to be early. I'm taking a deposition in the morning at eight, and I have to be in court by ten."

"Um, sure. I don't mind an early dinner. Shall I meet you somewhere?"

"How about if we find common ground? If I remember correctly, your last trip of the day is at a building near mine, on Fifth and Eighty-sixth—the Cranston Arms? We could get together in front of the Guggenheim, if that's good with you."

Impressed that he remembered one of the buildings

housing the dogs she walked, she said, "Sounds good. I'm usually through around six."

"Great. See you then."

Ellie flipped the phone closed and stared at it for a full ten seconds. With everything that had taken place over the past couple of days, she'd practically forgotten about meeting Kevin, but he'd kept her business card and called. Viv had been right. It really was time she made an effort to go out.

A horn blared, and she glanced at the taxi stopped at the curb. The back door opened, and a rotund man wearing a three-piece suit stepped out, waving in her direction.

"Hey! You Ellie Engleman?"

Figuring the man was Uncle Sal, she hurried to the cab and slid inside.

"Well, well, well," he said in a Dirty Harry tone of voice. "Joey didn't say you was a looker."

"Um, thanks."

He slapped a palm on the seat back, and the driver headed into traffic. Ellie smiled politely and held out her hand. "It's nice to meet you, Mr. Cantiglia. Thanks for agreeing to do this so quickly."

The attorney took her hand in both of his, and she noted the gumball-sized diamond in his pinkie ring. "Please, it's Uncle Sal to my friends—and all the pretty girls. How about, after this, we get a glass of vino? I know a great place in Little Italy; there's lotsa quiet corners, and it's real private. We could get to know each other better."

Uh-oh. "I'm sorry, but I already have a date for dinner." Bless Kevin McGowan for giving her a truthful excuse. "Maybe some other time."

Sal shrugged and his suit, a size too small and the color of snakeskin left too long in the sun, bunched around his shoulders. "Maybe. So, let's see what you got."

Ellie passed him the will, which he read while raising

and lowering a pair of caterpillar-like eyebrows. "Left the money to a dog, huh?"

"Why do you assume it's money?" she asked. How come everyone assumed a homeless person had cash in the bank?

"Just a guess. Either way, you're in charge of whatever it is. Lucky for you he says all you need to do is share it with your dog."

"It's been signed and notarized," she pointed out, "so I've been told we won't have any problems."

"Probably not. You got ID?"

"A driver's license, social security card, and a passport."

"Okay, we're all set." He loosened his tie, and she couldn't help but notice the ring-around-the-collar stain on his shirt. "It's a friggin' oven in here," Sal stated, sweat streaming from his temples to his cheeks. "Hey, buddy, crank up the air-conditioning on this heap."

The driver, Shadeesh Hepbaz according to the taxi license, didn't nod or acknowledge his passengers in any way. Instead, he hoisted a fist out the window, stepped on the gas, and shot across three lanes of traffic.

Sal rolled his eyes, mumbled something about camel jockeys, and gave her a damp smile. "So, Joey says this guy who named you in the will, you didn't know him."

Seeking relief from the overpowering scent of stale garlic lacing Sal's breath, Ellie inched back in the corner of her seat. "I knew him, but only in a roundabout way. Why?"

"Because you're gonna become a person of record for the deceased once the will is processed. Could be, creditors and nut jobs will swarm out of the woodwork after it's registered. You ready for that?"

Sam had mentioned the same thing might happen. "Could you explain what that means in plain English?"

Sal tugged on his pants, which had ridden up both calves to reveal a six-inch section of hairy white leg gaping over the tops of his ankle-high black socks. "Trans-actions like this are a matter of public record. Once it's posted, everyone who takes a look will see that you're the executor for this Garick Veridot. Could be second, third, even fourth cousins will try to get their sticky fingers on the estate. Sometimes, even people who don't have a legitimate claim try to stake one."

"I don't think Gary had any relatives, other than a brother, and he's been in prison."

"Sing Sing?" Sal asked, using the outdated term for the infamous New York State correctional institution.

"I'm not sure." Ellie swallowed. "Does it make a difference?"

"Prob'ly not. The slammer's the slammer, as far as I'm concerned. Don't get me wrong, I got a small contingent of miscreants for clients, but they're penny-ante, a couple of ladies of the evening, some purse snatchers, guys who'd do whatever they had to for a shot of juice. You know the type."

Ellie opened her mouth to tell him she most certainly did not know the type, but squeaked out instead, "Juice?"

He grinned. "Me, I'd rather handle the easy stuff, like what we're doin' today."

Thank God for the easy stuff. "Do you think this will take long? I have clients to walk in about ninety minutes."

"Clients to walk? Oh, right. Joey said you were a dog walker. And you call those fuzzballs clients. Cute." The driver swerved. Horns blared. "Jesus H. Christ! Take it easy! There's a lady back here!"

Clutching her tote bag to her chest with one hand, Ellie latched onto the door handle with the other. The taxi slammed to a stop at a red light.

"Only a couple more blocks," Uncle Sal grumbled. "If we're lucky, we'll get there in one piece."

She nodded, afraid to speak for fear the driver would

see to it they ended up in the Hudson River. Sal patted her knee. "You okay? You look a little sick."

She gave him a brave smile. "I'm fine." If she lived through this afternoon, she was going to kill Joe.

Mercifully, the driver brought the cab to a halt in a more subdued manner when they arrived at their destination. Uncle Sal tossed a bill in the front seat and hustled her out. Grasping her elbow, he gazed at the imposing building. "She's a beauty, ain't she?" he asked, though it didn't sound as if he expected an answer. "They film scenes from *Law and Order* here every once in a while. How's that for trivia?"

"Really? I don't usually watch television police dramas, so I wouldn't—"

"Come on, let's go." He tugged her inside, and they navigated the usual stopping points that secured a public building. "Okay, we go up to the fifth floor."

Ellie admired the building's majestic interior, encased in orangish salmon pink and white marble. If Sal hadn't led her to the elevators, she would have stopped to read a plaque explaining the structure's history, but he moved fast for an overweight sixty-year-old, and he obviously knew his way around.

Now on the correct floor, he escorted her to a door marked PROBATE CLERK. Inside, a stern-faced woman nodded to him. "Mr. Cantiglia. Nice to see you again."

"Hey, Gloria, you're lookin' good. Got a little business that needs takin' care of. Seems a no-brainer to me, but it's your call."

The woman read the will and turned to Ellie. "ID?"

She passed over her license and passport. Thirty minutes later, and fifty dollars poorer, Ellie was officially named as the executor of Garick Veridot's estate and the person of record for his debts and benefits.

Chapter 8

"You didn't call, so I assume everything went okay this morning," Ellie said to Hilary Blankenship when they met in the woman's apartment complex lobby at five. Frazzled over last evening's debacle with her houseguest and her trip to the Surrogate's Court, she'd called Hilary that morning and asked her to do the first walk of the day alone. She hoped this afternoon's round would make up for her neglect.

Wearing designer jogging gear, a pair of what appeared to be brand-new athletic shoes, and a paper mask resembling those a nail salon worker might wear, Hilary had three dogs in tow and carried her own in her arms. "I guess things went fine. All the dogs did their business. I just don't understand how such small animals can generate so much . . . waste. Even Cuddles makes a mess, and he's a baby." She glanced lovingly at her toy poodle. "Aren't you, sweetheart?"

Ellie bit back a flip comment about the mask and other paraphernalia the woman wore. "That's exactly why I only walk dogs of fifteen pounds or less. Anything bigger and it gets . . . daunting. Think about it. How much poop can one woman scoop and still keep her sanity?"

Hilary sniffed. "It's so demeaning, but this," she pointed to the mask, "helps with the odor."

Hilary's narrow-minded opinion was much the same as Georgette's, not a good sign for the future of her employment. They stood at the corner, waiting for the light to change when Ellie said, "If you decide this job isn't your cup of tea—"

"I'm sure I'll get used to it, and I really need the work. Richard's attorney is badgering my lawyer for that list of expenses, and my man is trying to hold him off as long as possible. It's so irritating, having to resort to menial labor while my husband refuses to let go of our assets."

Menial labor? I thought I was an entrepreneur, a successful businesswoman, independent of a man and proud of it. "I'm sure it's difficult, but you are making your own money again."

"Forgive me if I sound like a snob," Hilary clarified as they crossed Fifth Avenue. "It's just that everything I've known for the past fifteen years has suddenly been swept away, and I'm still not coping well. I've always been able to buy whatever I wanted, now I'm forced to live on an allowance so small no normal person could manage."

"Um, I don't mean to pry, but how much is your husband giving you?"

"Richard continues to pay the mortgage and the utilities, but he's cancelled the charge cards, except the one in my name for Bloomies. And he's agreed to deposit five thousand a month into my checking account, but that's it."

Ellie suppressed an eye roll. Entire families in this city lived on sixty thousand a year, and they paid rent and their own utilities. If she had that much to fritter away, she wouldn't be complaining.

"You'll have a salary come the first of August. I'll prorate it for the number of walks you're scheduled to do times your walk rate. How does that sound?"

"Acceptable. Still, it will be less than a thousand a month. That's barely enough to keep me in appointments at the Red Door. Richard might not care about my appearance now that we're divorcing, but I have to maintain myself in the manner to which I've become accustomed. Otherwise I'll lose all credibility with my friends." She stopped to let the dogs sniff a trash can. "Especially if I hope to find another husband."

Poor baby, Ellie almost said. She used to have spa appointments, too, and dates with a personal trainer, a fashion consultant, and a yoga instructor. But that was when the D wore her on his arm like a Rolex. Damn if she'd do it again. Why would any sane woman want to live under some controlling man's thumb when she could be her own person?

They strolled along the rock and iron fencing of Central Park. Up ahead, people wandered in front of the Guggenheim, and she wondered if Kevin McGowan was already there watching her do her thing with Hilary. She wasn't used to a handsome stranger taking an interest in her work, never mind remembering the buildings that housed her clients. He was either an extremely in-tune kind of person or he was actually interested in her. Since it was difficult to imagine a lawyer in either position, she had no idea how to act with him.

"Oh, no! Go on now. Shoo!" Hilary waved her free hand at a squirrel. The bushy-tailed rodent chattered, but continued to bound alongside the dogs. "Scat." She picked up a stick and raised it high, threatening to throw it. "Get away!"

"Hilary. Stop. It's a squirrel, not a wild boar."

The woman dropped her arm. "I hate the little bastards. And look at all these pigeons, soiling the sidewalk with their droppings. If I had my way—"

"They're not hurting anyone. Of course, if it bothers you so much, you could always scoop their poop when you picked up the dog waste."

Hilary frowned. "You may enjoy doing this, but I don't. If one of my friends spots me, I swear, I'll die of embarrassment." They waited while Sampson and Millie squatted. When the dogs finished, Hilary thrust the leads at Ellie, dug in her pocket, and slipped on a pair of latex gloves.

Now the woman looked like a worker at a hazmat site. Ellie sighed. Maybe Rudy was right. Hiring Hilary hadn't been such a bright idea, after all.

Hilary pulled a few plastic bags from her other pocket, bent, and gingerly picked up the waste. They traveled another two blocks while the rest of the pack pooped their hearts out and the scenario was repeated.

On the way back to the apartment complex, Ellie again scanned the museum. Finished with the renovations on the façade, the Guggenheim was back to its original beauty. People clustered in groups of two or three, most of them taking photos. Kevin could be anywhere, or still at home. Though he'd told her his apartment was near here, she decided she really should ask him where he lived.

Hilary continued making small talk while Ellie tuned out her whining and instead paid attention to their charges, who seemed subdued. When they reached Sampson's apartment, Hilary unlocked the door, unhooked and hung up his leash, and resecured the door.

"What about his treat?" asked Ellie.

"Treat?"

"His biscuit. Remember, I told you to buy a box and carry them on the outings. Each dog gets one when they've been good on a walk and are back in their home."

"I forgot. Is it really so important?" asked Hilary.

Ellie pulled a biscuit from her bag and corrected the error. "It's very important. I advertise special care for my guys. That means play time, biscuits, extra TLC. If you want to work for me, you have to do it, too. Ditto with the notes on how the pups did on their walk."

They took the elevator to the next two units, where Ellie passed out treats from her tote while Hilary composed notes. Now in front of her apartment, the woman shrugged. "I'm sorry. I'll try to remember the biscuit thing and the memo thing. I really do intend to make this work."

Divorce is traumatic, Ellie reminded herself, curtailing her temper. "I'll bring a box from home tomorrow. How soon do you think it'll be before you can do this alone?"

"Maybe another day or so." Her assistant held an ungloved hand to her forehead. "I might be coming down with something."

"I sent the paperwork to the bonding and insurance companies. You should be legal in a week or so."

"Well, that's good. Let me know if there's a problem."

She closed the door, and Ellie sighed. Good thing she'd left those "help wanted" sheets hanging at the local colleges. With Hilary's lackluster attitude, paper mask, and latex gloves, she'd probably need a new assistant before the week was over.

She stood on the corner of Fifth and Seventy-eighth, waiting for the light to change, when her phone rang. "This is Ellie," she answered, hoping it was someone calling about the assistant's job.

"I got a ticket about your dog walker ad." The male voice was muffled, as if the speaker held a hand or a towel over the receiver. "How about I come to your place tonight, so we can talk?"

Ellie heaved a breath. "Who is this?"

"Someone who wants the job. I'd like to come to your apartment, so we can discuss it."

Surprised a stranger who wanted a job would sound so demanding, she said, "I don't give people I've never met my address, but we can make a date for coffee. May I have your name?"

"Well, I don't give my name to someone I've never met. You think about that, and I'll call you later."

The line went dead before she could reply. Then the traffic signal changed, and she headed across the street, regaining her composure as she walked. That guy had nerve, rudely bossing her around when he was the one who needed work. If he called again, she'd tell him she'd already hired someone and hang up on him they way he'd done to her.

Putting the call behind her, she gazed at the Guggenheim, a beautiful museum shining in the sunlight, as stately and imposing as Frank Lloyd Wright had intended, and checked her outfit in a coffee shop window. She'd dressed nicely for her appointment with Sal Cantiglia, and she didn't want to make a mess of her dinner date with Kevin McGowan.

Ellie swallowed at the word "dinner." How could she have forgotten about Rudy and the boys? Not only would her petite protector be annoyed that she hadn't told him about her date, he'd be furious she wasn't home in time for his walk and supper. She dialed Viv's number as she continued toward the Guggenheim, and when they connected her best friend assured her she was on her way home at that very moment and would be happy to take care of Rudy and the Chihuahuas. Ellie even managed to hang up before Viv had the chance to grill her on the reason why she'd wouldn't be home in time to feed her dog.

Tucking her phone in her bag, she spotted Kevin, reading a glassed-in notice of an upcoming art event on the museum's front door. No doubt about it, the man was eye candy in the Godiva price range. Tall and dark-haired, with a killer set of buns, he was dressed in navy blue slacks and a pale yellow golf shirt.

She walked to him and whispered, "Think they allow dogs inside?"

He didn't glance her way, just continued perusing

the information. "Says here the only canines allowed are Yorkiepoos. Know anybody who has one?" Then he turned. "Oh, Ellie. I didn't know it was you."

"You're such a kidder," she responded, grinning.

"I try. I saw you walking a group of dogs with a woman a little earlier. Did she own all of them?"

"Hilary? Lord, no. Hers was the tiny white poodle. The rest are her charges."

"Her charges?" He nodded toward the curb, where a taxi was dropping off passengers.

"Yep," she said, sliding into the cab. "She's my new assistant-in-training. Until her bonding and insurance papers come through, I have to go with her on the walks."

"So you have an assistant. Good for you." He gave the driver the name of a restaurant and the address. "Do you pay her enough to make a living?"

"Hardly, since it's only part-time work. She's just hoping it will bolster her support money."

"But you and the judge said that anyone could make a good living at it, once they got a client list going. Correct?"

"Stanley and I have been over the numbers, so it's possible. But he's a financial genius, and I'm not."

"I imagine Georgette has an opinion on the matter?"

"Too much of an opinion." She relaxed in her seat. "According to Mother, I might be making money now, but the entire business could fall apart at any moment. She's the one who lent me the money to keep myself afloat during the separation and first few months after my divorce became final, and I'm going to pay her back every penny if it's the last thing I do."

"I take it your ex wasn't the generous type?"

"To put it mildly."

"And that woman—Hilary—is she having marital problems?"

"She's heading for the same deep water I was in, so I hired her. It might work out, and it might not. Only time will tell."

"I see."

They pulled up in front of an Italian restaurant with outdoor seating, and Kevin paid the driver. "The weather's good. Want to eat outside?"

The bistro had a dozen tables on the sidewalk, and it was early enough that most of them were empty. "That's fine."

He led her around the iron fencing and held out her chair. "Great. I'll get a waiter."

"I had a nice time." Ellie stood on the first step leading up to the porch of her apartment building, which made her eyes almost level with the six-foot-tall Kevin McGowan. "Thanks for dinner, and the escort home."

"I had a great time, too. If I didn't have to be at work so early in the morning, I'd ask you to invite me up for a while."

"Oh, um, maybe next time?"

"My calendar's full for the rest of the week, but what about Saturday night?"

She opened and closed her mouth. Perhaps it was time she reread the Book of Revelation, just to be certain it didn't mention the apocalypse was near when Ellie Engleman was asked on a second date by an articulate and handsome man.

"I'm free anytime," she said, in case he'd made a slip and really meant a Saturday night in 2011.

"Tickets to a play and dinner? Or are you up for something less serious? I think the Yankees are hosting the Angels."

The theater? A big-time sporting event? She almost swooned. "Either is fine with me. I just need to know which, so I'm dressed for the occasion."

"You'll look dynamite in whatever you wear. I'll call

you." Holding her elbows in his hands, he leaned forward and brushed his lips across her cheek. "Thanks again."

Frowning, she watched the taxi pull away. Kevin had just used the same line Sam had when he'd written that brush-off note, so she wasn't holding out hope she'd ever hear from him again, but she was still amazed by the evening. Climbing the steps, she entered the building and used her key to get her mail, then turned to open the main door.

And as she did, a man said, "It's about time you got home."

Ellie's thousand-decibel shriek bounced off the lobby walls, echoing like a fire alarm while she fumbled in her bag for her Mace. By the time she pulled it out, the surprise visitor had her pinned against the wall.

"Take it easy. It's me."

She stopped struggling, blew a flutter of curls from her forehead, and glared. "What the heck are you doing, sneaking up on me like some two-bit Jack the Ripper? I ought to get a restraining order, or better still call the cops, anything to keep you out of my hair."

Sam's teeth glinted in the darkness. "I am the cops, but go ahead if it'll make you feel any better."

She shrugged from his grasp, and he stepped back, raising his hands in surrender. "Sorry. I thought you saw me."

"Does it look like I'm wearing night-vision goggles? And why should I expect anyone to be hiding in the entryway of my complex at nine in the evening?" She pushed against the lobby door, but it didn't budge.

"Why didn't he come up?" Sam asked, changing topics.

"Now what are you talking about?"

"The guy who brought you home. Why didn't you invite him to your place?"

"Remind me to add stalking to the list when I apply for that restraining order." Fidgeting with her keys, she finally got the door open and stomped inside. "As for my date, Kevin is none of your business."

They made it to her landing before he asked, "Kevin? Are the two of you an item?"

Ellie rested her back against the wall next to her front door. "You've got to be kidding."

He stuffed his hands in his pockets like a first-grader unhappy with the rules of a game he was forced to play. "It's a reasonable question."

"It's a none-of-your-business question," she bit out. She entered her foyer and swung around to block the doorway before he stepped inside. "What do you want?"

"We need to talk."

"I doubt it."

"What's he doing here?" Rudy yipped by way of greeting. *"I thought he was out of our lives for good."*

She grabbed his leash and dropped to one knee. "Quiet. Where are the boys?"

"Those bean eaters? How the heck should I know?"

"You're supposed to keep them out of trouble," she whispered. Standing, she said to Sam, "I have to find my houseguests. Stay here."

Cheech and Chong were wide awake, tails wagging, in the kitchen. After hooking them to leads, she brought them to the door, where she found Sam and Rudy glaring at each other as if they wanted the same bone. Not willing to play referee, she tugged Rudy and the Chihuahuas into the hall, pulled the door closed, and led them outside for their evening walk.

Sam kept pace until the brothers stopped and found a spot to drop. "What are we waiting for?"

"Take a look, sport." She nodded to the squatting Chihuahuas. "It's not rocket science."

A second passed. "Oh."

She whipped a plastic bag from her tote and passed it to him. "Here. Do something useful."

He squinted at the bag. "Me?"

"I don't see anyone else making a pest of themselves. If you're going to tag along, you might as well pull your weight."

She grinned when he stooped and scooped. After pressing the seal, he held out the offering. "Now what?"

"Drop it in the nearest trash can." She took off at a clip, the dogs trotting alongside. Let him run to catch up if what he had to say was so important.

"Where are we going?" Sam asked when he reached her side.

"I don't know about you, but the boys and I are going to Carl Schurz Park."

"At this time of night? Do you have a death wish?"

"What I have is Mace and three canine companions." They crossed Third and continued east. "No crook worth his salt would dare bother me."

"Those hairy hamsters wouldn't hurt a fly—and neither would you. I had you pinned in your foyer before you pulled the can from your bag."

"Thanks for reminding me." She dug out the Mace and stuck it in her pants pocket. "Better?"

He mumbled a curse as he walked. Determined to make him work for the time he spent with her, Ellie ate up the sidewalk until they arrived at the gates to the park. At this hour of the night it was deserted, though she knew Sam was right about an unsavory element lurking somewhere in the vicinity. She led the dogs to the fenced run and unclipped their leashes, then sat on the nearest bench.

Sam plopped down beside her, breathing heavily. "Do you come here often?"

"A couple of nights a week. The boys have to take a trip outside before bed, and Viv claims she needs the exercise. I have the stamina, and she's safer if I'm by her side."

"Safer? With you?"

"Stop knocking my defensive skills. I did all right with Bibi and Fortensky, didn't I?"

"Two women brawling like cats in a sack isn't the same as protecting yourself from a felon with a handgun. You stroll this town alone. Anything could happen to you."

She folded her arms and humphed. "Like you care."

"I do care," he said crossly. "Protecting the citizens of this city is part of my job."

"Well, take me off your list of Manhattanites worthy of your concern, because I'm thinking of getting a gun," she threatened. "That way you won't have to lose sleep worrying about my safety."

"God help us." He cleared his throat when she glared at him. "Then you didn't suffer any permanent damage after the night we found Buddy and the others?"

You'd already know the answer if you'd bothered to pick up the phone, she almost blurted. "Rudy was in bad shape for a while, but the bruises and his cracked ribs healed. I was no worse for the incident."

They sat in silence, until Sam said, "I'm sorry I didn't call you like I wrote in the note."

"Don't give it another thought. Neither of us made any promises."

"Still, I said I'd be in touch and I—"

"What was it you wanted to talk to me about?" she interrupted. No way would she demean herself by whining.

He rested his elbows on his knees. "A couple of things. First, did you find an attorney and get the will registered?"

"It's taken care of. I'm now the person of record for Garick Veridot. According to Uncle Sal, I need to gird myself for an onslaught of creditors and distant relatives, each of whom will want a chunk of his estate."

"You have an uncle who's a lawyer?"

"He's the uncle of a friend, and he seems knowledgeable enough. Says I should be careful of anyone who asks about Gary and tell them to contact him if they have a problem."

"Do you have to report what you inherited to the government?"

"Sal says until you hit two million there's no need in this state, though it will have to go on my federal tax return, and I'll probably have to pay some sort of estate tax. He also thinks I'll hear from a lot of people, whether they're related or not. Apparently, there are scam artists who investigate the will registrations weekly, hoping to find a sucker. And there still may be some folks who remember the Veridot family and their fortune." She peered into the dog run and spotted Rudy giving the cold shoulder to Cheech and Chong. "They might cause trouble."

"Have you made any decisions about the money?"

"I plan to sit on it for a while, like you suggested, though I'll need some of it to have Gary cremated. And I probably should have his belongings hauled out of the park when the police say it's okay to disturb the crime scene." She heaved a sigh. "I'm not looking forward to the task."

"I talked to Gruning today. That's the other thing we need to go over." He leaned back on the bench and crossed his ankles. "What to do about Thompson Veridot."

She let the information settle before she spoke. "You're absolutely positive he's out?"

"As of the beginning of May. And no one's seen him since."

"I still don't see how he could simply disappear. Doesn't he have to check in with . . . someone?"

"Nope. He did every day of his thirty years, which means he paid his debt to society. He's free as a bird, no rules or constraints."

"So what Gary wrote in that note was probably right.

His brother could have killed him." Though her insides churned, she copied Sam's relaxed pose. "Does anybody have an idea where he might be?"

"I don't have a clue, and neither does Gruning."

"I'm beginning to believe you're right about him. The man is a jerk."

"I didn't tell him about the note you found in the bank box, because it would only lead to trouble, but I have a theory." He swiveled on the bench, and she knew he was studying her reaction. "These days, it's easy to disappear, buy a new identity, and get a fresh start without your past hanging over your head. Since Thompson has no family, he probably contacted some of the pals he met doing time. They may have helped him forge a new ID, get some cash, probably enough to see him through until he found a way to get money of his own."

"You mean money from his brother."

"It's a sensible answer. But if I explain the situation to Gruning, it will up the ante on your guilt."

Chapter 9

Sam walked beside Ellie as they made their way home from the park. It was late, and he had an early call in the morning, but he didn't care. The second Gruning informed him that Thompson Veridot had been released from jail, his insides had seized and he'd called the prison.

According to the warden, Veridot was a smart bastard who'd never tried for parole; without a sorry bone in his body, he knew he'd be denied. He probably figured his baby brother still had the family fortune and returned home to stalk him. Gary must have sensed it or seen the guy on the street, but had been too frightened to do anything about it.

When Thompson finally approached him, Gary probably refused to give him the cash. So the creep shot him, maybe in retaliation for Gary testifying against him, maybe for the hell of it. Then Thompson tore up the shelter searching for the money.

And if he'd been tailing Gary, he could have seen Ellie talking to his brother or visiting the shelter and figured she knew something. Now that the will was a matter of public record, all the scumbag had to do was go to the probate clerk and check the filings. When he saw Ellie's name as the person responsible for Gary's estate, he'd take it from there.

To think that Thompson might be watching her while she walked the dogs had Sam ready to blow a fuse. The creep might even have followed both of them to the bank the other afternoon, put the pieces together, and was waiting for the perfect moment to strike.

He'd tried to get this point across to Gruning, but the asshole wouldn't listen. Unless Ellie could prove there'd been a threat on her life, Gruning wasn't about to set up protection. In fact, if the idiot detective learned she was now in possession of Gary's cash, he'd probably reconsider his position and arrest her, as he'd wanted to do last week.

They arrived at her complex in silence, and she climbed a step before turning. Sam realized they were standing just about where she had been when that Kevin guy had kissed her. The man was a wuss. If Ellie had been Sam's date for the evening, their good-bye would have gone a lot further than a wimpy peck on the cheek.

He was about to show her the way a real man said good night when her dog wound itself around his ankles. Reaching down, he grabbed the leash, and all three mutts started yipping, growling, and jumping, making the tangle worse. Hopping on one foot, he loosened the leads and straightened. When he looked up, Ellie was grinning.

"What's so funny?"

"You. Big, tough detective, trying to corral a trio of 'hairy hamsters.' I should take a picture."

"Do that. In the meantime, we aren't finished talking."

She rolled her eyes. "You mean there's more?"

"Hell, yes, there's more, and you know it. I can tell by that tough-girl look on your face what you're thinking."

"You have no idea what's on my mind. But Gary's actions make more sense now."

"Just tell me you have no intention of doing what he suggested in that note."

She sighed. "Stop badgering me. I'm tired, and it's hard to think straight."

"Ellie, I'm ordering you not to go looking for Thompson Veridot, is that clear? Instead, we should discuss the things you can do to stay safe—besides buying a gun. Which is a terrible idea, I might add."

"That's exactly what I'd expect you to say." She looked down her nose at him. "You are such a—a—*cop*."

"A gun of any caliber is a serious piece of hardware, and it takes training, a strong arm, and a good eye to handle one properly. Never hold a weapon unless you know how to use it."

"There are places in the city that give lessons. I'll apply for a permit and pay someone to teach me how to fire a weapon. In case you haven't noticed, I'm responsible enough to learn how to do things right."

"It's not that simple."

"I know it's not simple. I'm willing to get instruction." She pulled out her keys. "Now, if you'll excuse me, it's time to say good night."

"Wait." He took her elbow. "Can I come up?"

"No."

"Just for a couple of minutes. I have more to say."

"More to say about what? Me and my stupid ideas? Me being too weak to defend myself?"

Okay, so he had to take a subtler approach. "Come on, fifteen minutes. I'll be nice, promise."

She raised a brow, but didn't say no. He followed her up the steps and into the apartment.

"Give me a minute to give the boys a nibble."

He sat at the kitchen table. "Don't tell me you didn't have someone walk them or feed them dinner."

"I asked Viv to do it, but she's not always generous. Besides, it's the least I can do for not being here on time."

"When did you and that guy meet?"

"Kevin? We met at six for an early dinner. He has to be in court in the morning."

Sam stifled a groan. A lawyer. It figured.

She put a handful of kibble in each bowl, then set down dishes with fresh water. After that, she peered in her fridge. "Do you want a beer or some ice water? If you'd prefer, I can make hot tea."

"Water's fine."

After pouring two glasses, she took a seat across from him. "What else did you want to say?"

"That you need to be extraordinarily careful. Don't go out alone, especially after dark."

"You already said that. What else?"

Her calm tone eased the stranglehold of worry from around his chest. "Pay attention to the people you meet. Don't walk anywhere that's isolated, and for God's sake, don't come into your building without that can of Mace in your hand, whether it's day or night. And if you think you spotted Thompson Veridot, call me."

"I wouldn't know the man if I tripped over him, so that'll be difficult."

"There must have been pictures in those online articles you read. Something you could use for identification."

"Thirty years have passed. I doubt he looks anything like he did back then."

"I'll phone the warden again, see if I can get a current photo and description."

She used a paper napkin to wipe a water ring off the table. "You really think he killed his own brother?"

"He murdered his parents, didn't he? Men like him don't change—unless they find religion and repent. From what the warden said, that wasn't the case with Thompson."

"Okay." She heaved a sigh. "Anything else?"

"Have you ever taken a self-defense class?"

She frowned. "You're joking."

"I'm serious. I know you don't believe in violence, but you should learn to protect yourself if attacked. Even if I'm wrong about Veridot, defensive training is a smart thing for a woman. I have a friend who owns a gym. He gives classes a couple of nights a week."

"And you want me to sign up for one of them?"

"Not one—a series of lessons. Learn how to scratch, bite, claw, kick with a vengeance, anything to break away from an attacker. It's worth it, believe me."

Rudy trotted over and put his paws on her thigh. She glanced down and gave his ears a scratch. "I know, thinking about it makes me tired, too." Then she gave Sam a look that told him his time was up. "I really have to get to bed."

He pushed away from the table, and she followed him to the door. "Promise me you'll be alert, careful. Don't talk to strangers and don't go into any park alone, especially at night."

"I'll try."

"Trying isn't good enough. I want your promise that you won't look for Thompson Veridot. If you think you're being followed, call me."

"I'm not making any promises. I have to think about what Gary asked me to do in that note, what I feel is right in my heart, too, and I can't do that with you on my case."

He sighed, then raised a hand and touched her cheek. Giving himself a mental kick, he drew her near. She was such a soft touch, she'd be an easy mark for Veridot or any jerk looking to do a hit and run. What could he do to make her see she was vulnerable?

Ellie grabbed his wrist as if to pull away, but he didn't let her go. He planned to make sure this was the good night she'd remember, not the puny peck she'd received from that wuss of an attorney.

When she opened her mouth to speak, he captured her lips, gently tasted and teased, then delved for more.

The kiss brought back all the old memories plus a few new ideas that kicked his heartbeat up a notch. Knowing it couldn't go any further, he drew back.

"I expect to hear from you at least once a day, and every night before you go to bed. If not, I'll be on your doorstep just like the postman, only I'll work on Sundays, too." He put a cocky grin on his face, gave her a small salute, and walked out the door.

Ellie was just about to go to bed when her cell rang. Striding into the kitchen, she dug in her purse and pulled out the phone. She needed to charge it, so the call was a good thing, no matter who was on the line. "This is Ellie." A bout of heavy breathing brought back the memory of the rude person who had called that morning to ask about the assistant's job. "Hello?"

"Did you give any thought to my coming to your place for an interview?"

When she heard the muffled voice, she knew it was the same man. "Look, Mr. . . . ?"

"You're still up. I can be to your place in five minutes."

"How do you know where I live?" she asked, telling herself to stand tough.

"I know lots about you . . . and your dog."

Ellie swallowed hard. This was too creepy for words. "Have you been following me?"

"In a manner of speaking. Now how about that interview?"

"I'm sorry, but I'm no longer looking for an assistant," she said, frowning. "And I don't appreciate your continued calls, especially since you won't give me your name."

His laugh raised goose bumps on her arms. "We'll meet, soon enough. I got plenty to say to you." With that, he disconnected the call.

"Stupid jerk," Ellie muttered, snapping her phone

closed. Then she rubbed her arms. What did she expect when she hung her phone number on public bulletin boards for every nut job to see? The guy's voice was downright ugly. She'd swear she'd heard it before, but couldn't for the life of her remember where. He'd pulled a slip off her flyer, but where? She'd gone to Columbia and a few other colleges, so he could have found out about her in several places.

Miffed, she stomped down the hall and into the bedroom, plugged her cell into the charger, and took care of business in the bathroom. Then she returned and glanced at Rudy, snuggled on the pillow next to her.

"Who was on the phone?"

"Some jerk trying to get an interview as my assistant."

"Hey, that means you can replace Hilary."

"No, I can't. Besides, this guy is rude, and he's a weirdo. I can't imagine putting any of our charges in his hands."

"Okay, whatever. By the way, I heard you and the dippy detective talking for a while. Did he have anything important to say?"

"Not much more than his usual warnings. But he did tell me to take a self-defense course."

"Karate? Tae Kwon Do? Kickboxing? Sounds good to me."

"Maybe so, but I don't think I can do it. I'd hate hurting anyone, even for practice."

Since Rudy had changed the subject, she forgot about the caller and thought further about Sam's visit. In a far corner of her brain, she had known exactly what he was going to say about taking care of herself. Now that she was certain Thompson Veridot had been released from prison, her homeless friend's spooky actions and the things he'd said in that note made more sense. Gary's strange comments about seeing ghosts, his odd conversation with Pops, his need to spell out his wishes on paper were all his way of coping with an ugly situation.

Gary had been planning to die, and though he wasn't sure when it would happen he knew there was only one person who wanted him dead. A man who held a grudge. The brother who blamed him for spending the last thirty years of his life in jail. And Gary, in his warped mind, thought that when he was gone, his friends Ellie and Rudy would know what to do about it.

She recalled how he'd admired her for discovering Professor Albright's killer. How he'd given her a tin medal he'd found in a Dumpster that proclaimed its owner "The World's Greatest Hero." He must have figured she could continue the heroics and bring closure to his family's story by catching his brother and putting him in prison for good.

"I doubt Gary expected you to actually capture his brother, Triple E. Maybe just point the cops in the right direction."

"It doesn't sound that way to me," she told Rudy, holding the note she kept on her nightstand up to the light. "He says right here, 'I'm counting on you to see to it justice is served once and for all.'" She heaved a breath. "He never mentions the police, just makes it sound as if he's leaving it all in our, er, my hands."

"The man had PTSD. You said so yourself. People like that aren't responsible for what they say or do. Gary was confused."

"I know he was, and that makes the situation more miserable. Imagine being so frightened you think evil lurks around every corner. You do what you can to keep the man who murdered your parents from getting a reward. And you ask your only friend—"

"Make that friends."

She ran a hand over his head. "Gary entrusted us with what was left of his family's fortune and expected us to take care of things."

"Taking care of things means disposing of him and his property, not getting ourselves killed."

"So we'll be careful, watch our step, do like Sam said and walk where there's good light and plenty of people. That doesn't mean we can't keep our eyes and ears open. We should talk to Pops. He sees everything that goes down on the Upper East Side. He'll know if strangers have been asking questions."

"But what if this Thompson creep is sneaky? Knows how to hide? Knows how to tail us?"

"Then we'll be sneakier, hide better than he does, and learn how to lose a tail."

Rudy sneezed his displeasure. *"I don't like the sound of this. For once I think Detective Dunce is right. Stay out of it and let the cops do their thing."*

"I'll try, but I'm not going to run from a monster who killed his own brother. Someone should tell Thompson what a wonderful man Gary grew into, no thanks to him." She switched off her bedside lamp and rolled to face her pal. "Maybe Sam's jumping to conclusions. It's been thirty years. It's possible Thompson never found him and Gary just thought he was being stalked. The killing was random, not on purpose."

"I don't know about that."

"Even if his brother had found him, he had to see that Gary lived in a cardboard box, ate from garbage cans, and led a pauper's existence. What would make Thompson think there was still money to be had?"

"Beats me why humans act the way they do. Look at how many mistreat their innocent four-legged friends, and it doesn't seem to bother them one bit." He yawned. *"Gary was sorta like an abandoned cat or dog, ya know? He looked for handouts, befriended people who treated him right, and wanted us to have everything that was his."*

She sniffed back a sob. "Keep it up and you'll have me in tears."

"Just don't do anything stupid."

"Now you're starting to sound like Sam."

"Who, me? Nuh-uh. Never." He curled into a tight ball on the pillow. *"What's with him anyway, stickin' his nose in our business like he cared?"*

"I think he does care, in his own might-makes-right way. Don't worry about Sam. I can handle him. Now go to sleep. We'll talk in the morning."

Seconds later, gentle snores told her Rudy was out for the night. That's when she faced another, more frightening truth. Kevin McGowan was handsome, intelligent, and fun to be with, not bossy or controlling. He seemed interested in what interested her, and he didn't speak to her as if she was too stupid to live.

Sam more than matched Kevin in the hunk department, but he also had a lock on bossy and controlling, as well as making it sound as if she was a dope with a capital D.

But when Sam kissed her, Kevin disappeared from her brain. Her lips had melted against Sam's and taken everything he had to give, reminding her all over again that he was strong, solid, and sexy as hell. She longed to be in his arms, where she felt protected and cared for even when she wanted to slap him silly.

If only she could wade through the mire of Gary's death and figure out what the devastating detective really wanted from her, she might be able to go on without him.

Chapter 10

The next morning dawned cool and bright, though Ellie was certain the temperature would return to the nineties as the day wore on. She'd pulled a thin black sweater over her hot pink T-shirt, planning to store it in her tote bag when the heat arrived. Now she and Viv stood on the sidewalk in front of their building, catching up on the past two days.

"Come on, spill. What happened between you and Dr. Dave the other night?" Ellie asked her.

Already dressed in a sleeveless red linen sheath, Viv had time before she was due at her office and was more than eager to talk as they walked their dogs—but not about her date. "Never mind about me and Dr. Dave. What about you and Kevin McGowan?"

"Kevin can wait. The big news concerns Rudy. To put it plainly, he's a rich puppy, and it's my job to manage the wealth."

Ellie grinned when Viv stopped in her tracks and opened and closed her mouth. It wasn't often her wise-cracking friend was at a loss for words.

"I know," she said, hoping to bring Viv out of her stupor. "I barely believe it myself. It's downright embarrassing telling people you got a bequest from a homeless person."

Viv blinked. "Are you telling me there was actual cash money in that safety-deposit box?"

"Over eight hundred thousand dollars. I just can't imagine what to do with it all. Probably give it away or—"

"Say what!" yipped Rudy, midpee.

"Say what?" echoed Viv.

"I'm seriously thinking of donating it to Best Friends, that wonderful no-kill shelter in Utah, or maybe sharing it with them and the ASPCA on Ninety-second, because without their care Rudy and I might never have found each other. I'll do it in Gary's name, of course. I'm sure he'd approve."

"Hang on. I'm still trying to absorb the details." Viv put a hand on her hip and waited for Mr. T to do his morning business. "Gary Veridot, a homeless bum, left you and your dog over half a million bucks? Do I have that right?"

Ellie nodded.

"Holy shit. That's un-fucking-believable."

"I agree. And we did nothing to deserve it." She dropped her tone to a near whisper in hopes that Rudy wouldn't hear. "That's why I'm giving it to charity."

"Don't go off the deep end. Give those animal charities a share, but keep the rest. Take a vacation, pay Georgette the money you owe her, buy a better wardrobe, do something nice for yourself." Viv's shapely brows drew together in concentration; then she snapped her fingers. "I have a brilliant idea. How long has it been since you've seen the Dickhead?"

They reached the corner and reversed direction, heading back toward home. Cheech and Chong squatted beside a trash can, and Ellie cleaned up before answering. "Larry? What does he have to do with anything?"

"The money is a perfect excuse to doll yourself up— hair, makeup, the works. Buy some bling and pay him a visit. Tell him you have a half million you want to invest and you need a good accountant, so maybe he could recommend someone. But don't offer him the job. That ought to make him cry loud and long, the way he made you cry when you realized you'd thrown away ten of the best years of your life on the schmuck."

"Revenge never made anyone feel better, not in the end. Besides, I don't want him to know that he sometimes crosses my mind . . . even when I wish he was floating on an iceberg somewhere in the Arctic Circle."

"Are you kidding? Remember Slim Jim? After I took care of him, I walked on air for a month."

"Six foot four and lean as a string bean. The man had nerve, picking up with his old girlfriend while he was still dating you, then denying it when you found out. I told you I didn't think he was playing with a full deck."

"Sometimes I wonder what he did with the eight cartons of protein powder I ordered online and had delivered to his apartment the day before I cancelled his credit cards and hacked them to pieces. And I would have paid money to see his face when the new-old girlfriend thanked him for those two-carat diamond studs she received via special messenger from Tiffany. They cost him six thousand, if I remember correctly." Viv grinned. "Proving that it never hurts to check the info in a man's wallet before you get too far along in the relationship."

They stopped in front of their building, where Ellie asked, "Which brings me back to Dr. Dave. What happened between the two of you?"

"Truth?"

"No, lie to me." Ellie rolled her eyes. "Of course I want the truth."

"Nothing." Viv's innocent expression screamed honesty. "Absolutely zero."

"What?"

"We walked Mr. T, and Dave was a perfect gentleman—held the umbrella, scooped T's poop, the whole nine yards. Then he dropped me off at my door and said a polite good night. Didn't even ask for my phone number." Instead of climbing the steps, she propped her model-perfect bottom on the balustrade. "I don't think I've ever felt so unattractive—or so confused."

"You want me to call him, do some fishing?"

"Don't you dare." Viv ran a hand through her fall of silky dark hair. "I have my pride."

"Unfortunately, I know what you mean."

"Hmm, that statement suggests you've seen Detective Ryder."

"Do I sound that miserable?" When Viv didn't comment, Ellie sat beside her on the railing. "He makes my blood boil . . . in too many ways."

"I assume he knows about the money."

"He was with me when I opened the safety-deposit box, and he wasn't a control freak or a pain in the ass, either. It's what he did last night that has me fried."

"Last night?"

"I had a date with Kevin McGowan—"

"I know. You asked me to take care of Rudy and the Chihuahuas, remember?"

"Yeah, sorry, I forgot. Anyway, after Kevin brought me home I entered the foyer and found Sam lying in wait like some nutty stalker. He scared the crap out of me."

"And . . ."

She wanted to forget about Sam's potent good night kiss but knew Viv should hear the rest of the story. "He came along when I walked the dogs, and we talked. He had some news to share."

"I'm almost afraid to ask what."

"It's not brain surgery. Thompson Veridot served his thirty years, and he's been out of jail for the past several months. Sam thinks he returned to Manhattan, found Gary, and killed him."

Viv put a hand over her mouth. "Shut up!"

"Wish I could, but it's true."

"Oh, my God. Does he think you're next?"

"He thinks I could be. Especially since Gary left a note in the safety-deposit book saying he was sure that if he was killed his brother would be the one to do it."

"Gary left a note?"

"I'll show it to you later, but the gist of it was that if Gary turned up dead he expected Rudy and me to find Thompson Veridot and bring him to justice."

"No wonder Sam's worried."

"There's no concrete proof Veridot murdered his brother. We don't even know if he's in town. Sam's going to call the warden and try to get a current photo—like that's supposed to help."

"And what else did Sam want?" Viv checked her watch and headed up the stairs. "Don't answer that. I have to get moving. Are you home tonight?"

"Far as I know."

"Great." She held open the door, and Ellie brought her charges inside. "I'll be over after work, and I want to hear the rest of the story." Waving good-bye, she and Mr. T disappeared into their apartment.

Ellie escorted her houseguests upstairs, collected their beds, and filled their bag with leftover food and treats. Janice Fallgrave should be home sometime today, and the singer expected to see Cheech and Chong when she got there. Back on the sidewalk in ten minutes, Ellie stepped to the curb, hailed a cab, and instructed the driver to drop her and the three canines at the Beaumont.

"Good morning, Natter," she said to the doorman when they arrived. "Looks like another nice day."

"Sure does," he replied. Then he nodded at the Chihuahuas. "Good to have the rodents back in residence. Miss Janice will be happy to see them."

"Do me a favor? Keep Rudy while I bring up Cheech

and Chong and their luggage and collect the other dogs? I'll be down with the crew in a couple of minutes."

Natter took Rudy's leash. "There's no need to rush."

Ellie did as promised, returned with her charges, retrieved her pal, and led the pack to the park.

"Did Viv really do what she said she did to that Jim guy's credit cards?" asked Rudy as they strolled down the sidewalk.

"Not only did she wield the scissors, she enjoyed every minute of it. Don't cross Viv . . . ever."

"Vivie loves me."

"Not as much as I do," Ellie teased.

"I thought you said she was gonna be my guardian?"

"We've discussed it, but there's nothing in writing."

He put on the brakes and skidded to a stop. *"What?"*

She struggled with the leads and calmed the grousing canines. "Hang on a second, everybody. Rudy and I have to talk." Sitting on a bench, she raised an eyebrow. "There's no need to get upset. Viv and I decided to share responsibility for you and Mr. T. We just haven't made it legal."

"How can you be so . . . so unconcerned? If anything happened to you, I'd be toast."

"Don't be a nitwit. Viv would take you to live with her and T, and if not her, I'm sure Mother would. Stanley would insist."

"Georgette? After what happened the last time she had me in her clutches? Are you high?"

"Speaking of the last time she had you, I'm still waiting to hear the story. When are you going to tell me how you ended up on Park Avenue in front of a speeding taxi?"

"Forget about the past. The judge could die any day, and your old lady doesn't care about anyone but herself."

"You're not being fair. She's doing okay with Stanley."

"Don't be surprised if something bad happens to him, too. She's not exactly Mother Teresa."

"Okay, so she won't win mother of the year, but she isn't mean." Ellie crossed mental fingers. "Georgette might not be an animal lover, but she'd follow my instructions."

Rudy sidled up to Lulu, instead of answering. *"If your owner kicks it, who's supposed to be your caregiver?"*

The self-absorbed Havanese held her tail high. *"I have no idea, but I'm sure there'd be a dozen people clamoring for the right to have me as their own. I've won a dozen Best of Breeds this past year, and a few Best in Shows, too."*

Ellie listened to the dogs chatter as she led them into the park, let them do their thing, and returned them to the Beaumont. Gary's will and Rudy demanding security for his future made her think. Maybe it was time she and Viv put things in writing, as they'd said. Uncle Sal could do it, and he wouldn't blab to her mother, either.

After dropping off each dog, passing biscuits, and writing the owner a report, she and Rudy moved on to the Davenport, where they met the dapper doorman tipping his hat to all who passed. "Good morning, Randall," Ellie said as they walked inside. "Is anything new going on?"

"Not a thing. How about your um . . . business?"

"You mean Gary's will?"

He huffed out a breath. "Please don't tell me you've gotten into more trouble."

"Me? Not a chance. I met with that attorney and registered the will like I was supposed to. Seeing to Gary's final request is next on my list."

"You mean his cremation?" Randall knitted his craggy brow. "Sorry, it's not a pleasant topic."

"Definitely not, but it is a part of life. I plan to go to the police station after lunch and see if they're ready to release the body."

She and Rudy rode the elevator up, collected their

charges, and headed for the park. When her phone rang as they crossed Fifth Avenue, she led the dogs to a bench and took the call. "Ellie here."

"It's Hilary." The woman gave a loud sniff. "I won't be able to take care of the dogs this morning."

"What's wrong? Is it your ex?"

Hilary's sob told her all she needed to know. "I—I—he—he— Come over, please. We have to talk."

Ellie gathered the dogs in Hilary Blankenship's building before she went to her assistant's aid. When the door opened, Hilary's blotchy face, red-rimmed eyes, and unkempt appearance wrenched at Ellie's heart.

"Come on, Hilary," she said, standing in the doorway. "It'll do you good to get out. I'll handle the dogs, and we can talk as we walk."

"I can't let anyone see me looking like this." Hilary ran a hand over her wrinkled silk blouse. "I'm just so angry."

"A little fresh air will make things better. Hurry up, put on your shoes."

Ten minutes later they crossed the avenue with Hilary wearing a huge pair of sunglasses and Ellie in charge of Millie, Cuddles, Sampson, Dilbert, and Rudy. "Now, tell me what's wrong. Is there something I can do to help?"

"You can answer a question," said Hilary. "Has anyone gotten in touch with you to ask about my employment?"

"You mean as my assistant? Certainly not, and even if they did, I'd probably tell whoever it was that it's none of their business. Why?"

"Because Richard called at the crack of dawn and told me he knew I was working. When we appear in court, he's going to make sure the judge knows, too. I have no idea how he found out, but he did."

"Maybe he's friends with one of the dog owners in

the building. You told me he hadn't met the Lowensteins, but what about the Eastons or the Parkers?"

"Possibly. Then again, he wasn't much for socializing with the other tenants. Is there some way you can find out?"

"I can call them and ask if they've spoken with him, but that's about it." She and Hilary took a seat on a park bench. "Did you tell him how little you were making? It hardly puts a dent in the amount you want for support."

"I tried, but he knows it's off the books and insinuated I could make a lot more if I went out on my own and set up my own dog-walking service." She sighed. "I never thought he'd use my getting a job against me."

"Have you phoned your lawyer?"

"He's in court, but I left word." She dabbed her red nose. "I imagine he'll get back to me when he can."

"It's never easy to second-guess an ex. My husband didn't want to give me a penny, either. In the end, I got the condo, though it came with a big fat mortgage, but it was worth it to be out from under his thumb. If things work out, I'm sure you'll feel the same. Just give it some time."

Ellie stood when the dogs grumped and pulled at their leads, and encouraged Hilary to walk with her. After the animals did their thing, the women headed for home. At Hilary's door, Ellie said, "I'll make a few phone calls and let you know what I find out. Will you be okay with the afternoon shift?"

"I suppose I'll have to be." Hilary inhaled a breath. "Thanks so much for listening. I appreciate it."

"That woman is trouble," said Rudy when he and Ellie rode down in the elevator. *"Next thing you know, you'll be in the hot seat, testifying in front of a pickle-faced judge during her divorce proceedings."*

"I don't see that happening. All I can attest to is how much I pay Hilary, and it's barely enough to cover her condo fees. Her husband can't possibly think she's able to live on such a trivial amount."

"It's not her husband who counts. It's the judge."

"True, but I wonder who her husband's lawyer is."

"Sounds like he's the bad ass in all of this. Which reminds me . . ."

"Oh, no. Don't tell me you have another lawyer joke."

"Come on, play along. It's a good one."

She rolled her eyes. "Okay, but just one."

Rudy cleared his throat, as if ready to spout Shakespeare. *"Why don't lawyers go to the beach?"*

Ellie shrugged. "I haven't the faintest idea."

"You're no fun. Come on, give it a try."

She scrunched her forehead. "I'm lousy at jokes. Can't ever remember the punch lines."

"Oh, yeah. Thanks for reminding me."

They were at the entrance to their next building before she looked down at him. "I'm still waiting."

"Waiting for what?"

"The joke, you knucklehead. Why don't lawyers go to the beach?"

"That's easy," he said with a doggie snigger. *"Because the cats keep trying to bury them in the sand."*

She hid a grin. "You're impossible."

"Aw, come on. Isn't that what you like best about me?"

"You're my true friend. That's what I like best about you." They entered the building, this one without a doorman, and took the elevator to the tenth floor, where they picked up the first of seven dogs. Forty-five minutes later, they stopped at Pops's hot dog stand for lunch.

"Ellie, Rudy." The elderly vendor nodded. "Where you two been lately?"

She removed her sweater and stuffed it into her tote before answering. As she'd suspected, the afternoon sun had kicked the temperature into the high eighties, and it was just twelve o'clock. "I had errands to run the last few days. I'm still sorting out Gary's death."

Pops opened his hopper and reached for their usual order: one dog with mustard and sauerkraut, one plain, and passed it to her. "Did that envelope I gave you help or was it more trouble?"

"Actually, a bit of both." She juggled the hot dogs as she accepted a can of Diet Coke. Thinking it might be time the vendor knew what Gary had done, she informed him of the will. "Now that you know the story, do you mind if I ask a few questions?"

Pops held up his hands. "I'm still tryin' to swallow that bit about Gary bein' rich."

"It shocked me, too. That's why I have questions."

"Ask away, as long as you don't mind me TCOB while you're doin' it."

She stood behind the cart while he attended to the small crowd that had gathered. When Rudy yipped, she broke off an end of the plain dog and dropped it for him. Then she took a bite of her own wiener and chewed.

Pops finished with his customers and wiped his hands on his apron. "All right, ask me what you want to know. I got nothin' to hide."

"Gary and you talked every once in a while, correct? I know you were kind to him and sometimes gave him free hot dogs."

"Yeah, we spoke, but it was usually about the weather or what he'd found in his latest Dumpster foray. As for givin' him food, I hate throwin' away what I don't sell for the day." Pops seemed embarrassed by his largesse. "Gary needed to eat, so it made sense he took my leftovers."

"I'm sure he appreciated it. I just wonder, while the two of you talked, did you ever notice anyone following him?"

The vendor propped me an elbow and leaned against the cart. "Give me a minute to think. It's been a while." He furrowed his brow. "I don't think so."

"How about when Gary entrusted you with the envelope? Did he say why he was giving it to you instead of a lawyer?"

Pops scratched his bald head, while she took a drink of soda. "Now that you mention it, Gary did act a little odd when he passed me that envelope, but I don't remember seein' anyone on his tail. I just figured he was bein' Gary."

"Did he say anything about a relative? Maybe a brother?"

"Nope."

"And he never told you he thought he was being followed?"

"Gary always thought he was bein' followed. It was just his way."

"Did the cops talk to you?"

He filled another order before responding. "Truth be told, that Gruning guy has been to see me twice, but he asked about you both times, never said much about our dead friend."

"Me?" Ellie huffed out a breath. That was just what she didn't want to hear. She tossed the empty paper sleeve from her hot dog in the trash. "Why me?"

"Don't have the faintest idea. But he seemed to think you knew more about Gary than what you were sayin'."

"That's crazy. Gary and I were passing acquaintances." She gave Rudy a second section of wiener, stuck the remainder in a plastic bag, and dropped it in her tote. "I hope you said so."

"Of course, but it didn't seem to matter. Oh, and he asked me if I knew what was in that envelope."

Well, crap. "Did you tell him?"

"I said I had no idea what it was when Gary gave it to me." Pops grinned, then wiped his damp forehead with a napkin. "That wasn't a lie."

"I guess I should be the one to give him the information. If he finds out the envelope contained a will, it'll look as if I've been withholding facts about the case, which will only be worse for me."

"Might be a good idea," the vendor agreed. "Get back to me if there's anything else I can do for you."

Ellie and Rudy waited for Gruning in her usual spot, a perpetually drab conference room at police head-quarters. She wasn't looking forward to the coming discussion, but she had no choice. If she didn't tell the despicable detective about the contents of Gary's will and he found out on his own, he'd figure a way to use it against her.

Then there was Gary. Surely the cops were through with his body. As his executor, she was bound by law to follow his wishes, and if not by the law, common decency told her to see to his cremation, as well as to his personal belongings, pathetic though they were.

"This is gettin' boring," Rudy told her as he paced. *"Doesn't Gruning realize we have work to do?"*

"I doubt Detective Gruning gives a thought to what's going on in our life. His only job is to catch Gary's killer."

"Maybe so, but I'll bet he isn't doin' much to see that happens. Cops don't care when the vic is a nobody."

"That's certainly no comfort. The police are supposed to enforce justice for all people, not only the wealthy or those with clout."

"Tell me about it."

The door opened without warning, and Gruning trundled in, his face wreathed in its usual patina of per-spiration. "Who were you talking to?" he asked by way of a greeting.

She straightened. "Myself."

The detective grunted, fished a red-and-white hard candy from his jacket pocket, popped it in his mouth, and chewed. "You wanted to see me?"

"Should I have called first?"

"Might have been nice. I got a lot of fish to fry."

Rudy muffled a laugh. *"Yeah, right."*

Gruning heaved his bulk into a chair. "I don't have all day, Ms. Engleman. You got something to tell me, spit it out."

"I want to tell you what was in the envelope Gary left me."

"I already know. His last will and testament."

She swallowed a gulp of air. "How did you find out?"

"We're the police. It's our job to find out." He crunched the candy while he stared at her. "Question is, did you know about your inheritance before he took a bullet in his chest?"

"How do you know it was an—"

"TMI, Triple E. TMI."

"So you did inherit something more than his junk and that cardboard box, eh? I thought that might be the case."

Ellie bit back a sigh. Great. She'd just added fuel to his arrest idea. "I hadn't the faintest idea he'd left me anything. The will was a shock." She leaned back in the molded chair and raised a brow. "How do you know it was an inheritance?"

The detective narrowed his gaze. "Didn't take a genius to figure it out. People go to the trouble of writing a will, they usually leave something important to those mentioned." He chewed on his candy. "Care to tell me what it was?"

She refused to give him another clue. "I've already registered the document with the probate clerk, but I have a copy if you'd like to see it."

"I had a look at Chambers Street. Thanks, anyway." He continued to chomp on the candy. "It would go better for you if you told me what you got."

When in doubt, follow Viv's rule and change the subject, she told herself. "There's something else. I'm now legally responsible for Gary's remains. Are you through doing whatever it is you do, so I can have control of the body?"

"Knock yourself out." He crossed his arms and leaned back in the chair. "I've already put in a court order, Ms. Engleman. I'll find out what you inherited eventually."

She clasped her hands on her lap to keep from reaching across the table and strangling him. "What about Gary's shelter. Can I go through it and remove what I want?"

"We took the crime scene tape down yesterday. But with the indigents roaming the park, I doubt there's anything left."

"Why didn't you tell me it was clear?"

"Tit for tat, Ms. Engleman. I would have, if you'd called and given me information on that envelope," he said with a slimy smile. "Now, is there anything further we need to talk about?"

"I hear Thompson Veridot has been out of jail for a few months now. I hope you're looking for him."

"You telling me how to run my investigation?"

She bit her tongue before uttering a "yes." "I'm merely wondering if you're covering all your bases where Gary is concerned. Just because he was homeless doesn't mean his killer should go free."

"Thanks for reminding me." Gruning stood and pushed away from the table. "I think we're through here."

Angry, Ellie nodded. "I can see myself out."

"You do that," said the detective as he left the room.

Chapter 11

"This is the most idiotic, half-assed—" Vivian's pained sigh was so gusty it almost fluttered the leaves on the trees. "I should have my head examined for letting you talk me into this."

Despite the fact that her best friend was probably correct, Ellie held firm. It would have been smarter for them to come to the Ramble earlier, but she and Viv had to work. By the time they'd arrived home, fed their dogs, changed and had dinner, dusk had settled. Besides, putting the task off until Saturday was dumb. It would only give the homeless people wandering the park more time to pilfer Gary's meager belongings.

"Stop whining. Central Park is one of the safest areas of the city," Ellie offered by way of apology. Getting Viv to accompany her had been a major coup. Unfortunately, she now owed her friend a no-strings favor, something she was not looking forward to providing anytime soon.

"Oh, really? Mind telling me who gave you that ridiculous bit of information?"

"The newspapers say so all the time, as do the police." She neglected to add that both agencies were often wrong in their assessment of safe havens in Manhattan.

"Now be patient and let Rudy get his bearings." She glanced at her Yorkiepoo. "Okay, big guy. You ready to lead us to Gary's home?"

"Sure, no problem. The nose knows and all that, right, T?"

"Yer nose, maybe. Mr. T ain't never been to Gary's crib."

She ignored the Jack Russell's tart comment and gave her pal the lead, calling over her shoulder to Viv, "Keep up. Rudy won't be happy if we lose you in the dark."

Nose to the ground as he muttered to himself, the dog took one of the many trampled grass trails that led into the Ramble. When the path forked, he didn't hesitate. *"It's a right and a right, then a left."*

"You sure he knows where he's going?" Viv huffed from behind. "Didn't you tell me you'd only been here a couple of times?"

"Four or five, but don't worry. Rudy knows the way. The night we found the body, the little stinker dragged me behind him as if I was a kite without a tail."

"Watching him now, I see what you mean."

Noting the lack of daylight as they got further into the underbrush, Ellie dug in her heels and pulled her dog to a halt. Not only was this area of the park shaded by overhanging trees, it also held an aura of gloom and doom. The knowledge that someone had gotten shot here didn't do much for her security quotient, either.

"Hang on a second," she whispered to Rudy. Then she called to Viv. "Find those flashlights and pass me one."

Vivian crept up beside them and dug into her bag. After Ellie turned on the flashlight, she recognized a pile of vine-covered rocks, or at least she thought she did, and pointed. "I think I have my bearings. We turn right here, and the shelter should be up ahead on the left."

"Jeez, can you imagine living here?" Viv peered into the forest. "The air is so thick it's hard to breathe."

"It's ninety-plus degrees outside, and the humidity's

been building. It's hard to breathe in this city, period."
Ducking under a swag of ropey vines, Ellie waited for
Viv and Mr. T to follow. "Just a little farther."

Viv stayed close, talking out loud. "I couldn't live without air-conditioning. It must be horrible to be poor."

"Poor? I don't think you know the meaning of the
word."

"I can't help it if I was born into wealth. Your family
didn't do so bad either, especially Georgette. Thanks to
her four divorces, the ex-terminator's got my mom and
dad beat by a couple of million in the disposable income
department."

Before Ellie could respond, Rudy brought them to
a clearing she remembered well. Except the last time
she'd been here, it had been overflowing with a platoon
of police, news vans, and inquisitive citizens.

"This is it."

"Now what?" said Viv.

Ellie passed her Rudy's lead, pulled a plastic bag and
a pair of rubber gloves from her tote, and gave Viv the
handbag as well. "You hang on to the dogs while I scope
the place out, see if there's anything the police missed.
Just sit tight."

She walked toward the tree Gary had used as the
backdrop for his shelter. Underneath, the cardboard
making up the roof sagged with the water weight from
the previous storm, and the surrounding ground was
covered in junk, almost as if a Dumpster had exploded.
Her throat swelled when she saw Rudy's shattered dish,
the one Gary had been so proud of. Picking up a shard
of the pottery, she sniffed back a tear.

Viv, oblivious to her friend's sorrow, stood with her
hands on her hips. "Ick, ick, and triple ick. Please tell me
I don't have to crawl in there."

"Stand guard while I look inside. Good thing I wore
jeans." Inching closer, Ellie dropped to her hands and
knees and forged into the remains of the shelter.

The flashlight cast an eerie glow on what was left of Gary's belongings. Though the cardboard box had been neat and tidy when it was his home, it was now a wreck. His burner was gone, as were his cups, plates, folding trays, and plastic utensils. The shoeboxes holding his treasures were shredded, their contents scattered. A pile of ashes ringed with rocks sat in the center of the earth-packed floor, proof that the shelter had housed others in need since Gary's death.

Inhaling a breath, she picked through the rubble. "Eww," she muttered when she lifted a soggy square of carpet.

"What! What is it?" Viv asked from somewhere outside.

"Bugs! Millions of 'em."

"What did you expect? Butterflies and fairies?"

"Ha-ha," Ellie said with a groan. She replaced the moldy section of rug and vowed to think before she spoke again, in hopes it would help keep Viv's lips zipped.

Scooting to a far wall, she sorted through a mound of filthy clothing, so unwearable even the homeless didn't want it. She then moved to the opposite corner and dug under a pile of old newspapers, but that, too, revealed nothing of value.

Heaving a sigh, she backed out and dusted the gloves on her thighs, then collected Rudy's lead. "There's nothing inside that will give us any clues. I guess it's all we can do."

Nose to the dirt, Rudy tugged on his leash, jerking Ellie forward a foot. "Hey! What are you doing?"

"That's the question I keep asking myself," Viv answered. "Why the hell am I here?"

"Got a scent . . . I got a scent. Let me and T go, Triple E. There's more here than meets the human eye."

"Hey, what the heck are you doing?" Viv asked when Ellie dropped Rudy's leash.

"I have a hunch, that's all. Release Twink. Let's see if the boys can do better than me."

Twink circled left while Rudy went right, their noses glued to the ground. Ellie heard them mumbling, but couldn't make out the words. Then both dogs stopped and stared at a pile of rocks set about twenty feet behind the main tree.

Walking to the spot, she dropped to her knees and dragged the largest rock from its shallow grave. "Is this where you want me to look? Is there something here I should see?"

"Yeah . . . yeah . . . yeah," Rudy panted, planting himself in front of Ellie and scratching at the muck. *"Come on, T, get the lead out. We need help here."*

"Not a chance. I done all the tough stuff I plan to do for the night," Mr. T said with a growl.

"Excuse me for asking," Viv chimed. "But what the hell is going on? And who are you talking to?"

Ellie sat back on her heels, dodging the mud Rudy shot her way. Seconds later, he backed out with a dirt-encrusted manila envelope in his muzzle and dropped it in front of her. Then he shook himself off, sending bits of crud in all directions.

"Hey, enough with the mud bath," Viv shouted. "What the heck did he find?"

"Something I'm guessing belonged to Gary, which means it now belongs to us." Ellie stood, shaking the dirt from the envelope as she walked to Viv. Then she grabbed her tote and stuffed the find in her bag.

"Are we through?" asked Viv, her voice a bit desperate. "It's getting dark . . . and I heard creepy noises while you were over there with the dogs."

Something rustled in the bushes and both women froze.

"There it goes again. What do you think it is?" Viv asked, her voice barely a whisper.

Rudy growled, his gaze fixed on the trees to the right,

and Ellie shuddered. "Beats me. Maybe squirrels or a raccoon?"

"More like rats. I bet this place is swarming with 'em."

"You got that right," Rudy agreed with another growl.

Ellie clutched the tote to her chest. "It's getting late. We should probably go."

"That's the smartest idea you've had all night," Viv pronounced as Mr. T pulled her down the path.

Sitting in Ellie's kitchen, she and Viv fortified themselves with single-serving pints of Häagen-Dazs while the dogs snored at their feet. In between bites of Caramel Cone, they stared at the photos on the table, as well as the key that was hidden in the envelope Rudy had found, comparing it to the safety-deposit box key she'd inherited.

"What do you think it's for?" asked Viv, scraping up a spoonful of ice cream.

"I don't have a clue, but I doubt it opens another bank box. It's too tiny."

"Maybe it belongs to a different bank, one that uses a smaller type of locking mechanism on their boxes."

"It's a possibility, but I doubt it. Besides, if it was something Gary wanted me to have, he would have mentioned it in the will."

"Gary was a nut job. He might have forgotten this key even existed, or forgot to put it in with the will."

"Maybe so, but without knowing what it opens, everything is conjecture. Worst case, it might simply be one of his special 'treasures,' something he found and liked, and it doesn't work anywhere."

"Then how do you explain those?" said Viv, nodding at the faded photos.

"Okay, so maybe it means something, but I don't know what."

"The key is stamped with a number, so it could open

a bus station locker or one of those boxes in a mail center. Are you sure this envelope was the only thing in that hole?"

Ellie rolled her eyes. "Gee, I think so, but there was someone standing a couple of feet away harping at me, so I didn't get a chance to dig any deeper."

"Hey, it was spooky in there," Viv said, her expression wounded. "Next time, we'll go in the daylight."

"Next time, I plan to tack a sign on the tree in Gary's memory. It's the least I can do for him."

"Before you forget, how about telling me what else Sam had to say about it all?"

At the mention of the detective's name, Ellie recalled his latest demand. She hadn't phoned him today, and she didn't intend to. "He wants me to take a self-defense course. Says he knows a guy who owns a gym and gives women lessons a couple of nights a week on how to defend themselves."

"Wow, he must really be worried about you."

"I have no idea why."

Viv drummed her fingers on the table. "Maybe because he believes Gary's brother killed him for the family fortune, which is now in your possession."

"I'm not about to go anywhere alone in this city after dark, nor would I open my door to a stranger," she said, remembering the creepy guy with the ugly deep voice. "So what's the problem? Besides, Rudy will protect me."

"Does Sam think this Veridot guy is stalking you?"

"Sam thinks a lot of things. It doesn't mean he's right."

Her cell phone rang, and Ellie ignored it, prodding the tarnished key with her index finger. "Stop dwelling on Ryder and help me figure out what this is for."

Viv glanced from Ellie to her tote bag holding the still ringing phone and back again. "Aren't you going to answer it? It might be someone answering your ad."

"Remind me to tell you about the call I had the other day. Then you'll see why I'm ignoring this one. If they want the job, they can leave a message."

"So Hilary is working out all right?"

"She's okay, but she'd be better if her personal life wasn't in such turmoil." The ringing stopped, then started all over again. She shrugged. "I really don't feel like talking to anyone."

Five seconds later, her cell stopped ringing. Thirty seconds after that, it began again.

Vivian frowned. "What's going on, Ellie?"

Three rings echoed before she answered, "Nothing."

"It doesn't sound like 'nothing' to me. Someone's trying to reach you, and they're serious about it."

Ellie scraped out her ice cream, slurped down the last spoonful, and brought the empty container to the trash. So what if she hadn't called Sam as he'd ordered? Had he actually thought she'd check in with him like a teenager on curfew?

A half minute passed in silence. Believing the barrage to be over, she was about to tell Viv she needed to go to bed, when someone pounded on her front door.

"I didn't hear the buzzer. Did you?"

"The phone was ringing so loud I couldn't hear myself think," said Viv. "Maybe you should answer the door."

"I didn't let anyone up, so it can't be for me. Besides, it's ten o'clock at night."

"Does Georgette still have a key?"

"Yes, but Mother wouldn't knock. She'd just storm through the door with her Jimmy Choos blazing."

"Well, I doubt a burglar would announce himself." Vivian stood. "Mr. T and I have to get going. You stay here, and we'll tell your visitor to get lost."

"No matter who it is."

Viv headed into the hall with her Jack Russell, and Ellie envisioned her peering out the peephole before opening the door. Then a deep baritone voice spoke, and Viv giggled. When heavy footsteps approached, she cursed. Damn Viv and her penchant for making trouble. Squaring her shoulders, she braced for the lecture to come.

"What in the hell have you been doing all day?" Sam asked, charging into the kitchen.

"My job," she shot back. "Like some detective I know should be doing."

He opened the fridge and snagged a beer. Popping the cap, he took a swig, then propped his butt against the counter and scowled at her. "You're driving me to drink."

She leaned back in her chair. "Oh, please, that is so not true. You just can't stand it when anyone ignores your orders."

He took a longer pull. "Are you saying you didn't call me on purpose?"

"Not really." She crossed mental fingers. "I—I forgot."

"You are the world's worst liar," he said after taking another swallow of his Bud Light.

"I got a spooky phone call, two actually, from someone who wanted the assistant's job."

"Spooky? What kind of spooky?"

"He wanted to come here, to my apartment, for an interview. I told him no. I doubt I'll hear from him again."

"Did you ever think it might be Veridot?"

Talk about paranoia. It was time to change the subject, she decided. "No. How did you get up here, by the way?"

"I was standing on your front porch trying your line when an elderly couple came home. I showed them my badge, told them I had business with someone in the building, and they were more than happy to let me in." He sat across from her at the table. "I believe their last name is Feldman."

"Great. Saul and Rita Feldman are two of the nosiest gossips in the building." And they'd had a lot to say when she was involved in the professor's murder. "By tomorrow, everyone in the complex will know I had a visit from a cop."

"I didn't tell them I was coming to see you."

"Did they watch you go up the stairs?"

"Maybe."

"Then they know it was me."

"If you'd called like I asked, I wouldn't be here right now," he reminded her. "I wasn't joking, Ellie. I did some more digging today."

She set an elbow on the table and propped her chin in her hand. "Me, too. Do you have any idea what this might open?"

Focusing on the key, he narrowed his gaze. "Where'd you find that?"

"Near where the cops found Gary's body. I saw Gruning, and he gave me clearance to take what I wanted from the shelter. He also told me I could claim the body." She frowned. "My next duty as his inheritor is to see that he's cremated."

"Does Gruning know about this key?"

"I only found it tonight, and technically it wasn't in the shelter, so I don't think I have to tell him. Want to see what else was in the envelope?"

"There was more?"

Ellie pushed the pile of faded photographs in his direction. The first was that of an older woman sitting in a high-back chair in front of a fireplace with a young man who could have been Gary sitting on the chair's arm. The date on the back said "May 1979."

"Gary must have been about sixteen and living with his grandmother when this was taken."

"The date is about right," Sam agreed.

He slid his chair closer and sized up the next photo: a man and woman perched on a sofa with two boys standing behind them. The setting, with the three males in suits and ties and the woman in lace and pearls, seemed forced. Only Gary smiled, while the others appeared to be staring at nothing.

Sam reached into his coat pocket and pulled out a folded sheet of paper. "Here's the photo the warden faxed me. Let's compare and see if there's a resemblance."

He placed the grainy image next to the oldest boy in the photo. "The bigger kid must be Thompson, but it's hard to tell after all this time. According to the prison photo, he's gone completely gray. Life in the pen will do that to a guy."

"Is there a description giving his height and weight? Eye color, birthmarks?"

"Say's he's five foot nine and a hundred eighty pounds. Eyes are brown, no identifying birthmarks, but he has a couple of tattoos on his upper arms."

"Of what?" Ellie asked.

Sam shook his head. "The guy was a real psycho. There's a red heart on his right arm with the word 'Mother' penned inside, and he's got the same on his left arm, only that one's dedicated to dear old Dad."

"The creep."

"You got that right. Let's see the last picture."

In the third photo, two boys, one about eight and the other a teenager, stood side by side in matching slacks and sweaters. While Gary was smiling in the other pictures, he looked terrified in this one. Stranger still, his older brother was grinning fiendishly, as if he knew a horrific secret.

"Not exactly a happy family, were they?" asked Sam.

"Not if Gary's expression tells the story." She held the photo to the light. "I wonder what Thompson is saying or doing to him. It can't be anything pleasant."

"Probably threatening to flush his goldfish down the toilet, or maybe suffocate him in his sleep."

"It must have been depressing, growing up with a brother strung out on drugs."

"The parents don't appear overjoyed with the burden, either. My guess is, after they saw how wild their eldest was, they put the screws to Gary, probably made him knuckle under no matter what. He had a bad time of it even before Thompson murdered Mom and Dad."

Ellie sniffed back a tear. "Makes me rethink my own childhood. I had loving parents, friends, an okay life."

"Maybe that's because you didn't do drugs or violate curfew."

"I did my share of goofing off, like any other teenager," she told him, miffed he thought her a Goody Two-shoes.

"You?" One corner of his mouth lifted. "You probably thought stealing a smoke was tantamount to doing drugs."

"I tried cigarettes once and hated the way they tasted, so I consider myself lucky to have avoided the addiction." She raised her nose. "And before you ask, I tried marijuana, too, but it made me throw up—and I hate throwing up."

"What about booze? Cutting school? Hanging with disreputable friends?" Still grinning, he raised a brow. "Premarital sex?"

Heat inched from her collarbone to her face. "My sex life is none of your business." He'd laugh his ass off if he heard she'd been a virgin until her second year of college. "My parents trusted me, and I didn't want to ruin what we had."

He leaned back and swallowed the last of his beer. "Sounds like your childhood was happier than most."

"What about yours? Did you do all those things?"

"Of course I did."

"No older brother to make you cry?"

"I'm the eldest of three, with two younger sisters. That's punishment enough."

Ellie sighed. "I always wished for a sister, but it wasn't in the cards."

"What did your mom and dad have to say about it?"

"Georgette refuses to talk about her life with my father or the fact that there were no other children. My dad died about fifteen years ago, so I can't ask him. What about you?"

"Lydia, that's my mom, sometimes talks as if my dad is still here, but he's been gone for five years." He stood and dropped his bottle in the trash. "My sisters think it's their duty to be matchmakers."

"Are they worried about what you do for a living?" Like I am, she thought. "You know, the whole chasing down the bad guy scenario."

"I guess." He turned his chair around and straddled it. "Mostly they just complain about the lousy hours and my lack of participation in family events."

"My mom doesn't let me get away with missing what she considers a family get-together either, at least not for long. As for matchmaking, I met that lawyer, Kevin, at a brunch she arranged. It's the first time since my divorce she's bothered introducing me to anyone."

Sam swallowed a smile. A fix-up by a parent was easier to accept than a sleazy meeting at a singles bar, though he couldn't imagine Ellie going to one.

"If he hangs out in your mother's circle, he must be well off."

"I guess. He lives on the Upper East Side, near the Guggenheim."

"Nice neighborhood." And about a hundred times the amount he paid for his apartment. "You seeing him again?"

Ellie fiddled with a paper napkin. "Maybe. He's supposed to ca—" She cleared her throat. "We should get back to the key."

Sam cursed to himself. If this Kevin guy was smart, he'd make that phone call and not blow her off the way he'd done. "Sure, fine. Let me have a closer look."

She pushed it across the table with a single finger.

"It's engraved with a number—2376B. Any idea what that means?"

"I don't think it's for a safety-deposit box. From what I understand, they aren't engraved for security reasons. Might be a bus or airport locker, or one of those places that allow you to use their mailing address as your own."

"Any clue how I can find out what it's for?"

"I'll ask around. And it's we. I'm in this thing with you, no matter how many times you deny it."

She sat up straight. "This is between me and Gary."

"It's between you and Thompson Veridot, and that makes me an add-on. Until I know for certain he isn't the killer, I'm going to be on you like white on rice."

Ellie stood, and her dog rose to its feet. "It's late, and I'm tired. I think you should go."

"Fine." He stood and righted the chair. "I want you to phone me tomorrow after your morning walks, and again when you get home." He took a step forward, and the dog growled. "Put a sock in it," he ordered the pint-sized Cujo.

The dog sneezed, and Sam swore he'd just been called a loser in canine speak. Then the animal padded into the hall and turned in the direction of the bedroom.

Sam followed Ellie to the foyer and stood at the door, deciding it might be time he came clean. "This is probably too little, too late, but I was an idiot when I didn't do what I said I would in that note. I don't know what else to say."

She folded her arms and rested her back against the wall. "I wish you'd forget that night, because I have."

He took a step closer. Raising his hand, he cupped her cheek. "It's tough pretending we didn't make love, Ellie."

She didn't pull away. "You should have thought about that the day after you left me. I waited for a week, then two. Then I did my best to file the experience under 'bad ideas I've had in my life' and move on."

They locked gazes, and he inched forward, then brushed her mouth with his. Relief washed through him when she let him tease her lips. This might be all she'd allow tonight, but it was a start.

Drawing back, he grinned at her baffled expression. "I'll talk to you tomorrow."

Chapter 12

"How did it go with your late-night visitor?" asked Viv, walking beside Ellie the next morning.

Ellie shrugged. She'd slept like a log—once she managed to erase Sam's parting kiss from her brain—but that had been around three. Now, at seven thirty, with the temperature and humidity in the high eighties, she was hot, sticky, and out of sorts.

"The pompous jerk has 'pain in the ass' down to an art form. No matter what I say, he insists he's right and expects me to obey his every command, no questions asked."

Looking cool and professional, Viv straightened the cuffs on her gray Yves Saint Laurent suit. "He's a police detective. He's used to people following his orders. And if I read him correctly, he's worried about you."

They waited while both Rudy and Mr. T lifted legs on a fire hydrant. "He needn't be. I'm not going to do anything stupid."

"If Thompson Veridot did kill his brother, it's a sure bet he knows about you, which means anything can happen. Sam's only trying to protect you."

"I plan to stay on my toes for that very reason. Right now, I'm bummed about this afternoon's errands."

"And what might those be?"

"Besides trying to stop in a couple of places that rent storage boxes so I can place the key, I have to call a crematorium and arrange for the disposal of Gary's body." She heaved a sigh. "I also have to order a memorial plaque for his tree. Once I pick up the ashes, I'll set a date for his dedication ceremony."

"Planning on inviting anyone I know?" Viv asked, a sour expression on her face.

"You don't have to be there. Rudy and I can do the deed all by our lonesome."

"Great—go tromping through the underbelly of Central Park alone and unprotected. Just remember, if you get mugged, I'll never forgive myself."

Ellie grabbed Viv's arm and planted her sneakered feet. "Why the heck does everyone think I need a bodyguard?" She blew an angry breath upward, ruffling the curls plastered to her forehead by the morning heat. "I am not a child. I'm an adult, with a brain, I might add. I don't follow you around warning you to be careful or watch who you're dating. And I never lecture you on how you should manage your life."

Viv crossed her arms and rolled her eyes. "Well, so-orr-ree. Can I help it if you're my best friend and I'd like to keep you around for a while?"

Deflated, Ellie hoisted her tote higher on her shoulder. "I'm not blaming you for my misery. Sam just makes me so mad." She bit her lower lip. "Last night, he accused me of being a Goody Two-shoes, intimated I'd lived a sheltered life and didn't know how to defend myself. He acted as if it was a crime to study hard and make your parents proud."

"You did that?" asked Viv. "I knew there was something about you I didn't like."

"Ha-ha." They reached the corner where Ellie decided enough was enough and turned for home with Viv and Mr. T on her heels. "You were a good kid, too. At least that's what you led me to believe."

"Define good."

"Just what I said. Studied hard, got decent grades, and told your parents when you did something they forbid you to do."

"Uh-oh."

"What?"

"I thought by good you meant not being sexually active until college. I hung on until freshman year."

Ellie groaned internally. Had any other women on the planet held on to her virginity as long as she had? "Yeah, me, too," she lied.

Viv raised an eyebrow. "Who was your first?"

"My first?"

"Yeah. Who did you give it up for?"

"My husband."

"Wait a second. You said you didn't meet him until your second year in college."

"First year, second. Who cares?"

"Okay, whatever. But you gave your cherry to Larry Lipschitz?" Viv's words bubbled out like irreverent squawks from a whoopee cushion. "Oh, God, you poor thing."

"I don't see what's so funny. No guy revved my engine, and I didn't want to do something I'd be sorry for later." All the male friends she'd made in college had treated her like a sister. Even Joe. "When the D asked me to marry him, there wasn't anything better on the horizon, so I said yes, and that was that."

"Shows what happens when women aren't raised to believe they're the ones in control. If I ever have a daughter—"

"Her birthday suit will be Gucci?"

"That, too. So tell me, does Sam know you're practically a virgin?"

She lowered her voice. "I've slept with several men since the divorce."

"Define several."

"Counting Sam?"

"I would if I wanted a decent number."

"Okay. Three." When Viv bit back a grin, Ellie wanted to slug her. "Can we discuss this later?"

"Sure, fine. Back to Gary's ceremony. If you promise to hold it in broad daylight, I'll come. I'm sure Sam will be there, too, if you ask him."

"Of course he will. Anything to annoy me."

They reached their complex steps, and Viv passed Ellie the Jack Russell's leash. "Do me a favor and bring T in. I'm running late."

"It's Friday," Ellie stated, hoping to get them back on even keel. "Do you have a date?"

"Possibly." Viv fiddled with the strap on her Fendi briefcase. "I was hoping Dr. Dave would call."

"I thought he didn't ask for your number?"

"He didn't, but he did ask where I worked, and I gave him my card. He could reach me at Kleinschmidt, Felder, and Wong."

"I'll keep my fingers crossed." Ellie climbed the stairs. "Like I said, I don't mind fishing."

Viv's eyes flashed a warning. "Absolutely not. I don't need anybody trawling for my dates." She ran a hand through her sleek dark hair. "What about that lawyer you had dinner with the other night? Wasn't he supposed to be in touch?"

"I'm not holding my breath. 'I'll call you' is the oldest line in the book."

"I thought Sam apologized for his faux pas."

"He did. That doesn't mean I can trust him." Ever again. "If I'm lucky, he's working late, which means he'll give this 'call me every day' crap a rest."

Viv headed for the subway, walking backward as she spoke. "I'll come up when I get home. We can talk then."

Ellie returned Mr. T to his apartment; then she and Rudy set out for the Beaumont while she thought about

Sam. He'd bossed her around from the first moment they met. When he'd decided she was too nice to have killed the professor, she'd gone ballistic, and even that hadn't changed his opinion of her. She was too tame, too innocent, too little-girlish to be woman enough for him. She simply didn't float his boat.

But if that was true, why did he continue to kiss her? He'd been too big a jerk to phone her after their one-night stand, so why did he care now?

After strolling in silence for the first three blocks, Rudy chimed into her thoughts. *"You don't need Detective Dunce to protect you, Triple E. I won't let that Thompson guy get you."*

"That's a very brave thing to say, my fuzzy friend, but you can't stop a bullet."

"I'd take a bullet for you if the opportunity arose. Honest."

They waited for the light at Park Avenue to change. "I know, but I wouldn't want you to do it. I wasn't around to protect you ten years ago, and I refuse to let anything hurt you again. That includes putting your life on the line for me."

While talking, the hairs on the back of Ellie's neck rose, and she took a look around. An older man standing next to her on the curb smiled.

"Chatting with your dog or yourself?" he asked.

When the WALK sign blinked, the pedestrians continued west. She focused in front of her, though she'd already seen his full head of gray hair and portly physique. Was she going to be suspicious of every older man she met, just because he matched Thompson Veridot's sketchy description?

"Myself," she muttered, wishing he'd disappear.

"He's a cute little guy," the man continued. "Kinda looks like a poodle, but not a poodle. What breed is he?"

"I could bite him for you," Rudy interjected. *"Just say the word and it's done."*

"He's a Yorkie-poodle mix."

The man started to say something else, but she ignored him and turned south at Fifth, heading for the Beaumont. She usually enjoyed talking to strangers, especially when they asked about Rudy, but Gary's death had put a damper on her life in just about every way imaginable.

"Hey, Engleman!"

Having finished walking the dogs at the Beaumont, Ellie ignored Eugene's nasal whine and plowed toward the Davenport. The last person she wanted to see before, during, or after her morning rounds was one of her competitors. Holding a conversation with him would only cause her further grief.

"Hey, Engleman! Wait up!" he continued. "I got something I need to talk to you about!"

She glanced skyward and prayed for patience, then turned to find her nemesis closing in like a heat-seeking missile. His summer wardrobe, a sleeveless, black mesh tee, a Band-Aid-sized pair of purple shorts, and ratty sneakers, only added to his sleaze quotient. She'd managed to avoid him for the past week, a nice move on her part. Sadly, it appeared as if her good luck was at an end.

"What do you want, Eugene?" she asked as he drew near.

His ferret face frowning, he took a drag on his cigarette and blew a stream of smoke in her direction. "I heard you're the person in charge of that homeless guy that died, what's-his-name—Gary?—his estate."

"You heard what?" How in the heck had word already reached the street that Gary had an *estate*, never mind that she was the one in charge of it? "And why is it any of your business?"

"It's my business"—he took another pull on the cigarette—"because the derelict owed me money. The

way I understand it, it's your responsibility to pay up."
Eugene dropped the butt and ground it under his heel.
"Gary bummed cash from me all the time, and I want
payback."

"He's got to be kidding," yipped Rudy.

Ellie agreed. "First of all, I was a friend of Gary's. and
he never asked me for a dime. So why would he leech off
you?" The biggest leech of all. "And secondly, I'd need
proof of the loans. Do you have signed IOUs? Anything
that says how much he owed you, or that he promised to
return the cash?"

Eugene raised a shaggy eyebrow. "Are you shittin'
me? The guy was a slug. He begged a buck here, a buck
there, but it all adds up, ya know. I did my duty helpin'
him out and all, but I'm not running a charity. He owed
me fair and square."

Amazed by Eugene's vitriol, she grimaced. "Of course
he did. Why would I think a nice guy like you would try
to pull a fast one?"

"Damn straight. Now about that money—"

"Just out of curiosity, where did you hear that Gary
left an estate? Homeless people rarely have anything of
value to give to others when they pass."

"I forget where. Back to the debt—"

Ellie folded her arms and leaned against the Davenport, intending to stare him down. "I refuse to discuss
this until you tell me where you heard the rumor. Once
your memory improves, we'll talk about the loans."

Slick as a snake, the distasteful dog walker grabbed
her wrist and gave it a yank. "Listen, you—"

Without warning, Rudy lashed out, growling like a
rabid wolf, and Eugene darted back. "Holy fuck. He bit
me! I'm calling animal control." He swiped at the doggie
drool dampening his knobby knee. "Little monster."

"You came after me first," Ellie said, tugging on Rudy's leash to hold him back. She squinted at Eugene's
hairy leg. "Besides, he didn't break the skin."

"Yeah, but not for lack of trying. The turd should be put down. He's a menace to society."

Squatting, she pulled Rudy near and picked him up, holding him close to stop his shivering. "You okay? Maybe you need a tetanus shot, something to kill the toxins."

"He tasted just like squirrel poop." Rudy groaned. *"Disgusting."*

"Keep talkin' to that canine of yours, and you'll be the next one to get blown away."

Shocked, she inhaled a breath. Did this idiot actually know something about Gary's murder? "What's that supposed to mean? If you have information the police can use—"

"Nope, not me. But Gary was nutty as a jar of Skippy, and so are you, specially when you hold those one-sided conversations with the dogs you walk."

She set Rudy on the ground and stepped toward Eugene. "Stay out of my life or I'm liable to prove you right." She dug in her bag and brought out her Mace. "I might even go off the deep end and give you a shot of this stuff."

He held up his hands. "Hey, hey, hey! Enough with that shit. You are one crazy bitch." He backed away, his face the color of a ripe tomato. "Just remember, I want my dough." Stumbling backward, he turned and took off at a jog.

Ellie returned the can to her bag and dusted off her hands. Too bad Sam hadn't been here to see her tough-girl act and kick-ass attitude. Kneeling, she cupped Rudy's muzzle in her palms. "You okay, big guy?"

"That was awesome," her pal yelped. *"He screamed like a girl when I went on the attack."*

"That's not too difficult a feat when you're a creep like Eugene. He didn't hurt you, did he?"

"I might be little, but I'm quick. He didn't even see me

comin'. I struck like a cobra, in and out. Almost got him, too."

"It's a good thing you didn't, or I'd be dealing with a lawsuit. Don't ever go after anyone again, unless you're positive I can't handle them." She stood. "Do you need a drink? Should I ask Dr. Dave to check you out?"

He gave a full-body shake. *"Nah. I'm fine. But a little mouthwash might be nice. Just to get the taste of squirrel poop out of my mouth."*

She grinned. "Are you sure you're okay?"

"Absolutely. Let's get cranking."

"Ellie," Randall began when they entered the Davenport lobby. "Do you want me to call the authorities? I heard the commotion and stuck my head out to see what was happening, but Eugene dashed off before I could think straight."

"We're fine," she told the doorman. "Just a little shook up. Rudy took care of him."

"Indeed." He stooped to pat the Yorkiepoo's head. "Your boy is quite the scrapper."

"He's my big man," she said with a smile.

"If you don't mind my asking, what was Eugene so upset about? Or was it simply his usual charming personality making its presence known?"

"He seems to think Gary owed him money and I'm the one who should pay his debt."

"Really?" The doorman scratched his jaw. "I can't imagine Eugene giving anyone spare change, even a homeless person. And from what you've told me about Gary, I doubt he'd make a friend of anyone of Eugene's ilk."

"I agree. But Eugene did say something odd. Maybe you can help me figure it out."

"I'll do what I can."

"He said people on the street know I'm in charge of Gary's estate. How would anyone have found out about an inheritance, or that Rudy and I are Gary's heirs?"

"I heard rumblings yesterday, but my shift was over

before you got here. My pat answer, of course, was a comment on how unreasonable it was to think a home-less person could even have such a thing as an estate."

"Do you remember who mentioned it?"

Randall's forehead wrinkled in concentration. "Eu-gene, naturally, and another dog walker. Said they heard it from a man they'd met in the park. That could be any-one, considering the riffraff hanging out there."

Or it could have been Thompson Veridot. Hiding a shiver, she led Rudy to the elevator. "Let me collect my charges. We'll talk when I get back."

Ellie and Rudy rode up, gathered the herd, and headed for the lobby. Forty-five minutes later, they returned the dogs to their homes, wrote progress notes, and stopped downstairs, but Randall was nowhere in sight.

"Guess we'll catch him tomorrow," she told Rudy as they took off for their next building. "Remind me to ask Kronk this afternoon. He seems to have his ear to the ground all the time."

On the walk to the Cranston, her phone rang.

"Ellie, here."

"Ellie, it's Kevin. Sorry I didn't call sooner."

She stopped in her tracks. It had been a while since she'd dealt with a man who kept his word. "It's not a problem. I've been busy."

"Too busy to go out tomorrow night for dinner and a show? I managed to get tickets to *Spamalot*."

"Oh, well, ah, sure. I hear that's a great musical."

"Good. I'll pick you up. Six o'clock. We can eat at a favorite place of mine in the Theater District, then walk to the theater. How does that sound?"

"Wonderful. See you tomorrow."

She closed her cell, dropped it in her bag, and put a spring in her step. Dinner and a show. She hadn't seen a Broadway play since the D had taken her and a dozen of his clients to the revival of *Man of La Mancha*. The evening had been fabulous, right up until her ex told her she was only allowed to order an appetizer for her meal. The night was costing him a fortune, and he didn't want to waste the money on her.

"What's the difference between a lawyer and a gigolo?" Rudy asked, interrupting her thoughts. *"And make it snappy."*

"Make it snappy? What's that supposed to mean?"

"It means if you think about that dweeb of a lawyer any longer, we're gonna walk right by our next stop." He dug his heels in and halted in front of the Cranston. *"Just because that McGowan guy called like he said he would doesn't mean he's any better than the rest of the legal profession."*

"You seemed to like him when you met him at Mother's."

"He was okay—barely."

"Then I have your approval to date him?"

"As long as he treats you right. But one false move and I'll take him down a peg or two."

"I'll make sure to tell him so."

They entered Hilary's complex and took the elevator to her floor. "Good morning," she said when the woman opened her apartment door. "How are you today?"

Hilary's Cole Haan sport shoes were an odd contrast to her yellow silk Dolce & Gabbana walking suit and the matching diamond necklace and bracelet adorning her size-four body. "I'm feeling better, thank you. Let's go."

Cuddles stood dancing at her feet. *"Rudy, hiya. I miss you lots 'n' lots, bud."*

"Well, I don't miss you, and I'm not your bud," he grumped. *"And stay away from my butt."*

Ellie pulled at his leash. "Be nice."

Hilary locked her door and followed them to the elevator. "I'm not sure I'll ever be comfortable talking to the dogs I walk the way you do."

They arrived at their first client's unit, and Hilary unlocked the door. "It's just a habit I've gotten into," Ellie explained. "After my divorce, it was nice having some- one listen who didn't argue or judge."

"There is that," Hilary agreed. "If I didn't have Cud- dles to talk to, I'd cry myself to sleep every night. It's just that when you speak, it sounds as if you actually expect an answer."

"I've been doing it for so long, it's become second nature. I hope that—I mean—you don't think I'm crazy, do you?"

"Crazy?"

"You know, for talking to them. Has anyone ever told you they thought I had a couple of screws loose?"

They continued their rounds, picking up Sampson, Millie, and Dilbert, but instead of handling the dogs, El- lie took stock of Hilary's expertise, though she contin- ued asking how she might be perceived by others.

"Heavens, no," said Hilary as they hit the street. "From what I can tell, your clients and their dogs love you."

Marginally buoyed by the comment, Ellie asked, "So, are you going to keep this job?"

"I'd like to. I'm just worried about my husband and his sleazy attorney." She rested her fingers on the multi- carat diamond necklace. "I'm thinking of selling my jew- elry and giving the money to my sister to hold for me. I wouldn't put it past them to convince the judge I should hock it and give Richard half the value."

"Is your husband still harping because you work for me?"

"What I'd really like to know is how he found out about the job to begin with. Have you had a chance to ask any of the people in my building?"

"I called and left a few messages, but no one got back to me, so I'm guessing they haven't spoken to him. Maybe he'll let it go."

They crossed Fifth Avenue and headed for the park. Once there, Hilary donned her mask and latex gloves, scooped the poop and bagged it, and dropped it in the trash in record time. In between, she continued to comment on her situation.

Half an hour later, they left Hilary at the entrance to her complex and went to their last building of the morning while Ellie continued to ponder Eugene's strange statements. How had he heard about Gary's estate or known she was the executor? What did he mean when he said she might be the next one blown away?

"Hey, stop thinkin' about Gary and get back to my question."

"What question?"

"What's the difference between a lawyer and a gigolo?"

She gave him an eye roll. "I don't know. What's the difference?"

"A gigolo only screws one person at a time."

Rudy's snorts of laughter were music to her ears. If she ever met a man with a personality like her fuzzy pal, she'd marry him in a heartbeat. Unfortunately, she doubted that would happen. Very few men had Rudy's sense of loyalty, his code of honor, and his deep-down love for the woman in his life.

"That's a good one, big guy," she praised. "I've been wondering, where do you get these jokes?" Surely he wasn't making them up.

"Here and there. I listen to people talk, and every once in a while Stanley tells me a couple."

"Stanley? Georgette's Stanley?"

"He's an ex-judge, and he's still in touch with his old cronies, even though he's condemned to that wheelchair. Trouble is, your mother doesn't get the humor in the riddles, so he tells 'em to me. I try to chuckle, but I'm not certain he realizes it."

Little did her stepfather know. "You're easy to talk to, which is probably why the judge enjoys chatting with you. I don't think Mother gives him the attention he deserves."

"The only person Georgette pays attention to is herself. Does she know about you and Gary?"

"Mother? Of course not. Besides Viv, Randall, and Sam I haven't told a soul. And Pops, of course."

"Fat lot of good that did you. If Eugene knows, everybody knows. He's such a putz."

"Okay, enough of that. We only have a couple more dogs to walk. Then we have errands to run."

"What kind of errands?"

They arrived at the last building and collected their charges while they talked. "I have to call the mortuary recommended by the coroner's office and make arrangements for Gary to be cremated. Then I have to stop at a couple of places I found that have a lockbox service."

"Sounds boring, if you ask me."

"It probably will be, but I still have to do it. Especially since I found that key. It's part of Gary's estate ... sort of."

"Does that mean whatever you find will belong to me?"

"Good question. Maybe I should give Sal Cantiglia a call first. He should be able to help us figure it out."

"Another lawyer? Jeez, this city is crawlin' with 'em."

"Uncle Sal helped me with the will, so cool it with the nasty cracks." Especially since he had yet to send her a bill. "After all, he's Joe's relative, and you like Joe."

"Joe, yes, but lawyers? No. Except for the judge, of course. Why don't you just ask him for help?"

"Because Mother would give me a lecture. Besides, the less she knows about this business with Gary, the better. As for lawyers, they're a necessary evil in today's world."

"You never said. Did Gary use one to write that will?"

"Nope. Sal said it looked like he bought one of those do-it-yourself forms at an office supply store and had it notarized at his bank. Pretty smart thing to do, don't you think?"

"*So you and Vivie could do the same thing for me and T, right? That way, we'd be covered, and it wouldn't cost much.*"

"Money is no object where you're concerned. It's just the time factor. And I haven't ironed out the details with Viv yet, but I will. Don't worry."

"*Okay, if you say so.*" He lifted his leg on a trash container. "*But can we stop for lunch before we go hunting? Cuz I'm starvin'.*"

Chapter 13

Ellie called Uncle Sal while they ate lunch, just to make certain she had the right to the contents of whatever kind of box the key opened. After he assured her they did, she and Rudy visited six different shops before they arrived at Mail It or Store It, tucked between a second-hand jeweler and a consignment shop on Lexington. According to the date on the window, the business had been around for years, which gave her hope that this might be the place she was searching for.

The pimply-faced kid behind the register examined the key, then returned it to the counter. "It could be one of ours." He narrowed his eyes. "But how come you got one of our keys if you don't know what it's for?"

Ellie snatched up the bit of metal and held it tight, in case the suspicious clerk decided to confiscate it. "It belongs—belonged—to a friend. He gave it to me, but he never got a chance to tell me exactly what it opened."

"Is that right?" The boy scratched his acne-covered cheek. "If you don't mind my asking, who are you?"

She hoisted her bag on the counter and fumbled for her driver's license, which gave her time to formulate a half-truth. "Here's my identification. The man who owned the key died, and I inherited everything he had, which, according to my lawyer, also includes the contents of the storage box the key fits."

He stared at her ID as if it were the plans for a nuclear bomb. "I gotta talk to my manager before you do anything."

"I don't see why." Ellie gave him her best sweet-and-innocent grin. "If I'd simply walked in off the street and used the key, you'd never know the box wasn't mine, would you?"

The kid tugged on his scraggly beard as his brow furrowed in concentration. "I guess not."

"Great. Pretend we've never met, and we'll play a new game." She set her bag on her shoulder and led Rudy outside. Then she walked back in and nodded. "Good morning. Nice day, isn't it?"

The clerk wore a befuddled expression, as if he couldn't wrap his dense brain around the scenario. "Uh, yeah, sure."

Holding her breath, Ellie continued on her errand, perusing the boxes lining the walls until she found one that matched the number on the key in a row at the bottom. "Here goes nothing," she muttered to Rudy as she squatted. "Keep your paws crossed."

Opening the box, she peered inside. "Oh, my."

"What! What?"

"Hang on a second." She pulled out a stack of brittle, yellowed sheets and went back for another. In seconds, a ten-inch pile of newspapers and ragtag envelopes rested beside her on the floor.

"What is all that junk?"

She raised the top newspaper and read the headline, then scanned the next one in the stack. "It looks like a collection of articles on the Veridots' murder," she whispered. "Gary must have saved them during the trial."

Gathering the documents, she tried sliding them into her tote, but there were too many. Luckily, she still had one of the shopping bags she'd brought to Gary's shelter. Snapping it open, she stuffed everything inside, stood, and carried her bundles to the counter.

"Can you look up the records on this box? Tell me when it was first opened, and how it was paid for?"

Still gazing at her as if she were certifiable, the counterman said, "I need the name of the real owner."

She spelled Gary's last name.

He tapped on a computer keyboard. "Says here it was first taken out in 1983 and paid for a year at a time in cash. Your friend also has a PO Box here."

"Really?" She reined in her excitement. "Can I have whatever's in there, too?"

His snide grin turned to one of superiority. "Sorry, postal regulations say I can't hand the mail over to just anybody . . . Unless you have that key, too?"

"Would I be asking you, if I did?" Ellie wanted to shout. Instead, she chewed her lower lip. She hadn't found another key, but that didn't mean one didn't exist. She simply wasn't crazy about digging around Gary's mucked up shelter again, even in broad daylight. "Without the key, what would I need to take possession of the mail?"

"I gotta ask my manager. Wait here."

Acne boy disappeared through a door marked OF-FICE, and Ellie gazed at Rudy. "Maybe I should talk to Sal again. There must be some type of legal document I can carry that will verify I'm entitled to Gary's possessions before I get arrested for stealing."

"Stealing, my butt. We own whatever you find. I say we call the cops and report this place for—for—robbin' us blind."

"I think another conversation with Sal is a better idea. I'll make the call if the manager doesn't cooperate."

Moments later, an older gentleman appeared, followed by the sales clerk. After she explained her predicament, the man was happy to give her what she wanted, including her own key to the postal box, while the sul-

len kid looked on with a scowl. She then cancelled the
storage box, collected Gary's mail and dumped it in the
shopping bag, and left with a mental note to check the
post office box in a month or so.

*"Feels like we just tried breakin' into freakin' Fort
Knox,"* Rudy griped as she hailed a cab. *"I'm worn out.
If you don't mind, I need a nap."*

They climbed in the taxi, and Ellie gave her home
address, then said, "I'm dumping this stuff at the apartment, so you can stay in while I do afternoon rounds.
How does that sound?"

"Fine by me. Can I take a look at those newspapers?"

"Take a look?" She glanced at the driver who was
wearing an iPod and doing a lap dance to the beat. "Oh,
that's right. I forgot you can read."

"One of my many talents," he answered with a doggie
grin.

"Maybe you should come clean and tell me now if
you have any other superpowers. These little revelations
you keep dropping are something of a shock."

"I can do lots of stuff humans can," he continued. *"If
I had fingers, I'd be a regular Harry Houdini. You could
enter me on Animal Planet's* Pet Star *program, and I'd
win, excuse the pun, paws down. There's not another canine that can touch me in the talent department."*

Ten minutes later, she led her bragging buddy into
the building, collecting her own mail on the way to their
apartment. If she had Rudy's confidence she'd be a star,
too. Well, maybe not a star in the television or movie
sense, and not an officer of the law or a private investi-
gator star, either. But she did plan to find the person who
murdered Gary. She owed the homeless man for leaving
them his fortune, and for writing that sweet hope-filled
letter charging her with avenging his murder.

It was Gruning's fault she had to dig this deep. It
didn't sound as if he had any intention of finding Gary's
killer. She was positive he'd finagle a way to doom the

case to an inactive file, which guaranteed the perpetrator would go free.

And Sam wasn't much better. If he gave her credit for having some smarts when it came to crime solving, she might not be so determined. Once she knew for certain who'd done the deed, she'd hang up her sleuthing shoes for good. No more hunting for clues, unlocking secret boxes, or crawling into fallen-down, bug-laden shelters in the dark of night.

She set the shopping bag on her kitchen table and sifted through her mail, pleased to open a letter from the bonding company that gave Hilary full approval. Planning to share the good news on their next meeting, she left for the Beaumont and her second set of scheduled walks.

Sam spent a half hour chatting up the snooty doorman at the Davenport. Once Randall verified that Ellie was due soon for her afternoon rounds, he decided to wait instead of ringing her cell. A sneak attack made sense, especially after the way she'd avoided his calls the other night.

Ellie had been on his mind every other minute for the past twenty-four hours, and it was driving him crazy. He had a job to do, cases to solve, and a reputation to uphold. He was a good cop, a man who didn't stop until he caught the bad guy, yet he'd spent more time worrying about a bossy, know-it-all bad penny than any criminal on his list.

He'd talked to Gruning earlier, and the incompetent fool still had no intention of putting out an APB on Thompson Veridot. As usual, the ass was more concerned about closing the file, not only because the victim was an indigent but also because there were no leads. He even hinted that, in light of the will and inheritance, he might charge Ellie with the crime. The attitude was typical Gruning, and annoying as hell to any decent detective.

On the bright side, Gruning made no bones about the fact that he thought Ellie a fluff-brained pain in the ass. If he knew the real Ellie Engleman, the man would run screaming into the night.

The idea that she was more than likely in the clear had taken a load off Sam's mind. If not for the fact that he saw her whenever he spotted a dog walker, or his thoughts wandered, or he closed his eyes to sleep, things would have been perfect.

He checked his watch for the fiftieth time since his arrival, spurring the doorman to say, "She should be along any minute now, Detective Ryder, though I'm not usually here when she does her afternoon rounds. Ms. Engleman is efficient, prompt, and dependable." He drew back his shoulders. "And, might I add, a woman of great personal character."

He didn't have to hear Randall twice. The aging doorman championed Ellie every chance he could. And knowing someone watched out for her when he couldn't gave him an inner peace he found confusing and comforting at the same time.

"I'm sure she is," he agreed. "I take it you've known the family for a while?"

Randall raised a brow. "Is that an official inquiry, or are you merely making conversation?"

"A bit of both, I guess."

The doorman gazed at him for a full ten seconds before answering. "The Englemans moved here when Ellie was little more than a child. After her father passed away, she and her mother stayed on until Mrs. Engleman found the second of her many husbands." He smiled. "Even back then, Ellie loved animals. She used to walk some of the tenants' dogs for free, because her mother wouldn't allow her to have a canine of her own."

Ah, thought Sam, that explained a lot. "What was the reason she couldn't have a pet?"

Randall's expression turned to one of disapproval.

"I don't enjoy speaking badly of tenants, but Mrs. Engleman—or whatever her most recent name is—no longer lives here, so I'm free to say that she ruled the roost where her husband and daughter were concerned. I imagine it's the reason she's been married so many times."

"How many is many?"

"According to Ellie five or six, but I never was crass enough to get the details." He raised his nose in the air. "Bear in mind, I don't approve of gossip."

Five or six husbands? No wonder his bad penny didn't have a lot to say about marriage. "It's not really gossip if I'm asking questions as a law enforcement officer."

"I can't see how Ellie's personal life has anything to do with an ongoing investigation," the doorman added, giving a sniff of disdain.

Sam shrugged. "Okay, it's more a need-to-know thing. I'm having a hard time figuring out what makes the woman tick."

"A kind heart, for one, just like her father." Randall considered before he spoke further. "I can only imagine how it must have been, growing up with a mother who judged her every move and being told she'd never meet the woman's strict requirements. It pained me when they moved, as I'd tried to be an anchor after Mr. Engleman died."

"That was a nice touch on your part." And it gave him an inside look at Ellie's fierce need to do the right thing. "I guess that's why she depends on you now."

"I'd like to think we're friends. And friends take care of each other . . . even after they're dead."

Sam didn't miss the veiled reference to Gary Veridot. "So she told you about her homeless pal and the inheritance?"

"Of course. And no one deserves the money more, though I know she plans to give most of it away as soon as things quiet down. Her mother collected settlement and alimony checks like a squirrel gathers nuts in September, and I'm certain everything she has will be her daughter's some day. Thus Ellie's willingness to donate to charity now."

Sam cringed internally. Chalk up another reason why the two of them didn't belong together. Ellie had been born to money and stood to inherit more. She deserved better than living off an NYC detective's pathetic excuse for a salary. "I'm not handling the case, but I was wondering, have you heard any street talk about who might have killed Veridot?"

"Not a word. Then again, I don't gossip," Randall insisted, as if erasing the last fifteen minutes of their conversation.

Seconds later, Boris Kronkovitz, the evening doorman, strolled jauntily through the door. When he spotted Sam, he stared with suspicion. "Someone *eez* dead?" he asked in a heavy Russian accent.

Sam gazed up at the six-foot-six bear of a man about fifteen years Randall's junior. "Not unless you know something I don't."

"I know only one *theenk*," said Kronk. "Too much *keel-ink* make me lose *slip* at night."

Randall waggled a finger at him. "It's about time you got here, Kronk. There are parcels in the storage room that need to be distributed. Follow me, and I'll show you what's what."

The Russian and Randall disappeared into a room behind the counter, and Ellie took that moment to stride through the door. Sam's heart kicked up a beat at the sight of her, looking cool and collected even in the July heat. Tousled curls feathered her forehead. Her sun-kissed nose scrunched under her oversized sunglasses. A bright yellow T-shirt clung to her dynamite curves, while plain khaki shorts showed off her tanned and toned legs.

"What are you doing here?"

"Waiting for you," he said, grinning. "Got a few minutes?"

"I'm running late, so make it short." Randall came out from the storage area in civilian dress, and she asked him, "You're here past time. Is there a problem?"

"Just waiting for Kronk."

"Ah, I see." She propped an elbow on the counter. "Has the detective been hassling you?"

"Not really. Though I must admit, the past half hour has been interesting," he said, exaggerating the time.

She set a hand on her hip and gave Sam a once-over. "You've been here for thirty minutes? Am I under arrest?"

"No, but—"

"Good." She headed for the elevator.

"Best of luck," Randall called as he left the building.

Sam raced after her and slipped into the elevator just as the doors closed. Neither he nor Ellie said a word until they reached the fifteenth floor. There, she walked briskly into the hall and he followed.

"Earth to Ellie. Where are we going?"

"Four of the dogs in this building get two walks a day," she said tersely. "Any other questions?"

"Only one. Can I come along?"

"What's wrong? Is the murder business slow today?"

"I'm off duty. I thought we should talk."

Ignoring him, she unlocked an apartment and smiled at the snow-white dog sitting in the doorway with a leash hanging from its fuzzy muzzle. "Hey, Sweetie Pie. Sorry I'm a couple of minutes late. Rudy and I had a busy afternoon."

The pooch gazed at Sam, then back to Ellie.

"Not at all," she said as she dropped to a squat and clipped the lead to the dog's collar. "If I'm lucky, he'll say what he has to say and leave."

Sam refrained from tossing out a smart-ass comment.

He still had a hard time understanding the one-sided conversations she held with her charges. "I thought I'd take you to dinner."

Without answering, she locked the door and headed for the elevator. Irritated by her silent treatment, he kept after her, following the canine cluster from floor to floor. He had no idea why he'd blurted the invitation to dinner, but now that he had he was looking forward to the experience. She'd say yes, if he got the words right.

"About dinner. You can pick the spot. I'll eat most anything."

"I'm not hungry."

"Really? I'd be starving if I got as much exercise as you. How many dogs have you got on your client list?"

"Not counting Viv's Jack Russell and Rudy, about thirty."

He gave a low whistle. "Sounds like your business has really taken off."

"It's a living," she commented.

Outside, they crossed Fifth Avenue and walked north along the edge of Central Park for three blocks. Sam made small talk while she did her job, though she only gave him one-word answers. Then they retraced their steps to the Davenport.

"So, you done for the day?" he asked when they entered the lobby.

"Hey, Kronk," she said in reply, heading for the elevator.

Sam stuffed his hands in his pockets and decided to wait. She had to come down eventually. After a moment, he locked gazes with the leering doorman.

"She is one fine *woo-man*, no?" the guy asked.

"Keep your eyes in your head, pal."

The doorman shrugged and disappeared in the room behind the counter while Sam nodded to incoming tenants, tapped his toes, paced the lobby, heaved impatient sighs—anything to pass the time. When the elevator door opened for the tenth time, he was relieved to see his dinner date. "What took you so long?"

"I have to write notes when I bring the dogs to their apartments." She aimed for the door.

He stayed at her side as she turned left. Since she wasn't heading home, he figured she had more dogs to walk. "Notes. Like a letter?"

"Notes as in what the dog did on its walk." She crossed Seventieth and kept going.

"You mean the owners want to know what they did? Like—"

"Exactly like," she answered. "If you want to talk, keep up. I have two more buildings."

She slowed her pace, and he smiled at the friendly gesture. Though he still hadn't received an answer to his dinner invitation, he figured there was a chance she'd say yes.

"About dinner—"

"Yes."

"Is that a 'yes' as in 'what?' or a 'yes' as in 'yes, I'll share a meal with you'?"

"Yes, I'll share a meal with you, but I can't be out late. I'm supposed to meet Viv for a walk to Carl Schurz."

His gut clenched, and he caught her arm. "Do you say things like that on purpose, just to drive me crazy?"

Ellie shook off his hand. "I don't have to do a thing to drive you crazy. It appears you're capable of getting there all by yourself."

He speared his fingers through his hair. "I told you that place is dangerous. I don't want you going there without me—day or night."

"Viv and I take the walk several times a week, and we've never had a problem."

"There's always a first time," he lectured. "And the first time might be your last."

They entered the next building, which didn't have a doorman, and walked to the elevator. Her failure to speak told him he'd offended her again, so he strove for middle ground. "How about if I go with the two of you tonight?"

"Viv and I are fine together." They got out on the third floor. "I'll keep my Mace handy, as you suggested. I'm sure we'll be safe."

The argumentative conversation wasn't doing either of them any good, so he decided to dole out more advice when they got to the restaurant. He'd done something she needed to be eased into, something he was prepared to defend, though she'd probably cry foul as soon as he gave her the news.

After walking five more dogs and bringing them home, they arrived at what Sam assumed was her final building. It was close to six, and he was hungry, tired, and running out of patience. When they stopped at the first door, a middle-aged woman carrying a tiny white dog and dressed for a fashion show answered the knock.

"Hey, Hilary. Good news. You passed the bonding agency's check with flying colors." Ellie took the pup from her arms and set it on the floor. "The insurance company should get back to me in a day or so, too."

"That's a relief," the woman responded. Then she caught Sam's eye, looked him over from head to toe, and smiled. "Something tells me this gentleman isn't training to be a dog walker."

"Sorry. Detective Sam Ryder, this is Hilary Blankenship. Hilary is my first assistant."

"Detective?" The woman locked her door and took the dog's lead. "Is this an official visit?"

Ellie steered Ms. Blankenship ahead as she answered. "Sam was the detective on Professor Albright's case. He's tagging along because he has nothing better to do with his time."

The woman glanced at him over her shoulder, and her expression told him she didn't believe a word Ellie said. Hanging back, he stayed mute while they collected two more canines and rode the elevator to the lobby.

"Have you heard any more from your attorney?" Ellie asked her assistant as they exited the building.

"No, thank God. For a while, I thought I was being stalked, but I guess Richard finding out about this job was just a fluke or something."

"Maybe," Ellie agreed. "Just remember, you're on your own starting Monday. Think you can handle it?"

They crossed Fifth Avenue and Sam decided to give the ladies some privacy. It sounded as if Ellie was branching out, building her business and getting help, and he approved. He was beat just following her on her second shorter round of walks. He couldn't imagine putting on the miles she trekked every day.

When she and Hilary turned north, he sat on a bench and scanned the street. Aside from a couple of homeless people, food and gizmo vendors, and the usual contingent of tourists milling in front of the Guggenheim, no one caught his eye. But that didn't mean Thompson Veridot wasn't out there, waiting for the right moment to pounce.

Crossing his legs, he counted the minutes while Ellie and her assistant did their thing, strolled back to the complex, and disappeared inside. Moments later, Ellie walked out of the building, spotted him on the bench, and waited for the light to change. Standing on the curb, she was approached by an older man with a stocky build and a full head of gray hair.

Jumping to his feet, Sam jogged in their direction. Veridot was older, on the heavy side, and gray-haired, too. Hair color could be changed, and there were plenty of men in their late fifties in this town, but it seemed too much of a coincidence that one would stop to chat with Ellie while she was without an escort or her pint-sized guard dog.

Dodging traffic, he darted across the intersection and

skidded to a stop. "Hold it right there, bud." He placed a hand on the man's shoulder. "Let's see some ID."

"What are you doing?" Ellie demanded.

"Keeping you safe." His gaze locked on the man. Reaching into his jacket, he pulled out his shield. "I asked if you had identification."

"Uh—um—uh—" The man fumbled in his pockets and withdrew a threadbare wallet. "I haven't done anything illegal, honest."

"Milton Fenwick," Sam continued, perusing the ID. "Says here you live on One-hundred-tenth. A little far from home, aren't you?"

"Sam—"

"I'm retired. I take long walks."

"Sam, this man—"

"Is that right?"

Trembling, Milton nodded.

"What's your business with this woman?"

"I wanted—I thought she still might be looking for help."

"Help?"

"As a dog walker, you dope," Ellie said, hands on her hips. "Mr. Fenwick picked up one of my advertisements on a college bulletin board." She snatched the wallet from his hands and passed it to Milton. "Here you go. And I'm sorry you were accosted by Detective Demento here. I have your card. I'll call you if I need more help."

Milton didn't say a word, just stuffed the wallet in his pocket and scuttled off like a drunken crab.

Sam didn't have to make eye contact with Ellie to know she was angry. The heat of her fury radiated waves. He stuffed his hands in his pockets and pasted a smile on his face. "So, you ready for that dinner?"

Folding her arms under her breasts, she stared. "You belong in a padded room—or a cave. I'm not sure which."

He opened his mouth to speak, and she held up a

hand. "Wait, I've got it. A cage in a zoo, where all the other crazed baboons live."

She stalked south, and he followed her. When they stopped at a crosswalk, he tried to take her elbow, but she shrugged him off. The light changed, and he kept after her. They were eating dinner whether she liked it or not. And if she didn't want to talk during the meal, fine. He'd spend the night staring at her across a table, but at least they'd be together.

They passed Sixty-sixth, got to Sixty-first, and turned left. Where the hell was she going? A few minutes later, they hit Lexington, and she took another left. Then she ducked into a Joe to Go and shot straight for the counter.

Chapter 14

Ellie made a beeline for Joe Cantiglia, behind the counter on register duty. Talking to her college buddy always lightened her spirits, and right now she needed a good laugh. Otherwise, she might finally commit that murder the police kept trying to pin on her.

"Hey, Ellie." Joe's grin flattened when he gazed over her shoulder. "What can I get for you?"

"The usual, but make it a decaf."

"One large decaf caramel bliss, on the double, Gina," he said to his barista. "And for your friend?"

"Friend?" She passed Joe her frequent buyer card. "What friend?"

Joe's smile returned full force. "Sorry, I thought the guy standing behind you was . . . um . . . your companion."

"The guy standing behind me is a pervert," she responded. "How about calling the police and reporting him for me?"

"My pleasure." He returned her punch card and reached for the phone.

Sam slapped his shield on the counter. "Back off, buddy. I am the cops."

Shaking his head, Joe gave her a look of chastisement. "Aw, Ellie, don't tell me you forgot to scoop Rudy's poop again. I hear the city's cracking down on pet owners who break the law with a seventy-five-dollar fine. The nice policeman's probably following you to make sure you comply."

Ellie hid a grin. The put-down was exactly what Ryder deserved for terrifying poor Mr. Fenwick. Thanks to Joe, she imagined Sam was ready to explode.

"I'm a detective, coffee boy, not a beat cop. I'm also Ms. Engleman's escort. She's just too stubborn to admit it."

"Nah! My Ellie's a smart girl," Joe taunted. "Hey, you wanna hang around and wait for me to close up?" he asked, looking directly at her. "I'll even spring for dinner. It'll be just you and me, babe."

"That would be—"

"Very stupid," Sam said in a threatening tone. "Like I already told you, the lady's with me, and we're having dinner together . . . alone."

"Hey, what's a threesome between friends? Ellie and I go all the way back to college." Joe's handsome face again wore a naughty grin. "I hear the Wickery special tonight is charbroiled rib eye, one of her favorites. I'm sure she'd love to have me along for company."

"But I wouldn't." Standing tall, Sam edged closer to Ellie. "Just pour me a regular coffee of the day, and hurry it up."

Joe gave a mock salute and turned to fill the order. The barista squirted thick caramel sauce over the frothy cap of white on Ellie's drink and set it in front of her. Joe handed the detective his black coffee, but before Ellie could pull out her money, Sam smacked a ten-dollar bill on the counter.

"Keep the change." He grabbed his coffee in one hand, her elbow in the other, and led her to a table. Pulling out a chair with his toe, he nodded. "Sit down and act like a big girl, or I'll be forced to take proper disciplinary action."

She glared at him over the top of her steaming drink. "After the idiotic macho displays you keep pulling, you have some nerve insinuating I'm a child. What are you going to do—make me stand in the corner?"

"I was thinking more of a spanking," he said, his eyes as dark as his drink. "At home. In your bedroom."

Heat raced from her chest to her cheeks. He'd had his hands on her butt before, and his lips, and she'd enjoyed every smoldering kiss and sensual caress, but she'd been naïve and foolish four months ago. Hell would freeze over before she fell into bed with him a second time. "What are you? Some kind of modern-day Neanderthal?"

Glowering, he took a swallow of coffee. "Look, let's call a truce. I'm no caveman, and I don't like to argue—"

"Then leave me alone. I can go to dinner with Joe, and he'll make sure I get home safe and sound. If I ask, he'll even go with Viv and me to Carl Schurz."

"I have a better idea. I'll take you to dinner, I'll walk you and your friend to the park, and I'll see to it you get home in one piece. End of discussion."

"You just can't give it a rest, can you?" She sipped the coffee, hoping the sweet caramel inching into her middle would calm her temper. "Okay, we'll do dinner, and you can walk us to the park. Vivian will appreciate it, especially since she wigged out at Gary's shelter the other night."

"What? Why was she there?"

"Because I didn't want to go alone. It wouldn't have been safe, remember?"

"Yeah, but what happened to upset her?"

"She kept hearing . . . things."

His expression grew concerned. "What kind of 'things'?"

"I don't know. Animals, maybe. Once I heard the rustling, we left in a big hurry." She took another swallow of coffee before confessing. "Nothing's ever happened at either location."

"You've never seen anyone suspicious at either park?"

"Not a soul." She set her cup on the table. "And I haven't noticed anything else out of the ordinary wherever I've walked since Gary's murder."

"Have you been approached by any strange men?"

"Only you."

He raised his eyes to the ceiling, his expression pained. "You know what I mean. Men you've never met before stopping to say hello or asking you about the dog walking business. Guys like Fenwick."

She recalled the older man who'd spoken to her at the crosswalk and the man she and Viv had met at Carl Schurz last week. "There was a guy who started to chat with me at a crosswalk, but I lost him. And a man at Carl Schurz spoke to Viv and me, but both conversations were about dogs. Dog lovers enjoy shooting the breeze about canines. And I did get that spooky call regarding my assistant's ad, which will also give me a shot at meeting strangers. Do you really believe Veridot would go to the trouble of getting a fake ID and pretending to want a job, just to cozy up to me?"

"You'd be surprised at what a killer will do to get close to their target. When was the first time you met Fenwick?"

"The day I posted the ads. He followed me, just to say that he'd seen me tacking the sheet up. Then he asked a couple of questions. I didn't see him again until tonight."

"Sounds like too much of a coincidence, his being there just as you were slapping up the info." Sam drained his coffee cup. "He's a senior citizen. What was he doing on a college campus?"

"I don't remember what he said. Do you think he looks like Thompson Veridot?"

"He fits the general description, but the faxed photo is dark and grainy, so it's hard to tell. Hair color can be changed, and some men grow a mustache or beard as a natural disguise. Spotting Thompson without a clear and current photo will be difficult."

"Wouldn't the tattoos be identification enough?"

"If his upper arms are exposed, but Veridot is smart. He'll keep his arms covered so you can't identify him."

"Great. What am I supposed to do?"

"I already told you, don't go anywhere alone after dark, and don't put yourself in a vulnerable position." He drummed his fingers on the tabletop. "I have a confession to make. I did something you need to know about."

She arched a brow at his hesitant tone. "Let me guess. You hired a bodyguard for me."

"It's an idea." When she didn't smile, he continued. "Remember that friend I mentioned—the one who teaches self-defense at his gym?" He cleared his throat. "I enrolled you in a course. Your first class is tomorrow afternoon at two."

"You did what?"

"Don't blow a gasket. I did it for my peace of mind. You're scheduled to go three times a week for the next four weeks, and I already paid for the lessons. There are a couple of times to choose from, but I took the liberty of making the first appointment . . . just to get you started."

She opened and closed her mouth. "You paid—"

"It's no big deal. Phil's a friend. He gave me a fifty percent discount." He pulled a card from his pocket and pushed it across the table. "Here's the gym address and phone number."

Cupping her temples with her hands, Ellie stared at the business card. Why did Sam continue to do things that interfered with her life instead of staying away and letting her exist at her own pace?

"Say something."

She ignored his plea, afraid if she raised her head she'd burst into tears. Was this his way of telling her she was an idiot, or was he trying to show that he truly cared?

He slipped a hand between her wrists, cupped her chin with his fingers, and lifted her face. "I don't want anything bad to happen to you, Ellie."

She clasped his hand in her palms. "I can't believe you haven't figured it out by now. I was Gary's friend. When I become someone's friend, I stick by them no matter what." She sniffed back a tear. "Even if they act like a crazed baboon every once in a while."

Sam leaned toward her, his expression as soft as she'd ever seen it. "I want you for more than a friend, even when you drive me nuts."

She opened her mouth to speak.

"And stop with the manic monkey references. The comparison isn't flattering."

Dropping her hands, she ignored the "more than a friend" comment and picked up her caramel bliss. "I'm not sure I can. What you did to Mr. Fenwick was so nasty I'm still simmering. Now I find out you've signed me up for classes in self-defense. It's demeaning—it's—why are you bossing me around?"

"I'm worried about you."

She slouched in her seat—too bad if it looked like a full-body pout. "What is everybody's problem?"

"Who, exactly, is everybody?"

"Mostly you and Vivian, but Randall and Pops have cautioned me about investigating this murder, as has Joe."

A muscle in his jaw clenched. "You are *not* investigating this murder."

"Not the way I did the professor's, but Gary did assign me to the case. Why can't people understand that?"

"They do understand, but they do not want to see you end up like Gary."

"Even so, I don't appreciate being treated like a kid who doesn't have enough sense to come in out of the rain. I have a brain, and it's filled with common sense. I try hard not to do stupid things, but every once in a while stupid wins, like it does with most people." She shrugged. "Even a hotshot officer of the law must know the feeling."

"The last time I did something stupid, I neglected to make a promised phone call. So, yes, I know how it feels."

Clasping her hand again, he circled her wrist with his thumb and forefinger. "I'd like for us to start over, but only if you want it, too."

She had no idea what she was supposed to say in response, so she stood. "I'm starving, and you promised me dinner, so let's get moving."

Ellie and Sam shared a comfortable meal at one of the Wickery's outdoor tables. Sam spent the time acting as the gracious host, something that took Ellie back to their one and only real date. The idea of starting up with him again was tempting, but something told her it would be smarter to go slow and make him work to get close to her. Besides, it was difficult thinking straight with this ordeal about Gary hanging over her head.

After an hour of pleasant conversation, she realized she had yet to let him in on her latest find and decided she might as well tell him. "I guess you should know what I did today, so you can't accuse me of keeping you in the dark."

His eyes narrowed. "What did you do?"

"I located the box that key is for—the one I found buried behind Gary's shelter."

"No kidding. Where?"

She filled him in, then said, "I wanted to go through the papers tonight, but it's late."

"I'd like to be there when you do. How about in the morning?" He grinned. "I'll bring breakfast."

At least he hadn't assumed he'd be sleeping over. "That would be fine, but what about your job?"

"I closed a couple of cases, so I have some downtime coming, like tonight. I'm not on call again until Sunday."

"And you're buying breakfast?"

"Damn straight, I am."

"Can I have anything I want?"

"Within reason, sure."

"How about a plain bagel, toasted, with lox, cream cheese, capers, and tomato? I'll have the coffee on. Say, nine o'clock?"

"That's good for me."

He signaled the waiter for the check, and she noticed the evening temperature had drifted to cool. When she realized the light was fading, she checked her watch and gasped. Thanks to Sam, she'd completely forgotten about Viv—and Rudy. Not that her friend would care, because Viv often made spur-of-the-moment dates with guys and left her hanging. They had an unwritten rule: accept a better offer if it came from a promising man. A good friend always forgave the slight.

But her fuzzy buddy would not be so kind, especially since he'd missed dinner.

"I have to call Viv," she told him, pulling out her cell. "I'm late for our walk." He signed the credit card slip while she made the connection. "Viv? I'm sorry, something came up—"

"Not a problem," Viv whispered. "I'm entertaining."

"Yeah, sometimes you're a real laugh riot, but that's not why I'm calling."

"I have company," she continued quietly.

"Male company?"

"Uh-huh."

"Can I guess?"

Viv's sigh echoed over the line. "One guess only. Then I'm hanging up."

"Hold on. I'm pulling out my crystal ball." Ellie waited a second before saying, "I see a big bird ... an eagle ... no, a heron ... no, wait ... a crane. Is it ... can it be Dr. David Crane, vet to the pampered pets of the Upper East Side?"

"We'll talk tomorrow, smarty pants. That's all I can say for now."

Smiling, Ellie snapped her phone closed.

Sam stood and pulled out her chair. "I take it Viv found a way to keep busy without you?"

"I'll say. I just hope it works out."

"She blew you off for a guy," he said sagely. "Happens all the time."

She followed him onto the sidewalk. "Viv and I have an understanding. Besides, I approve of the guy."

"You know who it is?"

"I know him fairly well." He took her arm as they crossed Lexington. "It's Rudy's vet."

"That dog doctor? The one who took care of Buddy?"

"Dr. David Crane. He's a very nice man."

Sam snorted.

"What's so funny?"

"I can't see him with a woman like Vivian."

They turned onto her street and headed for her apartment. "What do you mean 'a woman like Vivian'? You've only met her what ... twice? I doubt the two of you ever had more than a passing conversation."

"Doesn't matter. I know her type."

"Viv is not a 'type.' She's a good friend."

"Right. That's why she accepted a date with the vet instead of waiting for you."

"You don't know what you're talking about. If we'd planned something important, she'd have told him no, but it was just an evening walk. She knows I don't mind going alone."

"Which you won't be doing anymore." He followed

her into the lobby of her apartment. When she didn't comment on his dictum, he said, "Ellie, did you hear me?"

"I heard, but it doesn't mean I'm going to listen." She pounded up the steps. "Let me get Rudy, and we'll take off. He's probably crossing his hind legs and cursing me out—in doggie speak, of course."

She opened the apartment door and found her pal waiting with his leash in his mouth.

"Where have you been? I'm dyin' here." He glanced around her legs. *"Hey, you promised. No more Detective Doofus."*

"I promised no such thing," she said, adding, "I hope you've been a good dog," for Sam.

"Just promise me you'll never go to Carl Schurz alone again," Sam said. "Because it's not up for discussion."

Ellie refused to agree, so she hooked Rudy to his lead while Sam waited in the hall. Then she locked up and headed to street level. With her luck, her fuzzy pal would probably try to engage her in conversation, which would be next to impossible with the detective at her side.

Instead, Rudy stayed quiet while Sam fell into step beside her. "Why are you in such a hurry?"

"Because it's late and I'm tired, and my guy has to pee and then some. I said you could walk me to the park, so keep up. I need my beauty sleep."

"You fishing for compliments?"

"You always look good to me, Triple E."

"I never fish." She reached down and patted Rudy's head. "Do I, big guy?"

"Because you don't need to," Sam said.

"My bullshit detector is gonna pop a blood vessel," Rudy announced. *"You do realize he's only looking for a place to park his testosterone?"*

She tried for a faster pace, but Rudy lifted his leg a half dozen times as they walked, just because, she suspected, he wanted to annoy the detective.

"He's got a bladder the size of a cashew," muttered Sam on the ninth or tenth leg lift.

"Rudy's a small dog—"

"With a big temper, Bozo."

"But he's still my protector. I doubt he'd let anyone near me he didn't trust."

"He can't stop a bullet, Ellie. What more do I have to say to make you understand that?"

"I think you've said too much already." Rudy jerked her to a stop and squatted. "Okay, big business underway. Good boy." When he finished, she snapped open a plastic bag, collected the waste, and deposited it in the nearest trash receptacle. "We can go home now. I've decided it's too late to hike to Carl Schurz."

"Hey, that's not what I ordered."

"I said, 'It's too late to go to Carl Schurz,'" she repeated for the Yorkiepoo's benefit. "I'm ready to go home."

"I heard you the first time." Sam took her hand, and her skin tingled. "And it's the best idea you've had all night."

They walked together, but her canine pal lagged behind until they reached her building. Sam escorted her up the porch steps, took her key and unlocked the main door, then followed her to the apartment. After he opened her door, she shooed Rudy inside to shut out what she was sure would intrusive doggie comments.

"So, you're set for the night? No going to the park, or anywhere else, correct?" Sam propped his palms on the wall, caging her between his arms. "Say yes, because I don't have the energy to worry about you for the next ten hours."

Ellie rolled her eyes. "Yes, I'm done for the evening. I won't even look at the stuff I found in the box until you show up with breakfast. Is that what you want to hear?"

"For now."

He leaned toward her, and his breath feathered her curls, warmed her cheeks, invaded her senses. When his lips brushed hers, she thought she might melt. Then he wrapped an arm around her waist and pulled her tight to his chest, deepening the kiss.

Drawing away, he gazed into her eyes. "Get a good night's sleep. You need to be on your toes for your first self-defense lesson."

"I'm not taking—"

His mouth plundered again, moving over hers until she forgot what she wanted to say. Easing back, he wore a cocky grin. "I'll see you at nine. We'll talk about it then."

Chapter 15

Ellie woke at seven, took a shower, and opened her closet to inspect the clothes inside, most of which were folded on a wall of shelves across from a sparsely filled rod. She had a ton of jeans, shorts, tees, and sweaters, but few items that needed to be kept on hangers.

She had no idea how women dressed for breakfast with an ex-lover, a self-defense class, and a night on the town all in the same day and still kept their sanity. She'd hated staying current with fashion trends and designer togs when the D had nagged her to do so. She'd gotten rid of the high-end outfits he expected her to wear and dressed like a normal woman as soon as she'd tossed him out on his cheating ass. Since free of his dictates, she only wore comfortable clothes that felt good on her amply curved body, and she intended to keep it that way.

She didn't want to impress Sam, but she did want to look presentable, so she opted for a pair of tobacco-colored linen walking shorts, a cream tank top, and a gauzy burgundy shirt. She owned worn sweats and plenty of sneakers, which should suffice for the self-defense class. Unfortunately, nothing seemed right for an evening of dinner and the theater with Kevin Mc-Gowan, who, she suspected, knew the difference between a designer original and "off the rack" as well as Georgette did.

Returning to the bathroom, she blew her hair dry and let the glossy mop fall in disarray. She considered her shining cap of corkscrew curls her greatest asset, and thanks to Fredo, her all-knowing hair stylist, it was always in shape. If she'd thought ahead, she would have scheduled a trim, but Saturday was his busiest day. It would be impossible to fit in an appointment and do all the other errands on her list.

In the kitchen, she started a full pot of coffee, slid sandals on her feet, and called out, "Hey, lazy bones, time for your morning constitutional."

When Rudy didn't show his furry face, she went to look for him. He always started the night asleep on the pillow next to her and usually ended up there, but some mornings he found his way to a living room chair. There, he could stare out the window and keep tabs on whatever happened in the private fenced-in patio area on the ground floor.

The empty chair told her he might still be in bed or he was hiding, probably because he was ticked at her for allowing Sam to tag along on their walk last night. After she'd informed him the detective was bringing breakfast the next morning and then refused to read the stuff from Gary's storage box, he'd trotted into her bedroom with his snout held high, settled on his pillow, and ignored her.

Now in her bedroom, she scanned the area. "I know you're in here, so show yourself, tough guy."

Tsking at the silence, she opened her closet, in case she'd accidentally shut him inside. When that failed to produce him, she got down on her hands and knees, checked under the bed, and spotted him licking his privates at warp speed.

"Great. Just what I want to see before breakfast," she moaned. "Stop that and come out this instant."

Instead of glancing her way, Rudy picked up the pace, slurping so fast she thought he might choke.

Though the Yorkiepoo was her best nonhuman friend and she trusted him with her life, she'd realized from the beginning of their relationship that he would run rough-shod over her if she didn't assert herself. She accepted his laughable lawyer jokes, his off the wall thinking, and his savvy observations on the human condition, but in the end he was still a dog. He had to pay a penalty for outright disobedience, even though she felt lousy when she threatened punishment. She hated not feeding him almost as much as Rudy hated missing a meal.

"If you don't get out from under there right now, you can forget your morning nibble. You know the routine for acting like a baby."

He stopped midlick and glared at her.

"I didn't invite Sam for breakfast. He invited himself, and I said yes. It can't hurt to get his opinion on the stuff we found in Gary's box, and he's bringing food. I'll see to it you get a bite of bagel with a schmeer, but only if you behave."

"How about a little lox on the side?"

"If you promise to be nice."

"I won't bite him, if that's what you mean by nice."

She backed up and raised the dust ruffle. "No biting and no wisecracks. I can't think when you're in my head, spouting snide remarks."

"I can't help it." He crawled out and shook himself, then stretched onto his front paws and arched his back. *"The guy's a jerk. He hurt you. I'd never do that."*

They walked to the kitchen side by side. "I know you wouldn't. You're loyal and true, as are all canines devoted to their humans. Trouble is, Sam and I are— were—in what I thought was the start of a relationship. I get the impression he knows he was wrong when he didn't call, and now he's trying to atone. I have to think about how to handle that."

"If you forgive him, he'll want more of the same. What happens if—when he drops you again?"

"I'm not sure how I'll react, but I can tell you this. If I decide to see him on a personal level, and he repeats the transgression, he won't get a third chance."

"Humans are dopes. They never appreciate what they have until they lose it."

She couldn't fault his logic, so she grabbed his leash and clipped it to his collar. "It looks nice outside, not so steamy. Let's go around the block. Sam should be here by then, and we can enjoy a good breakfast."

Ellie turned the final corner toward home, noting the short walk had been uneventful for a Saturday morning. Because few people were trekking the pavement, the man beside her seemed to appear out of nowhere, causing her to inhale a breath.

"Hello again. Do you live around here?"

Growling, Rudy pulled her forward, and she took the hint, continuing on without acknowledging the comment. They would reach her front stoop in less than a minute if they kept going at this pace.

"I recognized you by your dog."

Her dog? She slowed her steps. The voice did sound vaguely familiar, and definitely friendly.

"Keep on truckin', Triple E," Rudy instructed. *"I got a bad feeling about this dude."*

Tugging on the leash to hold him at bay, Ellie turned to appraise the speaker.

"Remember me? We met in Carl Schurz about a week ago. You were with a friend, a lovely brunette, and her Jack Russell."

She sighed. It was the nice guy she and Viv had talked to on one of their visits to the park, the guy who liked dogs. "Sorry, I didn't recognize you. And I do remember the conversation. What are you doing so far from home, Mr. . . . ?"

"No mister. Just Benedict," he supplied, still smiling. "And you're Ellie, right?"

"You have a good memory."

"I may be old, but I don't forget meeting pretty young women. As for your question, it's a nice morning so I decided to take a stroll. Exercise is good for a weak ticker."

Rudy pulled on the lead. *"Stop talking and make tracks, Triple E. The doofus dick is coming, remember?"*

"I hope it's nothing serious."

He shrugged. "Time takes its toll, you know?" He scanned the sidewalk. "Coming back from the park, are you?"

"Not that far. We just took a quickie because we're having company for breakfast." Rudy sniffed the man's sneakers while he continued to growl, and Ellie realized the only way to calm him was to get rid of Benedict and return to their apartment. "Since he's done with business and we're almost home, I have to get moving. It was nice talking to you."

"Same here," he said. "Maybe I'll see you around."

His stride hesitant, he walked past her building, then hung a right and rounded the corner, and she heaved another sigh. Benedict was a nice guy who liked dogs, that was all. Unfortunately, even after this mess with Gary's murder was over, she doubted she'd ever be able to relax in the company of a solitary older man. And what was up with Rudy?

"Did you have to be so disagreeable?" she asked, heading toward their apartment. "The guy just wanted to talk."

"Don't you think it's strange, him finding you at this hour of the morning, in the middle of the millions of people in this city? I mean, what are the chances?"

"Very slim, I guess, but Milton found me, which made Sam crazy I might add."

"See, I'm not the only one watching out for you."

"So now you're on Ryder's side? Make up your mind." She jogged up the steps and into the building's foyer. "Benedict is no threat."

"I don't agree. There's something about him—"

"There's something about *you*. You find fault with every man who speaks to me. Old, young, tall, short, cop, lawyer, retired, it doesn't matter. This has got to stop."

"I'll stop as soon as you get wise."

"Wise? Are you saying I have to be on guard against all persons of the male persuasion?" They entered the lobby and climbed the stairs. "How about my doctor, my dentist, or Randall? I know you don't care for Sam, but he'd never hurt me . . . at least, not physically."

"Okay, so the dippy dick wouldn't shoot you or knock you around. Neither would Dr. Dave or Stanley or the doorman. If you'd let me have another sniff of that McGowan guy, I'd give you the skinny on him, too, raging pheromones or not."

"Why do you think all men are creeps looking to take advantage of a single woman? I know there aren't any bad guys in your history—unless you count that crazed taxi driver who mowed you down eleven years ago."

"Let's just say I can smell a psycho a mile away, and leave it at that."

"Fine, but unless your radar jumps off the screen and bites you in the butt, keep your thoughts to yourself. I'll tell you the same thing I've been telling Sam and Viv— I'm perfectly capable of taking care of myself."

"You don't get it, do you? It's my job to watch out for you. It's one of the reasons I was sent back."

"What?"

"You heard me. And before you start the grilling, no, I don't know it for sure. I just have a gut feeling. Call it canine instinct or whatever."

Unlocking her apartment door, Ellie gave up arguing. The idea that Karma had reunited them so Rudy could be her guardian angel was a shock akin to the first time she'd heard him speak in her head. Either way, she refused to think about it. She'd had enough surprises over the past week to last a lifetime.

"How about we talk this over later—or better yet, never. My brain hurts. Sam will be here soon, and I have to get the kitchen ready."

She unsnapped Rudy's lead, and he strutted to the kitchen with his tail and muzzle high. Great. He was angry with her.

"How about if I promise to be more alert . . . more vigilant, whatever you want to call it, from now on?" She dropped to a squat and scratched his ears. "If you get a really bad vibe, I promise to remove myself from the questionable person's presence as soon as it's politely possible."

"Is that the best you can do?" he grumped.

"Yes."

"Then I have to accept it . . . for now." Dancing in a circle, he changed the topic. *"Can't wait for the dope with the bagels, Triple E. I need my morning nibble, the sooner the better."*

Sam sat at Ellie's kitchen table sorting through the brittle newspapers she'd found in Gary's storage box. Stacking them in piles from oldest to most current, he placed them on the floor while Ellie took on the task of opening the yellowed packets of mail—even those dating back several years, on the off chance she'd uncover a clue related to the vagrant's murder.

They'd shared a friendly breakfast and worked in silence for the last thirty minutes. Thanks to fate, he had the day off, and he wasn't going to waste it. He'd thought about her last night and awakened with a decision. It was time to put their relationship back on the front burner.

Though Ellie didn't know it, he planned to buy her lunch, then accompany her to the gym and observe her first self-defense lesson. Phil knew his stuff, but Sam wanted to be certain she cooperated and took his pal's instructions to heart. Just imagining his bad penny, the queen of nonviolence, sparring with the bantam rooster ex-boxer made him smile. Unfortunately, he'd have to curtail his amusement or she'd probably read him the riot act and get on her high horse about everything on which they didn't agree.

He glanced over the top of the newspaper he'd been reading when she gasped. "What?"

"I found something." She held a crumpled envelope in one hand and an equally crumpled sheet of paper in the other. "From Thompson Veridot."

The sight of her pale face, coupled with the telling words, put him on alert. "You going to keep me in suspense, or tell me what it says?"

She licked her lips. "Shall I read it out loud?"

"It's an idea."

Clearing her throat, she began:

Gary,
Guess what, chickenshit. I've done my time, and I'll be out of the joint any day now. I know where you live, so don't try to hide. I'll find you, and if you don't have my money, well, let's just say you'll be seeing Mom and Dad a lot sooner than I will.
Your loving brother,   .
Thompson

Sam held out his hand, and Ellie shuddered as she passed him the page. "Now I understand why Gary wrote what he did in that note we found in the safety-deposit box. Gruning will have to pay attention to your theory after he reads this."

"Not necessarily," he warned after reading the letter. "A threat doesn't constitute guilt, though it might make Gruning move on that APB."

Ellie leaned forward in the chair. "But he's got to. Veridot is practically confessing to Gary's murder."

"Is there a legible postmark on that envelope?" he asked after reading the letter a second time.

"May something. The ink is smudged." She passed him the envelope. "Probably right about the time he was released from prison."

"I'll bring this to Gruning, but you have to understand, he'll have questions."

"Of course he will. He'll want to know more about Thompson Veridot."

"That's not what I mean. It's you he'll want to talk to."

She huffed out a breath. "Me?"

"Think about it. First, he'll ask how you got your hands on this letter. When you tell him where it came from, he'll ask how you knew about the box. After you explain that you found a key at the murder site, which you didn't bring to him, and took it upon yourself to locate whatever it opened, he'll explode, and charges of obstructing an ongoing investigation are sure to follow." He frowned at her indignant expression. "If I was the officer in charge, that's what I'd do. Remember, I told you not to snoop. Maybe next time you'll listen."

"You'd never do that to me . . . would you?"

He raised a brow. "I thought about it plenty of times during the Albright case."

"But you—we went out."

"After the case wrapped, not during, and I doubt Gruning has a single thought about getting to know you on a personal level, so the analogy won't fly."

"You're confusing things. Gruning insisted he didn't want my help. I took that to mean he didn't want to know about anything I found."

"What he meant was for you to keep your nose clean and let the police do their job."

Ellie thrust out her lower lip. "That's just your interpretation. You said yourself he's a terrible detective who always takes the easy way out. He should be happy I'm doing his legwork."

"He won't be happy with anything you do. And if he can find a way to screw your ass—er—you to the wall, he will."

"Well, great. Now what do we do?"

"Lie."

"Excuse me?"

"I'll rearrange the truth a little, tell him we went to the shelter together and I did the snooping and found the key. When I explained it was evidence, you let me keep it, even though it's yours by law. I was the one who decided to hunt up the storage place and find the box to save Gruning the time and effort. After you and I went over what was inside, I brought this letter to his attention like any good cop would do to help solve a case in progress."

"If he finds out you're lying, you could get in trouble." She placed a palm on the back of his hand. "I don't want you to do that for me."

"Yeah, well . . ." He tried to ignore the rush of feeling clogging his chest. Sometimes it paid to play the white knight. "If you keep the details to yourself, I'll be okay." He glanced at the clock over the sink. "It's close to noon. How about I take you to lunch, and then we go to the gym for your lesson?"

"Lunch?" Her cheeks turned pink. "Um, I can't."

"I know we just had breakfast, but . . . why not?"

Avoiding his gaze, she fiddled with a napkin. "I have to go shopping."

He swallowed his surprise. "You're blowing off a self-defense lesson to shop?"

"I'm going to the lesson, but I have to find a dress first." She carried their coffee cups to the sink and turned, resting her backside against the counter. "And before you ask, it's because of a previous engagement."

"A date?" When she bit her lower lip, he had his answer. "Never mind. I don't want to know."

"It's just dinner and the theater." Her face flamed red. "It's not a big deal."

"Let me guess. You're going out with that lawyer."

"Yes, but—"

"Hey, it's none of my business." He stuffed Thompson Veridot's letter in the envelope and stood. The sobering news was a great reward for his knightly services. "There's no need to show me to the door. I know the way."

"It's not what you think." Ellie stepped toward him, but he continued walking. When she touched his shoulder as he opened the front door, he turned. "Look, you can date whoever you want. Just promise me you won't skip that lesson at Phil's."

"I wasn't going to, honest."

His cell rang, and he pulled the phone from his belt. "Ryder."

"Hey, buddy," said his partner, Vince. "Sorry to call on your day off, but there's been a gang altercation. I was told to bring you in and report to the site. They expect every available body to show."

"Where?"

Vince rattled off the location, and Sam committed it to memory. "Got it. I'll be there ASAP."

"Did something bad happen?" asked Ellie.

"Sounds like. So things wouldn't have worked out anyway." I was stupid for thinking they could. "I'll take care of the letter and let you know what Gruning says." Heading out the door, he added, "See you around."

Chapter 16

After cabbing to Gramercy Park, Ellie opened the door next to a Greek restaurant and read the list of tenants posted on the wall above the mailboxes. According to the signs, the second floor was home to a CPA office, a security firm, and a nail salon, while the third floor hosted a one-word business: GYMNASIUM. After she climbed two flights of worn stairs that dead-ended on a small landing with a gray-painted metal door, she gave serious thought to going home. With no information on hours or the services available, she wondered if she even had the right place.

The D had insisted she belong to a health club. The one she used to visit regularly had a light and airy ground floor waiting room filled with the pleasant scent of flowers and aromatherapy candles. After signing in, clients walked to an immaculate dressing room, stored their street clothes in a roomy personal locker, and changed into workout gear. On the way to the actual gym area, customers passed a sauna, massage rooms, and a spa boasting facials, waxing, electrolysis, manicures, pedicures, and an array of other beauty treatments.

Judging by the sad condition of this particular entryway, if this was the correct business, she had zero chance of receiving the same intimate attention.

Juggling her tote bag and the hanger holding her new beaded navy blue sheath, she knocked. She'd spent so long shopping, she hadn't been able to drop the dress at home and still be on time for her class. After knocking a second time, she took a deep breath, opened the door, and peered inside.

In seconds, she was overcome by the intense odor of perspiration commingling with the smell of alcohol, some type of muscle balm, and the aroma of Greek cuisine. Inching her head through the doorway, she called a brave "Hello?"

A couple of men hitting an enormous leather bag gazed at her in silence, as did a jumbo-sized guy lifting free weights, and a slimmer slugger smacking a hanging bag. Each man was shirtless, showing a sweaty, well-muscled, and hairless chest, and each wore baggy shorts that flopped around their meaty legs like flags fluttering in a breeze.

"Is this Phil's gym?" she continued.

"Who wants to know?" asked the taller of the two men at the punching bag.

"May I come in? I have an appointment."

"Hey, Phil," he shouted. "Your three o'clock's here." He nodded his shaved head, indicating she should enter.

Ellie pretended not to notice the men's smug smiles and stepped into the room, jumping when the door slammed behind her. Waving a hand in front of her face to help defuse the odors, she sensed that thanks to her ensemble—pale pink sweatpants, a matching T-shirt, and sneakers touted as aerobically designed—she was laughably overdressed for this setting.

The four men went back to their exercises, and a figure approached from a door at the back of the room. Weaving between a few more hanging bags, a couple of stands holding free weights, and a bench press, the man strutted toward her like the person in charge.

As he neared, Ellie realized he was short, about five five in his black lace-up shoes, with arms like tree trunks and a chest as broad as a door. He held out his hand and his battered face, with a scar slicing his left eyebrow, a once-broken nose, and a pugnacious jaw, appeared almost presentable.

"Ms. Engleman?" He clasped her outstretched hand and gave it a punishing shake. Taking her in from head to toe, he continued to grin. Then he caught sight of her new dress. "I hope you're not planning to wear that for your lesson."

Despite her apprehension, she smiled at his teasing tone. Though she had to look down to meet his questioning gaze, it was obvious he was a take-charge man who enjoyed a good laugh. "No, but I do need to store it somewhere safe."

"No worries there. I doubt it would fit any of the boys. Follow me and I'll show you around."

They went through the door from which he'd entered, winding past equipment and punching bags, and walked through an archway into a larger room holding something Ellie knew existed but had never seen in person. "Is that a boxing ring?"

She regretted the words the moment they left her lips. Two men wearing padded helmets and baggy shorts were behind the ropes dancing and jabbing at each other, while a half dozen guys stood on the far side shouting encouragement. It couldn't be anything but a boxing ring, with real boxers pummeling flesh in place of leather bags.

He stopped and turned. "Yeah. Why?"

"Nothing, it's just that I—" Didn't expect to be given a tour of a torture chamber. "I thought this was a—a—"

"Health club?" The words shot from his mouth like a curse. "With a fitness room, fruity male trainers, and women who spend more time lookin' in a mirror than working out?"

"Yes—no!"

"That's okay. I'm not insulted. This is a professional gymnasium. We have some world-class hopefuls here, world-class trainers, too. Kid Shaneil came from that ring," he said, as if expecting her to know the name.

"Oh. How nice for you."

He grinned. "The Kid won a silver at the Olympics in China. He'll be in London in 2012, and this time, God willing, the medal will be gold."

"That's great." He was so proud of the accomplishment, Ellie didn't have the heart to admit that all she ever watched of the Olympics were gymnastics and the swimming and diving events. "When Sam said the lessons were at a gym, I just assumed . . ."

He folded his tree-trunk arms and the muscles bunched to mammoth proportions. "Ryder's a good guy. A little anal when it comes to his job, but still—" He blinked. "I thought he'd be with you."

"He planned to, until he got called out on a—a situation."

"Figures." Phil nodded, indicating she should proceed ahead of him through a door on the right.

This room, the largest of the three, was ringed with more weight training stations. The center of the floor was covered by a red padded mat about twenty feet square.

"You can hang the dress through there and to the left. It's the dressing room my female members use. Got a fancy shower, lockers, even a couple of razors and a bowl of smelly soaps, just like one of them froufrou spas. My wife tells me I gotta provide a little class for my ladies, so I comply."

Heartened by the fact that, eventually, she'd meet more feminine clientele, she entered a tidy area smelling of lavender. With a spotless tile floor and combination lockers lining the walls, it was clear the room was well tended.

Hanging her purchase in a vacant locker, she set her

tote bag inside and spun the combination dial. She'd trawled two designer showrooms and a half dozen high-priced boutiques searching for sales, and found the sheath on a fifty percent markdown rack for six hundred dollars. She wasn't about to lose it now.

Then she peeked into an adjacent room and took stock of the yellow-tiled bathroom. The spacious counter held double sinks under a mirrored wall and crystal clear bowls of disposable razors, cotton balls, and the aforementioned soaps. There was even a blow-dryer propped in a stand between the sinks. Checking out a smaller room exposed two sparkling commodes with locking doors, a large glassed-in shower stall, and a stack of fluffy yellow towels piled neatly on a white wicker table.

Feeling marginally better about the place, Ellie fought the urge to inspect the men's locker room and returned to the gym. She was brave, not crazy.

"So, you ready?" asked Phil, standing in the center of the huge mat.

She walked to meet him. "I have questions."

He placed his hands on his hips and grinned. "Ryder assured me you would."

She could only imagine what the dastardly detective had said about her. "Sam told me I was enrolled in classes, but he didn't say they were private."

"Just the first one. I try to get to know each of my ladies, learn what they're made of, that kind of thing. Hardly any show up on a Saturday, but you'll meet 'em during the week."

Digesting the info, she asked, "Am I dressed correctly or should I be wearing something more . . . casual?"

He again eyed her from head to toe. "You're a little overdressed. The AC's cranked to high, but thanks to the sweaty bodies and heaving breaths, it still gets warm in here." He raised the scarred eyebrow. "You might want to wear a pair of loose-fitting shorts instead of those fancy pants for your next lesson. I love lookin' at a tall, leggy woman."

Wondering about those sweaty bodies, she almost raised an eyebrow of her own, but changed her mind after his sexist remark. "Do I have my own locker?"

"If you find an empty, it's yours. Just give me the number and I'll give you the combination." He tapped his temple with a finger. "I got every key right up here."

She decided to ask a question she'd almost posed to Sam but hadn't because it would have caused a fight. "I'd like to pay for the classes. Is it possible you could refund Detective Ryder his money?"

He gave another cocky grin. "Ryder told me you'd ask. He also said I'd be dead meat if I did."

"Oh ... well." Darn Sam and his macho sense of honor.

"Don't worry about the detective. He still hasn't gotten in tune with women of the twenty-first century." He crossed his arms. "We'll begin with the usual. You ready?"

"I—I guess so."

"Okay. First thing you need to know is women have weapons, but most are either unaware of what's at their disposal, are afraid to use them, or don't know how. Which is it with you?"

Ellie shrugged. "Maybe a little of all three. I don't believe in violence."

"Oh, boy." Phil's mouth flattened, and he heaved a sigh. "Answer me this. If you were attacked, what would you do?"

"Uh, run?"

"The attacker surprises you from behind and grabs you around the waist."

"Scream?"

"He holds a knife to your throat."

"I can't imagine—"

"Read the papers, Ms. Engleman." His expression

turned to granite. "It happens all the time, especially in this city."

She did read the papers, but she skipped over those depressing stories. They made her sick to her stomach; they made her want to cry.

"I usually never walk alone. I have a dog."

"German shepherd? Doberman? Rotty?"

"A Yorkiepoo." When another idiot grin split his craggy face, she pressed on. "I know he sounds like a fluff ball, but he can be vicious if he's pushed."

"Ellie? May I call you Ellie?"

She nodded.

"Ellie, please. You're killin' me here. How about we get on with the lesson, and you'll see what I mean. First off, do you carry keys?"

"Sure, for my apartment."

He fished a key ring from the pocket of his baggy shorts and handed it to her. "Take these and show me what you'd do with them if you were attacked."

"I read somewhere you're supposed to make a fist and let the longest one stick out between your fingers."

"Okay, so do it."

She did.

"Good. Now come at me as if you're gonna stab me."

"Oh, I couldn't—"

"Sure you could." He stepped toward her and clasped her shoulder, squeezing tight.

She pushed against his forearm with her opposite hand.

"Nuh-uh. Use those keys, babe. Aim for the fleshy part of my arm."

Since his arm appeared to be a log of solid muscle, she wasn't sure where he wanted her to jab. She raised the hand holding the keys, and he slapped it away.

"Do it like you mean it."

She tried again, the movement faster.

He caught her wrist. "Better. One more time."

She shot her arm upward and almost hit her target before he grabbed her wrist. "Okay, that's better. We'll work on it. Let's move on." He held out his palm, and she dropped the keys. "Next step. Turn around."

Ellie swallowed, but did as he asked.

He slammed against her and wrapped his forearm across her throat. She screamed, but he cut her off with a choke hold.

Then he whispered, "Think, Ellie. Figure it out."

Almost by instinct, she raised her foot and brought it down on his arch.

"Harder."

"I don't want to hurt you."

He pulled tighter against her throat. "Sure you do. Because if you don't, I'm gonna hurt you."

She jammed an arm backward, and her elbow slammed into his ribs. He huffed out a breath, but didn't let go.

"A surprise attack. Nice move. But it wasn't enough. Try it again, but imagine you're fighting for your life."

Ellie slumped forward. It was going to be a long afternoon.

Kevin McGowan's handsome face stared down at her, the single bulb in her building entryway highlighting his elegantly arched brows and liquid gray eyes. "I had a good time. How about you?"

Ellie winced as she rotated her aching shoulder. Besides that, she was pretty sure she had a bruise on her upper thigh. Since Phil didn't believe in coddling his clients, she'd arrived home at five with nothing on her mind but a long soak in a hot tub. Instead, she'd taken a quick shower and started the tedious requirements for wowing her evening escort.

She hadn't gone to this much trouble for a guy since her date with Sam, and that had turned to crap. Yet she'd again spent an hour primping and using the standard bells and whistles needed to look her best for a night on the town.

"Think you might like to do it again?" he continued.

Her stomach gave a flip. The meal had been divine, the play entertaining, the night a success. And her attentive date was still trying to impress, lingering while he held her hands, letting her know he enjoyed her company and was amenable to more.

"I'd like that." She smiled. "Very much."

He inched forward. "Is it too soon to ask if I can come up to your place?"

"I don't believe in a timetable—"

"None of that 'can't go to bed until the third date' business for you, I hope?"

"I don't live my life, at least not my personal one, on a schedule. Business, yes, but that's understandable, considering what I do. My customers depend on me."

"Just like mine depend on me," he echoed. "We have a lot in common, in case you haven't already noticed."

As far as Ellie could tell, they had nothing in common. Most of the topics they discussed revolved around her job and the antics of her canine charges. Whenever she questioned him about his law practice, he changed the subject. She found that strange, because even the judge liked to gossip about his cases, though he never mentioned anyone by name and they were all in the past. Perhaps Kevin was simply too honorable to do anything he felt might break client confidentiality, but a few nameless incidents would have piqued her interest.

On the plus side, it was also nice that he thought she performed a valuable service, unlike some men she knew, and enjoyed talking about dogs.

"I have a feeling our conversation will extend to more private things eventually," he went on. "Either at your place or mine."

"It's just that I've had a long day." A day that felt more like punishment than a lesson in self-defense. "I need rest or I won't be able to move tomorrow."

"Are you inferring you won't get a good night's sleep if I'm involved?" Before she answered, he added, "If I came up, we could test that theory."

Not ready to be a *test* case, she shrugged. "I'm really beat, Kevin. Tonight's not possible."

He smiled again. "All right. How about if I call you sometime this week and we set up another meeting?"

"Fine." She heaved a sigh of relief. "I really have to go in. My dog is waiting for his last walk of the day."

"I'm willing to come along, if you want company."

She gazed over his shoulder through the glass entry door at his taxi, double-parked in front of the building. "Your ride is probably growing impatient."

He cocked his head in a "Who cares?" attitude. "So let him. Better yet, I'll set him free."

Ellie touched his shoulder. "No, it's okay. Go home. I'll be fine."

"You're sure?"

"Positive."

Leaning into her, he cupped her face and bent his head, grazing her lips with his own. Then he deepened the kiss, prodding with his tongue, searching the moist interior of her mouth when she opened to let him in. His arms slid to her waist and pulled her closer, then snaked around her back and pressed her spine.

The kiss stole her breath and heated her insides. Gasping for air, she rested her forehead on his jacket lapel. After a shuddering breath, she peered at him through her lashes, pleased to see the befuddled expression on his face.

"I—I'd better go inside. My dog—"

"Is waiting. Lucky dog," he said, running a finger down her cheek. "I'll call you."

Ellie climbed the stairs, still amazed by the evening.

When she opened her door, she almost stumbled over Rudy, sitting with his leash in his mouth.

"It's about time."

"I told you I'd be late." She strode down the hall and into the bedroom, unzipping the dress as she walked. After toeing off her sling backs, she skimmed the sheath down her hips, arranged it on a padded hanger, and inspected it for flaws. A few wrinkles creased the midsection, but there were no food stains or tears, a major miracle considering her klutz quotient.

The dress fit her like a second skin, with a scooped neck that showed off her boobs, well-placed darts that sculpted her waist, and a short skirt that complemented her toned legs. The look in Kevin's eyes when he'd first seen her told her he approved. Maybe the dress was worth the money she'd spent.

"You daydreaming, or are we going for my nightly constitutional?"

"As soon as I change."

"I suppose a trip to the dog run at Carl Schurz is out of the question?"

She tugged on the sweats and tee she'd worn earlier and carried socks and sneakers to the kitchen. "For tonight, yes. But I plan to get a good rest, so we'll go tomorrow. Promise."

"With Viv and Mr. T?"

"If they're up for it, sure."

She stuck her keys in her pocket, snapped the leash to his collar, and led him into the hall and down the stairs. Turning left, they were a distance from the building when she remembered she didn't have her tote, which meant she didn't have her Mace or her cleanup bags.

"I hope you don't have big business in mind," she told him. "I forgot the doggie bags."

He lifted his leg on a street sign stanchion. *"Just a couple of quickies and I'll be done."*

They walked in silence around the block, and she

did her best to ignore anyone who looked ready to give Rudy a pat or start a conversation, especially if it was an older man. By the time they arrived back home she was annoyed at the way Gary's murder had taken control of her life. She was a friendly person; she enjoyed talking about dogs, and she liked meeting new people. If she continued to be a fraidy cat, she'd never expand her business or her personal life.

To hell with Sam and his keep-to-yourself attitude. She was a big girl who could take care of herself.

Chapter 17

The next day, just before noon, Ellie grabbed detergent and stain remover from a shelf in her kitchen pantry and dropped the bottles in her wheeled hamper. "Sure you don't want to take a trip to the dungeon?" she asked Rudy. "You never know what might be lurking down there, just waiting to jump my bones. It could be your chance to shine."

The Yorkiepoo gave a huge and obviously bored yawn. *"The laundry room stinks, like something died behind the dryers. One of these days I'm gonna find out what smells, but not today."*

"Oh, I see. You're worried about me, but not enough to stop me from making the trip to the basement alone. Fat lot you care about my safety."

He walked in a circle, curled into a ball on the cream-colored tile, and settled down for a nap. *"Of course, I care. And you'll be sorry when I'm proven right."*

"Don't you mean 'if' you're proven right?" When he didn't answer, she opened a kitchen drawer and pulled out a roll of quarters stored there for feeding the washers and dryers. "I'll be back in twenty minutes. Think you can stay out of trouble that long?"

Resting his head on his paws, he closed his eyes. *"It's*

nap time. Try to keep the racket to a minimum when you get back."

Ellie stuck the change in her pocket, headed into the hall, and, dragging the clothes hamper behind her, reached the far end of the corridor. Thanks to the unwieldy carrier, she had to take the building's decrepit beast of an elevator to get to the basement. Depending on the outside humidity and the exploits of its last passengers, the confining space smelled alternately of three-day-old body odor, stale knockoff perfume, or recycled beer. She liked her condo too much to move, and this conveyance was the only thing about the building she despised.

Once she entered the elevator and pressed the correct button, the beast creaked and clanked its way to the bottom floor, then shuddered to a stop. Seconds passed while she waited for the contrary contraption to open its door. Finally, after she decided that next time she'd be better off wrestling the full hamper down three flights of stairs, the door slid wide with a harsh grating sound.

She stepped into the dim hall, noting the pale trickle of light emanating from a single dirt-encrusted casement window. Groping the wall, she flipped the switch, which allowed a bit more brightness from a naked bulb hanging overhead. Note to self: Call the maintenance company hired by the tenant's association and inform them this is a piss-poor way to keep the complex safe.

Opening the metal door marked LAUNDRY, she looked inside, surprised to find it empty. On weekends, the area was usually crowded with tenants lined up to use the half dozen washers, three dryers, and row of folding tables separating the machines. Then again, it was July, and many of the residents migrated to the Hamptons or Jersey Shore for a long weekend or a couple weeks' vacation.

After sorting her clothes, she used spray stain remover to take care of the damage she'd done to her casual clothing and T-shirts. Spritzing dabs of mustard, smears of chocolate, smudges of grease, and a variety of questionable marks that could be dog poop, piddle, or both, she sighed. No doubt about it, she was a danger to whatever she wore.

Sometimes she thought that along with walking dogs, she should offer herself to one of the major detergent manufacturers as an expert stain maker. If their product got her clothes clean, it would work on anything. But there weren't companies like that in the city, so the best she could do was carry a packet of personal wipes and a pen guaranteed to take out the most unsightly marks. Problem was, neither ever worked as well as was touted on the instructions.

She also took this time to sort through her unmentionables for anything too shabby or embarrassing to wear. Her mother paid a fortune for her lingerie, mostly La Perla, in a size so small the bits of lace looked more like colorful tissues than serviceable underwear. Ellie, on the other hand, preferred plain cotton bikinis in varying pastels.

She'd donned her frilliest lingerie last night, a fancy set she'd last worn on her date with Sam. Slipping into the dainty black panties, matching demi cup underwire bra, and sheer thigh-high stockings had made her feel sexy and adventurous, even naughty, if she was honest.

She hadn't anticipated going to bed with Kevin, but she'd figured the Boy Scout motto, "Be prepared," might serve her well. Kevin oozed sex appeal, and though he didn't make her damp in all the right places, she wanted to be ready if he did. Sadly, it was Ryder's searching hands and smoldering gaze that got her juices flowing, damn it.

Resting her elbows on the washer, she let her mind wander. She hadn't been intimate with a man since her one-night stand with Sam, and that single evening had probably ruined her for another guy. Kevin had his work cut out for him if he expected her to melt in his arms like a quivering mass of Jell-O.

Pushing away from the machine, she commandeered three of the six washers, poured in detergent, fed quarters into the slots, and added her clothes. The machines started filling as she rested her bottom against a folding table and glanced around.

Spooky, she thought, gazing at the crumbling cinder block walls covered in what might be moss, mold, or possibly one-hundred-year-old vomit. As far as she was concerned, the entire area smelled like the inside of a Dumpster in August. She couldn't pinpoint which particular spot was bad, the way Rudy could, but a dog's nose was more sensitive than that of a human. Staring at the beams overhead, she took note of the cobwebs, hanging low with the weight of insect husks. The building was ancient, as were many in the city. There were other rooms down here. Rooms used for storage, but storage of what?

She'd read horror stories about people finding skeletons, mummified bodies, even hidden treasure in the walls or deserted hidey-holes of aged structures. Did this building have a sordid past? Could it have housed mobsters and murderers bent on destruction? Or maybe crazed psychos intent on dismembering relatives for their fortunes?

The door creaked inward, and Ellie put her hand on her heart, ready to scream. A moment later, a man walked in carrying a plastic laundry basket in his arms.

"Morning." His wrinkled cheeks were covered in a three-day growth of beard, and he wore a short-sleeved white T-shirt and baggy chinos. "Any of these free?"

"Uh, free?" She took in his head of brown hair streaked with gray. "I guess so."

The man dropped his basket on the table and met her gaze with hooded brown eyes. "I'll only be a minute."

Hoping to calm her pounding heart, she inhaled a

breath. She'd attended the last tenant association meeting and thought she'd met every person in the building, but she'd never seen this guy before. On the short side, with a paunch and a shuffle to his step, he fit Veridot's description all too well.

He picked through his clothes and hefted an armful, and that's when she saw the red-pointed tip of a tattoo on his right bicep. Sidling to the nearest washer, she watched his arm as he dropped the clothes, added soap, and slid quarters into the slot. Though the red tattoo was still covered and she knew it could be anything, the shape and color screamed heart.

Swallowing hard, she did her best not to run. "I'm Ellie. I live in 3-A," she told him, hoping he'd offer a clue to his identity.

He rested a hip on the washer. "I'm staying in 4-D, visiting my sister." He moved to the next machine. "Name's Thompson. Verne Thompson."

Thompson? Veri—er—Verne Thompson? Her stomach churned. "I'm not familiar with the tenants in that apartment. What did you say your sister's name was?"

He loaded a second machine, and when he added soap the shirtsleeve rode up an inch. "I didn't."

Uh-oh.

Yep, that was definitely a heart tattoo, with writing in the center, but she couldn't make out the word. Inching closer, she gave him another sidelong glance.

" 'Scuse me," he muttered, reaching to open the washer she now stood in front of.

"Oh, uh, sorry." She took a step of retreat, figuring she had two choices. She could stay here and strike up a more intimate conversation or she could run to her apartment like a coward and call Sam.

Before she decided her next move, he turned. "Do you know the tenant in 2-B? The gorgeous brunette? The name above her mailbox just says V. McCready. Is she Virginia? Valerie? Vanessa?"

"Why do you want to know?"

"She's a looker is all."

"Her name is Vivian."

"Thanks, I appreciate it."

Ellie gave herself a mental slap. Great. She'd just given a strange man her best friend's name. Before she could think of a way to erase her stupidity, Thompson cleared his throat.

"You the gal that walks dogs?"

Her insides quivered. "I am. Why, do you have one that needs to be taken care of?"

"Nope. But my sister and I got to talking and she told me a tall redhead living in the building was a dog walker, and you fit the description. Seems Adrianne wants a little dog, but she works all day and can't get home to take it out. She'll be happy to know I asked you about it."

"What's your sister's last name?" she asked.

Finished loading the washers, he said, "Think it's safe to leave the stuff here and go back to the apartment?"

"Um, sure. It's what I do." She ran a shaky hand through her curls. Either he hadn't heard the question, or he wasn't answering on purpose. "I don't remember anyone in the building named Thompson or Adrianne," she said, smiling.

"She's married to a guy named Burns, and they're subletting the place." He walked around the table and nodded a good-bye. "So long. Maybe I'll see you again some time."

Ellie waited until the door closed and the elevator clanged its ascent before she took a breath. Then she shoved her hamper under the table and charged out the door and up the stairs. She had to take another look at that picture the warden had sent. Then she'd call Sam—no—she'd call Viv and ask her what she knew about the residents of 4-D. After that, she'd pour a shot of something with a higher alcohol content than a Bud Light and down it in one long swallow.

Then maybe she'd *think* about phoning Sam.

*   *   *

Ellie spent the rest of Sunday afternoon deep in thought. She didn't call Sam or Gruning or any other male trying to control her life, but she did phone Viv and, after listening to her rave about the night she'd spent with Dr. Dave, told her about the man in the laundry room. Then she'd taken a long, hot bubble bath, dressed in comfy clothes, and walked Rudy to the PETCO, where she bought a bag of gourmet dog food and a package of his favorite chew bones.

Now seven p.m., she and Viv had just finished eating Chinese takeout in Viv's apartment, where they'd again dissected Ellie's meeting with the man named Thompson and gone over what Viv discovered when she'd done a bit of snooping. The couple in 4-D was Adrianne and Stefan Burns, and they'd only lived in the building for three months, renting the furnished condo from the owner. No one Viv talked to knew much about them, and no one realized the woman's brother was visiting.

Feeling only marginally relieved at the info, Ellie convinced Viv to hook a lead to Mr. T and join her and Rudy in the promised walk to Carl Schurz Park.

"Oops, I almost forgot to tell you. Blackman's called and left a message on my machine while I went to the pet store," she said, vowing to drop all conversation about the mystery man for the remainder of the evening. "Gary's ready for retrieval."

"And you plan to pick him up in what? A coffee can?"

"Uh, I didn't think that far ahead. I figured Blackman's would supply something."

"Hah, I doubt it. They'll expect you to buy a container—maybe an urn—before they let you leave with the ashes. The urns are decorative and usually come in brass, pewter, even sterling silver. And the ginger jar containers can be stark as sand or painted in charming scenes or flowers. Then again, a plain wooden box . . ."

Viv's advice on storing a body's remains brought Ellie's mind around to the wooden box sitting on the high-
est shelf in her guest room closet, a box that held *old*
Rudy's ashes. It had been on her fireplace mantel until
the day she brought *new* Rudy home from the ASPCA,
when she'd . . .

"Hey. Pay attention." Viv gave her a poke. "Especially
when I'm offering free advice on a final resting place for
a dearly departed friend."

"Ow! Okay, okay." Ellie rubbed her forearm. "I was
just thinking about the day I brought the first Rudy
home."

"That was over ten years ago, and Rudy the second is
alive and well, so can the morose thoughts. This is about
Gary and his estate, which you are supposed to be caring
for. You say he was your friend, yet you'd let him blow
in the wind until there's nothing left to remember him
by?"

"You think I should do something else?"

"Of course."

Ellie scrunched her forehead. This executor business
was fast becoming a pain in the butt. "Like buy a container and bury it, ashes and all?"

"You could, but I bet another homeless person is already living there for real. What if you arrive at the site
and meet them? If they say, 'Yes, you can bury the container,' they'll probably dig it up the second you leave,
scrap the ashes, and take the empty to the nearest pawn-
shop. Unless you plan on a twenty-four-hour guard,
Gary will be gone and the money you spent wasted."

"That sounds so—so—depressing." Ellie waited
while Rudy lifted his leg on a fire hydrant. "Besides, how
would they get the container open? I thought they were
sealed."

"I'm not sure about the urns, but it's easy to open the
wooden boxes."

When they stopped at a light, she gave Viv a look.

"Sounds to me like you know a lot about this whole cremation thing."

"Just about the containers. I remember my mother talking about it after my grandmother died."

"And she was the one who worried about the safety of the different receptacles?"

Viv's face colored pink. "Not really."

"The idea that you've had a close encounter with human remains boggles the mind. What did you do, steal someone's ashes when you were a kid?"

They turned left on York Avenue before Viv confessed. "No. But Grandma O'Shea was cremated when I was eleven. My cousin Faith stayed overnight at our condo after the funeral."

"And Faith opened the box?"

"I was with her—but it was her idea."

"What did you do, exactly?"

"My mom was in charge of Gram. That night, after the memorial service, Faith and I sneaked into the parlor and took the box off the mantel to get a closer look. My cousin just happened to have a screwdriver in the pocket of her robe and . . . well . . ."

"You took a peek at Grandma?" Ellie shook her head. "That was so disrespectful."

"Yeah, but at that age it was more like creepy. We were into Ouija boards and other spooky stuff, and we'd just watched a movie about zombies. One thing led to another, and before I knew it, Faith and I were tiptoeing down the stairs and walking into the living room."

"What would you have done if Granny had been in one of those fancy jars?"

"Nothing, I guess. But she was in an inlaid wooden box with shiny brass screws at each corner. Swear to God, I've never seen a woman so fast with a tool. Before I knew it, my cousin opened the box and we were staring at the remains."

They headed east on Eighty-sixth, which put them in

front of Beth Israel North and about a block from their destination. "Which resembled . . ."

"It looked like the dust you find in a vacuum cleaner bag, but all I remember for certain is we heard a strange noise, slapped the lid back on, and Faith worked that screwdriver as if it was motorized. We shoved the box on the mantel and ran for the bedroom like we were on fire."

"And no one ever found out?"

"Nobody said a word. Then again, we had a cleaning woman. She probably straightened up the next day, righted the box, and kept on dusting." Viv stopped walking and waited for Mr. T, who had decided this was the place to do big business. "I have an idea. Why don't you keep Gary on your fireplace mantel? That way, you could talk to him the way you do Rudy."

"Very funny." Ellie scowled. She did her best to convince her pal, convince everyone, that talking to her dog was nothing more than a quirk. Putting it the way Viv just did irritated the Yorkiepoo, but, hey, if word got out that she thought she could actually converse with him . . . "Besides, I wouldn't have much to say to Gary. I hardly knew him."

"You'd think of something, I'm sure," Viv teased. "So, what are you going to do about a final resting place?"

"Discuss it with the people at the crematorium. They might have an area where they store the containers. I could pay a yearly fee, and Gary could rest in peace, like he deserves."

"I have a better idea. Find out where his parents and his grandmother are interred. If there's a family crypt, you could put him there."

"I hadn't thought about it, but you're probably right. I guess I need to do more research on the Veridots."

"Find their attorney. He'd know what happened to Gary's relatives." They walked through the park gate, let the dogs off leash in the run, and sat on a bench. "What was the grandmother's name?"

Ellie leaned back on the bench. "I don't remember, but it shouldn't take a lot of digging to find out. The bank guy would know, or her name and their attorney's name might be listed in those old newspaper clippings."

"I thought you read them already."

Sam had gone over the brittle pages on Saturday, right before he'd stomped out of the apartment, and they were still stacked on her kitchen table. "Ryder read them while I took care of the old mail, so I guess I'd better look them over myself."

The two dogs raced side by side in the run, chasing fireflies and whatever other night insects flitted about. After a couple of minutes, they slowed to a trot, gave a round of sniffs and leg lifts, and began wandering back to the bench.

Suddenly, Rudy veered off and fixed his gaze on a near corner surrounded by bushes. Moving slowly, he stopped and gave a low growl.

"What's got him so riled?" Ellie stood and, with Viv hot on her heels, hurried inside the gate. "Hey, guys. What's going on?"

"Rudy says somebody's spying from the bushes." Mr. T sat at Viv's feet. *"But I ain't about to find out who."*

"Maybe he sees something . . . or someone," Viv offered.

"You think so?" Ellie stepped nearer. "Rudy! Come!"

Instead of doing as told, the Yorkiepoo skulked closer to the corner.

"Do you think I should go after him?"

"Long as I don't have to follow you, be my guest," T responded with a growl of his own.

"I was talking to Vivian," Ellie said, frowning.

"I know you were talking to me. I'm just not sure what you should do."

With her heart pounding, Ellie moved closer. Rudy's short, curly coat, a cohesive blend of gray and white, barely showed in the darkness. "Rudy! I said come!"

When he continued to stare at the corner, Ellie walked in his direction, squatted, and pulled him near. "What's the matter? Is something going on?"

"Someone's been watching us, Triple E. He's gone now, but I smelled him on the breeze. I could hear him breathing, too. It really creeped me out."

"Did you recognize who it was?"

"A man, for sure. But the air here is filled with stink. The junk from the river, animals, bugs . . ."

"What do you think got him so hot and bothered?" asked Viv, joining them.

Ellie rose to her feet and snapped Rudy's lead to his collar. "He's not—I mean, I'm not sure, but just to be on the safe side, I think this should be our last trip to the park at night until they find Gary's killer."

"It's about time you started listening to Sam." Viv hooked Mr. T to his leash and the foursome headed toward the exit. "The man knows what he's talking about."

Sam again, thought Ellie. Just what she didn't want to hear. "I'm not coming here at night because *I* don't want to, not because of Ryder's orders. I put in enough miles each day without this long of a hike in the dark."

"What are you going to do about the guy you met in the basement?"

She shrugged. "There isn't much I can do. There's a very slim chance he got into the building without a key, so he must be staying in that apartment, just like he said. If he'd wanted to do me harm or grill me about Gary, he had all the time in the world to do so. It was just a coincidence that he has the same name as Veridot . . . and a heart tattoo."

"I suppose, but I'd still mention it to Sam."

"I'll think about it. Now let's move along. I've had all the excitement I can stand for one day."

Chapter 18

The next morning, after her first round of walks, Ellie dropped Rudy at Sutton Pets, a doggie day care on East Sixtieth, and arrived at the crematorium shortly after lunch. Standing in a showroom at Blackman's, she gazed openmouthed at the shelves of containers available for storing ashes. Intricately carved wooden boxes covered one entire wall, beautifully filigreed urns occupied another, and delicately painted ceramic ginger jars another.

A card hung beneath each sample, giving the name of the craftsman, the casting house of the urns, the composition of the wooden boxes, and the artists of the jars. The bottom of each card was stamped with a price, which ranged from modest to downright ostentatious.

Mr. Blackman, a jovial older man who looked more like Santa Claus than a mortician, had left her alone to "peruse at her leisure" for the past half hour, but studying the floor-to-ceiling shelves made her dizzy. If not for the fact that Gary was "ready for retrieval," she'd have left a while ago.

She enjoyed spending money on the finer things, but she wasn't a fool, which is why she'd shopped the sale racks for the dress she'd worn on her date with Kevin. She'd be using Gary's money for this purchase, and he'd been a simple guy, more at home with thirdhand knick-knacks than actual objets d'art. He'd thought that trite painting of dogs playing poker was the work of a genius, as was Elvis on velvet, so it stood to reason he'd be just as happy sealed in a coffee can as he would in an inlaid mahogany box, especially if it could be opened with a simple screwdriver.

The urns and ginger jars were even more costly—the least expensive she'd found was five hundred dollars—but Mr. Blackman had assured her they were guaranteed against contamination. More importantly, if someone wanted to remove the ashes and pawn the receptacle, they'd have to damage the container, thus rendering it useless for resale.

She checked her watch and calculated the time. After she made her decision, she'd have to cab to the first stop on her afternoon rounds in order to finish the day on schedule. Worse, she now had a crick in her neck, and she still couldn't make up her mind. As far as she could tell, there was only one way out of the dilemma.

Closing her eyes, Ellie spun in a circle. Then she stopped turning, raised her arm, and pointed. Opening her eyes, she kept her arm rigid as she walked toward the wall of ceramic jars. Her index finger landed on a squat black container painted with puppies of all breeds and sizes.

Viewing her choice as a sign from above, she grinned. Gary had liked dogs, and he'd been crazy about Rudy. If this was where he wanted to "rest in peace," he'd get his way. Best of all, this jar cost less than most of the other options.

"Has madam made a decision?" came a voice from behind. "Or do you need more time?"

Ellie caught herself before answering "Madam has a headache" and said instead, "I'll take this one."

Mr. Blackman strode to her side and slid the reading glasses dangling from a chain around his neck onto his cherry red nose. "You want this container for Mr. Veridot?"

"Uh ... yeah." Did he think she wanted it for someone else?

"Oh."

Uh-oh was more like it. "What's wrong? Is the jar out of stock? If so, the floor sample will be fine."

"The container is available, but ..." He pointed to a sign she hadn't noticed tacked on the wall next to the row, which read: FOR YOUR BELOVED FOUR-LEGGED FRIEND. "As you can see, this shelf is reserved for the remains of cats, dogs, and other family pets."

Squinting, she saw that each jar was imprinted with bunnies, birds, cats, or dogs. There were also a couple decorated with lizards, fish, even snakes and mice, and a few more with steak bones and dog biscuits.

"I guess I didn't read carefully enough," she said aloud. "It's just that Gary liked dogs and—" She closed her eyes and picked this one? "And I know he'd find this jar endearing."

The mortician raised a finger to his chubby chin. "There is no right or wrong in making this type of decision, but it is my duty to point out certain things to my customers. If you believe this is the correct container—"

"I'm sure Gary would like it ... if he were still alive."

"Then he'll enjoy it now. Shall I fill it with his remains and seal it, as well?"

"Yes, please. How long will it take?"

Mr. Blackman glanced at his watch. "Thirty minutes should do it. Would you like to wait or pick it up later?"

"Do you do the actual ... um ... transferal?"

"Not personally, no. It's handled by a staff member."

"Could you answer a few questions for me while I wait?"

"Of course. Just let me get my man started. Follow me to a seating area, and I'll join you shortly."

Left in a tastefully furnished room done in sedate yet boring black, gray, and white, Ellie sighed. The reality of considering what people wanted done with their remains was daunting. She couldn't imagine shouldering this task for her mother or anyone she cared about and made a mental note to talk to Viv and Georgette about how they wanted to be laid to rest. The judge had already told her his will was being taken care of by his sons, but she wasn't sure what her mother or her best friend had planned.

And she also had to think about Rudy. Granted, most owners outlived their pets, but life in Manhattan, anywhere really, couldn't be taken for granted. Her pooch was probably correct. She had to contact Sal and ask him to draw up a will giving directions for the care of her remains, her possessions, and most of all, her canine pal.

Several minutes passed. Then, smiling his Santa Claus smile, Mr. Blackman walked in and sat across from her. "All taken care of. Now what is it we need to discuss?"

"Is there some way I can find out where the remains of Gary's family are?"

"Through a family attorney, I would imagine."

"I suppose the family had one, but I thought maybe you had some connections and could do the legwork for me. I'd be willing to pay for your time, of course."

"Well, in that case, I'll see what I can do."

That evening, Ellie scarfed down dinner, left Rudy at the apartment, and caught a taxi to her second self-defense class. Mentally preparing for what would transpire in the next two hours, she climbed the dingy steps to Phil's gym. She planned to pay strict attention during the lesson, and get her—er—get Sam's money's worth, even if she ended up black-and-blue over every square inch of her body. No way would she give Detective Dreadful another reason to accuse her of being soft or cowardly.

On her side trip to the ladies' locker room, she noted a circle of women chatting on the red mat, while a couple of men watched from the weight machines spaced around the gym area. After storing her tote in a locker, she followed a woman back to the training room and took a spot on the fringes, hoping Phil would be prompt.

Moments later, he appeared, followed by a striking blonde Amazon with a killer body and six-pack abs. Phil didn't speak to her directly, just said a general hello, introduced the woman as his wife, Patty, and led them through ten minutes of bends and stretches to loosen their muscles. Then he called Patty front and center.

Ellie shuffled from foot to foot, wincing when the woman was put in several obviously painful positions. To her credit, Patty extricated herself from each one and even managed to get the better of her husband with a few quick moves. The words "joint lock" and "hapkido" were bandied about as Phil explained the techniques they would practice, and, except for Ellie, all the women seemed to know what he was talking about.

When the Amazon walked to Ellie's side, she glanced Patty's way, not sure if the woman was hanging around to keep an eye on her husband or because she enjoyed playing the would-be victim, but it was probably the latter. Any idiot could see that Phil was devoted to his "ball and chain" as he'd laughingly referred to his beautiful wife.

"You the new student? Ellie?" Patty asked, smoothing her long blond ponytail.

"That's me. Ellie Engelman." She held out her hand, and Patty gave it a shake.

"You look like you can take care of yourself."

"I can. Sort of."

The Amazon smiled. "Nothing like a positive attitude."

"I'm just apprehensive." She nodded toward Phil and Roseanne, a petite brunette with delicate, elflike features. "A girl could get hurt doing some of those things."

"Phil would never do anything painful to a woman on purpose."

"And you know this because . . ."

"Because I met him when I wrestled. He tried to break into the sport, but he was too soft. When he switched to career management, I hired him."

"You were a professional wrestler?"

Patty's baby blue eyes crinkled at the corners. "The Viking Vixen, at your service. Phil wanted me to change my name to Chyna, but that was already taken. And other than Melmac, we couldn't come up with a better moniker."

Ellie blinked. If the woman was making a joke, it was totally lost on her.

"China. Melmac. Get it?" Patty asked, still smiling.

"Uh, sure." Ellie scanned the group, noting that Phil had moved to his next victim, Marielle, a graying grandma-type who weighed at least two hundred pounds. Instead of flipping Marielle onto her back as he'd done to Roseanne, he put her in a choke hold and demanded she pass him her pretend handbag. Marielle responded by jamming the sole of her sneaker into Phil's kneecap and taking off at a run. After receiving high fives from a few of the girls, the grinning grandma resumed her place in the circle.

Phil next approached Jolene, an attractive bottle blonde with snapping brown eyes. Jolene had been in the locker room when Ellie arrived. Married with two kids, this was one of her three nights out for the week while her hubby babysat.

The other women, Lorna, Mary, and Phyllis, were preparing for their moment, as well, but Ellie got the impression they were a few lessons ahead of Marielle, Roseanne, and Jolene and wanted to be shown more advanced techniques.

At the sound of a shriek, she zeroed in on Jolene, now on the floor between Phil's feet. "That a girl," Phil said as he helped her to stand. "Practice that kick and hold with Roseanne, because next turn I want to be the one on my ass. Lorna, you're on deck."

He raised a brow and glanced in Ellie's direction. "Watch and learn, Red, because your shot is coming."

Red? What had she done to earn such an insulting nickname? Her hair was a honeyed russet, not red. It was probably Phil's way of getting her goat, so she'd toughen up when he showed her a move. If she wasn't careful, she'd be his victim in no time. Something she was not looking forward to.

" 'Scuse me for saying so, but you're white as a sheet. You aren't gonna hurl, are you?"

Whipping her head around, she locked gazes with Patty, whose blinding smile mirrored that of a toothpaste model. "I'm not planning on it, but I don't believe in violence," Ellie answered, hoping she didn't sound like a total wimp.

Patty snorted. "Honey, this class is *not* about violence. It's a course in self-defense, plain and simple. Besides, like I said, my husband would never deliberately harm a woman."

"Maybe so, but I had my first *lesson* on Saturday." She winced as she raised her knee and displayed her black-and-blue thigh. "And this is what I came home with."

"That bitty bruise?" The woman scoffed. "Shit, I get worse than that when Phil and I arm wrestle, though I like it better when we spar. That's when I really get to strut my stuff." The Amazon flexed her muscular arms and lowered to a crouch. "The first thing you need to learn is how to take a fall. You wanna go a round or two just for giggles, and I'll demonstrate?"

Patty made it sound as if Phil was a regular cupcake. If she had to tangle with someone, she'd chose the bantam boxer over this bloodthirsty giantess any day. "I think I need a little more experience first."

"Okay. Suit yourself," Patty muttered, disappointment lacing her tone.

At the sound of a thud, Ellie swung her head around in time to see Phil struggle to his feet. "That was a good one, Lorna," he said to the forty-something dark-haired woman. "Now you're getting the hang of it."

Bummed she'd missed Lorna's moment of glory, Ellie could tell from the woman's smile she was proud of herself. Then Phil reached out a hand to congratulate her, and Lorna took it, but instead of a shake, he pinned her arm behind her back and jammed his opposite forearm under her chin.

"Here's a repeat lesson, ladies. Remember what I said about complacency leading to a dangerous situation? The bad guy is always looking for a way to take you down."

"Come on, girls," Patty encouraged. "What should Lorna do to get out of this potentially harmful position?"

"Elbow jab and instep stomp?" asked Roseanne.

"Joint lock!" roared Jolene.

"Lorna, if I was for real, I'd already have you up against a brick wall. You wouldn't stand a snowball's chance in hell of executing a flip." He stared out at the surrounding women. "Pay attention and remember what you were taught."

When he tightened his hold on Lorna, the woman opened and closed her mouth. Then she shot from under Phil's arm, grabbed his wrist with both hands, snapped it down and up, and pinned it to his back. Ramming her knee into him from the rear, she dropped him to the mat.

From the sound of Jolene's cheer, Ellie assumed that was a joint lock. She smiled at the round of high fives. It was nice to see women being so supportive of each other, even if engaged in violence; and it was violent, no matter what Patty said.

Phil scrambled to his feet, gave Lorna a back slap, and moved to his next victim while the woman came to stand at Ellie's side. "That was great. How many lessons have you had?"

"This is my sixth," Lorna answered, panting. "It took me a while to get started. I don't like being mean."

"Me, neither, but someone thought I should take classes, so here I am."

"Your husband?"

"Not married."

"Boyfriend?"

"Uh . . . not exactly."

Lorna's brown eyes twinkled. "Oh, I see. He's a *friend*."

Ellie guessed Ryder was her friend, but the word didn't quite match their history. "It's complicated. Sometimes even I don't understand the relationship."

"I know where you're coming from. Men can be a pain in the ass. Who need's 'em?"

Instead of commenting, Ellie decided she'd better stay alert. Phyllis had taken Phil down on the last move, which meant she was next.

Their instructor dusted himself off and stood in front of her. "Nice to see you again, Red. I was afraid you wouldn't be back after our first go round. You ready for the next step in your training?"

"Ah . . ."

"Okay, first we'll go over what we did the other day." Phil stepped around her and put her in a choke hold. "You remember this one, don't you?"

Ellie envisioned his stance, very close to the one Phyllis had just gotten out of. She might not be as tall as Patty, but she topped Phil by a good three inches.

He tightened his forearm. "Time's a-wastin'." He jerked his arm. "You'll be out of breath in a couple more seconds."

Inhaling, she tried the elbow jab and instep stomp, but Phil twisted and drew back his leg. "Sorry. Not fast enough."

A couple of women jumped up and down, waving their hands like demented grade-schoolers begging to be called on for the right answer.

"Jam your heel into his shin!" one shouted.

"Grab a finger and snap it like a twig!" yelled another.

Too distraught to think rationally, Ellie struggled with no particular plan in mind. But she was able to bend over and raise Phil up onto her back, which left his feet dangling in the air. Then she jumped hard to dislodge him. When that didn't work, she dropped to her knees, flipped to her back and pinned him under her. If she couldn't shake him loose, maybe she could crush him into submission.

When Phil stopped wriggling, she stopped bouncing. He wheezed, then began to vibrate as though he was in the throes of a seizure. His arms fell to the side, and she rolled to freedom, terrified she'd brought on a debilitating attack. Panting, she rose to her knees. She didn't know the first thing about CPR, but she'd give it a try if . . .

It took her a few seconds to catch on. Phil, the big idiot, was laughing his head off.

As were the men now ringing the mat, while the women held their stomachs in an effort to stem their mirth. Ellie glared at them, realized how she and Phil must have looked, and gave an embarrassed grin. On the bright side, if she were attacked, she could always amuse her assailant until he let her go.

Patty held out a hand and helped her stand. Then she threw an arm over Ellie's shoulder and hugged her—hard. "That's the first time I've ever seen my honey fall apart during class. You're a stitch and a half."

Heat rose to Ellie's cheeks. Great. She'd always dreamed of being comic relief in a life-threatening situation. Could she be any more lame?

In the meantime, Phil righted himself and faced her. "Okay, Red, how about if we start with baby steps? Eye gouging, biting, things that might work if the bad guy was a novice." His smile grew condescending. "You know, girly stuff."

Girly stuff! Why didn't the man just say she was a wuss, a wimp, a poor female unable to stand up for herself or see to her own safety. Maybe Sam was right. She was a coward.

Ellie bit her lower lip. She would not cry . . . maybe.

Phil shook his head, as if he thought her pathetic. Then one of the men shouted, "Aw, poor widdle baby. You hurt her feelings, boss."

The taunt made her angry. She was sick and tired of being coddled and worried over. Damn Sam and damn the rest of them.

Crouching, she waggled her fingers. "Okay, tough guy. Let's go."

Chapter 19

Sam propped himself near the entrance to Phil's gym, called his sergeant, and clocked out for the night. He'd been on duty forty-eight hours straight. He needed a decent meal, a shower, and sleep, in that order.

He detested cleaning up after gang violence—all cops did. It was hell when young lives were wasted fighting over areas of the city in which no sane person wanted to live. But "turf" was the only thing these kids thought they had. Too bad they didn't want to hear that the best way to "own the streets" was to get an education, make something of themselves, and teach their younger brothers and sisters to do the same. The entire scenario made him angry and mean.

So why was he here, waiting for a woman he didn't deserve? A woman who had successful and snooty lawyer types calling her for dates. A woman who had just inherited a bundle and would probably be filthy rich when her mother died. A soft touch who would jump at the chance to put her own life on the line to rescue an abandoned cat or dog. Ditto a homeless man.

He saw the dregs of humanity, Ellie saw only the good. She wanted nothing to do with violence, wouldn't even admit it existed, while he knew the truth. They lived in a violent world where no one was safe, and that truth made them as different as sinners and saints.

And there was no confusion to which category Ellie belonged.

Most of the time she enjoyed lighting his fuse and watching him explode. Knowing that, he'd been a fool to come here when he was in a foul mood. Hell! Even if he was in a good one. But his body and his mind came alive when he and Ellie were together, as if being with her was the real reason for his existence. No doubt about it, he was a selfish bastard, using her because she made him smile, made him believe in the good things life had to offer.

Unless, of course, she was chattering about canine rights or the rights of street people, and how she could take care of herself. Which was a joke, because Thompson Veridot was out there, waiting for the opportunity to kill her. Sam felt the guy's presence in his bones just as Gary probably had when he wrote that damn note. A note that, according to Ellie, made her honor bound to do as Gary asked.

The door leading to Phil's gym opened and a cluster of women spilled onto the sidewalk. Laughing, they called out good nights and went in whatever direction took them home. He spotted Ellie immediately, her coppery curls shining in the light from the fixture over the entryway, and his irritability quotient dropped to low gear.

Pushing from the wall as she walked by, he said in his best street-tough voice, "Need a ride, little girl?"

She passed him like an express bus at rush hour.

Beating feet to catch up, he fell in step beside her. "I planned to be here to watch your lesson, but something happened at work."

They continued down the sidewalk in silence while his brain worked to come up with a more positive statement. When she stopped at the corner of Third and

Twentieth, he assumed she wanted to catch a cab. "I'll drive you home. My car is down the street."

Muttering a terse "No, thanks" she raised her arm, flagging a taxi as only a born New Yorker could.

"It's late. I'm parked close by."

She stepped farther out into Third Avenue. and he grabbed her shoulder, jerking her to safety as a stretch limo sped past. Back on the sidewalk, he held her by both elbows. "Christ, woman. Do you have a death wish?"

She twisted from his grip. "A taxi will take me directly to my front door, and if I get the standard driver, I won't have to answer any questions." Then she eyed him like a prosecuting attorney. "You should go home, take a shower, and get some sleep. You look like hell."

"You don't look so good yourself," he spouted. "Besides, I only live a couple of blocks from here."

She shifted her tote bag to the opposite shoulder. "You live in Gramercy?"

"Just a few streets up, on Twenty-fifth."

"Oh, I had no idea—"

"Where I lived. I know. I'd ask you over, but the place is a mess."

"Cleaning lady didn't make it this week?" She grinned. "Poor baby."

"I'm at work more than I'm home these days, and my mother has a key, which allows her to drop in a couple times a year." Dumb move, talking about what his mom did for her ungrateful son, but he was on a roll. "She decontaminates my fridge, tosses the empty pizza boxes and carryout cartons, even bug-bombs the place if she knows I'll be gone for twenty-four hours, which I usually am."

"She sounds like a nice woman—and a very caring mother."

"She is, if you can handle the weekly 'Why did you miss family dinner night?' phone calls." He took her hand and led her down the street. "Come on. I'm parked right around the corner."

Instead of commenting, she followed quietly. At the car, he opened the passenger door, and she slid inside. Then he settled behind the wheel, buckled up, and studied her while he started the engine.

Eyes closed, Ellie rested her head on the seat back and heaved a sigh. Figuring her day had been as rough as his, he decided to go easy on her. "Please take note. You didn't call me yesterday, and I'm not ragging you about it. That ought to get me a few brownie points."

"I've been too busy to call anyone."

"But you would have phoned me tonight, when you got home, right?"

She shrugged. "Maybe."

Not the answer she wanted to hear. He pulled into traffic. "You look beat."

"I had to choose Gary's final resting place today, and in typical idiot fashion I ended up buying a jar that's normally used for the ashes of a dog."

He smiled at her candor. "Seems to me that would be right up Veridot's alley. Didn't you tell me he loved dogs?"

"He did."

When she clammed up again, he asked, "How was tonight's lesson?"

"Fine."

The single syllable spoke volumes. "Did you meet Patty?"

"Uh-huh."

Two syllables. Things were looking up. "How many women in the class?"

"Seven, counting me."

Three entire words. Even better, though the conversation was going nowhere. "What did you learn?"

"Learn?"

"Learn as in self-defense. Did Phil show you how to foil a purse snatcher or evade some guy trying to grab you in an alley or your apartment lobby?" Or an ex-con bent on murdering you for the family fortune?

"We covered some of that."

"And?"

She heaved another sigh. "I don't want to talk about it."

He took the hint, and they rode in silence. Ten minutes later, he made a right on Sixty-fifth, crossed Second, took a left on First, and a left onto Sixty-sixth to double park in front of her building. Turning off the engine, he asked, "Why do I have the feeling something else happened today—something I should know about?"

"What happened occurred over the past two days, and it's nothing I want to repeat." She undid her seat belt and opened the door. "Thanks for the ride."

"Hang on. I'll see you up."

He made it to the outer lobby just as she unlocked the main door. Inside the body of the building, he wrested the keys from her hand. "Why do you always have to make a simple good night so difficult?"

She climbed the stairs, heaving a breath when she said, "Maybe because you always make it so complicated."

Groaning mentally, he followed her up the two flights. At her door, she stepped aside and allowed him to unlock it. Then she held out her palm.

He stuffed the keys in his pocket. "Can I come in?"

"Not a bright move. You're double-parked, remember?"

"Doesn't matter. I'll just add the ticket to my stash." Biting the bullet, he asked, "How about I tag along while you give Rudy his nightly walk?"

A smile flickered across her lips, and she opened the door. Sure enough, there sat her dog, a canine frown etched on his fuzzy muzzle.

"Hey, big guy. You ready for me?" She stooped to

take the leash from Rudy's mouth, then glanced over her shoulder. "I know, but he insisted on giving me a ride home. What could I do?" Focusing on the mutt, she snapped the lead to his collar. "He won't be here long."

Sam knew better than to criticize the one-sided dialogue. In fact, he was starting to enjoy the conversations she had with her cantankerous canine. Some of the things she said to her dog were things he was fairly certain she would never say to him.

Outside, she stopped at a trash can while Rudy lifted his leg. On the way to the corner, the mutt watered anything taller than a cigarette butt. Sam kept his eye on Ellie as they walked, noting the worry in her eyes and the way she chewed her lower lip. After a couple of minutes, they retraced their steps and arrived back at her building.

"It's late, and I'm beat," she told him, again holding out a hand for her keys.

"I'd feel a hell of a lot better if you told me what went on over the last few days."

She stared into the street. "It's no big deal, really. Just promise me you won't hire that bodyguard when I tell you."

He cursed under his breath and nodded toward the main door. "Inside. Now."

Ellie was simply too tired to argue. She let Sam march her up the stairs and into the apartment, where she unhooked Rudy's leash and whispered that she would join him soon. He gave Sam a doggie glare, then headed down the hall, and she shuffled to the kitchen. After filling a pair of mugs with water, she placed them in the microwave and set the timer. Then she removed two bags of Earl Grey from her tea caddy, put spoons and milk on the table, and removed the mugs when the nuker dinged. Aware that Sam had parked himself in a chair and now watched her every move, she brought the cups to the table and took a seat.

"Thanks for giving me time to think."

He dunked his tea bag a couple of times and laid it on a paper napkin. Reaching across the table, he clasped her hand. "And . . ."

Taking comfort in the feel of his warm fingers, Ellie fiddled with her own tea, adding milk to prolong the peaceful moment. She had no intention of describing her half-assed self-defense class, but he probably did need to hear about the tattooed man in the laundry room and Rudy's snarling battle with a bush in Carl Schurz.

"Okay, I'll fill you in, but don't jump down my throat until I'm finished."

Sam didn't say a word; he just sat with a frown etched on his face as he listened to her abbreviated replay of both incidents. When she stuttered to a stop, he asked, "You swear you didn't see anyone in the park? No one hanging around when you got there or following you when you left?"

"Nope, but it was unsettling." Creepy was more like it, but she could only give her impression, not use the exact words Rudy had spoken. "Viv and I decided that, aside from taking the dogs for a final walk around the block before bed, it was our last trip there at night until this mess is over."

"And the guy in the laundry room? Verne Thompson? He never made a threatening move or suspicious comment?"

"He wasn't terribly talkative, but he was pleasant. Why?"

Sam leaned back in his chair. "Because he's the one I'm most concerned about, not the invisible person in the shrubbery. If Veridot has access to your building, anything could happen to you at any time."

"So you don't think the laundry room guy was who he said he was? A man visiting his sister and brother-in-law?"

"It's too early to tell, but you're right about one thing.

If he was Thompson Veridot, he missed a perfect opportunity to drag the info out of you."

She straightened her shoulders. "Then I need to find out more about him."

He blew out a breath. "Finding out more is my job. You just watch yourself around strangers. And don't go to the basement alone again. Take your pal Vivian. Hell, take your dog. It couldn't hurt."

Pleased he made a suggestion she could live with instead of demanding she follow a ridiculous order, she nodded. "Okay, I can do that."

He stood and pulled her to her feet. "It's been a rough couple of days for both of us, so no more questions. Walk me out, and I'll leave."

At the door, she smiled. "Thanks for understanding."

"I'm going to Gruning in the morning to see if he's heard anything more about Veridot," Sam told her. "I'm also going to run a check on your neighbors in 4-D. And I'll expect a phone call tomorrow night, when you're through with the afternoon shift. Okay?"

At least he wasn't threatening to hunt her down if she didn't make the call. "I'll do it when I get in."

Cupping her jaw, he leaned forward, and Ellie closed her eyes. His kiss, firm yet gentle, made her toes tingle and her heart beat like a jackhammer. Lost in a sea of emotion, she melted in his arms and rode the feeling of care and safety surrounding her.

When he drew away, she rested her forehead on his chin. Sam had shown a new side tonight. A side she liked. A side she wouldn't mind seeing more often.

Stepping back, he opened the door and handed her the keys. "Lock up. We'll talk tomorrow."

"Well, well, well. That was a touching scene."

Ellie jumped a mile. Spinning around, she stared at her four-footed pal. "You scared the crap out of me. Aren't you supposed to be in the bedroom?"

"I only agreed to the suggestion because you promised to join me in a couple of minutes. When I realized I'd been lying alone for way too long, I decided to find out what was keeping you. It figures the deceitful dick was at fault."

"You're making too much of Sam's actions." She engaged both locks and hung her keys on the hook she used for Rudy's leash. "It was a simple good night kiss."

"Yeah, sure. If that kiss was simple, I'm a St. Bernard."

She headed down the hall, undressing as she walked. Right now, she just wanted to sink into a tub full of bubbles, then drop on her mattress and fall into a mind-numbing sleep. Too bad if Rudy didn't want Sam hanging around. He'd just have to get used to it—at least until this business with Veridot was over.

After dumping her clothes in the hamper, she gathered her robe and sleep shirt and walked to the bathroom, where she ran hot water in the tub and added a splash of gardenia-scented bubble bath. When she heard a knock on her front door, she assumed it was Sam.

No more talking for tonight, she told herself. She needed peace and quiet—not conversation.

A moment later, the bathroom door inched inward, and Rudy nosed his way into the room. *"And one more thing. I'm registering an official protest."*

So much for peace and quiet. "Good grief, now what?"

"You know exactly what. Don't ever do that to me again."

At the sound of another series of knocks, she stepped into the tub and willed her body to relax. Sam could leave a message on her cell if he had more to say. "I haven't the faintest idea what you're talking about."

Rudy plopped on the plush throw rug and curled into a ball. *"You try peeing in front of someone who thinks you're a useless dumb animal and let me know how it feels."*

"Sam doesn't think you're useless." She scrubbed her legs with a loofah, then moved the sponge to her belly. "He simply has a difficult time understanding canines."

"He doesn't like dogs, period. And I thought that was your numero uno criteria for bringing a new human into our life."

At the sound of footsteps in the hall, she froze. Since when had Sam gotten a key to her apartment?

"Ellie? Ellie, it's me," Viv said in an exaggerated whisper. "I knocked, but you didn't answer."

Rudy raised a leg and started licking his privates in double time.

Relieved, Ellie blew out a breath. This was turning into a lousy end to a perfectly lousy day. She and Viv had traded keys over a year ago, but aside from using Viv's when she walked T, they'd agreed the keys were for emergencies only. What the heck had happened that Vivian would consider an emergency?

The bathroom door opened wide. "Are you alone? I thought I heard you talking to someone."

Ellie slid deeper into the water. "What do you need?"

Viv sat on the commode, took one look at Rudy's canine machinations, and wrinkled her nose. "I promise I won't stay long, but I found out something tonight after work, and you need to hear it."

"Something that couldn't wait until tomorrow?"

"I don't think so."

After squeezing the water from her loofah, she set the sponge in its holder. "Well?"

"I ran into Stefan Burns—you know, the guy who's supposed to be the brother-in-law of the man you met in the laundry room, and we got to talking. He says his wife doesn't have a brother and neither does he."

No brother? A shiver tripped up Ellie's spine. "But that doesn't make sense. The guy gave me both their names and their apartment number. Are you sure it was the real Mr. Burns?"

"The man opened the box for 4-D and removed the mail. I couldn't see the name on the envelopes, but he didn't correct me when I asked about his wife Adrianne having a brother."

"So, unless he stole the mailbox key, it was probably Stefan, huh?"

"That's my guess. Look, I know you're almost ready for bed, but if I were you I'd let Sam know tonight. Maybe he can call in a background check or something."

"I already told Sam about the laundry room guy."

"Really? When did you see Detective Delicious?"

She ignored Viv's silly comment. "He came to the gym and offered me a ride home."

"I forgot you had a class tonight. How did it go?"

Ellie closed her eyes and leaned back into the bubbles. "How about if we discuss it tomorrow? I really need to get to sleep."

"You sure you want to wait?"

"I don't see what else I can do."

"Okay, then." Viv stood and sidled into the hall. "I'll lock up on my way out."

When her steps faded and the apartment door closed, Rudy said, *"Interesting bit of information Viv just gave us, huh?"*

"I'll say." She climbed out of the tub and let it drain.

"So, what are you gonna do about it?"

"I'm not sure."

"I know. Bring me wherever you go, even the gym for those karate lessons. Besides giving you my excellent canine impressions, I'll protect you."

Stifling a smile, she toweled off, then slipped into her sleep shirt. "They're self-defense lessons, not karate, you knucklehead." She brushed her teeth while he continued pestering. "All right, that's enough. You already go just about everywhere I do."

"But not the important places."

She headed for the bedroom with the Yorkiepoo on

her heels. After pulling down the comforter and sheet, she flicked off her bedside lamp and sank onto the mattress. "What kind of important places?"

Rudy hopped on the bed and took his usual spot on the pillow next to her. *The bank holding our money, for one. And Blackman's. If I'd been with you, I would have made sure you found the right container for Gary.*

Reaching out, Ellie ran her hand over his side. When he rolled to his back, she stroked his belly, then walked her fingers to his neck, scratching in his favorite spot— the underside of his chin. "Okay. Next time I plan to stop at either of those places, I'll think about bringing you along. And I guess I should tell Sam what Viv just said. I've filled him in on all the other stuff, so why not this?"

"I hate to say it, but it wouldn't hurt to give him the info." Rudy curled into a ball and gave her hand a comforting lick. *"Just remember, Ryder doesn't love you like I do."*

"I know, big guy. We only have each other. And no one will ever come between us."

"Hey, don't get me wrong. You deserve a first-class human male, but he's got to be as good to you as I am. He has to put you first, before his family, his job, before everything. And that's something the doofus detective will never do."

Ellie suspected Rudy was right, though she had no intention of telling him so. Sam was a dedicated officer of the law. She imagined that even the lectures he gave her were spoken in the line of duty. That's why tonight had been different. He'd been understanding, and instead of the usual lecture, he'd pulled a sweet and gentle act.

Since they'd reconnected, he'd hinted that he deserved a second chance but . . .

Too tired to guess Ryder's motives, she thought about Vivian's report. Had Stefan Burns told her pal the truth? Was there any way she could get the correct information without arousing suspicion?

Who was the man in the laundry room?

Chapter 20

The next morning, Ellie woke and stretched, moaning when her muscles bunched in protest. *Thank you, Sam, for insisting I take those horrific classes with Phil,* she grumbled mentally. For now, she needed the ibuprofen in her bathroom medicine cabinet, but from the nagging cramps in her arms and legs she doubted she'd make it there before she fell in a heap on the hardwood floor.

"I can wait a couple of minutes to go out," Rudy offered.

Glancing to her left, she found him stretching on the pillow while gazing at her through sympathetic brown eyes. "Thanks, big guy. It might take me a while to get moving."

He hopped off the bed and raced around to her side. *"I don't get it. Last week you had that ginormous bruise, and today you can barely move. What are they doing in that karate class? I thought their goal was teaching you to protect yourself, not turning you into a cripple."*

"It's not a karate—" She rose to a sitting position and grimaced, then swung her feet to the floor. "Oh, never mind. Let's just say I'm not the most stellar of students and leave it at that." Standing, she smiled when she realized the pain was bearable. "Give me a minute to get dressed and pop a couple of pills."

After collecting fresh underwear, black linen walking shorts, and a peach-colored skinny-strapped tee, she hobbled to the bathroom. Ten minutes later, pills swallowed, face washed, and minimal makeup applied, she felt almost human. Back in the bedroom, she grabbed her sneakers and her black cardigan and walked to the kitchen, where she found her fuzzy pal standing guard at the kibble cupboard.

Working through the pain, she sat at the table, slid her feet into her sneakers, and bent to lace them up. "Since it's our day to bring Natter and Randall their weekly drink, how about we walk to the nearest Joe to Go, then stop at Bread and Bones and splurge on a high-calorie breakfast for me and a gourmet goody for you?"

Rudy's doggie lips curved into a smile. *"Best idea you've had all week, but how about we get an extra biscuit for Lulu?"*

She slipped on her sweater and headed for the foyer. "Hang on a second. If Miss Pickypants gets a special treat, it's only fair we buy enough for the rest of the gang."

"Fair, schmair. I'm thinkin' about my gal pal. If a fancy nibble will keep me on her good side—"

"Nothing will happen." She clipped the leash to his collar. "You're *fixed*, and Lulu is being groomed for the next championship show at the Javits Convention Center. Mrs. Steinman would kill me if I let her baby mess around with another dog."

"I'm not 'another dog.' I'm the man." He trotted beside her down the stairs. *"Lulu told me so herself just last week."*

"Oh, really? I wish I'd heard that conversation."

"It was the morning those bean eaters had Montezuma's revenge. You were too busy scoopin' poop to hear."

Ellie remembered that mega-disaster all too clearly.

"The boys couldn't help it. You heard what Jan said when I reported the incident; they got into the garbage and ate something that didn't agree with them."

"Those illegals are too gross for words."

"Pay attention, because I'm not saying this again. Cheech and Chong were born here. They're upright canine citizens, though they might be a tad . . . odd."

"They're fools, I tell ya. Never mind too dopey to learn English—they don't even speak."

Tsking at his comment, Ellie stopped and pushed a note under Viv's door explaining that she had no time to walk Mr. T this morning and promising to be home so they could give the dogs their final walk outside together at nine o'clock that evening. After stopping at Bread and Bones, she had a list of things to do today, including a visit to Hilary's building. The woman had been on duty alone for the past few days, so it was time to check on her progress. The special treats would be an excuse to drop into Hilary's complex with Hilary none the wiser.

After that, they'd hike to Columbia and the other colleges where they'd hung a flyer to check the post sites. Aside from Milton and that rude guy who wanted to meet at her apartment, there hadn't been any interest in the assistant job. If someone had removed the notice or torn off the tabs, she'd tack up a new one and keep her fingers crossed.

Then she needed to phone Mr. Blackman regarding the final resting place of Gary's family. And somewhere in between, she planned to call Gruning and ask about Gary's toxicology report. In her heart, she knew the results would be clean. Gary wasn't a druggie, no matter what the detective thought, but it would make her day if she could nudge him with a pointed "I told you so" and score one for her dead pal at the same time.

Walking rapidly toward the nearest Joe to Go, Ellie gazed at the sun blazing in a brilliant blue sky. At this rate, her sweater would be too warm by the time they reached the bakery. Between the wretched heat and Gary's death, she needed a weekend off, even better a few days. If Hilary agreed to handle the workload, maybe she and Viv could bring the boys to the Hamptons or the Jersey Shore. Anywhere the air was cooler and the humidity lower.

When they arrived at the coffee shop, she hooked Rudy's lead under a table leg in the outdoor seating area and went in for Natter's coffee, Randall's tea, and her usual caramel bliss. With no sign of Joe, she paid for the order, carted the drinks outside, and released the Yorkiepoo's leash. A few blocks later, she hit Bread and Bones and bought three dozen of their best biscuits in assorted flavors.

Her stomach growled as she inspected the pastry case set aside for human customers. Unfortunately, everything she longed for was big and gooey, not something she could easily eat while balancing a tote bag, tray of drinks, and bag of dog treats. Settling for a sesame bagel with lox and a schmeer, she tossed Rudy a biscuit, stuffed her sweater in her bag, and added the canine goodies. Then, after making sure her best bud finished his nibble, she juggled it all and devoured breakfast while she walked to the Beaumont.

"Morning, Natter," she said, passing over his mocha java when they arrived. In the lobby, she set her drinks on the counter. "Mind if I leave this here while I collect the gang?"

The doorman raised his coffee in salute. "Not a problem. It'll be here when you're through."

Riding to the penthouse, she and Rudy collected Cheech and Chong first. "Say good morning to the boys," she encouraged when the Chihuahuas appeared in the foyer.

"Hah! It's a waste of time."

"Do it anyway, because I believe they understand every one of your nasty comments." Ellie snapped leashes to each of the tiny dogs' rhinestone-studded collars. "Doesn't that make you want to apologize to them?"

"Let me think about it . . . ah . . . nope."

He continued to mutter as she led them from the penthouse. A couple of floors down, they picked up Bruiser, the usually sullen Pomeranian, and Lulu, the champion Havanese and object of Rudy's fantasies. Three floors down, they collected Satchmo, a mini dachshund with an enormous ego, and Harvey, a strange-looking beagle mix with a boisterous personality, and rode the elevator to the lobby.

"If you're good on your walk, you'll all get a special treat when we bring you home," Ellie told them as they hit the sidewalk and dodged the strolling pedestrians.

"How special?" asked Lulu.

"Special enough to cost ten times the price of a Milk-Bone," Rudy said. *"But you're worth it, doll."*

"Hey, hey, hey! We're all worth it," Satchmo shouted, lifting a leg on a stanchion.

The Havanese raised her nose. *"Humph. I doubt that. How many of you have won Best in Show at a major competition?"*

The dogs strained at their leads, practically dragging Ellie across Fifth Avenue as they argued. So much for bribery. "Lulu, be nice. Not every owner wants a purebred with impeccable bloodlines, and some of those who do still don't bring them to shows."

"That's tellin' her, babe." Harvey shouted a high five.

Once they entered the park, the canines called a truce and concentrated on the giver of all good smells: the rich moist earth of Central Park. As usual, Cheech and Chong pulled one way while the other canines headed in the opposite direction, stretching Ellie to the max. After a few minutes, she gathered the leads and retrieved cleanup bags. When finished collecting the waste, she called out over the group's yappy chatter, "Okay, every-

body back home . . . and no treats for the lot of you unless you calm down!"

The pronouncement hit the unruly dogs like a bucket
of ice water. Banding together, they grew orderly and kept
in step, their paces identical and their tails high, a perfect
example of the name of Ellie's business—Paws in Motion. Grinning with pride, she realized her morning pain
reliever had finally kicked in and she felt good enough to
reward the mob for their overdue attempt at obedience.

Arriving inside the Beaumont, she led the dogs home
and gave each one a special biscuit. By the time she
dropped the canines in their apartments and wrote her
notes a half hour had passed. When she and Rudy got
into the elevator to ride it down they met Eugene, handling his own group of much larger dogs.

"Engleman," he said, his face set in a scowl.

"Eugene." She ruffled Rudy's ears when he growled.

"You still thinkin' about what I told you?"

In truth, she'd had a lot more on her mind than Eugene's ridiculous claim that Gary owed him money, and
if she discussed it with him now, she'd be late for her
next stop. When the elevator door took that moment to
slide open, she charged into the lobby.

"No time to talk. Catch me later." Grabbing the drink
carrier, she raced out the entrance while Rudy half-ran
to keep up.

Busy with a tenant, Randall merely smiled when
Ellie strode into the Davenport and set his tea on the
counter. Then she and Rudy retrieved their charges, led
them into the morning heat, and crossed Fifth to get to
the park. Once there, she gave them a heads-up on the
gourmet treats, but she didn't have to threaten. Sweetie
Pie, Buckley, Stinker, and Jett had been the first of her
doggie clients, and the newest, Bitsy, happily followed
their lead. They finished the walk, were delivered home,
and got their biscuits in record time.

Her next building didn't have a doorman, but Lily, Scooter, Fred, Barney, Pooh, and Tigger, all dogs with mixed pedigrees, were a pleasant group that rarely gave her trouble. With the promise of a special nibble, they behaved admirably, as well.

Setting her sights on Hilary's building a few blocks up, she and Rudy continued north. They would soon be in front of their intended high-rise, diagonally across from the Metropolitan Museum of Art. In the distance, a woman leading a group of tiny canines crossed Fifth at the light on Seventy-ninth, and Ellie thought it might be Hilary. Drawing near, she recognized her assistant holding a conversation with a tall man wearing a suit and carrying a briefcase.

Staring at the man, Ellie at first thought it might be Richard, Hilary's cheap bastard of a husband. But something about the way the guy stood, or maybe it was his hair, looked familiar ... too familiar. And the closer she got, the more certain she became.

She knew Hilary's companion.

They were a block short of their destination when the man flagged a taxi. She kept her eyes on the cab as it sped away, but the midmorning sunlight bouncing off the vehicle's rear window prevented her from making a more positive ID.

Raising her head, her gaze collided with Hilary's. The woman still wore her hazmat mask and gloves, but she held a tissue to her eyes with one hand as she clutched her charges' leashes in the other.

"Hilary," Ellie said when they met. "How are things going with the dogs?"

"Did you see him?" Hilary answered, clenching the tissue in her fingers.

"I saw you talking to someone."

Hilary heaved a sigh. "That was Richard's attorney."

The past two weeks came flooding back to Ellie in a haze of disbelief. Kevin McGowan was Richard Blankenship's attorney? If so, it was no wonder he hadn't mentioned what kind of law he practiced. Telling her he handled divorces would have made her more careful when she talked about her wounded assistant. But she had to be certain it was Kevin before she lost her head and did something she'd be sorry for.

"I didn't catch his name."

"It's Kevin McGowan. He and his father are involved in some of the biggest divorce disputes in Manhattan." Hilary narrowed her eyes. "Do you know him?"

Ellie figured she had two choices. Tell the truth and have Hilary quit her job or straight out lie. Both ideas went against her personal belief system, but doing the first would definitely erase any chance she had at a weekend getaway. And considering the upheaval in her life at the moment . . .

"You could always tell her one of my lawyer jokes," Rudy offered. *"Better still, what would Vivie do in this situation?"*

Knowing her girlfriend was the queen of sneaky tactics, she decided to channel Viv. "I've lost count of the number of attorneys Stanley's introduced me to since he and Georgette began dating." A true statement—and evasive as hell.

"Well, you'd remember this one," her assistant said. "He's very good-looking, and I've heard Kevin is quite a charmer with the ladies. But I'm his client's adversary, so I have yet to hear a pleasant sentence spring from his sneering lips."

Charming. A perfect word to describe the dirty rat.

"And you think he's the one advising Richard on how to handle the settlement—I mean the negative stuff about you working for me and what you might do with your jewelry?"

"Of course he is. He lives near here, so he probably saw me walking my charges and put things together." Hilary heaved a sigh. "If you don't mind, I'd like to bring the dogs home. I want to phone my lawyer and let him know what that despicable man just said."

Ellie stewed the entire time Hilary delivered the dogs home and wrote notes. But passing out the special biscuits didn't assuage the guilt she felt about her relationship with the deceitful louse of a lawyer. So much for thinking Kevin liked her for who she was. Instead, he'd been using her to help screw a friend!

Now at Hilary's door, she realized she had no time to consider her involvement with Kevin. She had a ton of things to do today, and—

"I'll be all right after I make a few calls," Hilary said, startling Ellie to attention. "Don't worry about me."

"I am worried. After all, I gave you the job, which seems to have sent Richard off the deep end."

"Maybe so, but you've also listened to my complaints, sat through my tears, and most importantly, helped me with Cuddles." Hilary picked the petite pooch off the floor and snuggled him to her chest. "I don't know what I'd do without my darling. He's even completely housebroken, thanks to you."

"I am, I am," Cuddles interjected.

"He's a good boy." Ellie scratched the toy poodle's head as she gazed at her assistant. "Positive you'll be okay?"

"I have to be, don't I?" Hilary answered, opening her apartment door. "After I speak to my attorney, I'll call my sister. She's been through three divorces already. I rely on her as my expert."

Maybe she could put Hilary in touch with Georgette and—

"Don't even think about it," Rudy warned.

Okay, so maybe introducing her to Georgette was a dumb idea. If her mother learned the name of Richard's attorney, she'd blab to Hilary that he'd been at her apartment and met her daughter, and that would be the end of Ellie's assistant. She'd have to think on it a while longer, later when she'd taken care of everything on her list. Still, if Hilary needed her—

"And don't suggest we take her afternoon shift," Rudy continued. *"We got too much to do today."*

"Hilary, I—"

"Yes?"

Rudy strained at his leash, tugging her toward the elevator. *"No, no, no. We got places to go, people to see."*

"Uh, nothing. Just let me know if there's anything I can do to help."

All of the notices she'd hung on college bulletin boards had been taken down, so she added a "Please do not remove" to the bottom of each new sign. She ended her trek at the Columbia University bookstore. Then she sat on the steps of the Butler Library and phoned the funeral home. Mr. Blackman reported that, as of yet, he'd had no luck locating the Veridot family's final resting place. Too tired to walk to Pops's lunch cart, she and Rudy caught a cab to the Guggenheim, or as she now referred to it in her mind, "the scene of the crime," and walked further south until she found Pops.

After chatting with him for a few minutes, she brought lunch to a bench and took a seat. The last twenty-four hours had been incredible. She'd made a fool of herself at her self-defense class, Sam had invaded her space and her senses, Vivian had found out that the man in the laundry room had lied, and now she'd learned that Kevin McGowan, a man she thought was a contender for her affection, had been stringing her along just so he could gain the advantage on a case. Aside from running into Thompson Veridot, she couldn't imagine things getting any worse.

Her cell phone chose that moment to ring, and she heaved a sigh. "I suppose I need to take this," she muttered. "Hello, it's Ellie."

"Hi. I'm, like, a student at Columbia, and I saw your ad . . . about the dog walker," the woman began.

"Can I have your name?" Ellie asked, keeping her fingers crossed that this person was normal.

"It's Cindy. So, like, what would I have to do to, like, get the job?"

"I'll tell you a little of what I need, and if you think you can work with me, we can arrange a meeting." And not at my apartment, she reminded herself. "First and most important, I'm looking for someone who enjoys working with dogs."

"That would be me," Cindy said in a little girl voice.

"Next, you'd have to allow yourself to be bonded and insured."

"Like, would I have to pay for that?"

"Nope. I'd pick up the charges. Next, you have to be available early in the morning and late in the afternoon."

"Like, how early is early?" Cindy asked.

"Like, uh, say eight a.m. five mornings a week, and around four each afternoon."

"Eight o'clock?"

"That's correct."

"I'm a night owl. I never get up before, like, ten. It took me weeks to arrange my schedule for the afternoons. I'm, like, still in class at four."

Ellie frowned. So much for Ms. Like Cindy. "Well, then, I guess we won't be able to arrange things. But you can call me again if your schedule changes."

"Okay," Cindy said, only her voice wasn't quite so perky. "Thanks for the chance."

After disconnecting the call, Ellie ran a hand through her hair. This finding-an-assistant business was a lot harder than she thought it would be. Maybe she needed to put an ad in the newspaper or—

Unable to process it all, she took a bite of hot dog and gazed down to find Rudy glaring at her. "Give me a break. It's been a rough morning."

"Another dope looking for a job?"

"Not a dope, exactly, just a girl with a schedule that won't mesh with ours. What really frosts my buns is Kevin McGowan, the big ass."

"I wouldn't give that sleazy lawyer another minute of brain pain. We have more important stuff to take care of, if you'll recall."

"That 'sleazy lawyer' used me to screw a friend. I want to confront him, but I need help figuring out the best way to do it. Maybe Vivian—"

"Vivian will know how to get him by the balls, but right now we have a killer to catch. And we still don't know where to store Gary."

"I called Mr. Blackman," she said, defending herself.

"How about talking to Gruning and getting the skinny on that toxicology report? While you're at it, ask him if there's anything new on Veridot."

"Gruning might give me the drug results, but I doubt he'd share info on Veridot. Besides, Sam told me to let him take care of it. He can get information from the police files I'm not entitled to, remember?"

Rudy sprang to his hind legs and put his paws next to her on the bench. *"Ryder has cases to solve. He's gonna let you down on this, the same way he let you down after your one date."*

"No, he won't. At least, not on finding Thompson Veridot. He's worried about me." She took a bite of hot dog and washed it down with Diet Coke. "If he wasn't, he wouldn't have paid for those self-defense classes."

Jumping up, Rudy parked his bottom beside her. *"He planned those lessons to weaken you. The next time he makes a pass, you'll be too sore to fight back. Before you know it, he'll have you in the—"*

"You are so full of it." Refusing to argue further, she offered him a chunk of the extra wiener, which he swallowed in two bites. "I know you want to protect me from dangerous men—"

"You mean unscrupulous cops and vicious murderers?"
She wrapped an arm around him, and he laid his head on her lap. "Them, too, but that's not Sam."

"Humph." He snuggled closer.

Ellie finished her lunch, then crumpled the paper sleeve and tossed everything into the trash. "Time to call Gruning. If he won't give me the report, I'll phone Sam and ask him to get it. He also needs to hear what Viv said about the guy in the laundry room. If I know Sam, he's already retrieved info on Stefan and Adrianne Burns."

Gruning wasn't in, so she left her number, but not the reason for the call. Then she tried Sam, but hung up before his voice mail kicked in. She'd promised to phone him tonight, and they could discuss things then.

Checking her watch, she saw that it was just about time to begin her second series of walks at the Beaumont. "Let's get moving." She stood, and Rudy hopped to the sidewalk. "Our next round awaits. If we hurry, we can be home early tonight."

"Let's stop at Joe's," Ellie said to Rudy when they left their final building. "He's usually at the Lexington store this time of day, and it's on our way home."

"I'm starvin', so hurry up. I'm lookin' forward to an early dinner and one of those gourmet biscuits for dessert."

Fifteen minutes later, they arrived at the coffeehouse, and she hooked Rudy's leash to an outside table leg, as usual. "I'll just be a couple of minutes. Don't move."

"Very funny. How about sneaking me inside, so I can say hello to Joe?"

"You know I can't do that, but if he's not busy I'll bring him out. Okay?" She moved to go inside, and he scuttled in front of her.

"What say you leave me something to drink? This miserable heat's turnin' me into a raisin."

Ellie swiped at the perspiration dotting her forehead. Rudy was right, the little stinker. She should have thought about his comfort before her own. She removed a small plastic dish and bottle of water from her bag, filled it, and set the bowl in front of him. He slurped, and she smiled. "Go slow. I don't want you to get sick."

He gazed at her with water dripping from his fuzzy muzzle. *"If you don't make it snappy, I'll be sick from hunger."*

"Be patient. Good things come to those who wait."

"Yeah, yeah, yeah. Hurry it up."

Striding inside, she spotted Joe behind the counter. The line was long, as was usual for this time of day, but she needed the caffeine. A caramel bliss would give her just enough zip to stay awake through tonight's walk with Viv and T.

Joe saw her in line and grinned when she arrived at the counter. "Haven't seen you since the night you stopped in with that cop."

"I've been busy," Ellie explained, hoping he'd lay off the topic of Sam.

He gave his barista Ellie's order and, like a dog with a bone, continued to gnaw. "So, are you and that guy . . . Ryder is it? Are you two an item?"

"Uh, no, of course not."

Accepting her payment, he passed her change and gazed at her frequent buyer card. "It looks like you've racked up another free cup of my joe." He punched the card and returned it to her. "Tell you what, next time you and Ryder are together, bring the detective around. I'll see to it you both get a cup on the house."

She tucked the money and card in her tote. "I don't think that'll happen anytime soon. We're not involved or anything."

"Really? Didn't look that way to me."

"Well, you're wrong. Sam's only on my case because of Gary's death—and a couple of other things." Still trying to change the subject, she said, "Rudy wants to see you."

Joe set her coffee on the counter. "Let me guess. The little guy told you that himself."

"As a matter of fact, he did." She sipped the strong, sweet brew and sighed in ecstasy. "Come outside and say hello."

"Okay, but only for a couple of sec—"

They jumped at a commotion somewhere on the sidewalk.

"What the hell?" Joe peered out the store's front window.

Ellie gasped at the sound of a familiar bark. "That's Rudy!" Dropping her coffee, she raced to the door.

Pedestrians speed walked past at their usual rush-hour pace. Staring openmouthed at the overturned chair and upended water dish, Ellie's heart dropped to the pit of her stomach.

"My dog," she said to a woman and her young son, sitting at the next station. "Did you see what happened to him?"

The boy gawked while his mother spoke. "Some guy walked over and put that envelope on the table, then dropped a sack over the dog's head and scooped him up. I screamed at him to stop, but he ignored me and took off that way." She pointed over her shoulder.

Joe grabbed the envelope and handed it to her. "Here. Want me to call the cops?"

Ellie couldn't think. She crumpled the paper to her chest and ran down the sidewalk, pushing pedestrians out of her way as she shouted Rudy's name.

Chapter 21

Gasping for air, Ellie stopped running, bent at the waist, and stared at the sidewalk. She'd focused all her energy on catching the dognapper while listening for Rudy's SOS, but she hadn't heard a thing above the sound of traffic on the busy street. In the last ten blocks she'd dodged, passed, or pushed about a thousand pedestrians, many of whom looked suspicious but none of whom had her dog.

She stood upright and, still heaving for breath, scanned the area around Lexington and Seventy-eighth. When she spotted a Pastrami Queen, one of Rudy's favorite quick-stop restaurants, her tears began to flow. Angry and confused, she swallowed the sobs and concentrated on what had happened.

Only an idiot would kidnap her dog. Rudy wasn't a champion like the canines she'd rescued a few months back. He didn't compete in shows, couldn't even father a pup. He wasn't worth a penny beyond the joy he'd bring to those he lived with, so why steal him? Anyone who wanted a pet could adopt from the ASPCA or other local shelters, and it was easy, safe, and legal.

For the first time, she looked at the envelope clutched in her hand—the one the thief had left on Joe's table.

Her name was scrawled across the front, the penciled letters smeared. That meant whoever had taken her dog knew her and had probably followed her to the coffee shop, where he'd waited until she was busy inside before doing the despicable deed.

Ripping open the envelope, she read:

> *If you want to see your mutt alive, bring my money to Carl Schurz Park at ten tonight. Come alone, or your boy is a goner. Same for your friend Vivian and that cop, Ryder, too. And don't try to cheat me out of the cash. It belongs to me.*

The note had no signature, but it wasn't necessary. Thompson Veridot had made himself clear.

Her body trembling, Ellie imagined Rudy in the hands of a man who had murdered his family in cold blood. Veridot's threat to kill her pal wasn't bravado.

It was real.

And though Rudy talked as if he could take over the world, he wasn't a Rottweiler or Doberman or any breed of attack dog. He was just a twelve-pound Yorkie mix, a sweet pooch with the sass of a shock jock, the guts of a high-wire artist, and a heart the size of Texas. He'd never be able to defend himself from a monster like Veridot.

To make matters worse, Veridot wasn't even giving her enough time to collect the money. It was close to six, when most financial institutions closed. What if First Trust was finished doing business for the day? Then what should she do?

Sidling between two parked cars, she stepped into the street next to a pair of older women dressed in Prada and pearls. After she caught a cab, she'd phone the bank to make sure she'd be allowed inside. If not ... well, she'd cross that bridge when she got to it.

Taxis roared by at NASCAR speed, confirming the horrific rush-hour traffic. When a cab stopped, she arm wrestled one of the seniors jostling her for ownership, then slid inside and slammed the door before the women made a scene. As the car took off, she tossed every bill in her wallet, about sixty dollars, onto the front seat.

"It's all yours if you get me to Fifth and Forty-eighth in five minutes."

The turbaned driver glanced over his shoulder, a smile on his dark, wrinkled face. "We go. You see."

Ellie grabbed the back of the front passenger seat when the cab shot across two lanes amidst a blare of horns. Gripping the strap hanging near the window, she held her breath as they weaved between delivery vans, cars, taxis, and buses, running yellow lights in the process.

About six blocks from the bank, she realized she hadn't called for their hours. Now stuck in hellish gridlock, she dialed 411, asked for the number, and let the phone company connect her. "You've reached First Trust, where your financial future is our main concern," a recording stated. "Our hours are seven a.m. to six p.m. Monday through Friday and—"

Closing the cell, she checked her watch again. There was still time to get to the bank, but if the traffic snarl didn't clear in the next minute, she'd hop out and start running. A second later, as if in answer to her prayer, the gridlock broke, and they sped ahead.

Arriving in front of First Trust, she stumbled to the street before the taxi stopped and charged into the building. Racing to the back, where the private viewing area for those handling safety-deposit boxes was located, she pulled out her ID and key, was approved, and followed the service rep to a room.

"We're about to close, Miss. You're welcome to take your time, but all customers must vacate the premises by six thirty, unless cleared with a bank official."

"I won't be long," Ellie promised.

A moment later, the rep hauled the box into the room

and left. She opened the lock and removed Sam's red canvas duffel bag. Glaring at the huge pile of banded bills, she wished the money hadn't been left to her and Rudy. Wished even more that she'd given it away, as she'd first thought to do, and had the magnanimous gift from Gary make the newspapers. That way, Veridot wouldn't be able to get his hands on the cash; he'd know it was gone for good.

She finished stuffing the money inside, hoisted the duffel over her shoulder, and groaned. The ibuprofen from this morning had worn off, and the darned bag weighed a ton. Lucky for her she was in decent shape, or she wouldn't get far carrying the load in this heat. Leaving the private room, she strode from the bank and stepped onto the sidewalk. Now what?

Think, Ellie. Think. Think. Think.

When nothing specific came to mind, she scanned the area, saw Rockefeller Center in the distance, and gave herself a pep talk as she walked. She was clever. There was plenty of time before she was due at Carl Schurz. She'd sit at a table, take stock of her predicament, and come up with a plan. Trudging the two blocks, she climbed the short flight of steps into the bar area and wended her way through groups of laughing tourists, most of whom were there to visit the Manhattan landmark.

Ordering a club soda with lime, she waited until the server left before opening the note a second time. The words "your dog is a goner" leapt out at her, and she swallowed a sob. If anything happened to her little pal . . .

She swiped away a round of tears with her paper napkin. No. Rudy would be fine. She'd make sure of it. But she couldn't call Vivian or Sam for help. She couldn't call anyone. She had no choice but to do what the letter said, and she had to do it on her own.

The waiter brought her drink, and she chugged half the cool liquid before setting the glass down. Blotting her still-damp forehead with another napkin, she told herself to be calm. Rational. Figure the problem out instead of diving in, as she'd done the last time a dog was in trouble.

Scanning the note again, she realized Veridot knew Vivian by name, and Sam, too. She and Sam had gone quite a few places together the last couple of days: the bank, the park, they'd even walked the dogs. And since he knew Sam was an officer, Veridot probably had checked out the precinct, too.

But what about Vivian?

When had they been out together in the past week, and who had they spoken to?

Ellie propped her chin in her hands and thought back to the morning she'd been in the basement of her building. She was the one who'd held a conversation with the tattooed guy in the laundry room, but Viv had talked to Stefan Burns the next day.

What if the man Viv met wasn't Burns, but the man who'd called himself Thompson? Viv hadn't described him, nor had she repeated her dialogue with Burns word for word, but Ellie was certain Viv would have introduced herself. If that was the case, the guy might have lied and just said he was Burns, when in fact he was really Veridot.

But how did he know she and Vivian were friends?

It only took a second for her to recall their dialogue. "Do you know the tenant in 2-B? The gorgeous brunette? The name above her mailbox just says V. McCready. Is she Virginia? Valerie? Vanessa?"

"Her name is Vivian."

Oh, God. She was such a sap, offering Viv's name as if she were a brand of ice cream or type of laundry detergent. When was she going to be more careful and not blab personal information to everyone she met?

Ellie finished her drink and asked the waiter for another. Then, tapping her fingers on the table, she reaf-

firmed her first decision. She couldn't let Viv or Sam
know about any of this because they'd insist on trying to
help. And if they did, they might be killed.

Rescuing Rudy was her job alone.

Standing in the bullpen, Sam glanced at the wall
clock across the room. He'd done paperwork for the
past hour, killing time while he waited for Ellie's call.
She'd promised to phone him when she got home, and
that was usually around six thirty. It was almost seven.
What the hell was taking her so long? He pulled out
his cell, began to dial, then snapped it closed. Dumb
move, asshole. He'd told Ellie he wouldn't push, that
he would trust her. If he called now, she'd take it the
wrong way and accuse him of not honoring his promise. Then she'd slam the phone in his ear and ignore
him for the next six months. Six months he didn't plan
to spend without her.

Gruning chose that moment to walk in the room.
Sam inhaled a breath and ambled in his direction. If he
played his cards right, he might be able to get some information and find out about Ellie, too.

"Detective Gruning," he said, forcing a smile. "Do
you have time to talk?"

Scowling, Gruning pulled a mint from the side pocket
of his rumpled, drab brown suit and popped it into his
mouth. "I've got two minutes. Hurry it up."

Though it pissed him off, Sam continued to make nice.
"Is the toxicology report back on Gary Veridot?"

The detective raised a brow. "Any special reason why
you want to know?"

Sam gritted his teeth. "Just doing a favor for a
friend."

Gruning's smile was more of a leer. "Your 'friend' already called today. Left a message on my voice mail."

"You spoke to Ms. Engleman?"

He propped a bulging hip on an empty desk. Crunch.

Crunch. Crunch. "I don't return calls to civilians who stick their nose in police business."

"I thought Ms. Engleman was a 'person of interest' in the case—unless you've dropped that misguided theory."

"She's still in the picture. But she isn't entitled to private information." He folded his arms, his expression smug. "I didn't take you for the pussy-whipped type, Ryder. Guess I was wrong."

Ignoring the rude comment, Sam said, "How about giving me a look at the tox results?"

Gruning's face flushed. "Can't. There's nothing to see."

"You mean the report came back clean?" Exactly like Ellie and I told you it would, fuckface. "No drugs were involved?"

"That's right. Now if you'll excuse me—"

He tried to barge past, but Sam raised a hand. "One more question."

The detective narrowed his eyes. "What?"

"Have you heard anything more on Thompson Veridot?"

"Who?"

"The victim's brother," Sam bit out. "The man who killed Gary Veridot."

"Not word one about the guy, and nothing on your lamebrained accusation, either. Now, if you'll excuse me, your two minutes are up." He pushed by without another word.

Sam swallowed a curse and made to go after him when his shoulder was grabbed from behind. "Easy, big guy. He's not worth a couple of weeks' suspension."

Turning, he saw Vince Fugazzo grinning. "Maybe not, but it would feel damn good if somebody rearranged Gruning's ugly face."

"I'm not arguing the idea, just don't want you to be that somebody. What would I do for a partner if you got suspended?"

"Find a new one." Sam stuffed his hands in his pockets. Vince was right. Even though it would be a plus to hear that someone had knocked out a few of Gruning's teeth, his doing it wasn't worth the downtime. "Just so you know, I finished the mound of paperwork we've had kicking around for the past week. Unless we get a call, our weekend is free."

"Great. Thanks. Just for that, you can come to our place for dinner tomorrow night. Natalie's family is coming over, and we're cooking out. She already told me to invite you."

"Can I bring someone?" Sam asked before thinking.

Vince's smile stretched from ear to ear. "You? Bring a friend? Besides me, I didn't think you had any."

"Har har. With jokes like that you'll never make it doing stand-up." Sam frowned. "Forget I asked."

"Hey, you're more than welcome to invite the lovely Ms. Engleman. Come to think of it, if you don't, I'll tell Nat about her, and maybe your moth—"

Flinching, Sam waved a hand. "All right, all right. We'll be there." If Ellie didn't have a date with that lame lawyer. "What time?"

"Six is good, and come empty-handed. We got it covered." He headed for their office, and Sam followed. "Ellie can even bring her dog, if it's good with kids. There'll be an entire herd at the house, ages six months and up."

"How many's a herd?" And what had Ellie said about her dog and kids?

Vince shrugged. "Six, maybe seven. I lost count."

"Okay, I'll tell her." Sam glanced at their desks and pinned a mental medal to his chest. They hadn't seen their blotter calendars in a month, maybe more. He slapped Vince's back. "I'll see you tomorrow night."

He strode out of the building, itching to use his phone, then realized Vince had given him a perfect reason to stop by Ellie's place. If she wasn't home, he'd visit her pal Vivian. Hadn't Ellie said they got together on nights when they didn't have a date?

Either way, he'd find her—wherever she was.

Sam stood in the entryway of Ellie's apartment complex, hoping the Feldmans or another of the tenants in her building would arrive so he could walk inside on their coattails. When ten minutes passed and no one showed, he accepted the fact that he'd have to do the deed himself, rang Ellie's outside buzzer, and waited. He'd promised himself on the ride over that he wouldn't lose his temper if she was sitting home eating her favorite ice cream instead of calling him. When she didn't answer, he even gave serious thought to getting hold of the McCready woman and asking her to let him in.

He'd only met Vivian twice and hadn't been impressed either time, but Ellie doted on her. It was possible he'd misjudged the woman, but since he prided himself on his ability to read personalities, he doubted it. Then again, maybe he should give Vivie, as Ellie sometimes called her, another chance.

Checking himself in the door window, he straightened his tie, took a breath, and pressed the button. A second passed; then he heard the scratchy rattle of the speaker.

"Yes?"

"Ms. McCready?"

"Yes."

"It's Sam Ryder . . . Ellie's friend."

"Detective Ryder?"

"Yes, ma'am."

"You rang the wrong buzzer. Ellie's in 3-A."

"I know, but she's not answering. I was hoping you might have some idea where she is."

"That's odd. She should be home by now. Did you two have a date?"

The personal question made him remember the reason Ms. McCready's charms escaped him. Both times they'd met, she'd stuck her nose in Ellie's business, especially where he was concerned. He still couldn't figure out if she approved of him or thought he was a jerk.

"Not exactly. I was hoping she'd call me, and she hasn't. So I came to ... uh ..."

"Check on her. She'll be really happy to hear that."

Sam nodded at a couple he didn't recognize coming through the door. If this discussion ever got back to Ellie, she wouldn't be happy about it, either. "Look, could I come up to talk about this?"

The buzzer sounded, and he pushed through, relieved Vivian let him in. If nothing else, he could hang out in the hall in front of Ellie's apartment until she arrived. Once on Vivian's floor, he found the door open and walked inside. When a dog growled, he glanced down and spotted one of the canines Ellie sometimes walked. What was the mutt's name? Master Bee? Mister Vee? Iced Tea?

"T, quiet now," said Vivian as she walked out from her kitchen. "Go watch Animal Planet, or I'm turning off the television."

Good God, now what had he gotten himself into? Yes, Ellie spoke to her dog, but he'd never heard her offer to put on a favorite TV program. The little black, white, and tan pup gave him a last nasty look and left.

"Sorry about that," said Vivian. "He can be a real stinker when he wants to be."

"I'll bet."

"Can I get you a drink? Soda, beer, something harder?"

"Uh, no, thanks. I just want to go over something you said a few minutes ago. You acted as if Ellie should be home."

"I thought she'd be back from wherever by now."

"What makes you say that?"

"Well, about an hour ago I heard her going down the

steps. Since we usually have a dog-walking date, I asked her where she was headed. She mumbled something about an errand, told me she'd see me in a little while, and that was it."

"Did she have the dog with her?"

"Rudy? No, she didn't. But she was carrying a huge red duffel bag, and it looked like it was full of bricks."

Sam's radar went off with a bang. "Oversized, with a yellow tag on the handle?"

"Yeah, that was it."

"And no dog?"

"No, which I found odd. Rudy and she go everywhere together, if at all possible."

"Was she dressed for a date or something special?"

"Actually, she wore a ratty pair of shorts and a loose tee. And she looked frazzled. But she took off before I could ask any more questions."

"Do you have a key to her apartment, by any chance?"

Vivian's mouth opened and closed. "You think maybe something bad happened to her?"

"Won't know until we investigate. First thing, let's see if she left any clues, say a phone message or a note with directions, and we can check on the dog."

"Hang on while I get my keys."

A moment later, they climbed the stairs, and Viv opened the door. "I'll go ahead and see if I can find Rudy while you do what you have to do."

She took off shouting Rudy's name at rock-concert volume while Sam checked out Ellie's kitchen, found her tote bag, and searched inside.

"He's not here," Vivian said after half a minute. "And that's really strange. If Ellie wanted him safe, she'd have left him with me instead of a doggie day care, but it wouldn't matter. It's past nine, so they'd be closed by now." She saw the contents of Ellie's tote, which Sam had spread across the table. "She left her handbag? No woman with a brain would forget theirs. Grabbing her purse is the first thing a woman does when she leaves her home." She frowned. "And forgetting this tote is something Ellie would never do."

"Can you tell what might be missing?"

Vivian sifted through the items. "Her cell phone, her keys, and her can of Mace, but that looks like it."

"Where does she go at night, when she takes the dogs?"

"You've been with her. It's just around the neighborhood. But we usually walk together if it's a long trip like going to Carl Schurz, and she didn't mention that tonight."

Damn. Something was wrong. Seriously wrong. It made no sense for Ellie to be transporting such an enormous amount of cash at this hour of the night. And where was her dog?

Worst-case scenario, Thompson Veridot was involved. But how?

Sam dialed Ellie's cell, which went directly to voice mail. "Ellie, it's Sam. I'm here at your place, and Vivian and I are worried. Where are you?" He snapped the phone closed. "Tell you what. I'm going to start canvassing the neighborhood. How about you call her mother and anyone else who might know where she'd be? Call me"—he passed her a card—"if you find her. If I come up empty, I'll expand the search, call in a missing person's report, and contact the black-and-whites on patrol. She won't be hard to spot carrying that huge duffel."

Before Viv could answer, he was out the door and on the street, cell phone in hand. Scanning the sidewalk, he went to his car and began Ellie's usual evening route, dialing while he drove. He figured Gruning would be useless, so he didn't bother asking for the jerk and instead talked to a desk sergeant.

His explanation and serious worry got a positive reaction from the officer on duty. Ellie's description and a description of the duffel would go out to all the patrol cars and foot soldiers on the Upper East Side. Other than that, there was nothing he could do, even though he knew something bad was taking place.

Something that had to do with Thompson Veridot.

Chapter 22

Ellie turned onto Second Avenue and headed toward Eighty-sixth, where she'd make a right and take a direct route to Carl Schurz Park. Though dusk had fallen, there was still enough light to see moving shadows, scary shapes, and small groups of people as they shuffled home or to Beth Israel North.

A feeling of being watched crept over her, but she refused to act the wimp. If Thompson Veridot was following her, there wasn't a thing she could do about it. Her only concern was seeing to it that Rudy was ransomed safely. There was no room in her brain for getting creative and cornering Veridot or doing anything stupid to screw things up.

As she shifted the overloaded duffel to her opposite shoulder, she passed the hospital where, as usual, things were jumping. At least, if Veridot shot her, she might be able to make it back here for treatment. If not, she'd tell her fuzzy friend she'd see him in heaven, kiss him good-bye, and trust that Vivian would take good care of him for the rest of his time on earth.

Inhaling a fortifying breath, she stopped at the park entrance to get her bearings. A brisk breeze blew in off the East River and suddenly her mind cleared. What the heck was she doing, talking like things were hopeless? Thinking she'd already lost? The battle hadn't even started, and she already sounded like a wussy . . . a fool.

A loser.

She was smarter than Thompson Veridot. She could be cagey . . . devious, even, if the need arose. She had no desire to capture him, but she did have a couple of self-defense lessons behind her. If Veridot came near her in any kind of threatening manner, she'd use the Mace, her keys, all the tricks she'd learned at Phil's gym to her advantage. Forget the money and forget what would happen to Veridot. If he made his escape with the cash, fine. Gary would forgive her for letting it happen. If Veridot ended up in the East River, even better. It was the perfect place for the slimy shark to land.

She just had to keep her cool and stick to her main goal: saving her dog.

Setting her sights on the park's dog run, she plowed ahead. Veridot's note hadn't said exactly where the meeting would take place, but the run made sense. If he'd been following her around town, he knew she came here often. Rudy could be penned in while Veridot grabbed his money, and she could walk inside to collect her boy.

Hoisting the bag higher onto her shoulder, she slapped at her right thigh and checked on her can of Mace and keys. She'd made sure the pockets of her shorts were spacious, with wide openings so she could reach what she needed with a mere slip of her fingers. Slowing to a measured pace, she scanned the area as she kept up her guard and her wits.

When she made it to the dog run entrance she set the bag at her feet and rotated her aching muscles. Then she slid her hand in her pocket and clasped the can of Mace. Prepared, she propped an arm on the fence and waited, still scrutinizing her surroundings.

At the sound of rustling leaves, she stilled, then

locked onto a figure shuffling in from the opposite side of the run, carrying a sack in one hand. The man's other hand appeared to be wrapped in white. As the guy neared, she saw that the odd-looking hand was bandaged from knuckles to wrist.

Raising her gaze, she tried to remain expressionless as she met the person who had called himself Benedict. When he stopped about fifteen feet away from her, his once-friendly face hardened into a frown.

"Ms. Engleman. Long time no see."

That voice. She knew it was familiar when he'd called about the assistant's job, but the connection hadn't registered.

She raised a brow, hoping it would mask the terror twisting her into a knot. "So you're Gary's brother. Do I call you Benedict or Veridot from here on out?" she asked. "Or do you want a job as my assistant?"

"No need to get snotty, girly. It's not my fault you wouldn't meet me in a more businesslike manner. And my full name is Thompson Benedict Veridot. Grandmother on my mother's side was Althea Benedict, bitch extraordinaire. The idiots thought they were doin' me a favor, naming me after Granny."

The bag jiggled, and he dropped it to the ground, then slammed a foot on the open end. "Oh, no, you don't, you little bastard."

"I want my dog," said Ellie, relieved to see the bag wriggling. "There'll be no exchange until Rudy is in my arms and I'm positive he's all right."

"Your mutt should be outlawed, better yet, put down," Benedict said, sneering. "Wouldn't take any of the sleeping pill concoction I offered him in food or the liquid I tried to pour down his gullet." He raised his bandaged hand. "Did this to me before I could tie him up. This, too."

He turned in profile, and Ellie saw a long scratch, almost a gash, running the length of his left cheek.

"Bastard almost bit my ear off before I dropped him, then he took a chunk out of my calf. I'm going to the ER for a tetanus shot and stitches first chance I get."

"Serves you right for taking him. What did he ever do to you?" Proud of Rudy's fighting spirit, Ellie was unsure of how to proceed. Did she let Benedict continue talking or was she the one who should take control, demand Rudy be set free, and pass the money?

"He didn't have to do nothin' but cooperate. He's a bargaining chip, is all. Him for the cash. I wasn't gonna hurt him. Just wanted my dough."

"About the money—"

"It's there, ain't it, in that bag?" He pointed to the duffel. "By my calculation, it should be a couple of million dollars, especially since my brother lived like a homeless bum. He couldn't have spent it all."

"Your brother was a bigger man than you will ever be. And for your information, he gave quite a bit of the money to food banks, homeless shelters, and other charities. Gary was kind, gentle, and considerate. He—"

Benedict lifted his good hand. "Stop, please. All this chitchat about the bleeding-heart traitor is killin' me. Just pass the cash. I'll take a look and be on my way."

"I'm not moving until you free my dog and let him come to me. When he does, I'll back away, and you can have the duffel."

"What do I look like, the Easter Bunny? First, I check out the money. Then you get your mutt."

Ellie didn't like that idea one bit. "How about we meet in the middle? I'll set the bag at your feet and pick up my dog. I won't move until you're satisfied." That way, she'd have Rudy in her arms, safe and sound. "Then you go where you need to, and I go home."

Benedict narrowed his eyes. "Sure, okay." He patted his right pocket. "Just remember I'm packin'. That means you do anything funny and I blow your little pal there away. Then I take you out, too."

*   *   *

Sam drove slowly, glancing up and down side streets as he zigzagged his way uptown. Ellie knew this area fairly well. It only made sense she'd stick to some place she felt comfortable as a meeting point with Veridot. It was the one small thing that might give her an edge.

His goal was Carl Schurz Park. He wasn't sure why, but something in his gut told him it was a prime spot for the rendezvous. Ellie had mentioned that she and Vivian thought someone had spied on them in the dog run one night, and she'd probably talked to other people there, too. Though the place emptied out at dusk, there was plenty of ambient light from the traffic on FDR Drive. The park was just far enough off the beaten path to afford privacy and space at the same time.

But if Ellie wasn't in the park, he was calling the precinct and asking them to extend the search while he continued up Fifth toward Columbia. She'd met that Fenwick character there. He could easily be Veridot, and he'd talked her into coming onto his turf.

Passing the hospital, he sighed. He'd been in his car for over an hour and had nothing to show for it but a headache and the need for a strong antacid. He had to get a break soon. After he rolled to the parking area in front of the green on East End Avenue, he killed the lights and engine and called the desk sergeant, asking him to send the nearest patrol car. Then he checked his Glock and returned it to its holster. He didn't want to use the weapon, but it might be the only language Thompson Veridot understood.

If that were the case, he'd have no choice. Keeping Ellie safe would be worth the internal investigation or suspension, or whatever they'd do to him for using his gun without cause.

Slipping from his car, he pressed the door closed to keep things quiet, sidled up the main path, and stayed to the right, creeping toward the dog run. As he neared, he squinted in the hazy light and heard voices about the same time he saw a man standing outside the pen and a woman standing in the entrance.

The voices were muffled, but he recognized Ellie when she said, "I won't move until you're satisfied. Then you go where you need to, and I go home."

"Sure, okay, but remember I'm packin'," said the man. "That means you do anything funny and I blow your little pal there away. Then I take you out, too."

Ah, thought Sam. He'd been right about why Rudy was missing. Ellie was here to rescue her dog. Veridot knew how much Rudy meant to her, and he'd kidnapped the canine in order to exchange it for the money.

Now that he knew what he was up against, he was certain there would be a perfect time to strike. Pulling out his Glock, he crouched and inched closer as Ellie hefted up the duffel and headed into the dog run. She stopped walking about three feet from Veridot and dropped the bag as if, like Vivian said, it held a ton of bricks.

"I hope you're in good physical shape, because this stuff is heavy," Ellie told Veridot. "You'll get a good cardio workout just hauling it around."

Veridot took his foot off a white bag squirming on the ground, and Ellie squatted. Sam let her retrieve her dog from the sack as he watched his target bend to open the bag and inspect the money. After racing to the entrance of the run, he assumed the position.

"Police! Freeze!"

Ellie turned around and saw Sam at the same time Rudy jumped from her arms. The little guy had shivered and whined the moment she'd touched the bag. Now, he took a flying leap and latched on to the good arm Veridot had digging inside the bag.

"Rudy! Stop! No!" she shouted.

Veridot took that moment to stand and shake Rudy from his forearm. Then he hoisted the bag and took off at a run, with the trio on his heels. Rudy reached him first, snarling and nipping at his ankles, and the older man stumbled, falling face-first into the grass. But Veridot sprang to his feet before Sam could tackle him, pulled his gun, and aimed it at Ellie.

"Throw your gun over there," he said, nodding toward a cluster of bushes, "and back away."

"Can't do it," Sam answered in a measured tone. "You're under arrest for the murder of Garick Veridot. Anything you say can and will be used against you. Drop the gun and come quietly, so no one gets hurt."

Brandishing the gun in Ellie's direction, Veridot's hand trembled as he spoke. "I'll get her before you get me, so I say we're at a bend in the road. All I want is my money. Toss your gun and tell her to step back, and I'll be gone in a heartbeat."

Ellie peered into the darkness, but Rudy had disappeared. Dropping her gaze to her feet, she saw the duffel easily within reach. If Rudy was in hiding, there was less than a one percent chance he'd be shot, which meant she could help Sam by distracting Veridot. But when she inched forward, Veridot trained his weapon on her again.

"Don't try to save the day, girly. Ain't nothin' more pathetic than a dead hero." He focused on Sam. "Back off and let me get my cash."

"You know I can't do that. Ellie, move behind me. Now."

"Don't do it, girly," Veridot ordered.

Instead, Ellie ducked, quickly lifted the duffel, and spun in place where she stood, twirling the bag like a discus with a handle. Her first spin knocked the gun from Veridot's fingers; her second go around smacked him in the head and knocked him on the ground. Continuing to whirl, she moved closer and closer to the fence separating the park from FDR Drive.

"Hey! Give me my money," shouted Veridot, charging her from behind.

"Ellie, get down!" yelled Sam.

She kept spinning right up to the fence, where she let go of the bag and watched it sail into the highway and land dead center in the far lane of speeding vehicles on the Drive.

Veridot roared, and she dropped to her knees, positive he was coming after her. But greed was the man's sole motivator, and he scrambled over the fence, jumped onto the highway and charged into traffic, dodging honking cars and blaring taxis as he headed for the duffel. Meanwhile, a passenger vehicle hit the bag and threw it into the air, where it came down in front of a cab that again smashed it toward the heavens.

Suddenly the sky was raining money.

Sam ran to Ellie's side, ready to climb the fence, when a squeal of tires caught them short. Veridot flew into the air much like the duffel had and landed in a heap at the side of the highway. Cars slowed, but several more smacked into the bag, moving it south on the Drive and pushing the money out and into the evening breeze.

A cop car slowed in the opposing lane of the highway, turned on its lights and siren, and hung a U-turn. Then another car pulled up onto the green behind them. Sam stared at Ellie. "I've got to get out there. You okay?"

"I—yes—sort of." She brushed the hair from her damp brow. "I've got to find Rudy."

"You do that." He holstered his gun, hoisted a foot against the fence, and vaulted over. "And once you do, sit on the bench outside the dog run and don't move. You got me?"

"I got you," she answered to his back. After watching him reach the other officers, she began a hunt for Rudy, positive he was close by and waiting for her.

Exhausted, Ellie blinked at the dial of her watch through bleary eyes. At three a.m. she was finally on her way home with Sam. She'd done as he'd told her and sat on the park bench with Rudy while an ambulance and fire trucks arrived on FDR Drive, followed closely by several more police vehicles and the usual flotilla of investigators and members of the press. When the dust settled, she'd been brought to the station for questioning and all the other necessary procedures she had to go through in a time of crisis.

While still on the scene, someone had brought the battered duffel bag to her and set it at her feet. Then a group of passengers from the vehicles stopped on the Drive had decided to do their good deed for the night and kill time by traveling up and down the highway collecting errant hundred-dollar bills and sending them to her via an officer.

When she'd glanced inside the bag an hour later, she'd noted it was only about half full, so there was no doubt in her mind that a couple of hundred thousand was now in the hands of the rescuers, though she wouldn't know for sure until the police did a final count. But so what? New Yorkers had done what they did best: help out in an emergency. They deserved a reward.

And, as she'd said all along, the money was Gary's, not hers. She'd planned to give it to charity. Now there'd just be less to spread around.

She heaved a sigh and gave Rudy a hug as a thoughtfully quiet Sam turned onto her street, pulled up in front of her building, and actually found a legal parking space. He'd been a rock during the night's proceedings, guiding her through each step, protecting her from Gruning, and assisting her in staying clearheaded and cool. Even Rudy hadn't complained when Sam was around.

But that was probably because he was all talked out. While on the bench, he'd told her in vivid detail about his battle with Veridot, how the guy had come at him from behind and dropped the sack over his head, how he'd refused to be drugged, and his heroic effort at getting away. Now that they were almost home, his relief coursed through her just as she was certain hers blanketed him.

Sam came around to open her car door, and she stepped out with Rudy in her arms. After five hours, she still couldn't put him down and let him walk. She'd held onto him from the time she'd found him curled in a ball under a group of bushes about twenty feet from the epicenter of the commotion, and she didn't intend to let him go until he was safely inside.

Until he said, *"Uh, Ellie, mind if I take care of a little business?"*

"Oh, sure. Sorry," she muttered in his ear. She set him on the sidewalk and smiled wanly at Sam. "He's been cooped up a long time. He deserves a break."

Sam nodded and held out his hand. "Give me your keys and I'll open up."

Too tired to argue, she complied and followed Rudy to the corner and back while Sam did as he'd said. Now at the stoop, Rudy hopped up the steps and trotted into the building as if the evening had been a night like any other and nothing dangerous or unusual had happened.

Sam kept his eyes on Rudy as he headed up the stairs. "He seems no worse for the wear."

Ellie heaved a sigh and went inside ahead of him. "I know, and I find that amazing. Did you see the damage he did to Veridot? He's one tough canine."

They climbed the steps side by side and met Rudy at the apartment door. Inside, she squatted, cupped his muzzle, and asked, "You going to be all right, big guy?"

He gave her cheek a sloppy lick. *"I'm better than all right, Triple E. Just dead . . . er . . . beat."*

"Okay, go to bed. Tomorrow's Saturday. We'll talk then."

He obeyed her without a complaint and took off down the hall. Ellie ran a hand through her hair and turned to Sam. "Thanks for everything. I really appreciate all the TLC you gave me tonight."

Sam propped his shoulder against the foyer wall. "You do realize there are a few issues we need to discuss?"

Oh boy, did she realize. "Um . . . yeah. But you heard me tell Gruning, tell everybody, why I didn't call you or anyone else when I got that ransom demand. You know how worried I was that you'd get hurt."

"That was no excuse, Ellie. It makes me think you didn't trust me to do my job. You interfered in a police investigation, almost allowed a felon to get away with murder, and God knows when the FDR Drive will be open to traffic. According to the captain, he plans to send a squadron out to search for more of the money in the daylight. Maybe even check out the East River. It was breezy tonight."

"I do trust you. I know you're good at what you do, honest. It's just that . . . I guess I was afraid Veridot would do what he said and figure out a way to kill you. I couldn't have lived with that, Sam, as much as I couldn't live without Rudy."

He pushed away from the wall. "Maybe so, but we can talk about it later. I still can't believe you're not upset about losing all that money."

"Letting the cash fly through the air and blow to kingdom come was exactly what he deserved. I just wish Veridot had been conscious, so he could have seen where his precious money went." She heaved a sigh. "Do you think he'll survive?"

"Beats me, but it'll save the state a hell of a lot of time, work, and funding if he doesn't. Once ballistics matches his gun with the bullet that killed Gary, he doesn't stand a chance at beating the rap."

She walked into the kitchen and set her Mace, cell phone, and keys on the kitchen table, where she found her bag upended and the contents spread around. "I guess you and Viv did this when you were trying to find me?"

"Sorry about that, but you gave us no choice. Once I knew your dog was missing and you were carrying that duffel, I figured something serious was up."

Ellie gave him a grin. "You're pretty smart for a detective. Guess that's why they pay you the big bucks and you have that fancy shield to show to everyone."

"I'm glad you're finally seeing the light." Sam brushed her bangs off her forehead, then took her elbow and led her down the hall. "You're dead on your feet. We can discuss all this tomorrow."

"I can put myself to bed, Sam. You need to go home and—"

"Not tonight, I don't. I'm using the guest bedroom, just so I know you're safe."

She straightened her shoulders, not happy with the idea. "What? No. I mean, that's silly. Veridot's unconscious and under guard at Beth Israel. I'll lock myself in and—"

"I'll lock us in and sleep in the guest room. Believe me, it's the only thing that will assure me a couple of hours' rest. There's just one thing . . ."

Telling herself that she was simply too tired to argue, she asked, "And what's that?"

"I want you to know now that I probably won't be here when you wake up in the morning. There's more to be done on the case, and I promised to lend Gruning a hand with the paperwork." He opened the guest bedroom door and turned. "I just don't want you to think I left you . . . the way I did before."

"The way you did . . . ? Oh. I mean, oh, I get it. I know you have police business to take care of. And if you'll remember, it wasn't the leaving that upset me the last time. It was what happened afterward that got me so ticked."

"Well, there's no worry on that point. I'll be back to pick you and Rudy up tomorrow, er, tonight at five thirty. We have an invitation to a barbeque."

Hands on her hips, she asked, "A what? Where?"

"My partner Vince's house. If you want to go. It's okay if you don't, because if not maybe the two of us could have dinner alone, which might be more comfortable for you. I just thought you'd enjoy yourself. Rudy, too."

"Rudy?"

"Yeah. Apparently, there's going to be a half dozen or more kids in attendance at this backyard shindig, and Vince somehow got the idea that your dog gets along great with children."

She opened and closed her mouth, thinking about her pal's reaction to that statement. Rudy had next to no patience with kids, especially those who were wild or misbehaved. In his own way, he was a very prissy pooch. But Sam was including him in the evening, a huge step in their relationship.

"Um, okay, I guess so." She stepped back into her bedroom. "So, you'll let yourself out, and I'll see you at five thirty?"

"That's right." Then, before she realized it, he was standing in front of her with his hands cradling her cheeks. When she gazed at him, he leaned forward and brushed her lips with his, gently, slowly, with care and feeling.

"Get a good night's sleep. I promise I'll see you later."

Chapter 23

"Why's your dog hidin' from us?" asked a five-year-old boy Ellie thought was named Johnny.

"I think you've worn him out," she answered the inquisitive child. "He needs a nap."

"I need a chiropractor. The little hellion tried to ride me like a pony," Rudy grumbled from beneath Ellie's chair.

"But my sister Jordan"—Johnny pointed to an adorable pixie-faced girl of about three—"wants to play wif him."

"I like Wu-dee," Jordan agreed. "He's a nice doggie."

"That kid needs a speech therapist. The sooner the better."

"He's the nicest dog on the planet, but he isn't happy when he's made to do things he doesn't want to do."

Jordon put a finger in her mouth. "I thought he was hung-wee, so I fed him."

"She tried to shove a pickle up my nose. I'm sick of these kids. Take me home."

Ellie grinned at her boy's grousing. "He's not hungry, but he does need some downtime. I'm sure he'll be ready to play in an hour or so."

"I plan to be on my way home sooner than that."

Johnny and Jordan walked away hand in hand, and Ellie hung her head between her knees. "Have to admit, you've been a very patient fellow with these children. I even saw you show your belly to that older girl in the red dress."

"You know I'm a sucker for a good tummy rub. And she told me she had a dog at home, so she knows how to treat us canines."

Ellie raised her head to make sure no one knew she was talking to her dog and saw Sam, carrying two bottles of beer, approaching. "Okay, put a sock in it. Here comes Sam."

"This is all his fault. Next time he invites the two of us anywhere, I'm a 'No, thanks.'"

"Shh." She grinned at the detective and accepted his offer of an ice-cold Bud Light. "Thanks. This will taste great right about now."

"I saw you talking to those rug rats and figured someone ought to rescue you, but you got rid of them all by yourself." He took a long swallow of his beer. "Good going."

"They're nice kids, just a bit . . . exuberant. They really liked Rudy."

"I'm surprised he moved around in this crowd for as long as he did. Thought you said he didn't like most people."

"What I said was he didn't *trust* most people. With two police detectives, two grade school teachers, a fireman, and a high school principal in attendance, these folks have to be as trustworthy as a troop of priests."

"Vince's family is okay. Natalie's too. But they only come together once or twice a year because of the numbers. Last time was the baby's christening."

"You never did tell me how your gift of a savings bond went over at that party," Ellie reminded him.

"It was much appreciated, especially when I told

Vince and Nat I'd be giving the kid one every birthday and Christmas."

"That's very nice of you." She took another drink, then before thinking asked, "Do you like children?"

"Me? They're okay, I guess. I only hope my sister's kid is a good one."

"Your sister Susan, correct?"

"Yep, that's the one. She and her husband are over the moon, happy as an expectant couple can be."

"And when is she due?"

"A couple more months. With my luck it'll be Halloween, and she'll have a goblin."

"That's not nice. I bet you'll change your tune when you become an uncle."

"Hey, the best part of being an uncle is the fact that my mom will be a grandmother. That should keep Lydia's nose out of my business for a good long time." He arched a brow and grinned at her. "I might even be able to have a personal life without her horning in."

"Too bad I can't say the same for Georgette," said Ellie. "Sometimes I think 'horning in' is her favorite pastime."

"I never got the impression your mother was a nudge. Didn't she do a good thing setting you up with that lawyer?"

The statement got Ellie thinking about Kevin Mc-Gowan, the big jerk. She'd been so busy with Veridot, she had yet to take her revenge on the sleazeball. "I'm afraid her matchmaking didn't work. I won't be seeing the attorney any time soon."

Sam's grin widened. "That's the first sensible thing I've heard you say in a couple of days."

"I've been making sense. You just don't want to admit I was right about the way I handled Benedict ... I mean Veridot."

"Not wanting to involve me in that ransom escapade

was a dumb move, and you know it. If I hadn't shown up, you might be dead right now."

Ellie finished her beer, noting that dusk had fallen. "Hah! Wouldn't have happened. Veridot and I had a deal. I didn't care if he got the cash, as long as I got Rudy back. And this isn't the time or place to discuss it. Looks like the group is getting ready to disband."

Sam gazed into the backyard, where a group of moms were corralling the children, another couple of women were clearing the picnic tables, and the men were collecting trash. "Looks like. Guess I'd better give Vince and Nat a hand or we won't be invited back."

At the sound of the word "we" Ellie's pulse sped up. She wasn't used to Sam, to any man, including her in his future plans. Maybe he was serious about starting their relationship over. Standing, she folded her chair, then pulled Rudy's leash from her tote and clipped it to his collar.

"Are we finally blowin' this joint?"

"It seems like. I just hope Sam realizes how tired we—I am and doesn't want to hang around. These people are nice, fun too, but I don't want to discuss what happened at Carl Schurz anymore." She'd spoken to Vince, Natalie, and a host of others about last evening's excitement and just wanted to forget it ever happened. "I'm afraid that's what they'll want to do if we go inside the house."

After she carried her chair to the patio and lined it up with the others, Sam came out of the sliding door, took her elbow, and led her out the back gate, along the side of the house, and into the street. "I said our good-byes, and everyone understood you've had a rough time of it. So we're good to go."

Relieved, Ellie settled Rudy in the rear seat of Sam's car, then climbed in the passenger side. "I had a nice time," she told him when he got behind the wheel. "They're good people."

"Vince is the best partner a cop could have, and Nat's a super lady. If you haven't noticed, they're a happy couple."

All their talk about happy couples and having children made Ellie curious. This new side to Sam was a big plus in the sensitivity column. Was he changing for the better?

"Um, so, thanks again for asking me to join you."

"No problem." They drove in silence for a few minutes; then he turned onto the Queensboro Bridge and headed for Manhattan. "We still have things to talk about."

She swallowed. "Things?"

The car eased across Second Avenue and made a right onto Third. "I know you're beat, but there's something I need to tell you."

Great. She was in trouble again. Gruning was probably trying to pin her with some trumped-up charge, or maybe she was going to have to let the police keep Gary's estate. "If this is about the money—"

"Oh, yeah, there's that, too. Gruning is angling to hold the cash for evidence, but I think a smart attorney can get him to back off. The money was never actually in Veridot's possession, and they have plenty of photos of the duffel, along with your statement and mine. I think you should show up on Monday morning with your lawyer and demand they release the bag and its contents to you for the reasons I just stated. I'm fairly certain that if Gruning is challenged, he'll lay off and shut up."

She'd have to call Uncle Sal and ask him to meet her at the station. If anyone was slippery enough to outtalk the cops, it was him. "I'll call the guy I used to record the will. He seemed to know enough about police procedure to take care of it. What else?"

Sam pulled in front of her building, got out of the car, and opened her door. "I'll come up and explain the rest."

*   *   *

Sam took a seat on the flowered sofa in Ellie's living room. After she sent Rudy to bed, she sat beside Sam, and he clasped her hand.

"So, what else is there to explain?" she asked warily. "Am I in more trouble?"

"You? Nah. But there are a couple of things you need to know. First off, that guy in your laundry room? The one with the tattoo?"

"You found out who he is?"

"Yep. Seems he wasn't Adrianne Burns's brother. He was her lover. Her husband was on a business trip last weekend, and the guy made himself at home. When I introduced myself and showed my badge, she spilled the beans but begged me not to tell her husband. And since there was no connection to the case, I agreed."

"So Viv did speak with the real Stefan Burns at the mailbox. That's good to know. I can't wait to hear what she has to say when I fill her in."

"There's more. I didn't tell you this next part earlier, for fear of spoiling your evening."

Ellie slumped on the cushion, as if ready for a major disappointment. "Okay, say what you have to say."

Letting go of her hand, Sam draped an arm over her shoulders, pulled her near, and leaned back on the cushions. This was going to be tough. "It's about Veridot."

She shifted to meet his gaze. "Please don't tell me they've let him go."

He ran his free hand over her cheek, then pushed a stray curl behind her ear. He had no idea how she'd react when she heard the news, but he imagined she'd be upset. "Veridot died this afternoon around three. He'll never bother you again."

Ellie's brows rose. Then her eyes teared up, and she sniffed. "Oh, no."

"Massive internal injuries will do that to a body. He never regained consciousness, by the way, so there's no way we'll get the entire story of what happened with Gary."

Her sniffle turned to a sob, and she swiped at her tears. "That is one of the saddest things I've ever heard."

"Sad? I think you should feel relieved."

She shook her head. "I'm not sad for Thompson Veridot. I'm sad for Gary and his parents. Imagine, an entire family is gone, stamped off the face of the earth for nothing more than some lousy money."

Leave it to Ellie to be miserable about a family she barely knew. "Bad things sometimes happen to good people. There's nothing you or anyone else could have done. It was all Veridot's fault, so I wouldn't waste my time crying over him."

Ellie reached for a tissue on the coffee table and blew her nose. After dabbing at her tears, she balled the tissue and set it on the table. "I know you're right, it's just that . . . Do you think I should be responsible for having Veridot cremated and laid to rest?"

"You? Why you?"

"Because I have his inheritance. It's probably the least I can do."

Sam frowned. "Think a minute. You have the family's money because Veridot killed them all. Hell, he might even have been responsible for his grandmother's death in some bizarre way. And if you had him cremated, what would you do with his ashes?" He cupped her jaw and looked into her eyes. "Something tells me the Veridots he murdered would not rest easy knowing the son who killed them was right next to them for all eternity."

Sighing, Ellie nodded. "You're probably right on that score, too." She shrugged. "So what happens to his body?"

"It gets turned over to the state, he's cremated, and they dispose of the remains. I'm not sure exactly where they go, but . . . Do you really have to know?"

She leaned back on the sofa and Sam drew her near.

"I guess not." She heaved another sigh and nestled into his shoulder. "This has been a long day. It's getting late, and I'm beat. Do you mind if we say good night?"

"No, I don't mind." He placed his palm on her cheek and turned her to face him. Dipping his head, he kissed her nose, then let his lips drop to hers. She tasted of kindness, and hope, and peace. All the good things he wanted in his life but never seemed to find. Deepening the kiss, he inhaled when Ellie opened and allowed him to explore the moist heat of her mouth.

Finally, he pulled away and rested his forehead on hers. "If I don't leave now, I'll never go."

"Just to be clear about our relationship, if you stayed, you'd have to spend another night in the guest room."

Sam kissed her forehead. "I figured as much, even though there's another bedroom I'd prefer. One I've slept in before."

She raised her gaze to meet his. "It's too soon, Sam. I don't think I'm ready for another . . . you know."

"I understand." Disentangling himself, he stood, reached for Ellie's hands, and pulled her to her feet. "How about seeing me to the door?"

They walked together side by side while he kept his arm around her waist. At the door, he faced her again and gave her another kiss, this one filled with the promise in his heart and all the emotion he could muster.

Then he stepped back and grinned. "I'll call you tomorrow to remind you about Monday morning. And I mean that with every breath in my body."

Ellie stared at him openmouthed. Then she smiled. "You'd better, because I'll find you if you don't."

"I like the sound of that," he said, caressing her cheek. "But don't worry, you won't have to."

He opened the door and stepped into the hall. "Lock up and have a good night. You'll need all your strength for our next date, say a week from now? I have to read the board and check my schedule before I know for sure if I'm free."

Still smiling, Ellie nodded and closed the door, and Sam headed down the stairs.

"Are you sure this is going to work?" Ellie asked Vivian as they took their seats in a back corner of the courtroom the Friday after Ellie had been to the Fugazzos' barbeque.

"Hey, I don't take days off for just anybody." Viv raised her nose in the air. "You're my dearest friend, and when I told Pete why you wanted to do this he jumped at the chance to make things right."

Ellie glanced around the room, noting it wasn't packed. But that wasn't unusual for a divorce hearing. The people who showed up came either to support a loved one or to wait for their case to be called. Hilary was already in place at one of the tables, and her sister was sitting behind her. So Ellie figured it wouldn't take long for the proceedings to start.

"This had better be good," she said to Viv. "Otherwise, I'm going to have to think of something else."

"It's going to be great," Viv pronounced in a whisper.

The door opened and two men walked in, one of whom Ellie thought was Kevin McGowan. When he took a seat next to Richard Blankenship at the table across from Hilary, she was sure.

"Let the games begin," Viv continued in a hushed tone.

Moments later, a judge entered from a door behind the bench, bringing to mind Ellie's own divorce proceedings. She and the D couldn't come to terms on a single thing, even with arbitration, so going to a judge had been their only choice, just as it now was with Hilary and her soon-to-be ex.

She had told Hilary she'd be there, and Hilary had said thank you but her sister was the only person she needed, which was fine with Ellie. Hilary's sister had come to offer moral support, while she had come for vengeance. There was no reason to mix the two.

The bailiff called the court to order, and she stiffened, planning to follow each argument carefully. Kevin stood and spouted all the reasons why Hilary didn't deserve spousal support, adding the part about her working for Paws in Motion and how much money she could make as a dog walker. Hilary's attorney countered with her past support of Richard when they were first married, citing that part of her earnings had gone to finance and furnish a percentage of the condo. The judge observed, commented, and gave orders as needed until neither attorney had anything further to say.

Viv left toward the end of the hearing and returned just as the judge gave his ruling. Hilary was allowed to keep her condo, and she would receive double her current support, but that was all. Ellie knew the money award was generous, but she felt certain Hilary wouldn't think so. And that was fine, because the woman's need for more cash meant she'd continue to walk the dogs in her building, giving Ellie a much needed break.

"He's here," Viv whispered, returning to her seat. "And he looks fabulous."

The lawyers stood and began putting folders and documents back in their briefcases. Richard Blankenship stormed out, and Hilary sidled around the railing and went to her sister. Then the rear door opened and a huge gorilla wearing a skirt and an enormous pink bow on its head danced into the room balancing a boom box on its shoulder. The song, a soulful rendition of "The Cheater" rang out so loudly the judge and bailiff stopped in their departure and turned, as did most of the viewing audience.

Kevin turned, too, and, when he saw the strutting

ape headed his way, blanched to a ghostly white. But that didn't stop the ape. She, really Pete, stepped lively to Kevin, smacked him on the chest, and shoved him into his seat. Then Pete continued to dance and, every time the singer vocalized with 'Cheat, cheat, cheat,' pointed to the shocked attorney as if he were the one on trial.

The judge and bailiff laughed out loud, as did most of the audience. It was clear Kevin had done something so heinous that someone, probably a woman from the looks of the gorilla, was furious. And what he'd done was obvious, too.

But the best part of the scenario was that this episode would get around to the other divorce lawyers with whom Kevin did business and hundreds of others in the legal world. He'd be a laughingstock for months to come.

The song was over all too soon. Ellie had grinned during the entire routine and waggled her fingers at Pete as he sashayed out the door. Then she looked to the front of the courtroom and found Kevin scowling at her. So she waggled her fingers at him, as well.

Hilary dabbed at the tears in her eyes, her smile so huge Ellie decided it was well worth the two hundred dollars she'd spent to put on the show.

Kevin slammed his briefcase closed, and she and Viv gave him another finger wave before they scooted from the courtroom. Outside, they found Pete on the street handing business cards advertising MONKEYSHINES to all who passed.

Ellie handed him a check and the ape, or rather Pete, gave her a salute, picked up the boom box, and danced up the street toward the nearest subway entrance.

"God, that was fun," Viv said, still sniggering.

"I should have borrowed Stanley's video camera. I don't think I've ever seen anything as hysterical as the expression on Kevin's face when he saw me."

"Saw you? What about when he saw Pete ... er ... Matilda fox-trot into the courtroom?" asked Viv.

"That, too." Ellie slid her hand into Vivian's elbow. "You got time for lunch? My treat."

"Don't you have dogs to walk?"

"My afternoon rounds don't start for another two hours. We can go wherever you want. Money is no object, as a thank-you for finding Pete."

"How about Tavern on the Green? That way, you'll be close to your canines so we can hang at the restaurant a little longer," Viv decided.

Ellie stepped into the street and hailed a cab. When a taxi stopped, she held open the door for her best human friend. Too bad Rudy hadn't been allowed in the courtroom. He would have loved the gorilla, the look of shock on Kevin's face, the whole nine yards.

She and Vivian arrived at Tavern on the Green, ate a delicious lunch, and said farewell. Four hours later, Ellie arrived home and found Rudy waiting at the door.

"So, was it as rewarding as you hoped it would be?" he asked as they headed down the stairs.

"I'll say. I only wish I'd had the sense to video it. The look on Kevin the creep's face was memorable."

"I can't stand the thought of you havin' fun without me, Triple E. Next time, find a way to bring me along."

They strolled around the block and made it home in twenty minutes. After Ellie put a Lean Cuisine in the nuker, she went to the kibble cupboard, poured her boy's dinner, and set his full dish on the place mat. Then she removed her meal and ate it at the kitchen table while Rudy finished his food.

When she tossed the plastic container in the trash, Rudy stood on his hind legs and did his own version of a fox-trot. *"Got anymore of those gourmet biscuits, huh, do ya?"*

Ellie retrieved the last of the special treats from the Bread and Bones sack and carried it to her living room.

There, she turned on the television, sat on the sofa, and passed Rudy his dessert. A few moments later, she found *Dogtown*, the show about her favorite charity, Best Friends, on the National Geographic Channel and settled back to watch.

Rudy ate his biscuit and rested his head in her lap until the show was over. Then he said, *"I pity those poor guys. They don't have someone in their life like I do, Triple E, and that's sad."*

"I think so, too." She pulled him to her chest and gave him a loving squeeze. "You're the best, big guy."

"So are you, Triple E. Just promise me one thing."

"And what might that be?"

"No more hunting for killers. It's too freakin' dangerous."

"I highly doubt we'll have the need to play detective again."

"Good, because this last fiasco scared the crap outta me."

"Oh, really? And here I thought you were the dog who could take on the world."

"Hah! I wasn't frightened for me. When I heard Veridot was holding a gun on you, I thought I was gonna die, too. In fact, I wanted to." He nudged her cheek with his nose, then gave her a sloppy lick. *"I couldn't live without you, Ellie. Even staying with Vivian and T wouldn't take away my sorrow."*

That comment caused Ellie's throat to close up and brought tears to her eyes. "Same here, little buddy. Same here." Drawing him near, she gave him another squeeze. "We're a matched set, and no one will ever separate us again."

Read on for a preview of Judi McCoy's

next Dog Walker mystery

DEATH IN SHOW

Coming from Obsidian in June 2010

Ellie pulled the lapels of her black wool blazer close as she crossed West End Avenue and headed for the Javits Convention Center. This was the best place for a dog lover to be on a cold November day, she told herself as she passed people leading canines of all shapes and sizes into the center. Though she'd sat in the viewing area of the Westminster Kennel Club show many times, this was her first visit to the Mid-Atlantic Canine Challenge.

And she was attending as a special guest, which allowed her backstage for the most exciting part of the competition. Flora Steinman, the owner of Lulu, a Havanese Ellie walked twice a day, had requested she be here to offer moral support for both her and her dog. In fact, since the petite pooch had come to her home to share a playdate with her own dog, Rudy, Ellie put Lulu on a par with Mr. T, her best friend's Jack Russell, and considered the Havanese a full-fledged member of her family.

She entered the crowded conference center and headed for the jammed escalator with a full heart. She was more than happy to spend today and tomorrow at the second-most prestigious of all dog shows. If Lulu won the MACC, she would be well on her way to Westminster in February. And even if she only got as far as Best in Breed or Best in Group, she would still be in a good position to take the big prize at Madison Square Garden.

Juggling her schedule had been daunting. Since losing Hilary Blankenship as her assistant a couple of months ago, Ellie had hired and fired several others. But just last week she'd found someone who might actually work out: a Columbia University student named Joy. The girl's usual chore was simple: walk five dogs in Paws in Motion's farthest north building for the next two days. But because of Ellie's commitment here, Joy now had to walk thirty dogs, some twice a day, in four different buildings. Definitely not an easy task.

It had been even more difficult explaining the rearranged schedule to her charges. Canines thrived on routine and weren't happy when their regular walk time changed. She'd promised special treats for the rest of the week if they agreed to the time adjustment, which they did, and she told herself again that her dogs were worth every extra penny.

Continuing her upward ride, she recalled the info Flora had given her on the ins and outs of the dog-show world. First and foremost, competition was fierce and beset by politics. Over the course of a competitive year, judges came to know each handler as well as the owners and their dogs, which brought friendship and a canine's reputation to every event. Right now the gossips predicted that tiny fur ball Lulu would handily take Best in Breed and go on to win Best in Group, but anything could happen to change that belief.

Ellie still wasn't sure of the reason the Havanese had amassed so many championships, but it was clear that Flora had taken a different route on the road to Lulu's success. Many canines were owned by multimember partnerships that had the dogs live with their handlers. Even the professor, Ellie's first client, had sent Buddy to his handler several weeks prior to a major outing in order to ensure the pair would appear as a single unit at the competition.

Instead, Lulu spent her life with Flora, who brought the dog to each conformation showing in which it was entered two days ahead of time. Arnie Harris then worked with Lulu long enough for them to compete as a synchronized team. The unusual practice had made getting here expensive and arduous for a woman in her seventies, but Flora had been adamant. Lulu would live with no one but her until forty-eight hours before a show.

Ellie still wasn't sure if the Havanese owed her success to continuous coddling or her stellar pedigree, but it didn't matter. Lulu had amassed enough points to be allowed entry here, and since today was one of the little dog's biggest appearances, she couldn't say no when Flora asked her, Lulu's secondary caregiver, to share the momentous experience.

She was determined to give Flora and Lulu the support they needed, and looked upon her attendance more like a mini-vacation, with the right to be near some of the most well-known and prestigious purebreds in the country.

After stepping off the escalator, Ellie flashed a guard her pass and received directions to the backstage area, where the contestants waited for their event. It was there the dogs in the morning rounds were made ready to compete. Inside the packed holding zone, filled with owners, groomers, handlers, hundreds of canines, show sponsors, and a variety of news reporters, she realized it was the most exhilarating place she'd ever been that had to do with her favorite four-legged friends.

Sidling past Malteses, Chihuahuas, Yorkies, and dozens of other miniature breeds, she took note of one oddity. The area was filled with the racket of human chatter, snipping scissors, and busy blow-dryers, but not a single sound came from the canines. At the very least, she'd expected to hear some of their excitement, but nothing penetrated her brain. These had to be the most focused hounds in the world.

Ellie almost sighed in ecstasy. She'd never been this close to so much pooch perfection. Rudy was a pound puppy, which was fine with her, but she'd never seen so many dogs of this caliber up close and personal. Nor had she ever spoken to a professional judge or handler, and she was looking forward to doing both.

Fighting her way through the crowd, she kept her tote bag under her arm and her eyes peeled for a sign that marked the holding area for the Havaneses. After several minutes of swimming through a mass of bodies, she decided this event was a pickpocket's dream. People had to walk sideways to get through the throng, brushing against one another like lovers sharing a group dance. If Lulu won today, Ellie planned to tuck her keys in an inside pocket and stuff cash in her bra for tomorrow's more important competition, instead of carrying her jumbo bag.

Rising on tiptoe, she saw Flora speaking to a man she thought might be Arnie, and headed in their direction.

"My darling girl, you made it," said the older woman when Ellie reached her. Dressed in a lilac-colored suit and matching pumps, Mrs. Steinman wore a double strand of pearls Ellie guessed cost more than her yearly income.

"I wouldn't have missed this for the world."

"Good, good. And here's someone you should meet." Flora smiled at her companion, a tall, burly man of about fifty wearing navy blue Armani. "This is Edward Nelson. He used to be Lulu's handler."

Used to be? Ellie held out her hand and she and Edward shook. "Hello. It's nice to meet you."

"Same here. Flora tells me we have something in common," Edward said in a deep voice thick with a New York accent. "I walk dogs too, some in the very building where Lulu, Flora, and I live."

Flora had fired Mr. Nelson, and he lived in the Beau-

mont? She raised a brow at Lulu. Ensconced on a pillow, the snobby Havanese pointed her muzzle in the air.

"Not my idea," the Havanese announced. *"Firing him was Flora's idea, but he always wore too much aftershave, so I approved. He made me sneeze up a storm."*

Ellie waggled her fingers at Lulu and returned her gaze to the handler. She'd never seen Edward Nelson before, and she thought she knew every dog walker on the Upper East Side. "In the Beaumont? I can't believe we haven't met before now."

"Oh, but I've seen you and your charges marching up and down the avenue like a marine platoon. Natter speaks very highly of you," he said, mentioning the Beaumont's doorman. "As does Flora."

She filed the information away, planning to bend Natter's ear about the handler/dog walker as soon as she saw him again. "We should compare notes sometime."

"Sounds good," said Edward, glancing over his shoulder. "Now, if you'll excuse me, I have to find my boy." A grin that seemed more of a smirk graced his ruddy face. "Flora, nothing against you and Lulu, but I look forward to bringing Fidel to the winner's circle today. No hard feelings, I hope."

"Of course not," Flora chimed as the man shouldered his way through the mob.

"Fidel?" Ellie asked, quirking her lips.

"The other Havanese I told you about, the one that gives Lulu so much competition," said the older woman. "If Edward hadn't found a dog in the toy group to handle today, I would have paid him a compensation fee for taking Lulu away. I'd only hired Arnie a few months ago, you see, and most handlers are booked well in advance for a show as prestigious as this one. I wasn't sure Edward would find another client in this group in such a short amount of time, but he managed, though it did surprise me that he found a second Havanese."

"Hey, Mrs. Steinman," a young man dressed in a navy

suit and matching tie called as he pushed his way through the crowd. When he neared, Ellie saw that he was accompanied by a twentysomething man wearing the same type of suit and tie in dark brown. The first guy, short and stocky, with a pleasant expression, spoke. "Jim Hiller." He took Mrs. Steinman's hand and shook it lightly. "We met at that open show in Connecticut last spring. Are you still using Edward Nelson to handle your prize bitch?"

"Why, no," Flora answered, not offering Arnie's name or Ellie's. She turned her gaze to the other man. "And who is this fine fellow?"

"My pal Josh. I've been telling him about Lulu ever since she won Winner's Bitch at that competition. We heard a rumor about Edward being out of the picture, and hoped you'd ask one of us to show her today. I sent you several e-mails but you never answered them, so I called and left a few phone messages. Guess I should have known you weren't interested when you didn't respond."

"I'm afraid I'm a total novice on a computer, and I'll have to speak to my housekeeper about those phone messages."

"Yeah, well, I still want you to know how much I admire your bitch. I don't have a dog in the toy group and . . ."

Ellie ignored the rest of their conversation, thinking instead of the terminology dog people used. She had a difficult time referring to female dogs as bitches, though it wasn't a slur but proper canine classification. Still, this kid's pushy attitude was hard to swallow. She'd been told handlers had a lot of confidence, but as far as she was concerned, his comments were just short of rude.

Flora didn't seem a bit flustered and spoke politely to the young men. They left a moment later, and she gave a loud harrumph. "Sorry I didn't introduce you, but those boys are brazen upstarts, too eager to push the pros out of the way. Inexperienced handlers looking to break into the big time often campaign for new customers, but not in such an unprofessional manner."

Then the older woman's eyes sparkled, and she nodded toward the crowd. "I think Arnie has arrived, and he's stopped to greet Edward. That means he'll be here any moment." She touched her head of silver hair. "How do I look?"

"Like you own the place," Ellie assured her.

Flora stopped fussing. "I hope the two of you get along."

Ellie peered through the crowd. Mrs. Steinman had to have radar or X-ray vision, because it was easy to spot Edward's tall figure but almost impossible to see who he was talking to. Then a short, dapper man, somewhere between Edward's age and Flora's, wearing an impeccable gray suit and matching tie, plowed through the human traffic jam, stopped in front of them, and grasped both of the woman's hands.

"Flora, my dear. Ready to celebrate Miss Lulu's big moment?"

"I'm all atwitter, Arnie," answered Flora, a blush gracing her papery cheeks. "At the very least, my little girl deserves to win Best in Breed, and I'm hoping you'll make that happen."

"I deserve Best in Breed no matter who the handler is," rang a voice in Ellie's ear.

She turned to Lulu, who watched from her pillowed throne, and sidled backward. "I wouldn't be so cocky if I were you. Fidel and the other seven Havaneses here have each won major competitions. They have the right to Best in Breed just as much as you do."

"Hah! I've beaten every one of them already. Any judge with a brain will see that I'm the most typey of my breed."

"Only time will tell, missy." Ellie noted that Flora Steinman and Arnie were involved in a discussion, and asked Lulu the big question. "So, besides too much aftershave, why did your mistress fire Edward Nelson?"

"You mean you can't tell?"

"Afraid not," she said, still staring at the senior couple.

"Ellie, Ellie, Ellie, Rudy is right. You are a babe in the woods when it comes to male-female relationships."

When Lulu's explanation sank in, Ellie blinked. "You mean Flora and Arnie are—are—"

"Not yet, but she hopes they will be. The moment she met Arnie it was bye-bye, Edward."

"Wow," Ellie muttered. "Who would have thunk it?" Her attention returned to Flora and Arnie, who were now grinning at her as if they had heard both sides of her conversation with the Havanese.

"I assume this is the young woman you've been telling me about, my dear," Arnie said to Flora as he reached to shake Ellie's hand. "You're Ellie Engleman, right? Flora's done nothing but sing your praises from the moment she and I met."

"Mrs. Steinman is a very kind lady," said Ellie. "It's nice meeting you too."

"I see Flora was right about your ability to communicate with canines. It appeared that you and Lulu were holding quite a discussion a few seconds ago."

"I know it's eccentric, but chatting with my charges is a habit I've developed over the course of my dog-walking career," she confessed.

"Good for you," praised Arnie. "You can never tell how much a dog understands, and Lulu is bright. I'll bet she's aware of everything you say to her."

You don't know the half of it, Ellie almost blurted, but she knew her unusual ability was inexplicable, even to the most fanatical dog lover. "Please forgive me if I stare like a Chihuahua milling with a pack of St. Bernards, but this is my first time behind the scenes at any kind of canine competition. I'm still trying to absorb it all."

"You'll get the hang of things soon enough. Once that little lady is in the ring, everything will come together like gin and vermouth, a fine cocktail and a fine win for our perfect Havanese."

"Uh, okay," she agreed, not certain the analogy fit.

A buzzer sounded and the mob grew quiet. "Attention, group twenty-seven. All Havaneses and their handlers, please report to ring number one."

Ellie checked her watch. "Oh, my gosh. It's almost time for the magic moment. We'd better get out there."

"I am so nervous," said Flora, stepping in front of Lulu with a brush raised.

"Now, Flora, that's my job." Arnie eased the grooming tool from her hand and stuffed it in his pocket, then gazed at Lulu. "How's my pretty baby today? Ready to wow the judges' socks off?"

Lulu answered him with a sneeze, and Flora giggled. "Isn't she something, acting as if this is an everyday occurrence instead of the biggest moment in her competitive career?"

Since Ellie was privy to Lulu's bossy outbursts and sometimes snotty innuendos, she said nothing. No one would ever believe her if she told them she knew exactly what the Havanese was thinking. Instead, she made an honest observation. "There are only nine dogs in her breed. I'd say she has a good shot at winning."

"Remember what I told you about the breed. Because they're one of the newest recognized by the American Kennel Club, there are only about thirty breeders in this country, hence the small number," offered Flora. "We've already met each of the competitors at other venues, and we've come in first several times. At each competition, Fidel has been the one who challenged my girl the most."

"Enough talk, ladies. It's time we got in line. We're next on the judging block." Arnie slipped over his jacket sleeve an armband, covered with a variety of statistics and the number nine on it, and moved it to his upper arm. Then he picked up Lulu and walked through the teeming mass with Flora and Ellie following.